I0769169

BOOKS BY TIM FRANKOVICH

Heart of Fire
Until All Curses Are Lifted
Until All Bonds Are Broken
Until All the Gods Return
Until All the Stars Fall

Dragontek Lore
Viridia
Incarnadine
Auric
Onyx
Amaranth
Atramentous
Chroma

The Certainty of Blood
Wolf Chosen
Under The Moon's Gaze

TIM FRANKOVICH

UNDER THE MOON'S GAZE

The Certainty of Blood, Book 3

*To Larry Hama,
who taught me what fight scenes
should look like*

Table of Contents

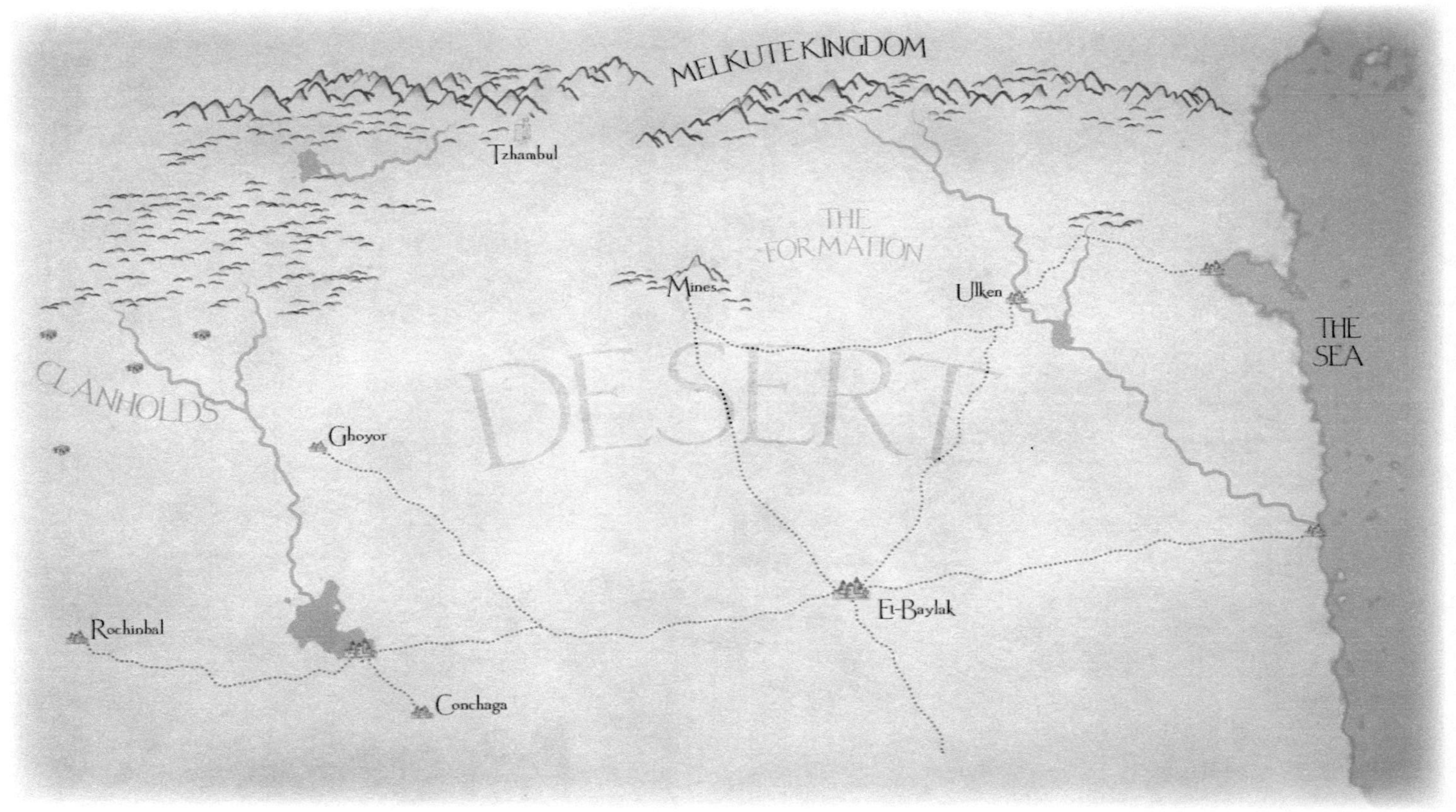

MELKUTE KINGDOM
Tzhambul
THE FORMATION
Mines
Ulken
THE SEA
CLANHOLDS
DESERT
Ghoyor
Rochinbal
Et-Baylak
Conchaga

Prologue

THE DEATH OF HOPE

His shattered legs left an all-too-visible trail of blood as he dragged himself through the snow. Tears flowed down his cheeks and sobs wracked his body, but not because of the agony of the broken bones or the knowledge of his impending death.

Daviland wept for shattered dreams, for the end of belief, and for the death of hope.

Everything had gone according to plan, according to the prophecy. He'd killed the Hawk King! And then… he didn't know. Something happened to him in the arena. Someone else took charge, someone else ruined everything, unleashing… that thing under the hill, the dark power soaked in blood.

Once he'd come to himself and understood all that had happened, he'd been horrified. General Ghan, left to his own devices after Clanless took the dark power down, gave the order: "Break both his legs and throw him outside the gate."

Maybe it was better this way. Better to die alone instead of continue to be used by that… that thing who possessed him for the past few months. But before she came, everything else… His faith had been unmatched, his labor unquestioned, and his vision unrestrained. He'd hoped to make such a difference in this land. And now it all lay in ruins. The Sar Empire would fall under the control of beings even worse than the Hawk King.

He craned his head to look up at the moon in despair. Did the goddess care? Did she even exist? Was she tormenting him for criticizing her priesthood?

He gasped at the sound of scampering feet in the rocks off to his right. The predators would find him soon, long before the freezing cold became a real problem. He didn't see the source of the footsteps, but it wouldn't be long now.

A hiss came from the left. He glanced in that direction and caught a glimpse of motion; something ran behind a large outcropping.

Why didn't they get it over with? He was helpless. He couldn't even crawl any further. Exhausted, he closed his eyes and lowered his face to the ground. Maybe the goddess would be merciful enough to let them kill him quick.

Heavy footsteps crunched in the snow not far away. He waited for the teeth to feed on his flesh. But nothing happened. Hesitantly, he lifted his face.

An enormous wolf stood before him, staring down at him with golden eyes. White streaks broke up its gray fur, but his vision blurred, and he couldn't be sure of further details. Even though he knew this creature would devour him, he couldn't help being awed by its magnificence.

"Do you desire death so much, son of the clans?"

Davil's mouth would have fallen open if his teeth hadn't been chattering so hard. The voice came within his head, but he knew with utter certainty that it came from the wolf.

"I see I must repeat myself. Do you desire death?"

"I… I don't want to die," Daviland managed to say.

"Your destiny is not what you thought, but neither should you die today, unless that is your choice."

The wolf stepped closer and breathed on his face. A flow of pleasant warmth swept over his body.

"If you are willing to be used by powers greater than yourself to accomplish a great victory for your people, you will live today."

He wanted to answer, but Daviland's consciousness faded. He struggled to keep his eyes open.

"It will be a long time of healing and preparation, but I believe you can be one of those who deliver salvation to this land."

One of those? Davil's eyelids fell. He jerked them back open, but the wolf had disappeared. Had it even been there? He let his head fall into the snow, and his eyes slid shut again.

Before he lost himself, he heard footsteps all around. They sounded human, but that made no sense. What kind of men would be out here?

Part One

CLANHOLD

SPEARS IN THE SNOW

Clanless scooped up a pile of snow and used it to rub blood from his face. Perplexed, he looked toward the pursuing sun over the hills and blinked at the brightness.

"How did I end up here?" he asked the moon before scanning the rest of the barren landscape before him. No blood. No footprints, at least not human. Some larger markings indicated some beast had been here, perhaps even used this cave as a home. But Bain had not come this way.

Clanless rubbed his hands together, letting the rest of the snow fall from his fingers. He thought he'd been following his former friend, now possessed by the chaos god, Suirel. But once he'd left behind the vast sea of blood and started his ascent through dark tunnels, he'd slowly lost the ability to see anything. The light of the crystals faded behind him, and any lingering blood-magic ability to see in the dark faded as well. He'd no way of knowing which way Suirel might have gone. He'd taken his best guess at each tunnel intersection, choosing passages that seemed to lead upward. A few times, he'd been forced to return to an intersection and take the other direction.

And this is where he'd ended up: a small cave opening nowhere near the mining caverns where it all begun. Markings on the cave's opening drew his attention. He ran his hand across several long gashes in the rock. Whatever creature made these had enormous claws. Better not to be here when it returned.

How had Suirel navigated the caves? Or had he? Maybe he'd taken a wrong turn and fallen in a pit. He was blind, after all. But Clanless doubted it. One didn't defeat a god of chaos that easily.

A thin wisp of smoke drifted in the air in the distance, the remains of someone's fire. Clanless rubbed his bare arms and shifted his wolf pelt to cover his shoulders. Damp and sticky with blood, like the rest of his clothes, the pelt would not be pleasant to wear as it grew colder, but he had no choice at the moment. The distant fire might be his only option, no matter who else waited beside it. He judged its exact direction based on the hills and the sun's pursuing position and set off out into the open.

The first gust of wind almost made him turn and run back to the cave. It might not be much warmer inside, but the wind's cruel bite felt colder than cold. The beastmen's many ideas about wind came to his mind. They would probably call this a wind from the chaos lord. What did they call him? The Lord of the Dead. That was it. Interesting how they associated him with death, not chaos.

He pushed thoughts of theology aside. He needed to focus on survival alone. He picked up the pace. He couldn't see the smoke any more, but he knew the direction. He clambered over rocks and slid down a long incline into a low hollow, finding temporary shelter from the wind.

More claw marks decorated the rocks in the hollow. The large creature, something he couldn't imagine, had climbed out of here as well. Maybe more than once. Clanless frowned. Anything that large should be sleeping well past the ending of High Winter, especially one such as this had been. Something had disturbed it and driven it from its hibernation. Perhaps Suirel had come this way, after all.

All the more reason to get to the fire. If he found Suirel there, Clanless would finish the fight. If the fire had been made by others, they might be in danger from Suirel. Or the creature. Or both. Clanless climbed out of the hollow and hurried on his way, trying to ignore the increasing intensity of the wind gusts.

Something stirred in his blood, bringing him pause. What was that? A moment later, he knew: his connection to Swift Claw had been restored. Since his descent into the sea of blood, he'd been aware of the beastman's existence but unable to pinpoint his location. Now, he could sense his friend straight ahead… and getting closer by the second.

Clanless found shelter behind a high crag and waited. Only a few moments later, Swift Claw bounded into view and slid to a stop in front of him. "Wolf Chosen. You live." His eyes and mouth were wider than Clanless remembered seeing. For a beastman, it communicated great happiness.

"Alive and cold. Is that fire yours?" For a brief moment, Clanless considered giving the beastman a hug. But he had no idea how Swift Claw would react to that.

"The humans wait there. Both of your women sleep beside it." Swift Claw cocked his head. "You are not wounded, but you are covered in blood not your own. The smells are… confusing."

"I imagine so." Clanless's heart beat a little faster on hearing of the women; although, Swift Claw apparently still had trouble accepting that Qara did not belong to him. "You all escaped then? Who else?"

"Your woman's sire and your battle brother. Mmh. Also the weak man."

Koland and Sugh. "Weak man?"

Swift Claw showed his teeth. "Your woman called him a priest."

Oh. The Ghamba Lam. Interesting. "I need to get to that fire before I freeze." He glanced around. "And I don't think we're alone out here."

Swift Claw stood aside and let him take the lead. "You are not wrong. I have seen its sign. Such a beast should not be waking yet."

"That's what I thought. Maybe Suirel woke it up."

"The Lord of the Dead still walks? You did not slay him?"

Clanless swallowed and tried to rub his arms harder. "I did the best I could. I thought I was following him when I came out here. I don't suppose you've seen signs of someone else passing this way?"

Swift Claw growled. "No one came this way before you."

Clanless grunted. His shivering grew. If only the gusts of wind would stop, maybe the sun would warm things a bit. High Winter was supposed to be ending. "Swift Claw… are these… his winds?"

"This is not the Dead Lord's Wind." The beastman shook his head as he scrambled over another large rock instead of going around it. "This wind is but cold."

"Yeah, I noticed that part."

Swift Claw stopped atop the rock and lifted his snout toward the air. "But the wind brings tidings still." He looked down at Clanless. "Other men are near. Very near."

"Some of General Ghan's soldiers, I would guess."

"We must hurry." The beastman leaped down from the rock and raced ahead.

"That's what I've been saying." Clanless shivered and chased after him.

Swift Claw rounded another large outcropping and came to an abrupt halt. Clanless almost ran into him. The beastman stepped aside and let him see.

Sheltered by the enormous rock, a small fire burned. Two women lay beside it, asleep. The man tending it stood up at their appearance. "Aldan," Koland said. "You look… terrible."

"It's just blood. Not mine." He moved closer to the fire, staring at Kekeen. He swallowed. The warmth flowing over him now came from more than the fire. "Kekeen," he whispered.

Sugh came around the other side of the rock. "Clanless!" he cried. "I knew you'd come back!"

Kekeen stirred. She blinked and lifted her head. "Aldan?"

"Others are here!" Swift Claw announced.

Clanless spun around to see a dozen or more soldiers spreading out in a crescent formation as they approached. Their leader, marked by a red cloth on his shoulder, lifted his hand to signal a halt. "You are ordered to surrender yourselves!" he called. "In the name of General Ghan and the Sar Empire!"

Koland stepped past Clanless and waved to the officer. "Young man, you were in the cave, weren't you? You've seen what these three"—he gestured back at the others—"are capable of. Do you really want to challenge them?"

"I have my orders." The officer made another gesture, and his troops widened the crescent, closing in around the small camp. All of them leveled spears, unusual weapons for Sar Empire soldiers.

"What's happening?" Kekeen asked.

"Clanless." Sugh tossed the moonblade to him. He caught it and took comfort in the familiarity of its handle. Reuniting with the blade completed him almost as much as finding these friends again. If he'd held the blade in his fight with Suirel, things might have been different.

"Koland. Let me." Clanless stepped forward. "You saw me take Suirel down the Throat, didn't you? But now I'm back, and he's not. Trust me. This is not a fight you can win."

"We outnumber you five to one."

"And I fought ten at once in the Hawk King's arena."

"I fought eight," Sugh put in.

The officer hesitated. His eyes darted from Clanless to Swift Claw to Sugh. He understood the danger, but would it override his commitment to the General?

"No one has to die here today," Koland said. "We can all… walk away."

Still the officer hesitated.

"I need you to take a message to General Ghan for me," Clanless said abruptly.

The officer's eyes narrowed. "What message?"

"Tell him that an army from the Melkute Kingdom is entering the Empire right now. He needs to get scouts out to locate them as soon as possible."

"There has been no sign of aggression from Melkute in years," the officer protested. "Where do you get this?"

"Suirel told me. He—"

"Wolf Chosen!" Swift Claw interrupted. "The beast is here!"

An enormous shape reared up almost right next to the officer, at least three times his height. Thick brown and white-streaked fur covered a heavy body with long limbs and a broad tail. Three massive curved claws extended from each of its four limbs. A roar exploded from a narrow snout on a head that looked almost too small for its body. It couldn't be a predator; something had disturbed it and pushed it into aggressive behavior when it should be hibernating.

"Soldiers! To me!" the officer shouted, backing away. He was too late; with another roar, the beast swung one of its huge arms and tossed him a dozen feet through the air. The momentum caused it to fall on all fours, curving its paws inward because of the huge claws.

A half a dozen spears flew toward the beast. Most bounced off its tough hide, but two managed to penetrate: one near its right shoulder and the other on its left side. As the creature reared back up on its hind legs, the two spears wobbled, their tips only an inch or two deep.

Clanless spared a look back toward Kekeen. Koland stood in front of her and Qara, holding a flaming brand from the fire. They would be all right.

"Swift Claw! What can you tell me about this creature?" he shouted, moving out into the open toward the beast's left. He waved the moonblade to attract its attention away from the others. It turned and took a ponderous step in his direction. Despite its initial attack, it did not appear agile.

"They do not fight," Swift Claw answered. He bounded past Clanless to distract the creature further away. "Unless they are attacked. Then they are very fierce."

"I could figure that much out!" Clanless tried to wave back some of the soldiers, but they ignored him. "How do we stop it?"

"I do not know. We have never killed one."

Wonderful.

Two of the soldiers moved in close to stab at the beast with their spears. At their attack, it swung its front leg, again with surprising speed. It snapped one of the spears and knocked the second aside. The second soldier lost his footing. The creature turned after him.

Sugh leaped in the way with a shout. His axe connected with the beast's front leg and cut deep. The monster screamed and jerked away, almost yanking Sugh with it.

"It can be hurt!" one of the soldiers yelled. "It can be killed!"

Clanless wasn't sure. Sugh's axe cut it, but… even at full depth, the axe blade didn't get far. Their weapons could not do much damage against a creature this massive. It might take dozens of similar wounds to weaken it. He reached for the Taint, but it eluded him. He tried again, but nothing happened. Had he lost it in the cave?

"Everyone! Attack together!" the same soldier commanded.

"No!" Clanless shouted. "Don't get too close!" Sugh, about to join in, stopped himself and took a step back. He wrinkled his brow, as if confused.

But the soldiers ignored him, circling in at the monster. It turned back and forth as they approached, growling and pawing at the earth. When they got close, it reared up on its hind legs again. Six soldiers charged in with maces and spears. The creature struck back left and right. Three soldiers went down screaming.

"Swift Claw!" Clanless beckoned him close.

"Do we fight as one?" the beastman asked.

"No, no. We'd be no more effective than they were." Clanless watched the soldiers regroup, dragging their wounded out of the way. "The only vulnerable spot I can see is the head. The moonblade might be able to cut it deep enough there, but I can't get to it…"

"I will go," Swift Claw said. "Be ready." The beastman bounded away to the right, circling around the creature.

Clanless moved closer, but stayed out of the reach of those enormous forelimbs. Several of the soldiers moved back in, including two who came around either side toward Clanless. He kept an eye on their movements. They might be allies for the moment, but he hadn't forgotten their purpose here. With their ranks depleted by this fight, he hoped they wouldn't want another one.

The beast took an awkward step forward. One of the soldiers threw a spear. They all cheered when it stuck into the monster's right forelimb. Clanless didn't cheer for another superficial wound. He stepped forward and waved the moonblade. "Hey, hey! This way!"

Its head swung toward him. The eyes, far smaller than expected for a beast this size, tried to focus on the motion of the blade. Clanless took a step back, pulling the moving blade with him.

"What are you doing?" the soldier to his right asked.

"Wait…" Clanless kept waving the moonblade. Swift Claw would be in position by now.

At last the beast took the bait. It stepped forward and crashed down to all fours. Clanless and the soldiers jumped back to stay out of its reach.

In that moment, Swift Claw leaped onto the beast from behind and ran up its spine. Clanless turned the moonblade and tossed it high. Swift Claw reached up and caught it. The beast reacted to the weight on its back, turning its head back and forth. It started to rise again.

Swift Claw brought the moonblade down with all the force he could muster. The blade penetrated deep into the monster's skull. It reared up with a scream. Swift Claw stabbed his own sword in as well, leaped free and backflipped away, leaving both blades buried in the creature's head. It wavered a moment longer, letting out a long moan, and crashed back to the ground. Its legs collapsed under it. The head with the embedded weapons twitched and lay still.

Clanless let out a sigh of relief. "Now we're getting somewhere." He stepped forward and reached for the moonblade.

"Take them now!" The voice sounded like the officer's, but strained, as if he were having difficulty speaking.

Clanless turned his head, looking for the speaker.

And a spear stabbed straight into his back.

TOO MUCH HEALING

Then

"What if I spill the blood?" the young priest asked, his voice shaking.

"Then you'll be expelled from the priesthood, sold as a slave, and spend the rest of your life working in the crystal mines," the old priest answered.

"What?" The younger man's voice rose in almost a screech.

The old priest put a hand on his shoulder. "Relax. That was a joke, son. If you spill blood, we'll mop it up. There's plenty more where that came from." He gestured at the enormous storage crystals around them.

"A-all right." He had no problem with the first part of the process: slicing open the pig's bladder and spreading it out on the table. His nervousness came from handling the Clan Ghamkiin blood. He picked up the dropper and dipped it into the bowl of already-catalyzed thick red liquid.

"It's only a few drops," his mentor said. "There's nothing to worry about."

Maybe not for him. He'd been doing this for years, perhaps decades. The young priest had never handled the sacred blood, prepared for magic by the power of the goddess herself. And he'd always been clumsy; his hands were so much bigger than others his age. He eyes never left the dropper as he moved it to the tiny crystal container he held in his other hand.

"Goddess above, use this blood for your glory," he whispered. The older priest joined him in the recitation: "Bless our work and our growth. Blood is life. Blood is precious. Blood is power."

Despite his worries, the transfer of blood into the crystal worked. He put the dropper aside and fumbled with the wax seal until he could be sure no blood would leak.

"There. You see?" The older priest patted him on the back. "Now you have only to sew the crystal into the bladder, attach the punch tube, and seal the bladder itself. Another Siphon for the arena."

"I… I don't fully understand, sir. I know that the Clan Ghamkiin blood can be used to manipulate other blood, but… how does it help here?"

The older priest picked up the tiny crystal. Its shape, a special design, was flatter than the vials used for currency and included special ridges for wrapping thin twine to sew it in place. "Since this blood is already catalyzed, the magic is already at work. Do you feel it?" He placed the crystal in his trainee's open palm.

The young man furrowed his brow. "It feels… strange. The tips of my fingers are colder, I think."

"Because the blood within your hand is being drawn toward the blood in the crystal. But this catalyzed blood has a limited life, which is why we at this temple make so many of these. The arena warriors use them up." He took the crystal back and held it up, letting light filter through the redness within. "When the punch tube is inserted into a fallen body, some blood naturally flows into it. But this causes the blood to flow more rapidly into the bladder, as the blood is drawn to it."

"Then how is the blood removed? Wouldn't it want to stay inside, next to the crystal?"

The older priest chuckled and placed the crystal back on to the bladder. "Blood is still blood, boy. It will flow when upended. This is not enough to counteract that."

His face burning, the young man turned back to his work.

"Ah." The older man shifted his feet. "I am too harsh. I apologize for calling you 'boy.' Old habits, I'm afraid." He chuckled again. "After all, few would think you're a boy based on your size. Fewer still would believe you're still only thirteen."

"I can't help being the biggest and strongest. I—"

"It's all right. It's all right, Sugh. Get back to your work here. I'm sure you're going to be an excellent priest."

Now

Koland grabbed Kekeen by the arm and held her back. "Qara, wait!" he snapped at the other woman who also started forward.

Qara fumbled at her belt and pulled out a blood vial. "I can heal him!" She pointed at the spot where Aldan had fallen.

"Aldan!" Kekeen shouted.

Koland's mind raced. Something didn't add up. The officer had been considering their arguments before the beast attacked. Now he'd lost at least half of his soldiers. Why attack now?

As if to underscore the point, Swift Claw bounded over the monster's body and tore into the soldier who'd stabbed Aldan. The soldier's screams as he fell beneath the beastman came to an abrupt and horrifying stop. Swift Claw whirled back around, slinging blood from his claws. The nearest soldier dropped his spear and held up both hands. "It wasn't me! It wasn't me!" He turned and tried to run, stumbling in the snow.

Koland released Kekeen and let the two women rush to Aldan's side. He couldn't see the wound from here, but the spear had penetrated deep in the center of the lower back. A horrible injury, but Qara's blood-magic should be able to heal it.

He looked around the battleground. The rest of the soldiers backed away, spears and maces at ready. None of them wanted to deal with the furious beastman. Or the enormous arena fighter who joined him in advancing toward them.

"Sugh!" Koland called. "Wait." He hurried to catch up. "Let me speak to them."

"They can leave now, or we will leave them for the scavengers," Sugh growled, shifting his axe from hand to hand.

Koland held up a palm and stepped toward the soldiers. "As I said at the beginning, this is not a fight you want. Take your injured comrades and go. We will not pursue you."

"Don't listen to him!" shouted the voice of the officer. "Kill them all!"

The other soldiers looked at each other, but didn't advance.

"Where is he?" Koland wondered.

Sugh pointed with his axe. "He lies over there."

"Should I remove his wind?" Swift Claw asked.

Koland blinked. "I... don't think that's necessary right now." He climbed over a rock and looked down at the wounded officer. The man held a hand to his side and glared back up at him.

"Don't ask your men to die for you, son," Koland said gently. "There's been enough bloodshed today. The goddess will not be pleased."

"Suirel will deal with your goddess. Soldiers! Kill them!"

Koland considered a moment, trying not to be distracted by the exclamations of dismay coming from the women. "Swift Claw, did I hear you say this beast was normally asleep?"

"It is so."

"Soldiers of the Empire!" Koland turned to face the others. "We have a beast that was behaving unlike itself, and now your leader seems not to be himself. Does this sound familiar?"

The troops murmured to each other. At last, one lifted his chin. "It sounds a bit like those… things in the cave. The ones taking control of people."

"Exactly. The blood-wraiths." Koland pointed down at the officer. "This one is no longer the man you knew. He belongs to Suirel now. Do not listen to him."

"He lies!" the officer shouted.

"Father!" Kekeen called. "We need you!"

"Take your wounded and go," Koland told the soldiers.

One of them pointed toward the officer. "What about him?"

"That's your decision." Koland scowled. "If it were up to me, I'd leave him here. Let that thing within him try to find something else to possess when he freezes to death."

"He was a good officer," one of the others mumbled. Another leaned in to whisper something. The others gathered around to join the discussion.

Koland jumped down from the rock and looked toward Aldan and the women. "What's wrong?"

Kekeen looked up at him, wide-eyed. "The healing blood isn't working!"

A wrongness swept through his own blood. Blood-magic always worked. How could… He didn't have time to think about it yet. He looked back to the soldiers. "Have you decided?"

One soldier hooked his mace to his belt. "We will take the wounded and leave. We will tell the General you escaped after killing our companions."

"Tell the General about the Melkute army Aldan told you about." Koland leaned toward Sugh. "Watch them." He and Swift Claw hurried to join the women.

"What is happening?"

Qara looked up, a wild look in her eyes. "The wound partially closed, and then it just stopped! This shouldn't be happening!"

Koland knelt beside Aldan. So much blood covered the warrior, he found it difficult to tell the new from the old. Qara held her hand over the wound, staunching any further blood flow. "Is that his only injury?"

"As far as we can tell," Kekeen said. She held Aldan's hand and stared intently at his face. "The rest of the blood is from something else."

Swift Claw picked up the discarded spear and sniffed it. "There is no poison."

Aldan still breathed, though his eyes were closed. Koland stood and looked around. One member of the party was missing. Finally, he spotted the Ghamba Lam emerging from behind another rock. "Priest!" he called. "If you're done hiding, we need your help over here!"

The Ghamba Lam scowled, but made his way to join them. "I was—" He broke off on seeing Aldan. "Goddess preserve him. Heal him, girl. Are you out of the proper blood?"

"I've been trying!" Qara snapped. "It's not working!"

"Have you ever heard of anything like this?" Koland asked. "Any time where blood-magic failed?"

"No, never. I..." The priest trailed off and cocked his head. "Of course, there's one possibility."

"What is it?" Kekeen demanded.

"He... if his body has been healed too much at once, it's possible the magic is... ah, overdone, I suppose."

"Overdone?" Qara said. "What do you mean?"

"Too much healing." The Ghamba Lam waved his arms in a frustrated gesture. "His body can't handle any more."

"This does not make sense," Sugh said, joining them. "We arena fighters have all been healed hundreds of time. It's always worked for us."

"I don't know!' The Ghamba Lam pointed at Aldan. "Look at him! He's covered in blood. He went down the Throat. Who knows what happened to him down there?"

"Swift Claw, did he say anything to you about what happened?" Koland asked.

The beastmen shook his head. "Nothing. But the blood has many smells."

"Koland..." The whisper came so low, he almost didn't hear it.

"He's awake!" Kekeen exclaimed.

Koland moved next to Aldan's head. "I'm here, Aldan."

"Need to know... army..."

"You said something about the Melkute Kingdom invading. Is that right?" He brought his head down close to hear the warrior's whispers.

In broken phrases, Aldan told an unbelievable story about a sea of blood and a battle between gods. The final part about an invading army fueled by righteous anger chilled Koland. His story finished, Aldan sighed and said no more.

"What did he say?" Sugh asked.

Koland stood. "A story more fantastic than anything I could come up with." He shook his head. "In other circumstances, I'd be jealous. But your theory now makes more sense, Ghamba Lam. He's been through some amazing things."

The priest folded his arms. "It is as I told you."

"We'll have to carry him. Sugh, help me find what we need to make a litter. I only wish we had blankets or something to help keep him warm."

"We'll bring the fire to him," Qara said, rising to her feet.

"That'll help for now. But we can't stay here for long. That huge corpse is going to attract predators pretty soon." He looked in every direction. "I'm unsure about our course, though. We're a long way from anyone who can help us."

"We go that way." The Ghamba Lam pointed. "Southwest. From here, we should intercept the main road within a few hours. With luck, my own wagons will be on their way back to Et-Baylak, and we can ride with them."

The others stared at him. The priest scowled. "What? I told you I didn't grow up in the big city. I know how to navigate outside."

"He's not wrong," Koland said. "Let's get to work."

A loud scream came from the direction of the wounded officer.

"What about that one?" Sugh asked.

"Stay far away from him." Koland looked toward him and sighed. "I wish we could do something for him, but the risk of the thing inside him possessing one of us is too great." His eyes drifted toward his daughter. Kekeen hadn't shown any sign of possession herself, but he still wondered.

Qara and Kekeen got busy with the fire while the men built a litter. Swift Claw found the highest spot from which to watch and surveyed the surrounding area for new threats.

In a short time, they were ready to move. They took great care in transferring Aldan onto the litter. Qara used every bit of spare cloth she could tear off other clothing to bandage his wound. Ironic that the biggest worry for a man covered in blood was that he might lose too much.

Throughout the process and as they started to leave, the officer continued to scream furious imprecations at them. Koland stepped as near as he dared to the fallen soldier and stared at him until he stopped.

"We're leaving now," Koland said. "You might want to consider whether your yelling will attract predators faster. Or if that's what you want."

"I need not this body. When it fails, I will seek out another."

"I suppose you will." He paused and considered. "But you haven't yet. Which tells me it's not so easy. Maybe you need that body to die before you can leave. Or maybe you're worried about what might happen if you try. I don't know. I wish I understood your kind better."

The officer's look softened from rage to something Koland couldn't identify. "There is an easy way for you to learn, storyteller. Step closer, and I will share what you want to know."

"Ha. I may be a fool in some regards, but not that much of one."

"You are missing so much." The officer shook his head and winced. "I could tell you stories far beyond your knowledge, stories of another world, of conflicts between beings whose power dwarfs that of your goddess. Stories of pain and triumph, wisdom and power. Stories of tyrants and rebellion, love and glory. You would gain access to so much I can't even express its magnitude."

"And all for the sake of surrendering my very being to you. No, thanks. Not for all the knowledge of this world or any other." He turned to go.

"I don't have to control you, you know. We could work together."

Koland paused.

"Take the fur from the fallen warrior and wear it yourself. It would protect you. I could come along as an advisor." He grunted and tried to shift his position. "Take me, and I will share all that I know with you."

Koland looked back. "Fascinating. You're truly desperate to escape this moment. I wonder what that means. If you don't have a body to possess, will you return to where you came from?" He glanced up toward the fading image of the chaos moon. "Or will you cease to exist?" He shook his head. "Either way, I wouldn't want to be you."

"Storyteller! Wait!"

Koland ignored him. He jogged over to the others. "Let's get out of here."

"Wait! I can help you!" The shouts followed them. "I know Suirel's secrets! I can tell you how to defeat him!"

The Ghamba Lam looked back. "Should we... I don't know. Should we listen to him? Would it be worth it to gain such knowledge?"

"He's a lying blood-wraith," Kekeen snapped. "Leave him to his fate."

"If Clanless were able, he could cast it out," Sugh said. "But he is not. Let us go."

Koland nodded and let them proceed ahead of him. The Ghamba Lam led the way with Sugh and Swift Claw carrying Aldan's litter. The women walked on either side, keeping an eye on him. Koland took one last look toward the fallen officer, one last moment of hesitation, and then joined them.

THE ROAD TO ET-BAYLAK

The Ghamba Lam's guidance proved accurate. A few hours after setting out, not long after midday, they found the road leading to Et-Baylak. But they could see no sign of wagons or carriages in either direction.

"What do we do now?" Qara wondered.

Sugh and Swift Claw lowered the litter with care. The arena fighter looked up the road toward the mines and hefted his axe. "Come, Swift Claw. Let us find what we need."

"Where are you going?" Koland asked.

Sugh gestured. "We will find a way to get home."

"You're going to steal a carriage out in front of the entire army?"

"It is a challenge! Ho, beastman! What think you? Will you join me in this?"

Swift Claw looked down at Aldan and took a few steps up the road. "Wolf Chosen needs aid. We will find it."

"Preposterous," the Ghamba Lam muttered. "We should wait here. My priests will be coming in time."

"You wait. We will go," Sugh said. He and Swift Claw moved on their way.

"Goddess go with you," Koland called. He sat on a rock beside the road and watched them.

"This is foolish," the priest complained. "Sending our warriors away." He looked out across the wilderness. "We could be attacked by anything while they are gone."

Koland pointed to the moonblade lying on the litter beside Aldan. "Then perhaps you should take a few practice swings with that while we wait."

The Ghamba Lam snorted and found his own place to sit. He brushed dirt from his robe, frowning mightily. Koland almost laughed. The priest's appearance was far from his usual magnificence. Then again, he supposed the rest of them didn't look much like themselves either.

Kekeen stepped beside him. "Do you think they have a chance?"

"If anyone does, they do." Koland stretched his fingers up and down. "I miss my dovshuur. Some music would be encouraging right now."

Kekeen lowered her head. "I don't think I could sing."

"Oh." He looked up quickly. "I didn't mean for you to. Just thinking out loud."

His daughter crouched on the road. "Do you think it will be safe to take Aldan to Et-Baylak?"

Koland brushed a bit of frost from his beard. "Why not?"

"I'm worried." She bit her lip. "So much has happened to him there. And he'll be recognized." She looked back at the litter where Qara sat watching Aldan. "I'm not..." She took a deep breath. "I'm not saying this just because I love him. If he's the only one who can fight these blood-wraiths, then we have to keep him safe until he can fight again."

He nodded slowly. "I suppose the capital city might not be the best place. General Ghan or Suirel may show up there soon. Or both. We have no idea of their plans. And yet... that is where I must go, at the least. Someone needs to warn the city about the Melkute threat."

"Can't the Ghamba Lam warn them?"

"Maybe. But would you trust him to be the best messenger to the various factions that control the city right now?"

Kekeen smiled. "No, I suppose not. I guess we'll have to split up."

Koland kept himself from frowning. He didn't like the idea of being separated from his daughter, especially as long as he couldn't be sure she remained herself. If Zektel did possess her, what could she gain by this separation? Did she mean to kill Aldan? No, she could do that now or in Et-Baylak. Maybe she planned to remove his protective fur and re-possess him. But that also could be done anywhere. What else could she be thinking? Maybe the idea came from Kekeen after all.

"Father?"

He shook his head and blinked. "Sorry. I was thinking. You're right, of course. But Aldan is recognizable almost anywhere. You can't go to Ulken, for instance."

"No. But I think I have an idea. Somewhere he'll be as safe as he can be."

"Where would that be?"

Kekeen smiled. "Home."

Before she could elaborate, Qara approached. "I'm worried about keeping him warm," she said, gesturing back to Aldan. "We have nothing to cover him. Can we build another fire?"

Koland rose. "Good thought. I'm sorry I didn't consider it first. The sun is warming things up, but it's not enough. Ghamba Lam!"

The priest looked up with shaded eyes.

"Help me gather wood for a fire?"

He gave an exaggerated sigh and pulled himself up. Together, the two men worked to find enough to fuel a small blaze. They found slim pickings near the road. Few trees of any size grew in this area. Koland borrowed Aldan's moonblade to cut apart what he could find. He marveled at the lightness of the weapon, considering its size. The intricate detail work—the craters carved into the blade itself, the engraving on the pommel—could not be denied. At some point, he needed to hear the story of how Clanless obtained this blade.

The afternoon wore away. Koland occupied himself by keeping the fire going. Aldan did not regain consciousness. Based on his story, his body had endured unbelievable violence and effort. The fact he'd made it this far was astonishing. It might yet take a long time for him to fully rest, let alone heal.

Kekeen alternated between praying at Aldan's side and pacing. Qara took inventory of her remaining blood supplies at least a dozen times. The Ghamba Lam, surprisingly, behaved the most patient of them all, waiting without movement or comment for an hour or more at a time.

"What are you doing?" Qara asked him at one point.

"Meditating, child. A worthwhile practice in times such as these. You should try it."

She rolled her eyes and left him alone after that.

About an hour before the sun's retreat concluded, the Ghamba Lam stood up. "A carriage is coming," he announced.

Koland's legs complained as he got up. He'd been sitting in one position for too long. He stared down the road at the approaching vehicle. "It's not military, at least," he observed. "They'd be coming for us with much more than a single carriage."

"The beastman rides on top," the priest said. "I don't recognize the carriage itself, however. It's not one of ours."

As it drew closer, Koland laughed. "It's one of the carriages we came in! How on earth did they manage to steal that from under the noses of Ghan's soldiers?"

"Greetings!" Sugh pulled back on the reins when the carriage arrived. "We thought this one looked like the best of the available options."

Koland clapped his hands. "You'll have to tell me how you did this. But not yet. We'd better get a move on before the sun completes its retreat."

Once Aldan had been carefully loaded into the carriage, they set out. Koland suggested traveling through the night to put as much distance between them and Suirel as possible. No one argued with him. They took turns handling the driving while one or two others tried to gain a little sleep. With Aldan already stretched out, they didn't have much room.

As the sun's pursuit began the next morning, Koland looked to the moon. A tinge of red shaded it, a sure sign of the season. The redness often appeared early and late each day at the beginning of High Spring. Koland gave the oxen a break and discussed their destination with the entire group. "Kekeen wishes to take Aldan somewhere safer to recover, but the Ghamba Lam and I must go to Et-Baylak. When we get nearer the city, we can easily find other transportation to split off."

"I will go with Wolf Chosen," Swift Claw said at once.

"I expected no less. Sugh?"

The big man grinned. "I promised to protect this one"—he patted Kekeen on her knee—"until she was reunited with Clanless. He is here, but is not able to protect her yet. So I must continue."

Kekeen smiled but said nothing.

"Qara?"

She looked at Aldan and sighed. "My heart says to go with Aldan, but… I can be of more use in Et-Baylak." She glanced at Kekeen before looking down at her own lap.

Koland understood. Unrequited love could be a heavy burden. "I will appreciate the help," he told her. "And the company. The priest here isn't the most pleasant of traveling companions."

"What does that mean?" the Ghamba Lam demanded.

"It's intended as a joke. I tell those as well as stories sometime."

"I fail to see the humor."

"Of course you do." Koland stood. "Let's get moving again."

Four days later, the carriage approached Et-Baylak. Koland turned from the window. He'd been thinking things through but needed to explore it out loud.

"We'll need a plan," he announced. "Ghamba Lam, what do you propose?"

"Me?" The priest relaxed on his carriage seat. "What makes you think I have a plan?"

"You've always got plans," Qara accused him. "You planned for Aldan's whole life!"

He raised his eyebrows. "I assure you, my dear: I did no such thing. I hoped he would become what was needed, and I pushed him in that direction. But a plan?" He shook his head. "No. I push people. I even manipulate from time to time. And I motivate. But it's all extemporaneous. I never know what may happen."

"Then it's time to use some of that manipulation," Koland said. "We need to convince the three Lords that this threat is real, so they'll prepare the city's defenses. Can I count on you for that much?"

The Ghamba Lam leaned forward. "This may come as a surprise to you, storyteller. But I am very much appreciative of my life, and I'd like to keep it. Of course I'll back you up."

"I think it would be better if you take the lead."

He nodded. "You're absolutely right. I'll call a meeting of the council at once. You can show up too, even though you quit on us."

"You know why I did that."

"Of course. But with you, your friend—I forget his name—and myself, we have but to convince one of the three Lords of our case, and that will be enough."

"Word will not have reached them yet," Koland mused. "They know nothing of Daviland and Suirel, General Ghan, or anything else."

"Unless some of the other priests made it back already," Qara put in.

The Ghamba Lam lowered his head. "I fear none of them ever left the mines. I saw no evidence along the road that they had traveled there."

"Then we have to decide what to tell them, exactly." Koland tapped his beard and looked out the window, thinking again.

"I'm sure they'll be happy to hear Daviland was possessed by a blood-wraith all along," Qara said. "And that he released the god of chaos onto the world. I'm sure the conversation will be ever-so-pleasant."

The Ghamba Lam scowled at her. "Leave the political maneuvering to your betters, girl."

"Have you really never heard sarcasm before? Were people too much in awe of your position to make jokes with you?"

"We tell them Daviland remained behind with the General," Koland said, still watching through the window. "They don't need to know anything more than that… except the Melkute threat, of course."

"Indeed. It may be more difficult to explain your presence than Daviland's absence."

Koland nodded. "I have an idea about that too." He hesitated and turned away from the window. "But we're leaving out one very important factor."

"What is that?" The Ghamba Lam straightened his robe, frowning at its dirtiness.

"Lord Ulakan is, at the very least, a supporter of the Suirel cult. We don't know how deep his involvement actually goes." Koland gripped the armrest beside the window. "Obviously, I have personal issues with him. And he's not likely to be pleased that neither Daviland nor Demujin have returned."

The Ghamba Lam nodded. "I had actually forgotten Demujin's status. Or rather, I blocked it from my mind once we left him behind."

"I can't blame you for that." Koland chuckled. The cult leader had been a thorn in the Ghamba Lam's side throughout High Winter.

"Would one of the Lords really be willing to sacrifice the entire city?" Qara asked. "Wouldn't he be destroying his, um, lordship?"

The Ghamba Lam steepled his fingers and cocked his head. "As ironic as it may sound coming from me, never underestimate the power of religious belief. That being said, I believe you are probably right. Ulakan has flirted with the cult, but surrendering the city to an invader? I don't think he'd go that far. In fact, I see no need to mention the cult's involvement with the invasion at all. Or even bring up Suirel."

"You're suggesting we portray this as a Melkute invasion and leave out everything else?" Koland tapped his beard again. "I can see the advantages of that. It should work, as long as no one else shows up to contradict us."

"I will order some trusted priests to watch the roads and report to me."

"Then I think we have a plan of sorts." Koland sat back and relaxed. He couldn't do anything about a god of chaos unleashed on the world, but he might be able to save this one city from destruction.

4

COUNCILS

Clanless wandered far in his dreams. He didn't remember how he got there, but somehow, he found himself walking behind a shining figure he knew to be the goddess. He could see almost nothing of their surroundings or much of anything of her form and appearance. Light infused everything, a warm light filling him with comfort and peace.

"Remember," her voice said in his mind, "do not speak. Your presence here is a courtesy only. Few mortals have experienced this… at least on your side of the veil."

He didn't quite know what that meant but nodded anyway. They emerged from whatever passage they had been traveling into a space so vast he couldn't imagine its dimensions. Though his vision continued to be limited by the dazzling light, he realized that thousands upon thousands of other beings moved about in this space. They radiated power and majesty, making him feel tiny and weak, like a small child walking into the presence of mighty warriors like Hagh and Sugh. Even that comparison fell far short of the reality.

The vast crowd's attention focused on a central area where a circle of thrones were placed. Clanless couldn't be sure of the number, but it must have been several dozen at the least. One of the thrones stood far larger than the others, surrounded by—or perhaps even composed of—blazing fire. The figure who sat on it dwarfed the others.

The goddess took a seat in one of the thrones. Clanless stood behind her, silent and watching. The gathering gave him the impression of a court or council where judgment could be decided upon or delivered.

Another shining figure stood before the largest throne, facing the others. "Suirel has been thwarted for the moment." The voice thundered in Clanless's head, and he staggered back. If he'd felt small before, the voice rendered him infinitesimal. "What say you now? Shall we leave the fallen peoples to his wrath? Or shall we intervene?"

Clanless wanted to jump forward and plead with them to intervene, to cast Suirel down once and for all. But the thought of stepping into the full view of these gods—especially the one on the largest throne—filled him with such dread he wanted to melt away into nothing.

Other voices spoke, but he heard not their words. The glory of the moment overwhelmed him. He sank down to his knees, face buried in his hands.

"Fear not," a voice whispered in his ear. A hand touched his shoulder, grasping him where his brand had always been. Yet in a sudden surge of realization, he understood the brand did not exist in this place.

With the hand on his shoulder, he could once again understand the larger voices speaking before him. He lifted his face, but did not rise from his knees.

"Then who shall go for us? Suirel and his forces are too much for the fallen peoples to resist alone." Clanless thought this voice came from the one standing near the largest throne, but he couldn't be sure.

"I will return to their world." For some reason, this voice sounded familiar. Clanless tried to see around the throne of the goddess to glimpse the speaker. He thought he saw a figure step down from a throne on the opposite side. He squinted, trying to discern anything about the shining figure.

"You have been a voice of wisdom at times," said the voice of the goddess. "Will you take a more direct role now?"

"I will do what must be done. Suirel knows that you are responsible for this people group. He expects your interference and thus plans for it. He does not expect me."

"His arrogance blinds him," said another voice. "Already, Suirel has suffered loss."

"It is a minor setback," the goddess said. "He will soon enact his plan to flood my world with his foul souls."

"It is not your world," answered the familiar-sounding voice. "Nor are they your people. Do not forget your place as steward. You are here now because you have chosen to repent and resume your designated role. Do not test our patience again."

The goddess lowered her head. "You are just to remind me."

Clanless trembled. He thought he understood the discussion, but pieces of it eluded him. The hand on his shoulder continued to give him comfort and courage but not total understanding. At the least, he grasped that the fate of his people was at stake.

The one who stood beside the throne crossed the open space to stand in front of the one with the familiar voice. "Go and do your part," he said. "But know this: the path to defeating Suirel requires surrender, as it ever has. Be on your guard. Do not be swayed by his words. And remember that you are not alone either."

At that, both of them turned their heads to look toward Clanless. He trembled even harder at the weight of their gaze and felt his consciousness fading, taking him away from this place. But one thing he knew and sought to hold on to even as the vision faded: the one who had volunteered to oppose Suirel looked at him with golden eyes.

((((●))))

"The Melkute Kingdom is invading!" The Ghamba Lam made his pronouncement and stepped back to watch the reactions. Koland stood just outside the door, listening.

"I've heard nothing of the sort!" Lord Ulakan exclaimed. "Once their ambassador returns from his High Winter recess, we have a new trade agreement to finalize."

"An agreement that cuts far too much into the profits of our own clans," Lord Ghayaktal said. "We—"

"This is not about trade agreements!" the Ghamba Lam interrupted. "A real army is marching toward us even now!"

Lord Ezen rubbed his beard. "Your holiness, this is… a rather difficult tale to drop on us this early in the morning. Can you, perhaps, shed some light on the absence of our dear leader first?" He gestured to the empty seat at the head of the table.

"Daviland and Demujin remained with General Ghan at the crystal mines," the priest said. "As I understand it, the General is planning some sort of holding action."

"A holding action?" Lord Ezen shook his head. "The General has most of our army with him. How large is this invading army that he does not believe he can stop them?"

Koland took that moment to push the door open and walk in. "It's large enough," he said. "Large enough that I accepted Daviland's plea to return with the Ghamba Lam and confirm his words to this council." He took his seat next to Sonkogh, who smiled.

Lord Ulakan's eyes narrowed. "This is nonsense. The two of you can't just barge in here and expect us to—"

"I expect you to accept my word in the matter," the Gamba Lam interrupted again. He lifted a hand to point toward the moon. "I swear to you by the goddess herself: what the storyteller and I describe for you is true."

The men at the table glanced at each other. Political differences or not, when the head of the state religion swore to the goddess, they couldn't ignore his words. Koland had counted on it.

"We have to prepare the city's defenses," he said. "Who is in charge?"

"Ah, that would be Captain Rakib," Lord Ezen said. He started to get up. "I'll summon him at once."

"Wait, wait…" Lord Ulakan lifted a hand to stop him.

Koland frowned. He'd hoped the oath would silence any serious argument.

Lord Ulakan shook his head. "You don't need to summon Captain Rakib. He's waiting in the outer chamber for an audience already."

"What for?" Sonkogh asked.

"An issue regarding blood dispersion. It means nothing before this issue."

In a few moments, Captain Rakib, a short man with broad shoulders, entered and was apprised of the situation. He did not react with surprise. "How much time do we have?" he wanted to know.

"We don't know, exactly," Koland said. "But it could be only days."

"I have scouts dispatched in every direction to be on the lookout," the Ghamba Lam added. "The moment I know more, you will know."

Captain Rakib nodded. "Then I will begin the preliminaries, but with an emphasis on haste. We'll start by evacuating the farmlands and small villages on the outskirts." He paused and took a deep breath. "There will be resistance. With the end of this Chaos Winter, the need for a good harvest this year is essential, and that process begins now. They won't want to leave."

"I would think the possibility of imminent death would be enough to persuade them," Lord Ghayaktal observed.

"Then you don't know farmers, sir," Rakib answered. "Uh, no disrespect intended."

"Nevertheless, get things started," Lord Ezen commanded. "And send out your own scouts as well."

The Ghamba Lam huffed.

"The walls of Et-Baylak have never fallen," the Captain said. "And they will not fall this time."

"Let it be known throughout the Empire and under the moon's gaze," the Ghamba Lam whispered.

"Let it be known," Koland echoed.

((((●))))

"The people are confused, but they are complying with the orders," Captain Rakib reported to the council a week later.

Koland watched each of the men around the table for their reactions. Only five of them were present to hear the captain's report. The Ghamba Lam had not arrived. He could only hope it didn't portend more trouble.

"This is problematic," Lord Ulakan said. "We're already seeing signs of panic at the markets. As supplies dwindle, prices will go up, and people will grow desperate. If we don't see evidence of this invading army soon, I must demand an end to these unnecessary and potentially ruinous impositions."

"Isn't it wise to be prepared?" Sonkogh asked.

"You know nothing of the way our city's business is conducted!" Ulakan snapped. "You are only here because of your relationship to the man who killed the Hawk King, the one person, I should add, who could have protected us without question if this threat were actually genuine." He leaned across the table and eyed both Sonkogh and Koland. "Without your leader present, for that matter, I see no reason why either of you should be here."

"Would you say the same about me, my lord?" the Ghamba Lam asked as he swept into the room, cape billowing behind him.

Lord Ulakan glared at the priest. "We handled Et-Baylak's administration just fine before this council was created by the insurgent."

Captain Rakib shifted his feet, clearly uncomfortable. Koland imagined the soldier would much rather be in the presence of a physical duel than this verbal debate.

The Ghamba Lam took his place at the table. "I am sorry for the delay, my friends. But I have just received information that will aid all of us in making decisions." His eyes narrowed as he focused on Lord Ulakan. "All of us," he repeated.

"What is this information?" Lord Ezen asked.

"The scout reports." The Ghamba Lam paused and licked his lips before placing a sheet of paper on the table in front of him. "They have delivered two important facts for us to consider. First and foremost... the enemy army is real and moving this way."

The table exploded as everyone tried to ask questions at once. Koland alone sank further back in his chair, contemplating. Until this moment, he had hoped Aldan had been wrong. Or that Suirel had lied to him. But now, the die was cast. After a generation of peace, war approached the Sar Empire. "Goddess help us," he whispered.

"The next scout report should have definite numbers," the Ghamba Lam explained once the furor died down. "All the initial glimpses were able to determine is that the Melkute army is very large. Definitely large enough to lay siege to this city."

"The vagueness of this report does not, ah, inspire confidence," Lord Ghayaktal said.

"I plead for your patience," the Ghamba Lam replied. "When you hear the second piece of information, perhaps you will understand why this scout chose to rush back and report, leaving the next scout to determine numbers."

"Then tell us," Lord Ulakan growled.

"General Ghan is on his way." The Ghamba Lam's eyes met Koland's as he spoke.

"What? This is excellent news!" Lord Ezen exclaimed. "No offense to our good Captain here, but the General will be very welcome in the defense of this city!"

"How many troops does he bring with him?" Lord Ghayaktal asked.

"Around three thousand," the priest reported.

"Three thousand? He commanded over ten times that many at Tzhambul!" Lord Ulakan almost jumped out of his chair. "What has become of the rest of our army?"

"Be sure to ask him that when he arrives," the Ghamba Lam retorted.

"If I may…" Captain Rakib offered.

"Yes, Captain?" Sonkogh said quickly. "What is it?"

"If I had to guess, sirs, the General must have left a significant number of troops at Tzhambul to guard the mountain passes," the Captain said. "How this Melkute army got past them is a mystery. Unless…"

"Unless what?" Lord Ulakan asked.

"Unless Melkute defeated our army at Tzhambul already."

The table quieted at that thought. Koland pondered what he already knew. When General Ghan arrived at the mines, he'd come with at least six thousand soldiers. After receiving Koland's message, he must have left half of them behind and hurried ahead of the enemy army. Or maybe he'd fought holding actions against the Melkute and had already lost half his force.

But neither theory answered the biggest question: when Ghan arrived, would he come as the Sar Empire's defender or as Suirel's servant?

"General Ghan appears to be moving as fast as he can drive his troops." The Ghamba Lam broke the silence. "He should be here within two days." He paused before adding, "The enemy army will be no more than a day and a half behind him."

Koland saw Captain Rakib's face turn pale. "We have less than four days?"

"It would seem so."

"Then, if your lordships will excuse me…"

"Yes, yes, of course," Lord Ezen said, waving at the Captain. "Notify all who need to know. But try not to let this spread to the general populace just yet."

As the Captain rushed from the room, Koland eyed the Ghamba Lam. Something else bothered the priest. His body language communicated greater unease than his words.

"I… suppose we all have more preparations to attend to." Lord Ghayaktal stood.

"Why should we keep this news from the general populace?" Sonkogh wanted to know. "Wouldn't it help them in their own preparations?"

"We must be guard against creating a panic," Lord Ezen said.

"But if we wait, won't the panic be greater?" Sonkogh gestured toward the door. "If we tell them an enemy is four days away, that's frightening, to be sure. But if we wait and tell them the enemy is only a day's journey, won't it be more terrifying?"

"It's a valid point," Koland said, "but Lord Ezen is also correct. This must be handled carefully. Ghamba Lam, do you have any suggestions in this regard?"

"Eh?" The Ghamba Lam appeared to startle out of some other thoughts. "Yes, yes. I suppose. Perhaps we should inform the populace in stages."

"Then let's inform the upper city first," Lord Ghayaktal said.

"What good would that do?" Sonkogh demanded. "They are the most protected already!"

"And thus, the least likely to panic," Lord Ulakan said. "If the lower classes see that the upper class is behaving appropriately, it may help their mindset as well."

Koland almost laughed out loud. Did the Lords really believe such things? Had they so convinced themselves of their superiority, or did they know they were being ridiculous? He leaned over and whispered to Sonkogh, "Don't worry about it. We'll inform the lower city ourselves. I'll get

Qara on it right away."

With a few parting comments, the Lords hastened out of the chamber. Sonkogh patted Koland on the back as he stood. "We'll get through this, goddess willing."

"Moon's stability to you, old friend."

"And to you."

Once he'd gone through the door, Koland turned at once to the Ghamba Lam. "What do we do about Ghan? Do you think he's coming to help or harm us?"

"Help the city, perhaps," the priest answered without looking up. "Help us? Almost certainly not. He swore allegiance to Suirel."

Koland got to his feet and walked around the council table. "Then we must decide between fighting and fleeing, I suppose."

The Ghamba Lam looked up with raised eyebrows. "Fight against the commander of the Empire's armies?"

"He is just a man. Men can be fought." Koland waited a moment before adding, "Or killed."

"Assassination may have been a tool in your fledgling rebellion, but not here and now. The Lords are right. Ghan is our best chance at saving this city."

"But what if he does not intend to save it?"

The Ghamba Lam shook his head. "I cannot accept that concept. You sent the message to him about the enemy, and now he comes this way? If he wanted the city to fall, he had only to stay where he was. Instead, he brings reinforcements and races to get here before the enemy."

"But Suirel…"

"Suirel wants chaos." The Ghamba Lam stood, hands pressed on the table's surface. "He cares not whether the city stands or falls. But Ghan… the good General loves the Empire, regardless of any other faults he may possess. I know him well, storyteller. He will not betray Et-Baylak."

Koland glanced toward the doors. "Then should we hide or flee ourselves and leave it to him?"

"I will not." The Ghamba Lam toyed with the scout report. "He would not dare to move against me here. I do possess some modicum of power myself, you know." He sighed and picked up the report. "You must make your own decision."

"Ghamba Lam…" Koland hesitated. "You seemed distracted earlier. Is there something else in the report you did not tell us?"

"In the report? No."

"Then…?"

"I mentioned my power just now. Ha." The laugh came without humor. "Most believe the position of the Ghamba Lam to be the supreme power beneath the goddess herself. But such is not the case. I answer to a council as well, a council of Daghilchs."

"Are there that many within the city?"

"Hm? Oh, yes. More than you know. And together, they hold much more power than I."

Koland again glanced toward the doors. "I fail to understand, I'm afraid. What is the problem?"

The Ghamba Lam crumpled the scout report into a ball. "I gathered the council and reported all that took place at the mines—all of it, mind you. They did not take it well."

"Did they expect you to prevent Suirel's release?"

"Some, perhaps. But not many." He waved a hand in dismissal. "Yet there are others who think I'm fabricating the entire thing in an attempt to solidify my own position and fame. They regard tales of blood-wraiths and chaos gods to be fanciful, relics of a more ignorant time."

Koland let the Ghamba Lam continue without interruption.

"And still others voice vague objections that don't make any sense! I suspect Suirel's cult has infiltrated the priesthood at a higher level than previously known."

"Ah."

The Ghamba Lam stalked several strides toward the door. "And when all these disparate groups unite, they counter all I have, all I am."

Koland caught up with him. "Do you think they will remove you? Has that ever been done before?"

"No, it has not." He stopped and faced Koland. "But that does not mean it cannot happen. If it does…" He sighed. "If it does, then you will be the only one who can fight, storyteller. The only one who knows… the whole story."

He turned again and pushed his way through the doors. Koland remained alone, gathering his thoughts.

HOME

"Why does the goddess not answer me when I pray?" Sugh stared up through the glass canopy at the moon.

Arban, his fellow priest and mentor, stopped sweeping the temple and regarded him. "What do you mean?"

Sugh turned and spread his arms. "I pray and pray and pray. But I never hear her voice."

"The goddess does not often speak in a voice we can hear with our ears, son."

"She did in the stories." Sugh frowned. "I always thought I would hear her myself once I became a priest."

"I have never heard her voice," Arban said. "And I do not know anyone who has."

"Not even the Ghamba Lam?"

"Having never met the highest priest myself, I could not tell you that." Arban held out the broom. "Finish up in here, please. I have some blood stores to move around."

Sugh took the broom, but Arban did not release it. "Are you happy here, Sugh? As a priest?"

Sugh's eyes widened. "There is nothing I would rather do!"

"Whether the goddess speaks to you or not?"

"My heart beats for her! I would never turn my back on our goddess!"

Arban smiled and released the broom. "Good, good. I merely wanted to be sure. Some are not fit for the priesthood, you know. And there is no shame in it."

"I will be the best priest in all of the Sar Empire!"

"Perhaps you will." Arban turned to go. "In the meantime, please finish with this floor."

Now

Clanless knew he'd been sleeping and dreaming, but everything blurred together. He'd fought a great beast with Swift Claw, but he couldn't remember what happened next. He recalled something about golden eyes, but little else. His brand. Something about the brand. Without opening his eyes, he felt his shoulder. The brand was unchanged. He sighed.

"Are you awake?" Kekeen's voice drifted to him from somewhere nearby.

"Mmm." Other sensations came to him: great pain in his lower back, the smell of bread cooking somewhere close, and the voice of a child playing outside.

He opened his eyes and looked up at a low ceiling. They weren't in the city. But this couldn't be what it seemed to be. "Wh-where?" He struggled to speak through a dry mouth.

"You need water. Just a moment." With a rustle of cloth, Kekeen came into view holding a leather canteen. "Here." She knelt and slid a hand behind his head. With her help, he lifted his head and drank. Cool, clean water poured down his throat. Deep well water. Also not from the city.

"Is that better?"

He started to answer, but Kekeen put a finger on his lips. "But maybe you'd rather drink from a different source." She leaned in and brought her lips to his. The kiss started gentle, but swiftly became deeper and more passionate. Surprised at first, Clanless let himself go and enjoyed the moment. Nothing else mattered right now.

At last, Kekeen pulled free and gasped for breath. "Oh. You can't believe how long I've been wanting to do that."

Clanless struggled to recover his own breath. "I… where are we?"

Kekeen glanced around. "You don't recognize it? We needed to take you somewhere safe, where no one would find you." She looked back at him with an unusual smile. He recognized it, but… it didn't seem exactly right. "Haven't you guessed yet?" She spread an arm out to indicate everything. "Welcome home, Aldan."

Home? "The clanhold?"

"Yes. There wasn't room in your parents' house, at least not without sharing with your little brother—who is a joy, by the way—so you've been sleeping here." She gestured again. "In your uncle's house."

Clanless erupted up from the bed but collapsed at once from the pain in his back.

Kekeen laughed, an almost tinkling giggle not like her at all. "Don't worry. He's working out in the fields right now. And you should know: he's absolutely terrified of you. It's quite hilarious."

He turned his eyes toward her face, a horrible thought dancing on the edges of his mind. "Kekeen, you…"

She raised her eyebrows. "Yes, dearheart?"

"No. No. No."

She put a hand on his chest and leaned in. "Whatever is the problem?"

"Zektel." He glared at her and swallowed.

"Very good. I can't fool you. Not that I was trying, really. I wanted you to know." She leaned even closer, almost lying on top of him. "Isn't this the best of all worlds, Aldan? You get both of us, both of the ones who loved you. And we get you. This will be so much better than before. So many wonderful possibilities." She kissed his chin.

"Stop it."

"You don't mean that. You want this. You love Kekeen, and you've missed me. You can't deny it." She kissed his cheek.

Her weight put extra pressure on his back. The pain grew with each moment, but he didn't care.

"I will drive you out of her," he struggled to say.

She shook her head. "No, you won't." She sat up, relieving the pressure. "And I'll tell you why." She put a hand over her chest. "You see, after Suirel ordered me to enter this body, I realized something. Precious Kekeen has a tiny… imperfection in her heart. It's not enough to cause her any problems for, oh, at least thirty or forty years under normal circumstances. In fact, it might never be a problem." Her smile widened. "But if you ever cut me and try to use your Taint on me… as I leave her, I'll agitate that imperfection." The smile vanished. "And poor Kekeen's heart will fail. She'll die, Aldan. So let's not try that, shall we?"

"I'll find a way," he whispered.

"I know you'll try. But it's pointless, dear Aldan." She ran her palm across his chest. "Let's just enjoy ourselves, shall we?"

The worst thing about it: she wasn't entirely wrong. He hated it. He despised Zektel and everything she stood for. But he had missed her. He couldn't deny the appeal of having her around to talk to... but not at the expense of Kekeen. He had to figure it out. He had to get her out.

"I'm not wearing the fur," he said as soon as he realized it. "Leave her. Take me instead."

She shook her head. "We've done that, Aldan. This is so much better. I have a body now. And I intend to keep it."

He gritted his teeth. Only the pain in his back convinced him this was real and not a nightmare. "Why are we here?"

Zektel sat back and related all that had happened. "So I persuaded everyone to bring you here to recover," she explained. "Everyone assumed you'd told Kekeen all about your home, so no one was suspicious at all. We've been here for almost a week. Your family was quite shocked at first, but they've adapted to the situation quite well."

A motion at the room's curtain door drew his attention. Clanless inhaled sharply as his mother entered, holding a platter. Her eyes widened at seeing him awake. Eight years had passed since he'd seen her—maybe nine by now; he couldn't remember exactly. Her hair showed a few streaks of gray, and the lines around her eyes were more pronounced. But otherwise, she looked almost the same as the day he'd left.

"Aldan..." she whispered. "My son."

Kekeen rose and took the platter, so his mother could sit beside his bed. Fighting the pain, Clanless pulled himself up on his elbow to face her. Tears trickled down her face. Clanless knew his own eyes weren't entirely dry. "Mother."

She put a hand on his cheek. "We failed you. We should have fought them. Your father... he hasn't entered the temple since that day. He blames himself. We... I'm so sorry, Aldan. I'm so sorry."

"I know," he said past the lump in his throat. "I... I've missed you."

"I kept you in my heart," she promised, patting her own chest. She bent in and kissed his forehead, her tears dripping onto his face. He closed his eyes, and for a moment, he was a small child again, about to go to bed for the night.

The blanket fell loose, exposing his torso. His mother's brow wrinkled. Her hand touched one of the scars on his chest. "How you must have suffered," she murmured. Her eyes drifted to the brand on his shoulder.

"I survived." He swallowed again. "Is that... do I smell flatbread?"

His mother laughed and turned. Kekeen handed her the platter. "Your girl here said you would want this when you finally woke up. I've made it every day. You just happened to wake up right when I finished this batch."

He reached for the platter, but she batted his hand. "Let me serve you. Please." She cut a sliver of butter and slathered it on a piece of the warm bread. She rolled it into a long cylinder and offered it to him. Clanless took a bite and closed his eyes again. The flatbread almost melted in his mouth. So good. He'd sought this flavor everywhere he'd been in the past eight years but never found a match to it.

More than the flavor moved him. His mother made this. For him. She cared. She still loved him, despite that day where he'd been taken away. For years, he'd believed she hadn't cared, that she'd comforted herself with, with…

His eyes opened and locked onto another pair of eyes staring back at him from the doorway. A small boy clutched the curtain door with one hand and watched this stranger in the bed.

"Could that be…?"

His mother turned and motioned for the boy to enter. "Come, Dimi. It is time you met your brother."

The boy inched forward. His mother reached for him, but he darted past her and grabbed a piece of the flatbread. He stepped back out of reach and stuffed it into his mouth.

Clanless laughed. "You love it too, don't you?" The boy's black hair fell down past his neck. Clanless wondered at their similarities. He'd looked the same as a boy. But had he ever been this skinny?

"This is Dimicin," their mother said. "We usually call him Dimi."

Dimi pointed at Kekeen. "She said you fought monsters."

"I have. Big ones."

"Like Otkerel the Wild?"

Clanless laughed again. How could this boy be so much like him? Well, why wouldn't he be? He'd grown up in the same place with the same parents. He slept in the same place, ate the same food, listened to the same stories from Father. Even… his laughter stopped. Dimi was seven, almost eight years old. Clanless's eyes darted back to the doorway. Zektel said Uncle Sejikdi was in the field. His hand clenched, grasping for the moonblade. Where had Zektel stashed it? He might need it.

Kekeen knelt next to Dimi. "Exactly like Otkerel. He even has a magic sword." She looked to Clanless. "Dimi and I have talked a lot while we were waiting for you to wake up."

Clanless accepted another piece of flatbread from his mother. "Dimicin. Dimi. You look strong. How is the back wall?"

Dimi straightened up and puffed out his chest. "We have the strongest back wall in the clanhold! I add to it all the time!"

"Good, good. I'm glad to hear you've taken that job." He winked. "I used to carry those rocks, you know."

Dimi stepped closer and wrinkled his brow. "You have big arms. You could carry the really big rocks."

"I do now. But my arms used to be the same size as yours."

His eyes widened. "Really?"

"The same," his mother confirmed.

"What of little Ot?" Clanless asked. "She must be... ten years by now?"

"She is with some of the hold women, learning her tasks. You will see her later this evening, I am sure." His mother eyed him. "Assuming you stay awake."

"Why did you sleep so long?" Dimi asked.

"I fought a very powerful monster. The fight lasted so long, I needed a lot of sleep."

Dimi's eyes narrowed, as if evaluating this story's truthfulness.

Clanless coughed. Kekeen hurried to bring him the water again. His mother smiled. "You've found a good woman here, Aldan. She's rarely left your side."

Clanless looked up into Zektel's eyes. This should be a magical moment: his mother and the woman he loved. But the blood-wraith ruined it all. "She's special," he said aloud.

His mother stood, setting the platter on the stool. Dimi grabbed another piece of flatbread from it and received a swat on his hand. "All right. Come, Dimi. Let's let your brother rest some more. We can talk more when the rest of the family returns."

"I wanted to hear about the monsters," the boy protested.

"Later," his mother warned. She pushed him toward the door. She gave Clanless a final smile before following her youngest out.

Clanless let himself fall back on the pillow. He put both hands on his face. So many emotions fought for dominance. Home. He was home. And yet that meant facing his uncle. As much as it terrified him, for the sake of Dimi, he must do it. Dimi. He had a little brother. And soon he would see his sister and father as well. So much reason for joy... but Zektel was here too, possessing Kekeen. He could not imagine a worse situation.

The emotions battled, but his consciousness lost. He fell back asleep in minutes.

RECONCILIATION & RETRIBUTION

When his eyes opened again, Clanless saw a much smaller pair of eyes looking back at him. "I thought you would sleep another day!" Dimi exclaimed.

Clanless rubbed his eyes. "Have I missed dinner?"

"No." Dimi sounded almost disappointed. "The men will be back any minute."

Wincing, Clanless pushed himself up on his elbow. "I'd better get dressed then. Are my clothes here?"

Dimi pointed at a pile on top of a stand next to the bed. Clanless breathed a sigh of relief on seeing the fur pelt. And then a thought occurred to him. Why not put it on Kekeen? He would have to do it when Zektel wasn't expecting it. She might use the opportunity to possess him instead, but it would still be better than the current situation.

The boy hopped up and scrambled over to the corner of the room. He retrieved a staff and brought it back. "Mother said you might need this."

Clanless took the smooth wood and admired it. "This is Father's. I remember it well."

"He only uses it when we go climbing," Dimi said.

Clanless nodded. "Yes, he does." He planted the staff and used it to pull himself upright. Pain shot through his back, and he gasped.

"Are you all right?" Dimi looked poised to run for help.

"I'll make it." Clanless took several deep breaths through his nose. Zektel had explained why the healing blood-magic hadn't worked on him, but he hoped it wasn't a permanent problem. This injury in his back could cause long-term issues. For now, he thought he could bear the pain as long as he didn't have to move around too much or walk too far.

He took a few practice steps with the staff. The clothes consisted of loose-fitting pants and a shirt, the usual clanhold man's working outfit. Dimi helped him with the pants, snickering almost the entire time. The shirt refused to fit; apparently his shoulders were much broader than who-ever owned these, Father or Uncle Sejikdi. He tossed it aside and pulled on the fur pelt. In many ways, he was more comfortable with it than a shirt.

"Is that from a wolf?" Dimi wanted to know.

"It is. A very special wolf."

"I thought so! Mother almost threw it away because it was so dirty. But your friend told her it was very important. She worked hard to clean it." He glanced at the door and stepped closer to Clanless. "Was that blood on it?" he whispered.

Clanless nodded. "Monster blood."

Dimi's eyes widened.

The curtain moved, and their mother slipped in. "Dimi, have you—oh!" She saw Aldan and put a hand over her mouth.

He smiled and leaned on the staff. "Hello, Mother. Is supper ready for us?"

She stepped forward, and he saw another tear in her eye. "You're so… big."

"Will I be that big someday?" Dimi asked.

"Keep lifting those rocks for the back wall," Clanless suggested.

His mother composed herself and wiped her eye. "Let me check your bandage." She hurried behind him and inspected the wrapping around his lower torso. She made a few adjustments, clicking her tongue. Satisfied, she stepped back and nodded. "All right. The others are waiting. Let's go."

Clanless almost sat down. He dreaded this moment more than any-thing since his fight with Daviland. For a moment, he even wished Zektel were here to whisper a few encouraging words. Maybe he could still skip this one. He could say he didn't feel strong enough. It wouldn't be much of an exaggeration; he wondered if he could move his feet. The knuckles on his right hand turned white from his grip on the staff.

And then a small hand slipped into his other hand. He looked down to find Dimi looking up at him. The boy didn't say anything. Clanless smiled and took a step. And then another. Mother led the way from the small bedroom into his uncle's primary living space and from there, into the courtyard.

He paused and looked out at the rest of the clanhold. Here at twilight, he couldn't see a single change since he'd left. Except it all seemed so much smaller now.

Dimi tugged at his hand. With a heavy dependence on the staff, Clanless followed him into his childhood home. The family's low dining table had been placed directly beneath the moon window and covered with more food than he could ever remember seeing in this room. His mother moved past him to join the five others waiting at the table. Before he could register everyone else, the man at the head of the table came to meet him.

For a moment, he didn't recognize his own father. He still possessed the powerful arms and hands he'd developed from years of labor. His hair hadn't even changed much. But Clanless had always looked up at this man, and now he found himself looking down. How did that happen?

"My son." The words came out broken and confusing, almost like a whispered shout.

"Father, I—"

Before he could finish, his father fell on his knees and bowed his head. "Please forgive me for failing you so greatly."

Clanless looked around, helpless. He wanted to lift his father back up, but he couldn't bend over without pain. Seeing his distress, his mother came and took hold of Father's elbow.

"Please get up," Clanless said. He'd never felt more awkward.

Both parents stood, but Father kept his head bowed. Clanless licked his lips and glanced at Kekeen. He couldn't help looking her way, even though it wasn't really her. She gave an encouraging nod.

"You… you were trapped, Father." He swallowed. "The priests control the clanhold. You… you had to choose between me and the rest of the family."

"I should have chosen all of us." His father looked up, tears streaking down his face. "I should have chosen you."

"They would have thrown us all out," his mother said gently.

"We would have been together." He stated an argument Clanless felt sure they'd repeated dozens of times over the years. "We could have made it to one of the cities, found a new life."

Clanless reached out and grasped his father's shoulder. "With Mother newly pregnant?" He shook his head. "She would not have made it. At the very least, we would not have Dimi here." He swallowed again, fighting his own emotions. "Hear me, Father. I hold no animosity to you for that day. We were all victims of a power too great for us to fight… at that time."

His father opened his mouth, but no words came out. Instead, he stepped forward and threw his arms around his son. Clanless heard applause, but didn't care where it came from. He closed his eyes and savored the embrace. For all the time he'd spent missing his mother, thinking about her flatbread, and wondering about Ot and his little brother… he'd never dared think much about his father. His father had been brave, strong, everything he'd wanted to be… and then he'd failed to protect his son. And here Clanless stood, forgiving him for that very act, arguing he'd done the right thing.

He and his father both knew he hadn't. They both knew he could have done more. But right here, right now: it didn't matter. They were together and reconciled.

Once the embrace ended and Clanless could take a breath again, he looked around at the rest of the diners. Kekeen and Sugh sat on one side of the low table, grinning at him. On the other sat a young girl. "Surely this cannot be little Ot?" he exclaimed.

She smiled and ducked her head. Mother moved next to her and patted her hair. "Not quite so little any more."

Clanless knelt to face his sister, despite the pain his back gave him. "You look very much like your cousin Borde once did," he told her. "And she is a very beautiful woman."

"You've seen Borde?" exclaimed his uncle. "Where?"

Clanless pulled himself back up with the staff and finally looked at the other man. Sejikdi had not weathered the years as well as Father. He looked more gaunt. His hairline had receded quite some distance, and what hair he had left was light gray now. Contempt welled up in Clanless's heart for this pathetic little man.

"We haven't heard from Borde in years," Mother chimed in.

Clanless turned to her. "She is in Et-Baylak, at least the last time I saw her. I'm surprised Kekeen didn't mention her." He gave her a side look.

"I'm so sorry," Kekeen said. "I was concerned about you and didn't remember everything."

"Et-Baylak," Sejikdi murmured. "It's a long trip, but maybe I should."

Clanless ignored him and sat down next to Kekeen, using the staff to slow his descent.

"Aldan!" his mother reproved him. "Have you no other words for your uncle?"

"What I have to say to him…" Clanless paused and inhaled through his nose. "…I will say in private. We will not discuss it here."

He gave his uncle a quick glance and felt some satisfaction on seeing the older man's face pale.

The others settled in to their places around the table. "We thank the goddess for this provision," Father said aloud.

"Where is Swift Claw?" Clanless asked Sugh quietly as everyone served themselves. He could sense the beastman was near, but not too near.

"He is somewhere outside the clanhold," Sugh whispered. "We decided he would create too much confusion among the people here."

Clanless grunted and grabbed two pieces of flatbread before his little brother could take it all.

Conversations came and went as the meal progressed. Clanless didn't speak much, though his mother kept trying to draw him in. The presence of his uncle soured his mood too much. Part of him—a large part—wanted to lunge across the table and strangle the man right now. Another part wanted to reveal his actions to the entire table... but his parents would have trouble believing it. And his mother had worked hard for this meal; it wouldn't be right to ruin it.

Kekeen leaned in and whispered in his ear. "You've made him nervous. That's good. Let him worry. But for now, you should go back to pretending nothing is wrong."

He narrowed his eyebrows and looked at her. "Why would I do that?"

"The rest of the family is nervous enough without you being so grumpy."

He nodded. She was right, despite whatever strange motivations she possessed.

"Sugh," he said aloud, "how did it feel to do a normal day's work?"

"A day? I have worked with your father for three days now! It is hard work, to be certain."

"But you're so strong!" Dimicin piped up.

"There are muscles for fighting, and there are muscles for working," Clanless said, remembering his first instructor, Kan. "Just because Sugh and I are strong for fighting does not mean we are as strong as Father here when it comes to working the fields."

Dimicin frowned, looking back and forth, comparing the men. "I don't think so."

Clanless chuckled. "Someday, you may understand."

The meal progressed more pleasantly from then on. As the last of the food disappeared, Clanless found his eyes drooping a bit. "Mother, it was delicious. But I'm afraid I'm still very tired."

"Of course." She rose to her feet. "You've only just awakened for the first time."

Kekeen jumped up. "I'll help him back to his bed."

A chorus of "good night" followed him as they headed back to his uncle's dwelling. Kekeen held his arm, not providing much support, but he appreciated her presence. In a few minutes, he would make his move.

Clanless exaggerated his need to lean on the staff while they crossed the courtyard. He kept an eye on Kekeen's reactions. She didn't make any moves to help him.

"Back to bed for you," she proclaimed as they entered the chamber. She set a candle on the stand next to his bed. "I suppose you're still too tired for me to join you."

Clanless glared at her. "That will not happen, Zektel. Not while you're within her."

"Oh, come. You can't deny that you want it. And it will be all three of us together. Won't that be special?"

"It will not happen."

"We'll see." She bumped her hip against his.

Clanless fumbled and dropped the staff. Kekeen laughed and bent to pick it up. In that moment, he swept the fur pelt off his shoulders and threw it on hers as she rose.

Kekeen stumbled. When she turned back to him, her eyes were wide and wet. "Aldan! It's…"

"I know." He pulled her into his arms. She trembled against him.

"I, I couldn't do anything. She controlled me all this time."

"I know, I know. It's all right."

She shook her head against his chest. "No. No, it's not. She's screaming at me right now."

He held her tighter. "You don't have to listen to her."

"She says… she says she'll kill me if you don't take it off." Kekeen looked up at him, her face inches from his. "Maybe… maybe that's for the best. I don't want to live if she's going to be in charge."

Clanless fought to keep his own breathing under control. "No. I won't lose you."

"I can't bear it! Watching her doing all, all the things I want to do. Meeting your parents." She choked. "Being with you."

"I'll find a way." He brought his face even closer. "I promise. I will find a way to free you. No matter what it takes." He kissed her. She welcomed it, pulling herself against him as hard as she could. Clanless never wanted the moment to end.

But Kekeen pulled loose. Tears ran down her face. "I don't think I can do it. To watch her with you when it should be me."

"Trust me." Clanless lifted his hands to her shoulders. "I will not do anything with her. And I will free you. I promise. I don't know how long it will take, but I will never give up. Will you trust me?"

"I, I'll try."

"I love you." He took hold of the pelt. With every pained breath, his chest rose and fell as if it were the last time.

"I love you," she whispered back.

"I will free you." He stared into her eyes and lifted the wolf pelt. He could see the exact moment Zektel took over. Kekeen's eyes hardened in an almost imperceptible way. No one else would have noticed it.

"That was foolish, Aldan. Did you think I would do nothing?" Her voice lost the stammer and emotion. "I told you I'm in charge here."

Clanless tossed the pelt back on his own shoulder. "I hate you."

"You don't mean that, of course. Not after all we've shared." She tried to move back against him, but he pulled away. "Didn't you enjoy that kiss? Let's try it again." She reached toward his head, but he pushed her hands away.

"Stop it. Leave me."

"You don't seem to understand our relationship here, Aldan." She sashayed across the room toward the door. "I hold Kekeen's life in my hands. That means I control everything. You do whatever I say."

"Why?" Clanless sat down on the bed. "Why are you even here?"

She looked back with pretend shock. "Whatever do you mean? Why wouldn't I be here with you?"

"You freed Suirel. He's... doing whatever he wants now. Why aren't you helping him?"

"Who says I'm not?"

"How? How does tormenting me here"—he gestured to their surroundings—"help the god of chaos in his work?"

She took a step back and crouched, putting both hands on her knees. "Do you think you can hide from a god? Even here?"

"You brought me here!"

"Yes, I did." She tilted her head. "I couldn't have you at Et-Baylak. Too much will be happening there. And besides... there's another player that may need to be dealt with. In the end, you're just a pawn, Aldan. A pawn in the hands of the gods. At least this time, you know which one is in control."

"What is that supposed to mean? What are you planning?"

She turned to leave. "When you're fully healed, we'll leave this place and visit another place you know well. I have questions to ask a certain hunchback."

Clanless sat in silence for a while, watching the candle flicker. Hunchback. She could only mean Nukai, Kan's assistant at the training arena. The fur pelt came from him. Without thinking, Clanless reached up and stroked the wolf fur. He thought of the great wolf in the snow… and something else, something that tugged at his memory but couldn't manifest itself in his mind. He sat alone as the candle burned lower. The darkness creeped in around the rest of the room, held back only by the tiny flicker of fire.

"What do you think you're doing?" The voice that came from the door wasn't entirely unexpected, but Clanless hadn't anticipated it so soon.

"Hello, Uncle."

Sejikdi did not enter; he spoke from beyond the curtain. "Your words at the table were hurtful, Aldan. Why would you say something like that in front of the family?"

"You know exactly why I said that. Or would you prefer I tell your brother what you did to me?"

"He would never believe you. The rest of the family sees me as the loving, supportive uncle." He chuckled. "In fact, I fought harder against the priests than your own father did when they took you away. He's felt guilty over that ever since."

"They would believe me."

"People believe what they want to believe."

Clanless hesitated before asking: "Have you done anything to Dimicin?"

"Dimi? Delightful boy. Reminds me so much of you."

Clanless tried to jump to his feet, but the pain in his back stopped him. He fell back on the bed. "If you so much as touch him, I will cut your head off."

"And how would that look to your parents?"

Clanless picked up the staff and used it to pull himself up. "Hear me now, Uncle. I care not what happens to me. If you hurt that boy, I will destroy you. I swear this by the goddess herself."

No answer came for almost a full minute. At last, Sejikdi's voice came in almost a whisper: "I never did anything to you that you didn't want."

"I was a child! I didn't understand what was happening!" Clanless looked around the room for his moonblade.

"You won't do anything to me," his uncle said. "We both know it. You just got your parents back. You're not going to risk that relationship so soon."

Clanless took a step toward the door. He would use the staff if he had to.

"In fact," Sejikdi said, "if you really—AAIIIEEEE!"

The scream of pure terror made Clanless lunge across the room. His back spasmed in agony, but he ignored it and swept the curtain aside. Another horrified scream met him.

Sejikdi lay on the floor, staring up at Swift Claw. The beastman crouched over him, teeth bared and claws at the ready.

"Swift Claw! Don't!" Clanless looked to the door, already hearing other voices reacting to the screams.

"This one deserves death," the beastman countered. He brought his claws down next to Sejikdi's face. The man whimpered, and the smell of spilled urine filled the room.

"Get out of here before they find you!" Clanless urged. "Leave him to me. Please!"

Swift Claw lowered his face to within an inch or two of Sejikdi's. Saliva dripped onto the terrified man's chin. "This one's wind is crook-ed."

"Please!" Clanless begged, limping forward.

A clatter at the main door drew his attention. It flew open, and his father rushed in, wielding a scythe. Behind him, several other men of the clanhold gathered in the courtyard.

Clanless spun back. Swift Claw was gone. Uncle Sejikdi lay on the floor, shaking.

"Brother! What happened?" Father ran to his side. Two other men came in, holding farm implements. Both looked toward Clanless with nar-rowed eyes.

"M-monster," Sejikdi murmured.

Clanless scanned the room. Where could Swift Claw have gone? His eyes at last turned up. The moon window. Of course. Clouds obscured the light of the goddess tonight. No one would even see a silhouette.

"Aldan! Did you see anything?"

He turned back to his father. "I heard him scream. I—"

"It must have gone up there." One of the other men pointed at the moon window, coming to the same conclusion.

Father gripped Sejikdi on the shoulder and stood. "If something got in here and attacked him, we need to find it."

"If an animal has learned how to climb on top of our houses and come in like that, no one is safe," the first man agreed.

The second pointed at Clanless. "Who is this?"

Father started back to the door. "It is my son, returned after many years. Come. Let's find this creature."

The other man didn't move. "He's the one who taints blood. The abomination."

"Don't be ridiculous," Father said. "Now is not the time for such things." He pushed the other two men through the door.

Clanless followed at a slow pace with the staff. In the courtyard, he saw a crowd gathering, drawn by the screams. Eight or ten men of the clanhold stood ready, holding tools and a couple of torches. The rest of his family stood at the door to their house, along with Kekeen and Sugh. The arena warrior stood in front of the others, holding his axe with a lightness that disguised his skill and readiness.

"Some kind of creature got in through the roof and attacked my brother," Father announced.

A clamor followed, including questions about Sejikdi's health. Father raised his hands. "He appears to be all right, but he's had the fright of his life. Let's spread out and see what we can find. If we stay in groups with a light, it shouldn't be able to surprise us."

"What is he doing here?" a loud voice cried. Everyone turned to see a priest pointing at Clanless.

"My son has returned after many years."

"He is clanless!" the priest shouted. "See where he was branded!"

A murmur swept through the crowd. Most of them remembered the day Clanless's abilities manifested. A few had experienced it. Words like "abomination" and "slave" could be heard.

"He probably brought the beast!" someone cried.

"He attacked Sejikdi himself! He is the beast!"

"Stop it!" Father shouted. "This is my son. He grew up here with us. He survived eight horrible years in the arena and has returned home at last. Let's—"

"He's an escaped slave!" the priest shouted, pushing his way to the front of the crowd. "He should not be here!"

"I won my freedom!" Clanless thundered, surprising himself with the force of his words. "I fought for the Hawk King. My bloodbond is no more, priest. I am a free man!"

"Lies! No one gains freedom from the arena!"

"You are the liar!" Sugh stepped closer. "I fought with him in the arena. We are all free men now."

"Another one!" The priest threw up his hands. "You will bring the Hawk King's judgment down on our entire clanhold! They will be looking for these two."

Kekeen slipped next to Clanless. He felt a familiar shape pressed into his free hand. Looking down, he saw the moonblade.

"The Hawk King is dead," Sugh said.

The crowd fell silent for a moment. "The Hawk King is immortal," someone whispered.

"He is not," Clanless said. "The rebel Daviland killed him. I was there."

"So was I," Kekeen added.

"Preposterous," someone muttered without conviction. They'd all heard rumors, at least.

"Who rules the Empire then?"

"There is a crisis in Et-Baylak," Clanless said. "Once I am recovered, we will return there to aid in whatever way we can." Even in the wavering torchlight, he caught the expression of dismay cross his mother's face. Did she think he was here to stay?

Father pointed outside the clanhold. "Are you all forgetting the beast? My brother was attacked! We need to find it!"

The priest tried to sway a few more to his side, but faced with the two imposing arena fighters and their huge weapons, most of the men decided hunting a mysterious beast sounded more interesting for the moment. Father divided them up into three groups. Sugh offered to go along with one of them. Before heading out, he whispered to Clanless: "We will not find him, will we?"

Clanless shook his head. "Not a chance in this world. Swift Claw is too clever to be found by these men."

"All the same, I will be sure to be loud." He strode over to join the searchers, almost shouting: "Ho! Let us go forth and find this monster! My axe craves its blood!"

With an effort, Clanless kept himself from laughing.

"If I let you keep the blade, will you use it on your uncle?" Kekeen asked.

"I think fear will keep him in line." Clanless turned back into the house. "But I'm keeping the moonblade."

Mother, carrying a lantern, came across to check on Sejikdi. He'd changed his clothes, but the smell of urine still filled the living area. Assured that he was unharmed, she followed Clanless into his room. With a glance back to make sure Sejikdi couldn't hear her, Mother said in a low voice: "Nothing like this has ever happened before. And I've heard your friends speak of another who came here with you. Is that who attacked your uncle? And is it related to what you said to him at our meal?"

Clanless raised his eyebrows. His mother was smarter than he remembered. He considered for a moment. "If I tell you all of the truth, Mother, will you accept it, even if it is hard to hear?"

Kekeen stood near the door, clearly wanting to listen in.

"Come, my son, let me put you to bed as if you were my child again," Mother said in a louder voice. "Kekeen, will you permit me this time?"

"Of course," she answered with a short curtsy, though her face revealed her irritation.

Mother set the lantern on the stand while Kekeen left. Clanless lowered himself onto the bed once again. His mother checked at the curtain and then joined him. "I do not think he will come back this way," she said, "but we should probably keep our voices low, just the same. I would not be surprised if Dimi tries to sneak in, and I suspect these words will not be for his ears."

"It is because of him that the words must be spoken at all," Clanless said. He took a deep breath. He'd never wanted to have this conversation. But with slow and careful words, he told her what her brother-in-law had done. She took it without interruption, but her jaw clenched and held through most of the story.

"Does your father know any of this?" she asked when he finished.

"No, I… don't know whether to tell him… or even if I can tell him."

Mother closed her eyes for a moment. The lantern's light grew lower. Clanless almost couldn't make out her face.

"If he is told, he will believe it or not," she said at last. "If he does not believe it, it will drive a schism between the two of you, which would be tragic. And it would make it harder to protect Dimi from, from his brother. But if he does believe it…" She sighed. "He will believe that he has failed his son yet again."

Clanless started to speak, but she shook her head. "In some ways, it is true. We did fail you again. How did we not see? How did we not know?"

"He is a deceiver."

"Yes." She took another deep breath. "Sejikdi is a vital part of this clanhold and this household. Your father would drive him out, creating a further rift with the rest of the hold men, who respect your uncle. For this cause alone, I hesitate to tell your father. But can we protect other children from this man?"

"I believe he can be persuaded to cease from his ways."

"Will you kill him?"

He hesitated. "I do not want to. And tonight, I believe he faced a terror he never imagined. Perhaps that will be enough."

"So you do know what he saw."

Clanless smiled. "Swift Claw is a friend, almost a brother to me. And he is a beastman."

"You must tell me that story." She rose from the bed. "But not now. You, my son, must sleep." She glanced toward the door. "After hearing your story, I would be concerned about your safety were it not for this other one who watches you."

"Thank you, Mother."

She bent and kissed his head. "May the goddess watch you as well."

TRAPPED

The men returned late in the night, having found no trace of the mysterious creature, of course. Clanless half-woke to hear his father trying to calm Sejikdi in the next room. He smiled to himself and returned to sleep.

In the morning, Kekeen slipped into his room early. "They're all heading out to the fields, despite being up so late," she announced. "It's fascinating how much their work means to them."

"It is the way things are done here." Clanless stretched tentatively. The injury to his back reacted with a burst of pain.

"You were masterful last night with your uncle," she said, twirling across the room. "It was all I could do not to erupt in laughter."

"Swift Claw did the real work."

"Yes, what a wonderful touch." She paused in her movements to look across the room at him. "But I don't believe he's suffered enough. Do you? After all he did to you?"

"I'm not here for revenge, Zektel."

"Why not?"

Clanless didn't answer at first. Part of him—a large part—wanted revenge. He'd told his mother he didn't want to kill his uncle. But he wavered. Sometimes he didn't want to. Other times, he wanted to see Swift Claw tear Uncle Sejikdi's face off, or better yet: to cut him apart with the moonblade himself. He wanted to see him suffer.

"I've killed hundreds of men," he said. "Some who deserved it, and… some who didn't. I'm tired of death."

"Are you saying he doesn't deserve it?"

"No. He, he does deserve it. Maybe more so than anyone else I've ever killed." He looked down at his hands. "But am I the one to decide that? This is not the arena."

"You're his victim. Who better to decide?" She sat down on the bed beside him. "And you shouldn't stop there. The priests here are the ones who sold you into slavery! You heard that one last night. You should deal with them too."

Clanless shifted away from her. "Where does it end? Should I punish my parents for failing to stop the priests? Do I hunt down the Ghamba Lam for his role?" Zektel's overreach pushed him in the opposite direction of what she wanted. He scowled, wondering if she realized that.

"Why not? You have the power to do all of it."

"I thought you had plans for me to help Suirel."

She smiled. "We do. But that doesn't mean you can't deal with these issues along the way. I'll even help you." She leaned toward him. "Do what we ask, and you can have everything you've ever wanted. Starting with your revenge."

"All I've ever wanted is Kekeen, and you've taken her from me."

"You can still have her." She tried to shift even closer to him. Clanless pushed off the bed and stood, wavering from the pain. Kekeen fell across his bed instead. She lay back on his pillow and held out her arms. "You can have her right now. And me too."

"You know what I mean."

"Aldan. You're not thinking this through. Who was with you throughout all the trials of your life? Who stayed with you when you were abandoned by your own family? Who supported you and encouraged you for all these years? Who did you talk to when you desperately needed someone? It was me. It was always me." She ran her hands down the sides of her body. "Kekeen was a beautiful girl you admired from afar. You've spent a handful of days with her. You don't even know her." She stared up into his eyes. "I warned you about her, but you wouldn't listen until she abandoned you. Remember?"

He didn't know what to say. She wasn't wrong, but...

"And now you get both of us. I could never be everything you needed so long as I was within you, but now..." She licked her lips and pushed up a little from the bed. "Now you can have it all. We both can."

For a brief moment, he felt the temptation. "You... you abandoned me too," he remembered.

"Only because you left me no choice at the time. Come, Aldan. We both—"

"You killed Hagh!" He snatched up the moonblade. "Maybe I should get revenge on you!"

She chuckled. "All right." She rolled over and pulled her hair aside, exposing her neck. "Would you like to cut off your beloved's head?"

"I, I'll find a way. I'll get rid of you if it's the last thing I do."

She rolled back onto her side and lifted up on one elbow. "The last thing? No one wants you dead, dear Aldan. Well, except Suirel, I suppose. Taking his eye wasn't very nice of you. But he's left you to me for now." She wrinkled her nose. "This bed smells too much of her sweat." She sat up and jumped to her feet. "I have a new idea."

Clanless watched her with narrowed eyes, not trusting himself to speak again.

"You seem to have fully rested now, so maybe you've recovered from that fight in the cave with all the blood. If so, your body might be able to handle a little more blood-magic." She headed toward the door. "I'll check the temple and see if they have any Clan Kurav blood. I'm sure they'd be willing to give me some if it meant getting you out of here sooner."

When she'd gone, Clanless dropped the moonblade and collapsed onto the bed again. He was trapped. As long as Zektel controlled Kekeen, he had no choice but to do as she said. No matter the cost, he couldn't lose Kekeen. Suirel could have the Empire and everything else.

He sighed and stretched on the bed. Kekeen was right: it did smell of his sweat. Mother would insist on changing it as soon as she found out. He smiled at the thought. Such a simple thing: someone who cared enough to worry about odorous bedclothes. And yet, he'd not experienced that for eight years. It would be hard to leave it behind again.

☾ ☾ ☾ ☾ ● ☽ ☽ ☽ ☽

Clanless twisted his torso back and forth. He no longer experienced the debilitating pain, but something still hurt inside when he twisted to the right. The healing blood Kekeen had acquired from the temple worked as much as could be expected. He bent over and strained to touch his toes. Muscles he hadn't used in days complained.

He picked up the moonblade and swung it in a few controlled arcs. He didn't have enough space to do much in this room. Might as well go outside and get some more exercise. He needed it.

He pushed aside the curtain, stepped into the living area, and stopped.

Uncle Sejikdi sat at his own small table, eating a bowl of porridge. He looked up at Clanless but showed no emotion.

"I suppose you'll be leaving soon then," he said.

"Yes." Clanless shifted his grip on the moonblade. The earlier conversation with Zektel repeated in his mind. He could kill this man. Who could stop him? And who could do anything to him in response?

The murder would destroy his family's reputation within the clanhold. His parents, Ot, and Dimi would suffer. Others would not do business with them. The priests might even cast them out.

But he could take them with him to a city somewhere. Get them started in a new life. No. It would take a lot of blood, and any of his that remained would be in Et-Baylak. He couldn't take anyone there, not with an enemy army on the way.

"Are you going to stand there watching me eat?" Sejikdi asked.

"I'm considering my course of action."

"You want to kill me."

"Yes."

Silence.

Sejikdi sighed. "I will not touch Dimicin. You have my word."

"That is not enough." Clanless took a step toward him. He could sense Swift Claw very close. His own conflicted emotions drew the beastman toward him.

"What do you want from me?" His uncle's tone grew higher.

Clanless closed his eyes for a moment and calmed himself. He opened them and stared at his uncle. "First, swear by the goddess that you will never touch a child again."

Sejikdi licked his lips, then looked up to the moon. "I swear by the goddess that I will not touch Dimicin."

"Any child!"

"I, I swear by the goddess that I will not touch another child."

"Second. The monster that attacked you. Do you know what it was?"

Sejikdi shook his head.

"It was a beastman, Uncle. And he is my friend. Should you ever— ever—violate your sworn oath... should your hand so much as brush against my little brother... he will return. And he will devour you, beginning with your manhood." Clanless pointed his moonblade. And a low growl came from the moon window above, punctuating his statement.

Sejikdi paled and may have trembled a little. "I... I understand."

"See that you do. There are others here who also know what you did, and they will be watching you." Clanless took two long steps forward and swung the moonblade. It thunked into the table and bisected the porridge bowl. "May your remaining days be filled with a fear so great it motivates everything you ever do." He pulled his own shirt down to reveal his clanless brand. "You are not branded in the flesh as I am. But you are branded by your oath. The goddess may not have been watching when you… when you hurt me. But she will be watching now." He shook his head. "And your punishment in the life after this will be far worse than anything I can ever do."

Clanless yanked the moonblade free and walked to the door. The smell of fresh urine followed him.

Outside, he swung the moonblade in a wide arc, testing his reach. His muscles felt tight from little use. He used the momentum of the swing to continue into a series of practice moves. How long had it been since he'd done this? Weeks? Months? If he stepped into an arena tomorrow, he'd be a laughing stock.

He moved outside of his family's courtyard and into the wider common grounds of the clanhold. People coming and going from their homes stopped and stared. Clanless didn't care. The clanholders had made their opinions known the previous night. He wouldn't be staying much longer.

Sugh approached, his axe slung over his shoulder. "Mind if I join you?"

"Like old times." Clanless smiled and lifted the moonblade. Sugh lifted his axe to match him. Together, they launched into a new set of maneuvers. Attack, defend, step, dodge. Tight muscles stretched and grew limber. Aches multiplied but felt good at the same time. Sweat poured down both of their bodies.

At last, Clanless slammed the moonblade down into the dirt a second before Sugh did the same. They both leaned on their weapons, breathing hard.

"I may not have the 'fight as one' thing like the beastman," Sugh said, "but I'd say that was pretty close."

"We did the same routine back at the arena for years." Clanless pushed his hair away from his face.

"So we did." Sugh grinned. "Did I say we didn't?"

Clanless laughed. He glanced toward the nearest courtyard and saw a young girl duck down behind the boundary wall. "We had an audience here too."

Sugh straightened, lifted his arms above his head and stretched. "These people are not used to warriors such as we."

"They're not strangers to a fight," Clanless said. "But no, nothing like us."

"It is good we brought you here. Kekeen was smart to do so." Sugh nodded.

Clanless hesitated. "Sugh… there's something you should know about Kekeen."

"Worry not." Sugh waved dismissively. "I vowed to serve her until you returned, and now here you are! I surrender her to your keeping." He sighed. "But I think I will stay around, just in case you die. My heart could beat for that one if you were not here. You have a good woman there."

"Uh… yes. I do." Clanless looked to be sure no one else could hear their conversation. "Sugh… back at the mine… something happened."

Sugh nodded. "Many things happened. Some I still do not understand."

"Kekeen is being controlled by one of those blood-wraiths!" Clanless said it as fast as he could, worried he might not get it out otherwise.

Sugh pulled his axe from the dirt. "Are you certain?"

"Very certain. It's Zektel, the one who used to be inside me."

Sugh's eyes narrowed. "This is part of what I don't understand yet, but I will let that go. You used your power to free me from their influence. Can you not do the same for her?"

"No…" Quickly, he explained all that Zektel had told him.

Sugh wiped dirt from his axe blade. "We must find a way to free her. I will do whatever you ask."

"Thank you." Clanless swallowed. "For now, treat her as if she were Kekeen. If she doesn't know that you know the truth, maybe we can use that somehow."

"I will pretend that we did not talk about this." Sugh wiped the dirt from his hand on his trousers. "It vanishes from my head like this dirt from my hand."

"Heh." Clanless pushed his hair back again. "Let's get something to drink. And then we'll need to tell the others we're leaving. Tomorrow, if we can."

"You are only just out of bed," Sugh pointed out. "Are you sure you're ready for a journey?"

"The priests will be sending word to their Daghilch." Clanless pointed toward the clanhold's temple. "We can't keep my presence here a secret any more. And the longer we stay here, the more nervous I am about my family." He looked toward their home. "I worry about what Zektel might tell them."

TURNING POINTS

Sugh stepped out of the temple and looked up toward the moon. "Thank you," he breathed. Today, he'd counseled four people and been commended by the Daghilch himself for his compassionate manner. And he'd only been here two years! Life was good in the service of the goddess. Why would anyone want to do anything else?

The streets of Conchaga grew dark as the sun completed its daily retreat. Sugh smiled to himself. One of the priests today told him of a foreign nation where people actually worshipped the sun. What foolishness! Why would you worship something that retreated from the true power of the skies each and every day?

On the other hand, he did appreciate the sun's presence. Light and warmth were not trivial matters. Days would be strange without them. Even so, he would always choose the moon for her ever-present glory and stability. Almost in mockery of his thoughts, a cloud moved across the moon's surface, hiding her light. Well, even deities needed breaks, he supposed.

His stomach growled as he started walking, reminding him that he'd skipped the midday meal again. He'd been so caught up in a counseling session, he'd forgotten to eat. Thankfully, the walk to his boarding was a short one. He could eat when he arrived. The thought of the meat pastries at the eating house inspired him to pick up his pace.

He almost didn't hear her. And when he did, he almost kept walking. The Daghilch had warned him numerous times over the past two years about his interest in women. "The goddess is the only woman for you," he'd said. "Think not of those who walk this land, but of the one who walks the heavens."

Well, yes. But the ones who walked here were so… pleasant to look at. And think about.

"No, please…" The woman's voice came from a narrow alley to his right.

Sugh stopped and peered into the semi-darkness. "Is everything all right?" he called.

"Mind to yourself," a man's voice responded. Sugh took a step away, but a soft feminine whimper came next. That did not sound right.

He took several steps into the alley. Toward the end, he made out two figures standing close together. "Moon's stability to you," he said. "May I be of any assistance?"

The cloud gave up trying to disguise the moon's glory, and her full brightness illuminated the alley. A man, scruffy and wearing the clothes of a common worker, stepped away from the other figure to face Sugh. "A bleeding priest? Go away! You're not wanted here!"

Sugh looked past him. His eyes widened to see a young woman near his own age, her hair and clothing disheveled. He even caught a glimpse of her bare breast before she pulled her shirt back up onto her shoulder to cover it. "I… Are you all right, my lady?"

"She's no lady!" The man took another step toward Sugh. "This moon-calf is my slave. Mine to do with as I wish. You can move along." He puffed up his chest, trying to look impressive, though he had to look up at Sugh's face.

Sugh kept his eyes on the woman, his heart racing. "Is this true?"

"I… I'm not a slave," she whispered.

Sugh turned to the man. "She is not a slave. Which means it is you that is not wanted here. I advise you, in the name of the goddess, to remove yourself and leave her alone." His anger rose at this man, something else the Daghilch had warned him against.

"How dare you?" The man made some kind of motion and suddenly held a short knife in his hand. "Leave now, you blood-damned fool, and I won't cut you. Your stupid robes won't protect you here."

"Please," the woman said. She took a step away from the wall. "Let me go home."

Sugh's eyes narrowed. "You are welcome to leave, my lady. This one will not stop you. So I vow."

"Blood-cursed idiot!" The man lunged forward, leading with his knife. The woman shrieked.

Sugh stepped to one side. In a smooth motion, he trapped the man's knife-hand between his left arm and side, then punched him in the face with his right fist. He released the attacker and stepped back, trying to control his own anger. "I assume that was sufficient. Now—"

The man howled in anger and slashed at Sugh. The knife cut through the first layer of his robe, but didn't reach his skin. Sugh caught his hand and twisted it. "You require more convincing, I see." He grasped the front of the man's shirt, lifted him off his feet, and slammed him against the building's wall.

The man staggered a bit, as if drunk. He glared up at Sugh. "Never met a priest who could fight. Fine. I'll let her go. But you won't be here next time. That whore will be mine, and—"

With a roar, Sugh seized the man, lifted him off his feet, and threw him to the ground. His head bounced off a large rock. Sugh picked him up again and slammed him down once more. The knife clattered on the hard ground, fallen from his hand. He didn't move again.

The woman stepped forward, hand over her mouth. "You… you killed him!"

Now

Clanless approached the two-wheeled wagon with trepidation. "You brought me here in that?"

Kekeen shoved a bag into the back of the wagon. "It's better than walking."

"Maybe." Clanless eyed the lone ox waiting patiently to set out again.

"We could walk faster," Sugh said as he came up behind him. "Maybe. But it would be a long walk." He shook his head. "And we would have to carry all this food." He displayed a large basket. The smell of fresh flatbread drifted from within.

"That one will stay near me." Clanless snatched it from his friend. "I've thought about this bread for eight years."

"Is that all you've thought about, Aldan?" His mother's voice made him turn and face the rest of his assembled family. They'd gathered outside the courtyard to see him off.

"Of course not, Mother. I thought of all of you. All the time." He set the basket on the ground and pulled her into a hug.

"You really don't have to go," his father said.

He took a deep breath. "Yes. Yes, I do. A great evil threatens us all. And it's walking around in the body of a friend. I have to go."

"Will you fight more monsters?" Dimicin asked.

"I will probably have to." Clanless crouched to face his little brother. "Can I have a hug from you also?"

Dimicin hesitated a moment, then threw his arms around his neck. Clanless held him and closed his eyes. He'd never anticipated a moment like this. How could a world so full of pain still contain such joys? And what kind of fool would leave this behind?

He looked to his sister, who stood behind her mother. "Ot?" She shook her head.

"You're still a stranger to her, Aldan," his mother said. "She hasn't had enough time to get to know you. Perhaps if you stayed longer…"

"I will try to come back," he promised.

"When?" his father asked.

"I… don't know. When this is done." He lowered his head. "I don't want to go. I don't want to be involved in these things. I want to take the woman I love"—he glanced at Kekeen—"and escape from all of it. But I can't. Not yet. Not when everyone is in danger."

Father put a hand on his shoulder. "You have grown into a good man, Aldan. I am proud of you."

"You defended me in front of the crowd," Clanless said. "I won't forget that."

"If… if only I'd done the same nine years ago…"

Clanless pulled his father into an embrace. "It's behind us now. I love you. Thank you for, for being my father."

They pulled apart, both clearing their throats as if they'd caught something in them at the same time. Father looked back at the houses. "I'm not sure where my brother is…"

"I said farewell to him already," Clanless said. "He had some things to do." He looked to his mother. She placed a hand on Dimicin's head and nodded.

Kekeen slipped up beside him and took his arm. "It's not too late to make sure he never harms another child," she whispered.

"Between the threat of Swift Claw and my mother's watchfulness, I'm confident it will be all right." Even so, Clanless hesitated before helping Kekeen onto the wagon. A part of him would always want the revenge

Zektel urged him toward.

He climbed up beside Kekeen. Sugh bid everyone farewell once more before hopping onto the back end of the cart. His sudden weight rocked the small vehicle. "Careful!" Kekeen laughed. If he didn't know better, Clanless would have sworn the laugh came from Kekeen herself. She sounded so… carefree and happy.

The actual farewell took a great deal longer. Clanless flicked the reins, and the ox started walking. They made slow progress across the clanhold while the family followed along, calling out further farewells and advice for the journey. Clanless smiled when Ot joined in at last.

Then they passed through the gates. The family stopped and waved. Sugh, facing the rear, waved back most enthusiastically. Clanless and Kekeen joined in, but took turns keeping an eye on the road. After all, they wouldn't want to suddenly find themselves plowing into one of the fields that lined the road. Men of the clanhold stopped their work to watch the cart make its slow way between their labors.

Sugh twisted around to face front. He shifted some of their luggage in the process, causing a familiar clinking sound. Clanless glanced back. "We have blood vials?"

"Yes!" Sugh shoved a bag to produce more clinking. "Are we rich?"

"No, we are not." Kekeen twisted to look back at Sugh. "Those are from Qara."

"Blood from different clans? For magic?" Clanless asked.

"No." She faced him. "It's all your blood."

"Mine? Why?"

"You were losing a lot of it, so we captured some in her empty crystals. They could come in handy at some point."

Sugh hopped off the cart and started walking beside it.

"You know how this works now, right?" Kekeen asked. "Your blood, Aldan. It's a catalyst for the other types of blood. So if we need some magic, and we have the other blood, we can use yours to activate it." She smiled. "Without having to cut you open."

Clanless nodded. "I can see that."

Sugh scratched his head. "So if we take blood from Clan Berge and combine it with the blood of Clanless, we get the magic strength?"

"Yes, exactly."

"What if I cut myself"—Sugh held up his arm and pointed at it—"and pour some Clanless blood on that. Would the blood-magic flow through all of my blood? In my entire body?"

"Huh." Clanless cocked his head. "I've never thought of that. But I'm sure my blood mixed with others in the arena. I don't remember anything special happening."

Kekeen gave him a knowing smile. "You don't remember anyone suddenly displaying blood-magic powers late in a fight?"

He frowned. "Maybe. I guess I thought they were holding back at first."

"It may not be that at all," she went on. "I would assume that if your blood touched someone else's while still flowing from their body, it would have an effect like the Taint."

"That would not be pleasant," Sugh said.

"That's right." She looked over at him. "You've experienced it now."

"Twice. But I asked for the first time. And the second time was not really me."

"You asked for it?" Clanless wrinkled his brow. "Why don't I remember that?"

"It was soon after you joined us with the Dohor." Sugh waved at a farmer as they passed. "Hagh and I asked you to use it on us, so we'd know what it felt like."

"Ohhh, right. Now I remember."

"Hagh fell almost right away. I did not." Sugh chuckled.

"You lasted longer than most people," Clanless admitted. In fact, while Sugh had fallen, he hadn't passed out. That almost never happened.

The cart rolled on, eventually leaving the fields behind. The road itself faded, becoming almost non-existent. "Do you remember the way to Rochinbal?" Kekeen asked.

"South," Clanless answered. "It's hard to miss. First real city we'll discover."

Sugh pointed off to the right. "Swift Claw approaches."

The bond with the beastman had been growing since they left the clanhold. Now, it sprang to full life within Clanless. He smiled as Swift Claw bounded into view. "You took longer than I expected to catch up to us."

"I made one last visit to your sire's brother," the beastman said. "In the field. He did not see me coming."

"You didn't kill him, did you?" Clanless straightened up, eyes wide.

"No. You told me not to." Swift Claw's eyes and mouth grew large. "But he will not forget me."

Kekeen laughed. "All right. I wanted you to kill him, but this might be as much fun, after all."

Clanless scowled at her. "Not even hiding it any more," he grumbled.

"Why should I? You've already told Sugh about me. You may as well tell the beastman."

Swift Claw caught hold of the side of the car and hung on it. "What does she mean, Wolf Chosen?"

"Her wind is not her own." Clanless gripped the reins tighter. "And there's nothing we can do about it."

"Mmh." Swift Claw ran one hand through his hair. "Then we do as she says?"

"For now."

"For now," Sugh echoed.

"And where do we go?" The beastman dropped off the cart and trotted along beside it and Sugh.

Kekeen patted the pelt on Clanless's shoulder. "To talk with the man who gave him this."

# GHAN

Koland tapped his fingers on the table, but stopped at a glare from Lord Ezen. All six members of the council sat silent, waiting for the moment they all anticipated or dreaded or both. A full minute passed without anyone speaking.

"We should have gone to meet him!" Lord Ghayaktal burst out.

"He is a military commander, not a sovereign," Lord Ezen said. "He should report to us, not we to him."

"He's clan Shukan, same as the Hawk King," Ghayaktal said. "If anyone can claim to take the throne, he can!"

"Daviland will return," Sonkogh said.

Koland doubted that much. Suirel would have seen little value in keeping the upstart leader around.

"He holds no power here any more," Lord Ulakan said. "He effectively abdicated when he left the city to us."

The door to the chamber burst open. General Ghan strode into the room, pulling gloves from his hands. Like the last time Koland had seen him, the general's pristine uniform showed no signs of having traveled any distance. Captain Rakib trailed behind, a nervous hitch in his gait.

The general's deliberate strides brought him to the table, where the council stood to greet him. He looked first to the empty throne before surveying the men waiting for him.

"I am told," he said, "that you men have been governing the city in the absence of… royal leadership."

"This council has been formed from leaders of all branches," the Ghamba Lam began. "We—"

"If that were true, there would be twelve of you," Ghan interrupted. "One for each clan, thus having leaders from all branches, as you say."

"In time, I'm sure that will be done. This is but a beginning or interim leadership."

"I see." He looked from one to the other, sizing them up. His eyes settled on Sonkogh. "You are the only one here I do not recognize."

"My name is Sonkogh of clan Dariachin. It is—"

"Unimportant," General Ghan interrupted. "I assume you're here as a sop to that rebel leader, Daviland. It will interest you all to know that he is dead."

Koland bowed his head, ignoring the outcry of the other council members. He said a quiet prayer for the man he'd known, the man who'd dared so much to save his people, before he'd been corrupted by the blood-wraith.

"I do not know how this affects the balance of power in this room," the General said, lifting his voice to silence the others. "And right now, it does not matter. I am here for one reason only: the defense of this city."

"Then you have seen the Melkute army?" Lord Ezen asked.

"I have not only seen it, I have engaged it in a series of raids." General Ghan moved to the head of the table, standing next to Daviland's former seat. "I attempted to cause damage to their supply wagons with limited success. They are well prepared and well organized."

"How many are they?" Lord Ghayaktal asked.

"My scouts estimate the entire army to be composed of approximately 90,000 men."

Silence fell. Koland closed his eyes. An army of that size would have no difficulty placing Et-Baylak under a complete siege. This was far worse than he'd anticipated.

"And… and you brought only three thousand with you?" Lord Ezen looked ready to run from the room. "Combined with the soldiers here, that is, that is…"

"Not enough," Sonkogh whispered.

"The walls of Et-Baylak have never fallen," Ghan said. "And I do not intend for them to fall under my leadership. Captain Rakib has explained the actions taken thus far. Now that I am here, I will assume command of the defense and accelerate the process." He looked around the table. "Unless you gentlemen have any objections?"

"None whatsoever," Lord Ulakan said.

"It would be appreciated if you would keep us apprised of your actions," Koland spoke up. "So that we can aid the rest of the populace in responding to your needs or new developments."

General Ghan's perpetual frown did not move as he focused on Koland. After a few moments of locked eyes, he turned to the others and said, "I will, of course, inform the council of… developments. But as of now, I assume complete command of every soldier in this city. None of you have any experience in warfare. As such, I will not have my orders countermanded by anyone."

"Of course," Lord Ghayaktal said.

"As you said," the Ghamba Lam answered, "you are here for the defense of this city. It is our priority as well. We hope to work with you for the good of all. In this matter, we bow to your specific expertise."

"Excellent." Ghan's eyes darted around the table again, as if measuring each man's worthiness. "I would speak with you directly, Ghamba Lam, if we are finished here."

Everyone else rose at once. After a few more words of gratitude, the three Lords filed out. Sonkogh followed. Koland started to leave, but Captain Rakib caught his arm. "The General would prefer that you stay as well." Koland nodded and turned back.

Ghan took a seat but kept his posture stiff and upright. "Well, gentlemen, we face each other again."

"Sir?" Rakib asked.

"Oh. You are dismissed, Captain. I will meet with you again shortly."

The Captain saluted and hurried from the chamber. He glanced back before reaching the door, obviously wondering about the odd trio. Koland gave him a smile and a wave before turning back. He stood behind his chair and waited.

"Let us be blunt, General," the Ghamba Lam said once the Captain had gone. "There is no reason for ambiguity among us. Are you truly here to defend the city, or to serve Suirel?"

"Can a man not serve his city and his god at the same time? Why do you believe they are at odds?"

"Because," Koland said, "your Lord of Chaos is the one who convinced the Melkute Kingdom to invade."

General Ghan unbuttoned the top button of his outer coat. Koland thought it might be the closest the man got to relaxing. "I am told that you are a storyteller by profession," Ghan said. "I see that it is true."

"How did you find out about the army?" Koland challenged. "Wasn't it from one of your own soldiers who returned from trying to capture us?"

"And?"

"Clanless is the one who warned him. And he found out from Suirel himself."

The General turned his head back and forth as if scanning the entire room. "Where is the great Clanless, now that you mention him?"

"He is not in the city."

"Pity. We can use every good fighter." Ghan sighed. "Gentlemen, you request bluntness. Very well. I could have both of you seized this very moment and held for the murders of both the Hawk King and Daviland."

"Preposterous!" the Ghamba Lam exploded.

"I can produce twenty good men who would testify against you. It would be simplicity itself."

"Your own soldiers! Would you create a legal struggle between the priesthood and the military?"

Koland gripped the back of the chair. "I notice, General, that you used the word 'could.' I gather that you do not intend to do as you threaten. May I ask why not?"

"At this point, it would not serve any good purpose. As members of this council, you may yet be useful in the defense of the city. And should it come down to the worst, any man who can lift a sword will be needed." He nodded toward the Ghamba Lam. "And as he says, it would not be useful to create such a large-scale conflict within the city when the larger threat looms without."

"Then we will work together," Koland said. "For the good of all."

General Ghan gave a crisp nod. "At least for the present. I will warn you, however, that Suirel will be coming here."

"My scouts have not seen this," the Ghamba Lam said. "The Melkute will be here in less than two days."

"Nevertheless, he will come. Sometime later, I assume."

"If so, it will be interesting to see which side of the battle he joins," Koland observed.

General Ghan did not react. "Indeed."

((((●))))

"I'm glad you could make it." Koland took Qara's hand to assist her up the last few stairs.

"Looks like everyone made it," she answered, looking up and down the wall of Et-Baylak, "or at least tried to." Crowds gathered all along the wall. Soldiers chased some of the onlookers away but allowed others to stay.

In most cases, it came down to status.

Koland nodded to the nearest soldier, who returned the gesture with a grin. Over the past three days, he'd made regular trips to the wall and become acquainted with a number of those on duty. They had no objections to his presence or his guest… especially when the guest was an attractive young woman.

"I've never been here before." Qara stepped up to the outer parapet. "Everything looks so different from up here."

Koland looked out over the empty fields and dwellings outside the city. On a normal day, he would see dozens of people at work or coming and going through the gates. Now, nothing moved. Soldiers had closed and sealed the four gates of the city an hour earlier. They would not open again. Everyone who lived outside the walls had come inside. Or run away somewhere. "It's quiet," he murmured.

"Quiet is good," said the soldier. "When it's loud, bad things happen."

"Yes. Kansukh, wasn't it?" Koland asked. A light breeze blew from the north, breaking some of the stillness.

"Aye, sir."

"I thought so." Koland introduced Qara, to the soldier's delight.

"Where will they come from?" Qara asked.

"Ah, well, we're on the north wall here, ma'am." Kansukh pointed off to the left. "Our best guess is that they'll come from there, the northwest. But they could shift before their arrival and come straight on instead."

An officer hurried past them. Kansukh stood stiff at attention until he passed.

"I know it was unlikely," Qara whispered to Koland, "but I'd hoped Aldan would make it back before the enemy arrived. I would feel safer if he were here, as ridiculous as that sounds."

"I understand. But from what Kekeen told me of her plans, they won't be returning here for some time."

"And now they can't." Qara looked over the parapet toward the city's north gate a few hundred yards to their right. "No one can."

The breeze danced over them, playing with Qara's hair. "I'm surprised the wind isn't stronger up here," Koland observed.

"It usually is, sir," the soldier said. "It's calmed down today."

"The beastmen have a lot to say about winds," Qara said. "I wonder what they would say about this."

"You must tell me more about your time with them." Koland's mind danced at the idea of learning about a whole new race of beings.

Qara hugged herself. "We may have plenty of time for stories if this siege happens as you say."

"There!" Kansukh pointed again to the northwest. "They come!"

At first, Koland saw nothing. The soldier's young eyes could see further. A moment later, the distant landscape changed.

"I see a moving shadow," Qara said.

"An apt metaphor." Koland shaded his eyes and squinted. "Like the opening of Oketei's recitation of the Battle of Eaton."

"What?"

"A story. Never mind." But the description of a shadow fit. "A dark shadow on the edge of the world, growing, ever growing. A threat to all life and peace. It is birthed in darkness, nursed on the high hills, and embraces the opportunity to suffocate life itself."

He didn't realize he'd spoken the words aloud until he noticed Qara and Kansukh staring at him.

"Goddess, sir. I knew you were a fine fabler, but that's…" The soldier shook his head.

"It's terrifying," Qara finished for him.

"Sorry. Habits." He watched the shadow grow. Shouts echoed up and down the wall as the word spread. Messengers raced away to inform those who needed to know. The watchers moved to the very edge of the parapet, straining to see as much as they could.

The shadow separated itself into smaller shadows, distinct groups and men, wagons and creatures. As it did, the sound arrived: the tramp of thousands of feet and the rotation of hundreds of wheels. Distant shouts echoed from foreign tongues, speaking words they could not understand.

Qara shifted next to him. "Koland, there's… so many…"

The growing shadow spread across the land, now moving outward to the west and east even as it drew closer to the city. Even from this distance, Koland could tell there would be far more than enough troops to encircle the city. If anything, General Ghan's estimate of their numbers had been too low.

The shadow came down over a short set of hills, transforming from a shadow to more of a wave in Koland's mind. A dark wave of humanity rolling across the plains now, sweeping toward the wall of the city where it would crash against the stone. But no, it wasn't composed of humanity alone. The wagons were pulled by armored creatures, larger than most oxen. And other beasts moved among the enemy soldiers, unfamiliar creatures as large as the wagons themselves, some with horns or tusks.

A sudden gust of wind from the north pushed against the watchers.

The enemy forces split into ranks, moving into pre-arranged positions around the city, spreading out even further. Yet their lines were not thin; more troops poured in behind them, reinforcing every step along the way.

"I… I never dreamed there would be this many," Kansukh said.

"If you had dreamed it, it would have been a nightmare, son." Koland formed his hands into fists to press against the parapet. He'd told stories of great battles and sieges hundreds of times over the years, yet he'd never fully grasped the concept until now. These were people, tens of thousands of people, who'd come hundreds of miles with but one purpose: to kill the people of this city and take all they owned. What kind of hate could propel men on such an endeavor?

They stood watching in silence for a good quarter hour or more. The dread mounted in all those who beheld. Word spread throughout the city and dozens more of the curious and worried tried to obtain a moment on the wall to see for themselves.

"What do we do now?" Qara asked.

Koland shook his head. "Have you told everyone to evacuate the buildings closest to the wall?"

"Yes, but they're debating how close is too close." Qara rolled her eyes. "No one wants to leave their homes or businesses."

Koland pointed at structures moving among the soldiers. "They'll know exactly how close is too close once those catapults begin their work."

Qara bit her lip. "Is there nothing else we can do?"

"Pray, I suppose. Our fate is not in our hands." Koland took one last look before escorting her toward the stairs. Another gust of wind struck his face.

The siege of Et-Baylak had begun.

Part Two
ROADS

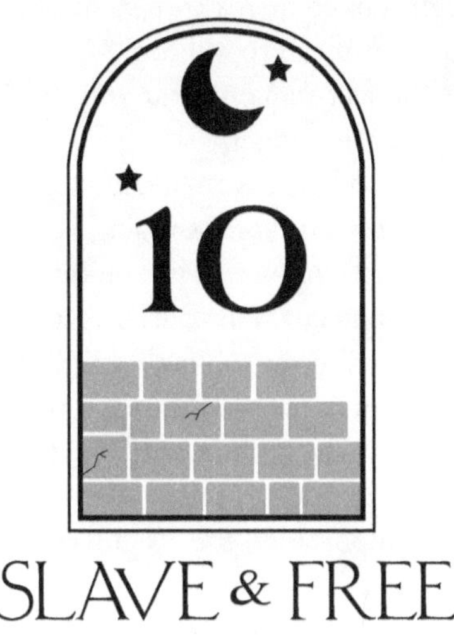

SLAVE & FREE

Sugh paced within the temple, glancing from time to time at the moon window above. More clouds obscured the light of the goddess. The lack of her presence enhanced his nervousness as he waited for word of his fate. The Daghilch had been in conclave with the other priests of Conchaga for three hours now. Two temple guards stood at the door to prevent his escape, but the very idea baffled him. Why would he flee? He'd only sought to protect the weak. Was it not one of the highest principles of the goddess herself?

At last the door opened. The Daghilch entered, followed by Arban, six other priests, and three more temple guards. Sugh met them and lowered his head in deference.

"Priest Sugh, we have carefully considered your account of the night's events," the Daghilch declared. "As a whole, we are very disappointed in you."

Sugh looked up in shock. "Sir?"

"You had a most promising career ahead of you," one of the other priests said. "Such a shame."

"W-what do you mean?" Sugh looked from one to the other. Arban would not meet his eyes.

"You have killed a man," the Daghilch said. "You cannot remain a priest of the goddess with this blood on your hands."

Instinctively, Sugh looked at his own hands, as if the statement had been literal. "I… I did not mean to kill him."

"It matters not. The fact remains that you did." The Daghilch shook his head. "You are a priest no longer."

"What? But, but I saved that woman from his attack! Ask her!" Sugh pointed toward the outside. His voice shook.

Arban stepped forward and put a hand on his shoulder, as he'd done so often. "Sugh. I know you meant well. But… you went too far."

"Murder is more than simply 'too far,'" another priest muttered.

Sugh jerked away from Arban and stared at the other priest. "Murder? I fought to protect! He had the knife, not I!" He grabbed the slashed edges of his robe and displayed them.

"The details are unimportant," the Daghilch said. "You killed a man. You cannot remain a priest."

Sugh looked around and saw impassive faces. Arban alone had the courtesy to appear concerned. As the finality of the situation sank in, Sugh fell to his knees. "All I ever wanted was to be a priest," he murmured. "To serve the goddess."

"You may continue to serve her, but in other ways," Arban said. He bent to be closer to Sugh. "The priesthood is not the only place of service. You—"

"It is not his choice to make," the Daghilch interrupted.

Arban looked back at him. "What do you mean?"

"I have spoken with the city guard. Considering the presence of the dishonorable blade, they are willing to show leniency. There will be no life-for-life."

Sugh reeled and almost collapsed. There had been a chance he'd be executed?

"But we are in agreement on how to proceed," he continued. "They have requested slavery, and I am inclined to agree, under one caveat."

Sugh looked up at him, feeling like he might pass out at any moment. He'd never thought, never dreamed it would come to this. Slavery? What would his parents think?

"Since you have demonstrated the capability and perhaps even a predilection for taking life," the Daghilch intoned, "it is the judgment of the city guard and this office that you be delivered to the arena trainers and, should you survive their ministrations, sold to the arena owner most interested in your future. Let it be known throughout the Empire and under the moon's gaze."

"Let it be known," the other priests echoed. Arban only shook his head.

Sugh clambered to his feet. His despair gave way to a swiftly-growing wrath. Arena slavery? Him? After all his dedication? All his work? "This is not just!" he shouted.

"You are judged by your spiritual and civil betters," the Daghilch said. "There is no higher court."

"The goddess would not agree with this!" Sugh cried. "She defends the weak and helpless. I did what I did to be like her, in honor of her!"

"This is the law of the goddess," one of the other priests said. "As it is written."

"Then I question those who wrote this law! I did nothing wrong!"

The Daghilch's eyes narrowed. "Be careful that you add not blasphemy to your crimes, young Sugh. The law was written by a Ghamba Lam, inspired by the goddess herself. These are her words you question."

Sugh's eyes darted upward. The moon remained hidden. "She cannot even watch," he groaned and lowered his head. The guards moved in from either side. Arban stepped back, shaking his head further.

Sugh stood and allowed the guards to seize his arms. They attempted to guide him away, but he stood firm. He raised his head and glared at the Daghilch. "Then I have more to say."

"Don't," Arban whispered.

"If this is the justice of this priesthood, then I say it is a false justice."

The priests murmured.

"And," he hastened to add, resisting the guards' pressure to move, "if this is the justice of the goddess, who cannot watch and refuses to speak, then I will no longer serve her!"

"Silence!"

"I will not be silent! From this day forward, I serve no one but myself. You send me to the arena? So be it. I will fight, but not for her." He threw his head back and stared up. The clouds parted, and the moon's brightness filled the room. "Never for her!"

Now

Clanless had no words for the feelings that came over him at the sight of the arena outside Rochinbal.

His feelings when they passed the walls of Rochibal itself were easier to define. He'd been inside the city only once and met Kekeen there. He knew happiness in those memories but also grief that the real Kekeen couldn't share the moment with him.

But looking at the arena structure itself, he couldn't translate his feelings. Here, he'd become a man and a warrior. Here, he'd made friends and lost them. Here, boys were trained to become killers. Here, boys… died.

Tunt. Nerlesen. Uyan. How many others over the years? Hundreds? He put a hand on the metal doors with their faded engravings of warriors. And his feelings coalesced into one very simple: anger.

"Zektel," he said as Kekeen walked up beside him. "We'll try to find Nukai, as you wish. But then we're burning this place down."

"Aldan, dear. I love the way you're thinking." She reached up and rapped on the doors. The sound echoed through empty halls and chambers beyond.

Sugh walked up behind them, leaving Swift Claw to watch the cart. "This is a dour place," he said. "Not at all like the one where I trained."

"You trained in a happy place?" Clanless asked.

"No, not happy." Sugh patted the wall, and a puff of dust came loose. "But colorful and busy. All the time."

Clanless frowned. "There should be boys here training right now. Graduation isn't until the end of High Spring."

"Perhaps they've already heard the news of the Hawk King's fall," Sugh suggested. "No more arenas!"

"I doubt it," Kekeen said. She banged on the door again. "Remember Ulken? Societal change takes time, boys. You can't end an entire industry overnight."

"This part of it ends today." Clanless shoved the door. To his surprise, it moved. He narrowed his eyes and pushed it the rest of the way open.

The three of them entered the wide hallway, lit only by the open door behind them. Clanless could make out faint light from the edges of another set of double doors in the distance, doors that led into the seating for the arena itself. He tried to push back his rising anger.

Kekeen took hold of his arm. "You would never have survived this place without me," she whispered.

She was right, but he didn't answer. Zektel had suppressed memories of many things that happened here, some of them horrible, some for her own twisted reasons. He still hadn't sorted them all out in his mind or dealt with some of the worst. But she'd also been there with him through it all, providing a friend, someone he could talk to. He couldn't discount that.

Sugh headed toward the opposite doors. "Wait," Kekeen called. "This door to the right leads to the offices. We should go that way."

Clanless stopped her. "Do you hear that?"

"What?"

He shook her hand off and pushed past Sugh toward the doors. "Shouts." He shoved the doors open, his fury rising.

For a brief moment, Clanless was thirteen years old. Kan screamed at him to keep his buckler up. Nerleson took advantage of his hesitation and… He snapped out of it and stared at real life in front of him.

The arena looked much the same as it had so many years ago, if a bit more disheveled and broken down. The condition of the seats, especially, had degraded. On the sand floor below, an unfamiliar man shouted orders at eight boys who faced each other in pairs, wielding maces and bucklers.

Catching sight of them, the trainer stalked across the sand in their direction. "No visitors at this time!" he shouted. "Nukai! Where are you? Who left the door open?"

Clanless seized the railing overlooking the arena and vaulted over it. His feet hit the sand hard and sank deep. He pulled the moonblade free and spun it around into a threatening stance. Sugh landed behind him a moment later.

The trainer backed up a couple of steps. The boys all stopped their dueling to watch this unprecedented interruption. "W-what's going on here?" the trainer demanded. "You're arena fighters, aren't you? What are you doing here?"

Clanless strode forward, every step a walk through his memories. "The Hawk King is dead! And with him died the arena system. You will release these young men at once!"

A murmur swept through the boys. Several of them lowered their maces. Two moved to back up the trainer.

"He speaks the truth," Sugh said. "We are members of the Dohor and witnesses to the Hawk King's death."

"I don't care who you are," the trainer said. "You can't come in here and tell me what to do." He tightened his grip on his own mace but glanced around with nervous eyes.

Clanless took a step toward him. His eyes darted across the boys watching. He saw a variety of emotions. The two with the trainer appeared ready to fight for him. Two or three others looked hopeful, but the rest only looked… frightened? Of him? Or of what would happen if he were telling the truth? One of the frightened ones, a little more stout than the others, dropped his mace. Clanless winced, thinking of Tunt.

He stuck the moonblade into the sand and released it, showing empty hands. He glanced around until he found what he wanted: a rock. He took a few steps to the side and picked it up. "So much smaller than I remember," he murmured. Turning to the boys, he held it up with one hand. "Listen to me. I am Clanless the arena fighter. Some of you may have heard of me. I was trained in this arena by a man named Kan." He pointed to the far door across the arena. "He would make us run from this door to that one, back and forth. And sometimes, we would have to carry these rocks. Have you ever had to do that?"

A few of the boys murmured in the affirmation.

Clanless threw the stone into the seats. He looked about until he spotted what he'd expected: a blood-priest standing next to the door, poised to run. "And I suppose some of you have suffered horrible injuries and needed his blood-magic to heal you." He pointed at the priest.

This time, at least four of the boys answered "Yes," while two others nodded.

"That never has to happen again!" He picked the moonblade back up and turned to the trainer. "Because this man is going to give me all of your bloodbonds, and I am going to free each and every one of you."

Loud gasps erupted. The priest ran.

Clanless stepped closer to the trainer and looked him over. "You are not Kan. You are not even worth bloodying my blade. Give me the bloodbonds." He pointed to a bag hanging from the man's belt.

"You… you can't do this."

"Yes, he can." Sugh joined him, brandishing his axe. "You need to find a new job."

The trainer backed up. "Boys! Defend me!"

The first two stepped up but didn't advance. Two of the others started forward but their comrades pulled them back. The trainer looked about. "I still own you! Do what I say!"

Clanless pointed the moonblade at him. "They do not have to. Your day is over. This arena is over."

The trainer looked around for support and found none. "You will all pay for this," he growled.

"I do not think so," Sugh said, slinging his axe back over his shoulder.

The trainer dropped his mace and ran. As he passed by the boys, one of them stuck out his foot and tripped him. It was the one who'd reminded Clanless of Tunt. Sugh ran and yanked the man up out of the sand. "You have forgotten something, friend." He pulled the bag of bloodbonds from his belt. "And you've forgotten to do something."

"Free them," Clanless ordered. "You do it willingly, or I will kill you and set them free myself."

The trainer looked from him to Sugh and gave up. He took the bloodbonds, one at a time, and recited the necessary words to end each boy's enslavement. The boys stood around watching with wide eyes, as if they couldn't believe their fortune. When it was done, Clanless took the metal plates and tossed them away into the sand. "Powerless now," he said. "You're all free."

The sound of clapping came from behind him. He turned to the arena doors and saw Kekeen approaching, followed by a shuffling hunched-over man wearing heavy clothes. "Well done," she called. "But I found who we were looking for."

"Nukai?" Clanless stared at him. The older man looked up hesitantly. A dirty cape slid off his back into the sand. Nukai scrambled to pick it back up. Behind them, the trainer took advantage of the distraction to run away. Sugh took a couple of steps after him, then shrugged and turned back.

"It's me. Clanless. Do you remember me?" Clanless took off the fur pelt and held it out.

Nukai stared at the pelt as though seeing it for the first time. "Clanless," he repeated in his raspy voice. "It's been… years." He touched the pelt and looked up at him. "Did you honor me in this?"

"I tried to." Clanless hesitated for a moment before replacing the pelt onto his own shoulder. "And it turns out this thing is far more important than I understood."

"And we think you know more about it," Kekeen put in.

Nukai glanced at her with lowered eyebrows. "I know who you are," he muttered.

"Excuse me, sir?" One of the boys stepped up with a nudge from one of his friends. "What are we to do now?"

"You're free," Clanless said. "You can do whatever you want."

The boys looked at one another. "How?" one of them asked.

"Gather your personal items, if you have any, and walk out," Clanless said. "Head for the city. Someone there…" He trailed off. Goddess. What was he supposed to tell them?

"Didn't think this one through, did you?" Kekeen said. She stepped past him and looked over the boys. "You should also gather whatever you can find from your former master's rooms. And bring the best weapons too. If you have far to travel, you can sell those things to pay your way."

"We will take you to the city ourselves," Sugh said. He looked back at Clanless. "We can do that much, yes?"

"Sure." He took a breath and looked around. "And we're burning this place down as we leave."

The boys ran through the doors. Clanless watched them go with a mixture of pride and satisfaction. Regardless of other failures in his life, at least he could accomplish this one good thing.

"You have one place left you want to visit, don't you?" Nukai asked.

Clanless looked down at the hunched man. "I do?"

"First, you need to answer our questions," Kekeen said.

Nukai ignored her. "Behind the arena?" he prompted.

Clanless sucked air in through his nose. He hadn't thought of that in years. And before, he'd tried not to think about it. Kan's words on his first day here echoed in his memory: "Sixteen boys will fight that day, and eight will become true arena fighters. The other eight will be buried in the ditch behind the arena."

"Take me there," he ordered.

As before, Nukai moved far faster than Clanless would have expected for someone in his age and condition. Upon understanding their destination, Kekeen left them to help Sugh prepare for the fire.

"You know that Dokhon will return with the city guard," Nukai said as he led the way through several doors and passages.

"Dokhon? The trainer?" Clanless frowned. Another complication. "We'll deal with it when they get here," he said. "We only came here to find you."

"I know." Nukai brought out a set of heavy keys to unlock the final metal door. "I am prepared to go with you."

Clanless furrowed his brow. "What? I don't think…" He trailed off as the door opened and he saw what lay beyond.

Graves. Dozens of graves. Based on Kan's words, Clanless had expected some kind of mass grave: the "ditch." Instead, someone had buried the dead individually and placed a small stone to mark them. It wasn't much, but it had required a lot of work. Clanless was pretty sure he knew who had done it.

He stepped out of the arena and walked between the graves. "So many," he murmured.

"One hundred and three," Nukai said. "Between six and ten for every year. Class sizes varied."

Clanless knelt and examined one of the stones. It was a simple rock, not unlike the ones Kan made them carry within the arena, with a rough symbol carved on the top. "What do these mean?"

"It's how I keep track." Nukai shuffled past him. "The ones you're looking for are over here."

Clanless stood and followed him. One hundred and three graves. So many. And yet… "Shouldn't there be even more?" he realized. "Kan had been doing this for many years."

"But I hadn't." Nukai stopped and pointed at a set of eight stone-marked graves. "These are the ones from your graduation. The first three are the ones you knew."

Clanless knelt again, unsure what he should feel. Two of these—Nerleson and Uyan—he hadn't known well. He'd fought with and against both of them and listened to their stories by the fire. But he'd kept his distance. Nerleson wanted to be the best and didn't care about friendships. Uyan had been Yeltek's ally and little more. But the third… Clanless shifted, staring at the carved stone.

"It's the one you're looking at," Nukai said softly.

Tunt. He'd tried so hard to be a friend, even when Clanless pushed him away. Maybe if he hadn't done that, Tunt would have survived. But even if he had, could he have lived very long as an arena fighter? No. Tunt didn't belong in that world. Zektel would have said he was too weak. But that wasn't it. Tunt's spirit was too bright for the darkness of the arena.

Clanless brushed his fingers against the stone. "I'm sorry," he whispered. "I miss you."

Nukai said nothing, waiting while Clanless spent a few more minutes in the dirt. "Goddess," Clanless whispered as he stood, "if you've taken Tunt to somewhere celestial… tell him…" He stopped, losing the words.

"She knows what you mean," Nukai said. "Your groanings are understood."

Clanless pushed his hair back. He looked around the graves again. "Why did you stay, Nukai? You obviously cared about… about us. Why be a part of this system for so long?"

Nukai pointed to Tunt's stone. "He needed someone to cry to in a place no one else could hear." He walked to another stone in a different row. "This one needed someone to change his bedding when he peed on it the first week he was here." He pointed at a third stone. "This one needed his night terrors kept secret from the others." He looked back at Clanless. "And you needed a push to use what was given you. So that you would survive."

Clanless shook his head. "But you helped. Kan and, and the newer trainer. You helped them do what they did."

"You were slaves, Aldan. All of you. Your only hope was to find a way to survive. And that meant becoming very good at fighting." Nukai paused. "Maybe… maybe you would have done something different. Maybe I should have. I don't know."

"You were an arena fighter once."

Nukai nodded.

Clanless wanted to ask more, because he still didn't understand. Wanting to help slave boys survive was one thing. But helping them through a system that would lead to them killing others? It was too much. He looked around at all the stones again, an ache filling his chest.

"The people of Rochibal need to see this," he said at last.

"They cheered when boys died. Do you think the graves will make a difference?"

"They need to see the consequences of their entertainment," Clanless growled. "I'll make them see."

"You're going to take on an entire city now?" Nukai moved away from him, leaving the organized graves and stopping at one set apart from the others.

"Who's that?" Clanless asked, curiosity overriding his anger for a moment.

Nukai stood with head bowed for a moment without answering. He lifted his head, sighed, and turned back toward the arena. "My predecessor," he said. "A complicated man."

One of the boys appeared at the door. "The lady sent me to find you," he said with a tremor in his voice. "And to tell you that they're… oh." His eyes widened, taking in the graves.

"This is where you were headed," Clanless said, walking toward him. "Half of you, at least." He gestured widely. "This is graduation day."

The boy stared, unable to answer.

Nukai sighed. "He knows, Clanless. No need to traumatize him further." He moved on. "Come, Naran, let's get out of here."

Clanless let them go ahead. He paused one more time to look over the graves. The sight made him want to find every one of these places throughout the Sar Empire and destroy them all. But a literal god of chaos walked the earth right now. And a blood-wraith owned the woman he loved. How could one man right so many wrongs?

Nukai looked back from inside the door. "One step at a time, Clanless," he called. "One step at a time."

NUKAI

Clanless could hear the crackle of the flames, but they didn't reach high enough to be seen yet. As he watched, a large section of the stands collapsed, disappearing into the rising smoke.

He stood with Sugh, Kekeen, Nukai, and the rescued boys. Swift Claw had wisely chosen to fade into the wilderness rather than try to explain his presence to the young ones.

"The stone walls will contain the blaze," Nukai said. "Everything within will be destroyed."

Clanless nodded. He didn't know what the others had used to get the fire going and didn't care. It would take an enormous amount of work and funding to restore this place. The arena owners from the cities would have to all agree to take care of it, and by then, the news of the Hawk King's fall would have spread everywhere. As long as Suirel didn't ruin everything…

"Old wood. It burns well," Sugh said. He paused before adding: "This is a good thing. I am glad we were a part of it."

"We should get moving," Kekeen said, "especially if you want to get these boys to the city before dark."

Clanless glanced up. The sun had begun its daily retreat, but they still had plenty of time. He inhaled, letting the smell of the smoke fill his nostrils. Maybe he had no chance to stop a god of chaos, but he could do this much.

"The city guard is coming!" one of the boys shouted.

They all turned toward the city and saw a small band approaching.

Dokhon, the trainer, led the way.

"How do we handle this?" Sugh asked, hefting his axe.

"I don't want to fight them," Clanless said. "But I won't give these boys back to that man."

"Maybe we kill him then."

Kekeen pushed in front of both of them. "The guard is not going to react well if you murder him in front of them," she pointed out. "Let me handle this."

Sugh looked at Clanless. "Is that a good idea?"

As much as he hated to admit it, Zektel probably had the best chance of talking her way out of this. Nukai might be able to help, but he had withdrawn back behind the cart with the boys. "Go ahead," Clanless said, but he readied the moonblade as well. He counted eight guardsmen with the trainer. Four other men, all younger, followed at a distance, curious onlookers attracted by the commotion.

When the crowd drew close enough, Dokhon stopped and pointed at them. "There they are!" His shout did not seem necessary. "We've got them now!"

"We're not going anywhere," Kekeen said loudly. "I'm so glad you brought the guard. They can help us get these boys to their homes."

The leader of the city guard, a middle-aged man with a close-cropped gray beard, stepped to the front. "I'm afraid I must ask the three of you to come with us," he said. "This man has made some serious charges against you."

"For what?" Kekeen asked. "He's the one who's been running a criminal organization here."

The guard leader wrinkled his brow. "This arena has been a part of our city for longer than I've been alive, miss." He gestured toward the boys. "They train arena fighters here for the whole Empire."

"They used to, you mean. I'm afraid that all ended when the previous trainer, Kan, retired. You remember Kan, don't you?"

Several of the guards nodded.

"Don't be ridiculous!" Dokhon shouted. "Kan turned everything over to me! Nothing has changed! This arena is mine! Those boys are my slaves!"

"Then I'm sure you can produce their bloodbonds," Kekeen said calmly.

The guard leader looked to Dokhon. "Can you?"

"They took them from me! Forced me to release them all!"

"So by your own words, these boys are not slaves at all, are they?" Kekeen asked.

"They were! You took them!"

Kekeen let out a huge sigh. "The truth, good men of Rochibal, is that he had no bloodbonds at all. We came here at the behest of a family in one of the clanholds to the north. Cousins of Aldan here. The mother, Borde, told us a harrowing tale of how her son was kidnapped and taken here by mercenaries serving this man." She gestured at Dokhor. "Unable to afford slaves of his own, he resorted to stealing young men against their will."

Clanless marveled at Zektel's skill at weaving in bits of truth into an elaborate lie. Then again, most of what she'd ever told him over the past eight years might be the same.

"You can't believe any of this!" The trainer stared at the guard leader. "None of this is true!"

"Can you prove it?" Kekeen asked. "Show us the bloodbonds. Or show us your riches that would enable you to purchase eight slaves."

"My blood was in there!" He pointed at the burning arena. "They probably stole it for themselves!"

"You're welcome to search all that we have," Clanless put in. "We have nothing to hide."

Kekeen shot him an annoyed look for speaking up.

The guard leader scratched his head. "This has become a lot more confusing than I expected it to be."

"I can send word to the arena owners," Dokhon said. The timber of his voice grew with each interchange. "They'll all support me!"

"That seems fair," the guard leader said. "And while we wait for them to answer, we can—"

"You're saying people from the big city arenas will support you?" Kekeen asked.

"Yes, of course they will!" Dokhon threw up his hands. "They all know me!"

Kekeen stepped back next to Clanless. "Have any of you ever traveled to Et-Baylak?" she asked. "Or heard of the arena fights there with the Hawk King's Dohor?"

"What difference does that make?" the trainer snapped.

"Perhaps you've heard of Clanless, the greatest arena fighter of our time." Kekeen pulled on Clanless's shirt. He helped her expose his brand. "And this other huge man is Sugh, another of the Dohor."

A crash sounded behind them as another section of the stands collapsed.

"I saw him fight once!" one of the guards exclaimed. "I knew he looked familiar!" He nudged the man next to him. "I said so as we walked up, didn't I?"

Two of the others murmured about recognizing the brand.

Dokhon stumbled over his words. "They... no, that's not... they're escaped slaves too! They must be!"

Kekeen's mouth dropped open. "You're suggesting the Hawk King is foolish enough to lose track of his most valuable slaves?"

"Then what are they doing here?" he almost screeched.

"We heard about your illegal activities, of course," Sugh said. "Seems only right we should be the ones to shut it down."

Dokhon's face grew so red, Clanless wondered if it would burst into flame. "This... this is preposterous!"

"Ask the boys," Kekeen suggested. "Boys, are any of you slaves?"

"No," several of them answered at once. "I want to go home!" the one named Naran shouted, looking as if he might start crying at any moment.

"There, you see?" Kekeen turned back to the city guard. "You have eleven witnesses to one."

"Nukai!" Dokhon shouted. He shoved past Sugh and ran to the cart. "Nukai, tell them! Tell them how you have served me so faithfully all these years!"

Nukai straightened enough to look the trainer in the eyes. "Your actions abhor me," he said.

Dokhon stumbled back. "W-what?"

Kekeen lifted both palms and cocked her head. The guard leader sighed. "I guess I can't see past all this. Looks like we'd best get these boys home." He shook his head. "I'm going to miss this place, though. Saw some good fights."

"Perhaps you'll change your mind when you see what's behind it," Clanless said.

A few minutes later, three of the guards and two of the onlookers reacted in horror at the sight of the graves. The others, including the leader, stood around awkwardly. Clanless felt a fury rising within. He wanted to force these men to care. Maybe if he made them dig up the most recent graves and see the bodies...

A gentle hand touched his back. "The greatest evil is that which is simply accepted as normal," Nukai said in a quiet voice behind him. "Before you condemn these men too harshly, consider: if we laid out the graves of all those you've killed in the arena, would it be smaller or greater than this?"

"The ones I killed weren't boys!"

Nukai pointed to a grave next to Tunt's. "That one would disagree with you."

Clanless closed his eyes. The boy he'd killed in his own graduation. He could argue with Nukai, of course. He'd had no real choice in the matter. He'd had to kill or be killed. But did that make it right?

Nukai gestured again toward the guards. "They will tell the story now. Some will listen. Not all. But some."

"Then we made a difference today."

"For Naran and the other seven boys? Most definitely. For the future? That remains to be seen."

Clanless furrowed his brow as he looked at Nukai. The hunched man had always had words of wisdom and knowledge to dispense, but… "You're not as grumpy as you used to be," he said.

"I'm not?" Nukai chuckled and adjusted his furs. "I'll work on that."

With no allies remaining, Dokhon fled back to the city alone. Clanless gathered up the boys and, together with the city guard, returned that way as well. Within Rochinbal, they found an inn that could hold all of them, at least for one night. The innkeeper, a mother herself, joined them in determining where each boy had come from. Together, they arranged transportation for all of them, paid for by Kekeen, who seemed to have a significant supply of blood vials after all. Clanless suspected she'd taken it from Dokhon's office.

Zektel made a half-hearted offer for Clanless to share her bedroom, but even she knew he wouldn't agree. He shared a room with Sugh and Nukai instead. As he started to fall asleep, he sensed Swift Claw somewhere outside the city. The beastman might be growing irritated with always being left outside. He could handle the nighttime cold better than the humans could, but that didn't mean he liked it. Before he drifted off, Clanless reminded himself to apologize to Swift Claw.

((((●))))

"All right. We've waited long enough," Kekeen proclaimed at the breakfast table the next morning. She leaned across and pointed at Nukai. "Tell me about the wolf."

Clanless winced at her tone. He'd meant to tell Nukai about Zektel, but everything had happened too fast yesterday.

Nukai finished chewing his pastry and swallowed. "The Wolf was an arena fighter, perhaps the greatest of his day," he began. "He wasn't owned by any of the arenas, however. He—"

"That's not what I meant!" Kekeen interrupted. She grabbed Clanless's pelt and pulled on it. "This wolf."

Nukai regarded her with sad eyes before taking a drink of water.

"I think it's all tied together," Clanless said. "Let him tell it his way."

Kekeen rolled her eyes and leaned back.

"The Wolf was an arena fighter, perhaps the greatest of his day," Nukai repeated. "He wasn't owned by any of the arenas, however. He fought, not as a slave, but as a free man. He traveled from arena to arena, challenging their mightiest."

"I am a free man now," Sugh said. "Maybe I should do this."

"The arenas will be shutting down," Clanless reminded him.

"Will they?" Kekeen asked. "I wouldn't bet on it."

"The Wolf was called by his name because he'd won his fame fighting the largest wolf anyone had ever seen in the arena at Et-Baylak," Nukai went on, as if no one had said anything.

Clanless fingered the pelt. "Not this wolf, though."

"No. That one came later. Much later."

"But Orgina told me the Wolf wore, um, a wolf pelt."

"He did." Nukai nodded and picked up another pastry. "These are good. Why didn't I come here before? It's not far."

They waited while he consumed the pastry and drank some more water.

"Yes, the Wolf wore fur. Always. But from different wolves, depending on how he felt." He paused and stared off into the distance. "Some of them had very odd coloring."

"This is getting us nowhere," Kekeen grumbled.

"Oh, do we need to leave?" Nukai started to get up.

"Not yet." Clanless caught his arm. "Finish the story."

"Of course." Nukai hesitated, as if trying to remember. "The Wolf fought everywhere. He had fame, fortune, whatever he wanted. Until the day he received an invitation from the Melkute Kingdom. They wanted him to come fight in their capital arena."

"The Melkute Kingdom has arena fighting too?" Clanless exclaimed.

"Oh yes," Sugh said. "I fought one of their champions the month before you joined us in the Dohor." He shrugged. "He did not fight well."

"But on the trip north, the Wolf's caravan was attacked by barbarians," Nukai went on. "Everyone else was killed or taken prisoner. But not the Wolf." He shook his head. "He fought hard, perhaps harder than he ever had in his life. But in the end, there were too many barbarians."

Clanless looked down. He knew the feeling.

"They laughed over his furs and took them all. They left him for dead beside the road. But he was not dead." This time, Nukai touched the fur on

Clanless's shoulder. "And that is where the real wolf found him."

Kekeen straightened up. "The real wolf? The giant one?"

Nukai looked at Clanless. "You have met the wolf. Have you told her?"

"She knows everything I know, which isn't much. The wolf saved me in the wilderness. And he talked… not that I understood much of what he said."

Nukai nodded. "It is the same."

"But what is he?" Kekeen demanded. "Wolves don't talk. Who is he, really?"

"This wolf talked," Nukai said. "He said he'd bathed in the blood of the ancestors."

"Yes! That's what he said to me!" Clanless interjected.

Kekeen threw her hands up. "The blood doesn't make animals into giants or give them intelligence! There's no blood-magic anything like that!"

"Are you so certain? Perhaps this world contains powers beyond your comprehension," Nukai suggested.

Kekeen glared at him. "I comprehend far more than you do about powers, old man. You have no idea who you're dealing with here."

He watched her without moving. "Perhaps it is you who does not possess the correct idea."

Clanless considered bringing up the story his father had told him, but Zektel knew it already. In fact, she'd blocked his memory of it. But now she claimed the whole thing was nonsense. His eyes narrowed as he watched her argue with Nukai. The blood-wraith wanted some kind of specific information, but he couldn't figure it out. Her own lies and concealments contradicted things she said now. Why?

Nukai might have deduced some of her intent on his own. "But you clearly believe something different," he added before Kekeen could respond. "What do you believe about this wolf creature?"

"I believe you are hiding something, old man."

"Old, am I?" He chuckled. "I suppose from your point of view, I might be. But come: I have not yet finished my story of the Wolf."

"Yes, what happened after you met the, uh, wolf?" Clanless asked.

Kekeen folded her arms and kept silent.

"Most believed the Wolf died that day," the hunched man said. "He never fought in an arena again. Not that anyone saw, at any rate. But he did not die." He paused. "Not yet, anyway."

Kekeen rolled her eyes again.

"He returned to the arena, but not as a fighter."

"He went to work for Kan," Clanless said. "To help the training of new fighters."

Nukai inclined his head but did not respond.

"Did you see it as, as some sort of penance?" Clanless wanted to know.

Nukai's dark eyes pierced into his. "Penance for what?"

Clanless shifted uncomfortably. "For, um, all the lives taken in the arena, I suppose."

"Do you feel the need for penance, Clanless?"

"This isn't my story."

"Is it not?"

Kekeen buried her face in her arms on the table. "This is completely pointless."

Clanless got to his feet. "It was your idea." The words about penance reawakened the thoughts he'd experienced looking at the graves. And if there were so many at this arena, where only one event took place each year… how many dead lay in mass graves outside the other arenas? The priests always took the bodies for their blood, but he'd never thought—perhaps intentionally—about what they did with the remains afterward.

"Regardless, I suppose it is time to move on?" Nukai made to get up as well.

Kekeen lifted her head and frowned. "We don't need you any more."

"And yet, I am going with you to Et-Baylak."

"You can find your own transportation."

"He can travel with us," Clanless said. "There's no harm in it."

Kekeen appeared about to argue but paused. "Hm. Very well." She stood and nudged Sugh. "Let's go, big man."

"I am not done eating!" he complained.

"When are you ever done?"

He grabbed one more pastry and got up to follow them out the door.

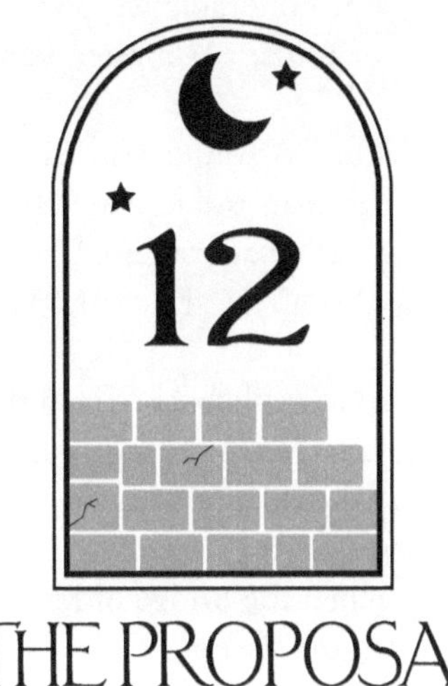

THE PROPOSAL

A full year of training had led to this point. Sugh's future would be decided in the next few minutes. He took a deep breath to steady himself. He'd survived the training, but from this point on, he would be facing death on a constant basis. He knew his own abilities now but couldn't help but wonder how long he would survive.

"This one fought extraordinarily well in the exhibition," the trainer said, gesturing to Sugh. "One of my best, despite coming to me at such a late age."

"He certainly looks the part." Baduhan, the arena master, looked Sugh over as if he were a slab of beef in the market. "How tall is he?"

"Well, he, uh…" The trainer scratched his head. "Taller than any of us."

With an effort, Sugh kept from rolling his eyes. Late age. Taller. What nonsense. "I never lose," he said. "If that's what you want, then here I am. If not…" He shrugged. He'd heard some rumors about Baduhan's treatment of his slaves. He might run the most profitable arena in the Empire, but it came at a cost to his fighters.

Baduhan, an overweight man with a meager beard, chuckled. "He has a mouth, does he?" He frowned at the axe sitting on the nearby table. "Dishonorable weapon too."

"Aye," the trainer said. "Had some dispute with priests before coming to me. Insisted on using a dishonorable weapon." He shook his head. "I trained him on the mace, of course. As master, you can force him to fight the way you want."

"Oh, I don't know, Father." A young woman, Sugh's age or a little less, stepped out from behind Baduhan and his three aides. "Your other fighters are boring now. Maybe this is what you need." She moved over to Sugh and patted the muscles on his upper arm. "Big. Dark. Scary." She looked up at Sugh and smiled.

He swallowed and tried to smile back. The girl was voluptuous with a red tint to her long, dark hair. Maybe being an arena fighter for this man wouldn't be all bad. One of the aides, a bodyguard of some kind, narrowed his eyes and stepped closer, readying a mace.

"Chabi." Baduhan pinched the bridge of his nose. "How many times have I told you not to touch the slaves?"

She spun back to face him but stayed tantalizingly close to Sugh. "I want this one, Father. Trust me on this."

He waved a hand to the trainer. "Very well. Bring me his bloodbond. I'm already overdue for a massage before the trip home."

Chabi followed him, but not without a cocked eyebrow back at Sugh. He opened his mouth, but didn't know what to say. Would anything be appropriate in such a situation?

His trainer shook his head. "You're in for it now, big man."

Now

Koland stopped in the middle of the street near the palace and listened. For the first time in three days, he didn't hear the sound of the siege engines. They'd been bombarding almost non-stop since the enemy's arrival. At first, they'd tried bringing down the city walls or gates with massive rocks, but that hadn't worked. They'd shifted their strategy after a few hours to launching their projectiles over the walls into the fringes of the lower city. Sometimes they launched rocks, but they threw fire as well, igniting larger conflagrations.

But now… he hadn't heard a new attack in the past two hours. And he'd received an urgent summons to the council. In his trip to the palace, his mind had raced through the possibilities. Surely General Ghan wasn't surrendering already. Did the Melkute army have a new strategy in mind? Were they about to launch a full assault against the walls?

In a few moments, he arrived in the throne room to find the rest of the council already assembled and waiting with General Ghan. He walked to the table, feeling every eye watching him.

"At last," the General said. "I was beginning to think you'd gotten caught in one of the fires. I'd hate to ask this council to rule on something without every member present."

"I appreciate your patience," Koland answered, taking his seat. "As a matter of fact, I was near the fires, encouraging people to move inward in the city and stop trying to save buildings that are already lost."

"Indeed." General Ghan put his hands behind his back. "I summoned you all because we have received a messenger from the invading army."

The council members murmured. Lord Ezen whispered something to Lord Ghayaktal.

"He came under signs of truce, and, as you have no doubt noticed, the attack has stopped for the moment," the General went on. "As such, we allowed him to enter. He has communicated his request to me, but I thought it would better serve the city for the rest of you to hear it as well."

After a pause, the Ghamba Lam spoke up. "We appreciate your consideration, General. Are you saying that the Melkute messenger is here right now?"

"Correct." The General gestured toward the door where Captain Rakib waited. The Captain nodded and opened the door.

A clean-shaven young man strode into the room with a confident smile. Koland's eyes noticed the obvious, like everyone else: the man's skin was lighter and his hair longer than most men within the Empire. Under one arm, he carried a helmet decorated with a plume of even longer hair. Koland also noticed things the others would probably miss: the man's confident demeanor was a sham. Something bothered him. A twitch of the jaw, a tremble of the hand: these things gave him away. Koland narrowed his gaze, trying to understand. What could possibly trouble a man who, by all accounts, was on the winning side of this siege?

The messenger stopped a few feet from the table and looked over the council. "I am to understand that you are the leaders of this city now?" He spoke the language easily, with barely a hint of accent. This was a man who'd been involved in dealings with the Sar Empire, either as a diplomat or merchant.

"We are," Lord Ulakan said. "Why have you broken decades of peace and invaded our land?"

"I am not here to debate the causes of the conflict," he answered. "I am here to work toward a resolution."

"State your message," the Ghamba Lam said. "Questions can wait until we have heard what you have to say."

The messenger gave him a curt nod. He stared across the table, above the council's heads as he spoke: "My king and lord, Kataat Ghun the Almighty, commands that you surrender the city to save further bloodshed."

"Is that it?" Lord Ezen exclaimed. "You wanted to see us for a simple surrender demand?"

"The King is aware that you will not acquiesce to this command, as the Sar Empire is known for its obstinacy and its pagan beliefs. Perhaps you expect your so-called goddess to rescue you."

Koland shot a glance at the Ghamba Lam, who looked vaguely amused at the religious attack.

"This will not happen. In time, our army will breach your walls, and everyone within will die or become our slaves. And so," he hastened to continue before they could interrupt, "Kataat Ghun the Almighty, being ever merciful and gracious to those beneath him, is prepared to offer an alternative." He paused.

"And this alternative is…?" Sonkogh prompted.

"The King has heard much of the fabled arena warriors of the Sar Empire. The all-knowing Sama El has revealed the truth of such things to King Kataat Ghun."

Sama El? Koland frowned. It was a deity name, obviously, but it did not sound like any of the names of the Melkute god he'd heard before. A new god, perhaps?

"And so, the King offers a way to prevent the mass bloodshed: a battle of champions. The King's Champion, Ular, stands ready. We ask that you send forth your mightiest warrior to face him." He stopped speaking and waited for their response. Distracted by the "Sama El" name, Koland almost didn't notice the subtle change in the messenger's demeanor. The initial concern faded, replaced by… a mild smirk?

"This battle of champions… its outcome would determine the entire war?" Lord Ghayaktal asked.

"In the unlikely event your champion wins, we will withdraw our army," the messenger said. "When the mighty Ular wins, you will open the gates of the city and surrender. Your people will be treated fairly as new subjects of the Melkute Kingdom."

"I'm sure they will," Koland murmured. "Tell me," he said louder, "why should we accept this offer? We are secure here."

"For the time being, you are. However, we can wait. Even if we do not breach the walls, the outcome is inevitable. You have no aid to come to your rescue. When your people begin eating one another to prevent starvation, you will beg for our mercy." His eyes narrowed. "And because you rejected the king's gracious offer, the mercy will not come."

"Even assuming we accept this offer," Lord Ezen said, "and we choose our own champion, what assurances do you give—"

"Your pardon," the messenger interrupted. "The terms of this offer do not require you to choose a champion. There is only one whom King Kataat Ghun will accept as your representative."

"You choose our champion for us?" Lord Ulakan exclaimed. "What nonsense is this?"

"We do not choose him. You have chosen him already, proclaiming him as the greatest warrior the Sar Empire has ever known."

Koland swallowed as he realized what was about to be said. And there could be no doubt of the messenger's smirk now.

"Your champion must be the mighty arena warrior," the messenger said. "The one you call Clanless!"

A moment of shock followed. If not for the seriousness of the situation, Koland would have laughed at how many mouths fell agape around the table. After a few more questions that revealed nothing more, the council dismissed the messenger with a promise to send a response as soon as possible. Once he'd gone, General Ghan looked straight at Koland. "The question must be asked. Where is Clanless?"

"I don't know," Koland said.

The Ghamba Lam almost erupted out of his seat. "This is no time for secrets, storyteller! He left us with your daughter! Where were they going?"

"I don't know," Koland repeated. "They did not tell us, in order to keep it secret. Clanless has enemies and needed time to recover from injuries."

"Goddess above!" Lord Ezen swore. "Do you mean to tell me that the man who could save our city is off on a pleasure trip with your daughter somewhere, and we have no way of finding him?"

"General Ghan." Koland turned to face him. "Do you believe this offer of theirs is sincere? Would they really stake this entire war effort on a single one-on-one battle?"

"It is not without precedent," the General said. "A battle of champions has been used many times in the past as a means of saving lives and avoiding difficulty. It was often seen as a spiritual thing as well. For a battle of such significance, surely the gods would interfere to make sure the correct man won."

"Yes, yes. I've told the stories myself of such things," Koland said. "They are relics of the past. But here and now: are they serious?"

General Ghan hesitated before answering. "I do not know. I have not heard of it being done in my lifetime."

"Can we risk it on a single fighter?" Lord Ghayaktal wondered.

"What does it matter?" Lord Ezen exclaimed. "Clanless isn't even here!"

As the debate erupted, Koland sat back and pondered. Sama El. There was something familiar about that title. And the messenger said Sama El had revealed "the truth" about arena fighters to the Melkute King. What truth would that be? And then the smirk…

"He knows," Koland said out loud.

The council stopped arguing and looked at him. "Who knows what?" Sonkogh asked.

"The messenger. He knows Clanless isn't here. That's why he smirked in making the challenge. He knows we can't produce him."

"You're basing this revelation on… a smirk?" General Ghan asked. "If true, what does that mean? That the offer is not sincere? So why make it?"

"Why indeed?" Koland stared at the table's surface while he spoke. "Is it a taunt? Is he dangling salvation in front of us, knowing we cannot achieve it? Does he want us to suggest a different champion? If so, does he believe no one else can equal Clanless? So many questions."

"Is there anyone else?" Lord Ulakan asked. "I know Clanless was exceptional, but surely there are others we could suggest?"

"Ghouk took all of the Dohor, remember?" the Ghamba Lam said. "There are none left in the city."

"Need it be an arena fighter?" Sonkogh asked. "General, what about your soldiers? Don't you have someone you could suggest?"

General Ghan stirred as if he'd been thinking of something else. "I could, if I thought it would work."

"Why not?" Lord Ulakan demanded. "We choose the best warrior we can find, enhance him with every possible blood-magic advantage and—"

"They won't allow that," the Ghamba Lam interrupted. "The Melkute believe our blood-magic is an abomination."

"The Melkute ambassador was a regular visitor in the Hawk King's arena box," Lord Ghayaktal pointed out. "I never heard any such objections from him."

"Diplomats are not Kings," the priest said.

As the conversation devolved again, Koland returned to his earlier thoughts. Could Sama El be Suirel? He considered the implications. General Ghan insisted Suirel had no connection to the Melkute invasion. But if he did, perhaps he'd suggested this battle of champions. Yet why? Koland could see no real advantage in the maneuver. Unless… Suirel was searching for Clanless? Was this a way of establishing his location? Did the Lord of Chaos fear Clanless?

"All of these pieces do not fit together," he muttered to himself.

After further debate, the council agreed to send a return message explaining that Clanless was not available. Would the Melkute King be satisfied with a different challenger?

Koland felt certain he would not. But the reason eluded him.

WHY DO YOU CARE?

Then

Sugh winced and stretched out on his bed. His feet dangled off the end. He'd pointed out this problem to the attendant, who'd only laughed. "Do you see this room? This isn't a luxury suite. You're here to sleep and not much else." He paused. "Except once a week, I suppose. You might just want to throw the mattress on the floor then." He laughed again and left without explaining his joke.

Sugh's first battle in Baduhan's arena had gone well. He'd overcome two other fighters, neither possessing great skill. But it went over well with the crowd. One of his opponents bruised the right side of his rib cage, though. He'd asked about healing magic but been told it was for serious injuries only.

"Does your heart still beat for me?"

He looked around the room, but saw no one else. The voice came again, suffusing him in warmth and a sense of peace: "Does your heart still beat for me?" And then he understood.

"Now you speak to me? Now?"

No answer.

He pushed up on his elbows and stared at the ceiling. Though these tiny dwellings for the arena fighters had no windows, he imagined the moon above it all. "You wouldn't speak when I begged you, but now… now that I'm abandoned by everyone, including you… you want… what do you want?"

"…your heart…"

"My heart was yours!" he cried. "It belonged to no other! But you didn't want me!"

Silence filled his room.

"Goddess?"

No answer.

Sugh collapsed back onto the mattress. "You didn't want me," he muttered. "No one does. Not really."

Now

Nukai rode on the back of the cart. Kekeen would allow no one other than Clanless to sit beside her, leaving Sugh and Swift Claw to walk. Fortunately, neither of them minded, despite the cold temperatures. Sugh regaled the beastman with tales of his arena life and pressed him for more details about the beastmen community.

Their conversation spurred a thought in Clanless. "Swift Claw," he called. "You said the Melkute Kingdom were worse than us. What did you mean by that?"

"Mmh. We lost entire tribe to them. Not good. Not good at all."

"But you spent some time with them?"

"Too much." Swift Claw showed his teeth in displeasure. "Their winds are false."

"I don't know much about them at all," Clanless said. "In the books I've read, they're barely discussed. There's a lot about how they've been both allies and enemies over the years." He glanced at Kekeen. "What do you know about them?"

She laughed. "Dear, I know less about this world than you do, remember? My knowledge comes from… elsewhere."

"I never know whether you know something or not. You've lied about it often enough."

"The Melkute Kingdom lies to the north," she recited. "Their people are very similar to your own. You may have been one people originally. And now, thanks to encouragement from Lord Suirel, they are invading. They believe your Empire to be oppressors, so they are morally justified in destroying you." She shrugged. "That is literally all I know."

Clanless watched the ox plod along and shivered. "It's been weeks. It took too long for my recovery. Their army is probably already here."

"Why do you care? You've never loved the Sar Empire." Kekeen nudged him. "Their policies took you from your family and put you in the arena system, after all."

"We still live here," Sugh pointed out.

"You don't have to."

Clanless thought for a few moments before answering. "I've fought in small fights. And once, I fought an invading band of barbarians. It was horrible. I do not want that to happen to anyone."

"Not even the rich fools of Et-Baylak? The ones who cheered on the Hawk King's excesses?" She leaned in to look up into his face. "The one who threatened your beloved?"

"I can't choose who lives and who dies."

She laughed. "But you've been doing that for your entire life, Aldan darling. Every arena fight was a decision about who lived and who died."

He growled at her. "You can't compare slaves fighting to a full-scale war!"

"Humans die, Aldan. It's what they do."

"I have a question!" Sugh announced loudly. When they looked at him, he turned in a circle, arms outspread, as he kept pace with the cart. "We here are a very strong group. Clanless and I are mighty arena fighters, and Swift Claw is terrifying. But… what can we do against an entire army?"

"I don't know," Clanless admitted. "But I can't run away or do nothing. If all we do is stop Bain—Suirel—then at least we've taken care of the biggest problem."

Kekeen laughed again. "And how do you plan on doing that? You couldn't stop him before."

"I blinded him."

"You had an entire sea of blood-magic then. Now you have nothing."

"We are not nothing!" Sugh protested.

"I don't know," Clanless repeated. "But I have to try."

"New choices present themselves in life every day," Nukai murmured from behind them.

Kekeen glanced back at him with a scowl. Then she leaned in against Clanless and took his arm. "Besides," she whispered, "how do you plan to do anything against Suirel when I am here. If he orders it, I could kill your beloved."

The thought had not escaped him. The truth? Just by walking into Suirel's presence, he might be surrendering himself. And yet… "I owe it to

Bain," he said. "And Badaar. And Duurald too. I can't do nothing."

Kekeen sighed. "All right. I have no reason to stop you yet." She ran her fingers through his fur pelt. "And there are still answers I'm searching for."

"This is the beginning of High Spring, yet it's still so cold," Nukai said. "I'll never understand how you people survive without warmer clothes." He adjusted one of the furs on his back.

The ox, oblivious to their discussion, kept moving down the road.

((((●))))

Clanless and his companions made slow and tedious progress traveling from Rochinbal to Et-Baylak. Swift Claw, who appeared to understand distances better than any of them, estimated it would take at least a week. Three days in, an early High Spring rainstorm slowed them further. Clanless chafed at the delay. Even though he had no idea what he would do once they arrived, he wanted the journey to be over.

Kekeen's situation drove him to near insanity on a daily basis. He spent each day with her, mostly sitting beside her, their bodies constantly touching. But she wasn't there. Or more accurately, she remained a prisoner within her own body. He wanted her. He wanted to free her. But no matter how he racked his brain, he couldn't think of any way to banish Zektel. Whispered discussions with the others when she wasn't around produced nothing substantial.

He broached the topic with Nukai one day on the road when Kekeen had gone to relieve herself. The hunched man did not express surprise when Clanless explained the possession. He offered only one suggestion: "Treat her well," he said. "For if your beloved still sees you from within, she will see your true character in this adversity."

"I'm not going to treat her like she's really Kekeen!"

"That is not what I said."

Clanless sighed. He supposed Nukai did have somewhat of a point. When he'd used the fur, Kekeen said she was watching what Zektel did with her body.

"You gave me the fur," Clanless pointed out. "You know the wolf. It blocks control, but it's not enough. I'd give it to Kekeen in a moment if it would save her. But Zektel says she can kill her."

"What do you want me to say?" Nukai asked.

"If we… if we found the wolf again, could he save her? If his fur alone is so powerful, could he drive Zektel out without hurting Kekeen?"

Nukai pursed his lips. "You ask a hard thing. You heard my story, and I yours. Did anyone find the wolf while seeking for him?"

"No…"

"Then we must trust that providence will present a way."

"But maybe if we headed north to, to the places where we've seen him," Clanless suggested.

"I do not think he can be found in that way."

Clanless threw up his hands and stalked away.

He asked Sugh to bring up the subject with the goddess in their next conversation. The big man agreed, but added that he hadn't heard anything from her in some time. "I do not know what this means." He hesitated. "And I do not know if I want to hear from her soon."

"Why?"

Sugh shook his head. "She will ask for something I am not ready to give." He sighed. "But perhaps that is what I need to work on." He walked away without saying anything else.

Kekeen returned a few moments later. She sidled up to Clanless. "Miss me?"

He looked into her eyes. "I miss Kekeen."

She spread her arms. "I'm right here."

"You are not her."

"Aldan, Aldan, Aldan. How many times must we go over this?" She slipped her arm around his and leaned against him. "Fine. I'll be brutally honest. You never loved Kekeen."

He pulled away and glared at her. "That's a lie!"

"You loved the idea of Kekeen, not Kekeen herself." She twirled in a sensuous manner. "How could you not? The friendly, innocent girl who wants only you. The good girl, not tainted by your violent world. The one who's willing to overlook your past deeds in that world." She stopped and folded her arms across her chest. "Face it, Aldan. That's a dream, not reality."

"No. That's Kekeen. She is good, so much better than me."

"You barely know her!" She laughed. "You met over eight years ago. Since that day, you've hardly spent a full week's time together."

"It's more than that!"

"Barely." She laughed again. "You spent years with me. We talked almost every day. I know you better than anyone in this world or any other." She grabbed his arm and pulled. "Come on. We can continue this talk on the way."

He followed her back to the cart and watched her climb aboard. "Why are you suddenly in a hurry to get going?"

"I'm not. But I thought you were."

He glanced at the other three. Sugh helped Nukai get back in the cart.

"You don't want to lose me!" Clanless understood at last. "You really did miss me while you were with Daviland!"

"Of course I did," she answered. "That's what I've been saying for days now. I've always cared about you, Aldan."

"That's not what you said when you left me in the arena."

"We spent eight years together. Why hold a momentary lapse against me? Kekeen abandoned you too, remember?" She patted the seat beside her. "Come on up."

Clanless looked down the road, then pulled himself up. "Zektel," he said quietly, "maybe we can work something out here. I… did appreciate all you did for me. But I want Kekeen back. Do you have to… I mean, could you be inside someone else?"

She reached up and ran her hand through his hair. "But I like touching you. And you touching me."

He jerked away. "I wish you wouldn't do that."

"One day." She gave an exaggerated sigh. "You'll come around. You can't stay in such close proximity to this body and to me without something happening eventually."

Clanless took up the reins and kept his eyes forward. A terrifying thought filled his mind: she might be right.

THE RECLAMATION OF HOPE

Then

Sugh entered his tiny room with a huge smile on his face. Two years in Baduhan's service, undefeated in the arena, and this room hadn't changed a bit. It never would. And yet he couldn't lose the smile today. All of the fighters had done well, and Baduhan had been pleased. It meant tonight would be a night of pleasure.

The arena master would never allow his slaves to wander the city, of course. But on days like today, he rewarded them. The fighters couldn't visit a brothel, but the brothel could visit them. Soon, Sugh would hear a knock at the door, and a pleasant companion would join him for the night.

He'd been shocked the first time it happened, of course. But he soon lost himself, short mattress or not. He had little else to look forward to here. If he wasn't practicing or competing, he was confined to this building where he could sleep, eat, and bathe. Nothing more. Except this night.

He'd barely pulled his shirt off when the knock came. His heart sped up as he turned, eager to see who would be joining him this evening. A hooded woman shut the door behind her before turning to face him. When she pulled the hood back, Sugh's smile vanished. His jaw dropped.

"Chabi?" Baduhan's daughter. He saw her in her father's box watching his fights almost every week. They'd exchanged a few words in fleeting moments here and there, but never more than that. "What are you doing here?"

She pulled the hooded cloak off and tossed it onto his one chair. "I had to spread a lot of blood vials around to get myself in with the girls tonight, and then yet another bribe to get to your door." She shook her head. "You have a reputation, big man."

"But… but why?"

She crossed the short space between them and put both hands on his bare chest. "I would have thought that would be obvious. I told Father I wanted you, back on the first day we met."

Sugh's mind pulled in multiple directions at once. "He. But. He'll kill us both if he finds out!"

"No." She ran one of her hands up his chest and tapped his chin. "He'll kill you. He'll scream at me, but that's all. He dotes on me too much for anything else." She stepped back. "So you need to decide: am I worth the risk?" She started to undo the buttons on her tunic.

Sugh swallowed. His smile returned.

Some time later, Chabi lay atop him as they rested. She toyed with his hair. "You are a perfect specimen of a man, Sugh. Do you know that?"

"So I have been told."

"You have these bare spots on your head, though." She ran her fingers across one of them. "Why?"

"I fought a man with a flaming whip a few months ago. Burned some of my hair right off." Sugh reached up and scratched one of the spots. "Those spots have never grown back."

"You should shave the rest of your hair so it matches."

"Perhaps I will."

She chuckled. "My father complains about how much healing you require."

"It is how I fight." He ran his fingers down her back. "When an opponent thinks he has me, that is when I strike."

"You take too many risks."

"Like this one?"

She let her head rest on his chest, her reddish-black hair falling across it. "Mmmm. I can hear your heart beating."

He hesitated only a moment before answering, "It beats for you."

Now

Clanless brought the cart to a stop. They'd reached a dividing line in the Sar Empire, an escarpment descending from the high hills into the lower plains. The road curved down, down in front of them. From their vantage point, they could see one small group moving some distance ahead.

"How far are we from Et-Baylak?" Clanless asked.

"Perhaps… perhaps two days," Swift Claw said. "Maybe three." He snorted at the ox. "I am always forgetting how slow this creature moves."

"Shouldn't the road be busier then? We encountered many more people around the last city."

"You're right," said Sugh as he stepped up beside the cart. "High Spring is just begun. The road should be full of people coming and going from the busy city. This road leads nowhere else."

Kekeen stretched her arms above her head. "The city may be under siege by now," she said. "That tends to cut down on the travelers."

"If that's true, maybe we should warn those people." Clanless pointed at the group in the distance.

"Something strange there." Swift Claw sniffed, his snout elevated. "The winds bring smells I do not know."

Sugh shaded his eyes. "I cannot see much from here."

"Swift Claw, scout ahead," Clanless suggested. "We'll follow, at our usual speed. Come back when you know something more."

The beastman bounded off at once. "Useful to have around," Kekeen noted.

"He's my friend." Clanless snapped the reins to urge the ox on again.

"More than that, I would think. There's some kind of… connection between you two."

Clanless kept his eyes on the dwindling form of Swift Claw. "You can sense that?"

"He helped you do some things back in the mines. Things you should not have been able to do."

"Does that bother you?"

Kekeen flinched. "No. Why would it? It's just a magic I'm unfamiliar with. Makes me curious."

Clanless thought about that. Zektel was not from this world. She'd needed him to explain blood-magic to her years ago. There were still things she did not know, which meant Suirel didn't know everything either. Maybe… maybe the keys to their defeat were hidden in that knowledge. He considered all he'd learned about the beastmen, searching for something useful.

"Swift Claw returns," Sugh said.

Clanless brought the ox to a stop again and waited. Swift Claw joined them in moments. "They are not your people," he reported.

"Melkute?"

The beastman nodded. "Four of them. They have a cart like yours. But also creatures. Two of them."

"What kind of creatures?" Sugh asked.

Swift Claw showed his teeth. "Like wolves but not. I have seen them before, beyond the mountains. Very dangerous."

"They're a scouting party of some kind," Kekeen said. "Maybe they've been looking around and are now returning to the main army."

Clanless reached back in the cart and picked up the moonblade. "We wanted to find out what was going on. Who better to ask?"

"Four soldiers and two creatures." Sugh also retrieved his axe. "It sounds like a fair fight. And we have a very wide arena floor here."

"Stay with the cart," Clanless told Kekeen as he got down.

"Are you sure you're healed enough for this?" she asked.

Clanless didn't answer. He still experienced pain in his gut from time to time, but it wasn't enough to mention. And he refused to believe Zektel cared.

"I'll stay as well," Nukai said.

Clanless nodded and joined Sugh and Swift Claw. The three of them descended the hill and moved toward the scouting party.

"Should we spread out?" Sugh wondered.

"No. It's a good way for them to pick us off individually," Clanless said. "We fight together."

"Fight as one," Swift Claw said.

They kept walking. Clanless watched the enemy forces getting closer. The sound of laughter drifted from them. And then two dark shapes rushed from the scouting party toward Clanless and his friends.

"The wolf creatures come," Swift Claw noted.

"They'll be the most difficult," Clanless said. "I never know how the Taint will work against animals. After we deal with them, the soldiers will be easy. I want them alive for questioning." He hadn't used the Taint since the fight with Suirel. Would it even work?

"That should not be hard." Sugh stopped and took a defensive stance with his axe at ready. "You're good at leaving them alive."

Clanless also took his stance and braced himself. "Swift Claw, step back a bit. When they attack the two of us, you jump in."

As the creatures drew near, Clanless saw they weren't so much like wolves as they were like enormous rats. Enormous, heavily muscled rats, at least seven feet long, not including their tails. Their huge heads featured long snouts and jaws. They were covered in fur, but it looked thicker on the front half of their bodies, especially on the higher musculature—like a hump—above their shoulders. The tawny coloration on the front transitioned into darker stripes on the shorter fur of the back and the long, thin tails. Their jaws opened, revealing more teeth than any rat or wolf should ever have.

"Sidestep?" Sugh asked.

"You go left; I'll go right."

The beasts charged at them, slavering and growling. As one, Clanless and Sugh sidestepped at the last minute in opposite directions and swung their weapons. Clanless's swing came a little slower than he'd wanted, catching the rat-beast just above its left shoulder. The moonblade hit at a bad angle and didn't cut deep enough for blood. Like the giant cat he'd fought in the arena, these creatures possessed a hairy and thick layer of skin almost like leather armor.

Before he could evaluate further, the beast spun to snap at him. It could move faster than any creature he'd could remember, but its jaws were its only real weapon. As long as he could avoid them, he'd be all right.

Swift Claw leaped atop the beast and slammed his own sword down at it. He cut into the shoulder hump, deeper than the moonblade but still not enough to draw blood.

"Ho!" Sugh shouted. "Their undersides are weaker!"

Did that mean Sugh had cut his beast? Clanless couldn't see; everything was happening too fast. And if he used the Taint indiscriminately, he might affect his friends.

Swift Claw leaped free as the beast rolled over to dislodge him. At the same time, it whipped its tail around at Clanless. He managed to jump over it, but stumbled as he came back down. All right, maybe the tail counted as a weapon too.

The creature lunged at him before he could fully recover his balance. With both hands, he shoved the moonblade sideways between its jaws to keep it from biting his head off. Its weight landed on him, knocking the wind out of his chest. Swift Claw attacked again, hacking at it from the side, but the beast ignored him.

Clanless couldn't breathe. Enormous weight pressed down on his chest. He held on to the moonblade as the beast jerked its head back and forth. Saliva splattered across his face, and a horrible stench of rotted meat filled the air.

Swift Claw shouted something he couldn't hear.

Clanless twisted the moonblade. The edge caught the thinner skin where the upper and lower jaws met and sliced through it. A trickle of blood flowed out.

He still couldn't breathe. His ribs felt like they were being crushed. Darkness threatened the edges of his vision. With one desperate thought, he activated the Taint.

The familiar burning filled his eyes. The creature howled and jerked back, freeing him. He rolled over, gasping, trying desperately to suck in air. He didn't know how he managed to hold on to the moonblade. It worked. The Taint worked.

When he finally got a short breath, he rolled to see Swift Claw on top of the creature again. The beastman had dropped his sword and held on with his claws. He still couldn't harm the monster, but it thrashed about in fury at the unwanted rider. Beyond them, Clanless caught a glimpse of Sugh still standing and fighting.

He pulled himself up on to his own feet, still struggling for air. "Show me… its… belly," he gasped.

Swift Claw shifted his weight back and forth with the creature's movements, then yanked it to the side. He threw all his weight to pull it off-balance. The creature fell on its side, pinning Swift Claw's arm and leg. Had he been alone, it would have been Swift Claw's last action.

But he'd done what Clanless wanted. He swung the moonblade as hard as he could into the creature's underbelly. It sliced deep. Blood erupted. Clanless activated the Taint again.

The creature writhed and made obscene noises. Swift Claw pulled loose and rolled to his feet. Clanless waited until the creature stopped flailing. He stepped up to it, looked down at its twitching head, and brought the moonblade down into its face. It spasmed a couple times more and lay still.

Sugh clapped. Clanless turned to see him standing nearby, blood soaking his left arm. The other beast lay dead with Sugh's axe inside its jaws. He'd somehow managed to cut up into its brain through its open mouth, an astounding feat.

"You were slow," Sugh said.

"I'm out of practice," Clanless answered. And he felt it. He'd moved too slow through the entire fight. More shocking, he'd never felt the bloodrush. That could not be good.

Something thunked into the ground not far away. "Arrows!" Sugh exclaimed.

Clanless turned to see the four soldiers near their own wagon, a four-wheeled transport with a canvas cover. Two of them pulled back on short bows. They could barely make the distance between them with those weapons. "Swift Claw! Make them bleed!"

The beastman raced off to the left to circle wide around the enemy. Clanless and Sugh retrieved their weapons and started moving down the road again.

"Is it wise to walk toward the archers?" Sugh asked.

"We want to keep them focused on us." From this distance, they could see the arrows coming in high arcs. It wasn't too difficult to avoid them, but that would change the closer they came.

"A shield would be helpful now," Sugh said. He grunted as an arrow nicked his thigh.

"I haven't used one in years." Clanless picked up his pace. He could see the Melkute scouts clearly now. They wore leather armor on their chests and pointed helmets, each with a topknot of long hair. Otherwise, they looked remarkably similar to soldiers of the Sar Empire.

Pain flared in his right shoulder as an arrow struck. He stumbled but kept moving, switching the moonblade to his left hand.

The scouts erupted in cries of dismay as Swift Claw leaped among them. Sugh and Clanless broke into a run; the archers were busy trying to defend themselves. The beastman spun and slashed, dove and rolled, evading any response. "They bleed!" he shouted.

Clanless focused on the four soldiers and activated the Taint. In unison, they cried out in pain, wavered, and fell. The battle was over.

Swift Claw stood and hastened to the fallen men. He collected their weapons before Clanless and Sugh arrived. "One is dead," the beastman reported, "but three still live." Clanless pointed at a coil of rope hanging from the side of the wagon. "Tie them."

"You, ah, have an arrow in your shoulder," Sugh pointed out.

"We'll take care of it when Kekeen and Nukai get here." He turned and waved the moonblade back at their cart. Kekeen started forward to join them.

With everything settled, Clanless sank to a knee. No bloodrush the entire time. Had he lost his edge during his convalescence?

"Let's hear what they know," Sugh said. He picked up one of the bound soldiers by his chest armor and knocked his helmet off. "Wake up! I have questions!" He slapped the scout's face. The man shook his head, glared at Sugh, and babbled something in another language.

Clanless cursed himself. He hadn't even thought about a language difference. "Do you understand him?"

"Not I."

"I can speak his words," Swift Claw said.

"Really?" Clanless immediately regretted the surprise in his voice. "Of course. You said you spent time there."

"Ask him where they have come from," Sugh said, still holding the man off the ground.

Swift Claw spoke in a rush. The scout stared at him for a moment, then answered in the same way. Clanless tried to listen. Some of their words sounded familiar but not quite right. He felt like he could almost grasp a word or phrase, but it slipped past his understanding in the rapid cacophony. Swift Claw and the scout talked back and forth several times. The scout started with clear arrogance but lost it when the beastman moved in close, baring his teeth.

"They are scouts," he confirmed, stepping back. "They and some others left their army three days ago. They burned a village two days ago and then split up."

"Where is the main army?" Clanless asked.

"It is at your big city."

"Et-Baylak," Sugh said. He dropped the scout. "Do we know anything about this village?"

Hearing a sound, Clanless looked back to see Kekeen pulling the cart up nearby. But that wasn't the sound he'd heard. It was more of a moan…

"Wolf Chosen!" Swift Claw exclaimed. "There is more blood!" He scrambled to the wagon and leaped up to look inside it. At once, he fell back, snarling. "These men have foul winds."

"What is it?" Sugh strode to join him, pushed aside the canvas and peered into the shaded darkness within. "Goddess!" he exclaimed.

Nukai appeared beside Clanless. "Do you need assistance with this?" He pointed at the arrow.

Clanless nodded but kept watching Sugh. The big man climbed into the wagon.

"This has not penetrated too deep, but it will hurt a lot when I remove it," Nukai warned. Kekeen stepped up beside him and looked around at everything. One of the scouts shouted something at her. Even with the language barrier, Clanless knew it had to be obscene.

He gasped as Nukai yanked the arrow free. It hurt far more than he'd anticipated. His vision swam, and he ducked his head for a moment. Nukai muttered to himself as he slapped a wadded cloth over the wound to staunch the bleeding.

Clanless lifted his head again in time to see Sugh stepping down from the wagon carrying a young woman. Bruises covered her face and blood stained the remains of her ripped-apart clothing. Kekeen gasped and hurried to them. Sugh laid the woman gently on the ground. Kekeen took her head in her own lap and wiped blood from a gash on her forehead.

"There is another in the wagon," Sugh said, "but she is already dead." His face was harder than Clanless had ever seen it. "They have been…" He didn't finish, nor did he need to.

Clanless looked to Swift Claw. "Ask them where these women came from."

Swift Claw exchanged words with the scouts. "They are from the village they burned. They kept these two for themselves."

Clanless lowered his head. Nukai said something about "evil" and applied healing blood to the arrow wound. Clanless gasped again as it took effect. Healing blood-magic always hurt as much as the original injury, if not more.

He looked up to see Kekeen staring back at him, infinite sadness in her eyes. In that moment, he believed he could see the real Kekeen. Maybe Zektel had pulled back inside, leaving her in control for this. If so, what did that say about her? Did the blood-wraith actually care about the innocent?

Kekeen looked down at the woman in her lap. "She is beyond healing," she said quietly.

Sugh picked up his axe. "And soon they will be, as well."

Clanless opened his mouth to stop him but said nothing. He could see what the scouts had done to this woman. He could only imagine the horror and anguish she and her companion had gone through over the past two days. Two days! And they…

The soldiers shouted and begged for mercy in their language, but Sugh had none.

☾☾☾●☽☽☽

Nukai found Clanless sitting alone behind a terebinth tree. He heard the hunched man approach but didn't acknowledge him. The moonblade, still coated with blood, lay beside him in the dirt. His mind struggled between despair, surrender, anger, and a touch of guilt for not taking care of his weapon.

"You fight as well as ever," Nukai said. He took hold of one of the tree's branches, as if to hold himself steady.

"No. I don't." Clanless stared blankly into the distance. The sun's retreat would end soon. The dried blood and sweat on his body grew cold as a breeze stirred the tree's leaves.

"The three of you defeated a larger force. Isn't that a success?"

"Is it? Sugh killed those men. And I let him." He paused before adding in a lower voice, "If he hadn't done it, I would have." He thought of Salkhi and what he'd done to the man who'd hurt her. This was the same thing. Wasn't it?

Where would Salkhi be now? She must still be within the walls of Et-Baylak, surrounded by the Melkute army. Along with Qara and Koland and thousands of others.

"You've experienced a taste of the horrors of war," Nukai said. "No one can blame you for being upset."

Clanless ran his hands through his hair and clasped them behind his head. He leaned forward and squeezed the sides of his head with his forearms. "What am I doing, Nukai?"

"Only you can answer that."

"The city is already under siege. I can't do anything about that. We didn't even arrive in time to help those two girls. Or the village they came from. We don't know where Bain is or what he's planning." The words tumbled out in a rush. "Even if we did, what can I do? Zektel's right about that. Without all the blood-magic, I can't defeat him. Or save him. I can't even save Kekeen!" He shook his head back and forth. "It's hopeless. Everything is hopeless."

"Never hopeless." Nukai's raspy voice remained calm. "Dark? Yes. Dangerous? Yes. But never without hope."

Clanless released his hands and let them fall into his lap. "I cannot hope in something for which I have no confidence."

"Ah, so you believe you can only hope in things that are certain. I hope the moon will be there tomorrow. I hope the sun will shine."

"Not just certain things. Of course not. But... possible things."

"Defeating Suirel is impossible, you say."

"It seems like it!" Clanless threw his hands up. "I'm an ordinary man. I can fight, but I can't defeat a god!"

"And rescuing the city is also impossible."

"There's an army!" Clanless finally turned to look at him as he pointed off down the road. "An entire army! The five of us can't do anything about that!"

"Your beloved is also doomed because saving her is impossible."

"Why are you repeating what I said? Yes! All of it's impossible!"

"Then why have you come so far?"

"What?"

"Why have you come so far?" Nukai repeated. "You could have stayed in the clanhold with your family. Let the Lord of Chaos sweep over the rest of the world. He probably won't pay any attention to distant clanholds for years to come. But here you are, instead."

"Zektel wanted to talk to you." Clanless turned away. He dug his fingers into the dirt. "I had to bring her or she would hurt Kekeen. But I thought, after that, we could go to Et-Baylak and help Koland. Maybe. Or find Bain. Or… I don't know. I don't know what I was thinking. And I don't know what to do now."

"Do you think that everything depends on you?"

Clanless didn't answer.

"Suirel, Lord of Chaos, will only be defeated by you. The mighty Melkute army will only be put to flight by you. Even Kekeen will only be rescued by you." Nukai made a noise somewhere between a chuckle and a snort. "The great Clanless will save the world and everyone in it."

"Everything is my fault, anyway."

"What do you mean?"

Clanless spoke slowly, putting it together. "If I had killed Daviland in the arena, as I was told to do… the Hawk King would still rule and have the power to protect the city. Suirel would never have taken Bain. Kekeen and I would be free and away from all of it."

"And she would have forgiven you for killing Daviland?"

"In time. Maybe."

Nukai looked back toward the others. "Sugh over there would still be a slave, wouldn't he?"

"Yes, but… Hagh would be alive!"

"Would he? He was getting older, Clanless. He couldn't fight in the arena forever."

"I don't know." He looked down at his hand in the dirt. "Zektel wouldn't be in Kekeen."

"No. She'd still be in you."

"That would be better!"

"Would it?" Nukai pointed at the fur pelt. "Would you have worn this after leaving the arena? Would you have worn it on your wedding night?"

"I…"

"You would have lost yourself to the blood-wraith instead. And who knows what chaos it would have created with you under its control." He sighed. "You cannot blame yourself. Even the gods cannot see all ends or trace all beginnings."

Clanless grunted.

"So we are back to you here and now, the only one who can save the world."

"No one else is doing anything," he muttered.

"No? You think those within the city are doing nothing? That they have surrendered to their fate?"

"No." Clanless inhaled through his nose and let it out slowly. "Koland will be helping them. They'll be doing whatever they can."

Nukai looked over his shoulder. "And what of these companions of yours? You think they will do nothing?"

"Of course not. But we're… we're not enough."

Nukai nodded with a smile. "That much is true. So it is good that you brought me along."

Clanless laughed, a bitter sound. He looked at Nukai, expecting to see a twinkle in his eye, but the hunched man appeared completely serious. Clanless looked down again and sighed. He lifted a handful of dirt and let it trickle out between his fingers.

"Zektel," he whispered. "Even if, as you say, the other things aren't hopeless… she won't let me do anything against Suirel. She holds Kekeen's life. She… she might even order me to help him. And what could I do?"

"Again, do you think that everything depends on you?"

"I don't know! What do you want me to say?"

Nukai crouched down and placed his hand on the fur pelt on Clanless's shoulder. "There is hope. There is always hope. Because not everything depends on you. Or me. There are other powers at work besides Suirel. Trust, Clanless. And reclaim your hope. All is not lost. Not yet."

Clanless picked up his moonblade. "I should clean this," he whispered.

"Yes. That is something you can do." Nukai grasped the tree and pulled himself back up. "And then do the next thing you can do. And the next. Until… hope takes over."

Clanless wrinkled his brow. "What does that mean? Hope takes over?"

"It is often the darkest moment." Nukai paused and took a deep breath. He adjusted his own furs. "And then something happens. Something you did not expect." He turned to go. "And in that moment, hope bursts into power and takes control." He took a step before glancing back. "If I am not wrong, Clanless, you will see that again. And, if we are fortunate, I will see it with you."

Chilled by another breeze, Clanless rubbed some of the dried blood from his shoulder. He ran his fingers over the brand. It puzzled him how healing magic never touched that scar. The arrow had torn through it, but after healing, the brand remained the same as it had always been. "Nukai."

The other man stopped and looked back. "Yes?"

"You couldn't use blood-magic when I was a boy."

"I am not the same man I was then."

Clanless grunted and pulled himself up. "You certainly talk a lot more than you did back then."

"Do I? Are you certain your memories of our time together are intact?"

Clanless froze. "How do you know about my memories?"

Nukai shrugged. "You have said much, both to me, and to your friends, who have also spoken to me. And years ago, I watched your memories vanish."

"Zektel hid so many of my memories, for all sorts of reasons." He looked across the road. Sugh and Swift Claw dug graves while Kekeen prepared the bodies. "But Kekeen said she sees everything while Zektel is in control. Bain said something similar. Why were my memories tampered with and not theirs?"

"You don't know?"

"Of course I don't know! Why would I ask the question, old man?"

Nukai sighed. "The blood-wraith makes use of what it finds, Clanless. When I met you, you had already locked memories away. On your own."

"What?"

Nukai looked up into his face. "You did it, Clanless. You locked your earliest traumas away. Your mind created it as a way of coping with what happened to you as a child."

His uncle.

"I learned this about you on the second night in the arena. You fled from the other boys and talked about many things."

"I... don't remember that at all."

"As I said. When the blood-wraith entered your mind, it discovered your... locked memories and how you had done it. She took advantage of it."

Clanless processed that. It made sense, but... "Does this mean I still have other memories locked away? Memories I put there?"

Nukai shrugged. "I cannot see your mind, so I cannot say."

"Clanless!" Sugh called.

"Are you going to make us do all the work here?" Kekeen added.

"Coming!" He looked back at Nukai. "Thank you. You've given me a lot to think about."

"Ponder hope, Clanless. Ponder hope."

SUIREL IS COMING

Then

Two months after Sugh and Chabi began their clandestine relationship, he heard the voice again. This time, it came while he trained alone in the arena.

"Your heart beats for another?" The words sounded like a question.

Sugh lowered his axe and looked up at the moon, shaded with a red hue this day. Early days in High Spring often gave it such an appearance.

"She wants my heart," he answered. "You never did."

"Not true..." the voice whispered.

"If you want my heart, why am I here?" He shook his axe at the moon. "You had it, but you sent me here instead!"

"If I asked, would you give it?"

Sugh lowered the axe. She'd never spoken this much to him. And the question... disturbed him.

"Why would you ask for something you once held but gave away?" he wondered.

"I will ask again one day."

Sugh stared at the moon a while longer. If she did ask, what would he say? Half of him wanted to run back to the goddess, throw himself into her service once again, and hope that she would see fit to deliver him from this life. But the other half warned that to do so would mean giving up Chabi.

"I could never do that."

◖ ◖ ◖ ◖ ● ◗ ◗ ◗ ◗

Now

"How did this happen?" Koland demanded. His fist hit the table, drawing the attention of the handful of other customers in the eating house.

Qara shrugged. "Who knows? Someone started it, and now it's everywhere."

Koland slumped back into his seat and shook his head. A distant crash gave reminder of the enemy's catapults in play again. He'd chosen this lower city eating house for its proximity to the inner walls. The bombardment over the outer walls could not reach this far. Even so, the occasional impact sounds were disturbing. No one slept well down here.

"The only ones who knew about the Melkute challenge were the council members," he said. "And General Ghan and Captain Rakib, I suppose."

"It could have been any of them." Qara glanced around and took a seat across from him. "But the whole city knows now, or at least the whole lower city. Everyone wants to know where Clanless is, and why he doesn't save us from the invading army."

"What have you told them?"

Qara threw her hands up. "What can I tell them? I don't know! I didn't even know it was true until you confirmed it!"

Koland put his head down on his arms and chuckled. "I did, didn't I? So much for secrecy."

"Does it matter, though? I mean, he's not here, so…"

"You're right." He lifted his head. "Even so, I don't like his reputation being destroyed this way. He can't get into a city under siege. But the longer the challenge goes unanswered, the more rumors will spread about him."

"Should we start our own? Rumors, I mean?" Qara almost laughed. "Or maybe just the truth?"

"It can't hurt, I suppose. Tell people he's not in the city, so he can't accept the challenge."

"And what if they ask where he is?"

"The truth, I suppose. You don't know. And neither do I."

Qara glanced around. "It's all true, though? They really did offer to resolve the whole thing with an arena duel?"

"Something like that. I don't understand it. I think Suirel is behind it somehow." Koland sighed. "It's all nonsense. Even if Clanless were here and won their fight, I doubt they'd turn around and march home."

"Maybe they would. The Melkute have a strange idea of honor, from what I've experienced."

Koland cocked his head. "You've had some experience with them?"

"Bits and pieces. I was required to give the Melkute ambassador frequent tours of the arena and answer his questions." She smiled at the memory. "He was the most polite and careful man I ever escorted."

"Interesting. I've encountered a number of them in my travels." He paused. "Wait. Now that I think about it, I do remember a couple of them being… careful, as you put it. Very circumspect about paying their precise bills and asking if they were required to pay me as well. They had a phrase they repeated. 'Every obligation met,' I think it was. It may not be everyone in their culture, but at least some follow it. Hm. I need to ponder this."

They sat in silence at the table for a few moments. Lost in his thoughts, Koland didn't even notice Qara's continued presence for a while. When he looked up, he jerked his head. "Oh. Sorry. Was there something else we needed to talk about?"

"Yes. Dinner. You need to buy it for me. In case you hadn't noticed, I don't exactly have a job any more."

Koland laughed. "Right, right. I'll take care of it." He got up and sought out the proprietor. Though his own blood supply had run out over a week ago, he'd persuaded the Ghamba Lam to help fund their current work. Perhaps he'd need to ask for a bit more.

❨❨❨❨●❩❩❩❩

"Suirel is coming," General Ghan announced.

Koland and the Ghamba Lam looked at each other and back at the General. "Here?" Koland asked. "To the city?"

He hadn't known what to expect when the General requested a meeting with the three of them. Part of him had been prepared for some kind of retaliation for their opposition in the mines. But he hadn't expected this.

"He has obtained permission from the Melkute invaders for safe passage into the city," Ghan explained. "They will allow him and those with him to enter through the gates without any interference."

"For what purpose?" the Ghamba Lam asked.

"That is not our business."

"General." Koland tried to let his earnestness be obvious. "Suirel does not have Et-Baylak's best interests in mind. He is the very reason these invaders are here!"

"I have communicated with him regarding the defense of the city," he answered with his usual straight demeanor. "He will not interfere with my orders. Moreover, by entering the city, he binds himself to the city's fate. If it falls, he falls with it."

"Not if he can negotiate safe passage through enemy armies!" the Ghamba Lam exploded. "He'll let us all die, and then walk back the way he came!"

"I am giving him the arena facility," the General went on. "It is unused and provides space for his purposes. He will be there, and we will be here, in the palace. There will be no interference with each other."

"What then are his purposes?" Koland asked.

"Again, it is not our business. He has work to do, he says, and the arena will be sufficient for that work."

An awkward silence settled over the three men. Koland's curiosity finally prompted him to ask another question: "Why are you telling us this? Have you reconsidered your decision not to arrest us?"

The General didn't move, but his eyes darted toward the door and back. "As I said before, you are useful in the defense of this city as members of the council and also within your own particular… congregations. And it would not be useful for us to be in conflict within the city."

"If Suirel will be hiding out in the arena, what conflict will there be?" The Ghamba Lam's voice dripped with sarcasm.

"As long as you do not create any, there will be none." After a pause, he added, "As far as I am concerned."

"As the leader of the priesthood of the goddess, you know I cannot support or ignore this thing," the Ghamba Lam said. "We cannot sit idly by while an enemy of the goddess makes his home within ours."

General Ghan looked down and flicked a speck of dirt from his uniform sleeve. "I suggest, Ghamba Lam, that you consult with your council of Daghilchs about the proper course of action."

The Ghamba Lam took a step back. Koland inhaled deeply. So the General knew about and had influence within the priestly council. How far had Suirel's followers infiltrated every aspect of the Empire's life? The General controlled the military. The council of Daghilchs controlled the religion. The three Lords controlled the city. And all of them might be controlled by Suirel.

Koland couldn't help wondering: were the enemies without or within the greater threat? And would they remain opposed to each other… or unite under the Lord of Chaos himself?

THIS IS WAR

Then

Sugh relaxed in the bath and closed his eyes. Baduhan kept his fighters busy even during High Winter. Sugh understood his master's desire to keep them at their peak, but the number of workouts in the freezing weather bordered on the ridiculous. At least they kept the bath water warm. And later tonight, if he was lucky, his bed would be even warmer.

Someone grunted as he descended into the bath from the other side. Sugh opened one of his eyes a slit to see Raki. Out of the current arena fighters belonging to Baduhan, Raki came closest to a friend. Sugh had decided early not to grow too attached to any of them. After all, death was an ever-present possibility. In some cases, an ever-present probability.

"You are not being very smart, young Sugh," Raki said after a few moments of silence.

"What do you mean?"

"I've been here far longer than you."

Sugh waited. Raki took his own time when making a point. He spoke very little and took great care with what he did say.

At last, the older fighter sighed and continued, "You are not the first arena fighter Chabi has claimed for herself."

Sugh's eyes opened. "What are you saying?"

"Chabi is… variable. She will proclaim her undying love one day… and forget your existence the next. When Baduhan buys a new man, if he's handsome enough, she'll claim him for herself. For a time."

Sugh frowned. He didn't want to dismiss Raki out of hand; the older fighter's wisdom usually made sense. But…

"Chabi is the one bright spot in my miserable life," he answered at last. "But I will think on your words."

Raki grunted and said no more.

His warning persisted in Sugh's mind, gnawing at him throughout the rest of the day. When Chabi came to him that night and leaped into his arms, he kissed her once and pulled away.

"What am I to you?" he asked.

Chabi laughed and nibbled at his shoulder. "What do you mean?"

He set her on the floor. "I'm serious, Chabi. What am I to you? Am I"—he hesitated, not wanting to say it—"important to you at all?"

She wrinkled her brow, which somehow managed to look even cuter than normal. "Of course you are. Why would I be here?"

"Because it's fun? I don't deny that part. But… do you care about me? Would you mourn if I died in the arena in my next fight?"

"Don't be silly. You're not going to die. You're the best. Even my father says so."

He stared down into her eyes. "You didn't answer the first question."

Chabi reached up and entwined her fingers together behind his neck. She pulled his head down toward her own. "I care about you, Sugh. And you alone."

"Truly?"

"What is it you say to me? About your heart?"

"It beats for you," he said automatically.

She released his neck, took his hand, and put it to her chest. "And mine beats for you. Feel that?"

He smiled. "I do."

"Good. Now put that hand to better use." She shifted it.

Sugh growled and swept her off her feet again.

Now

Clanless walked to the front of the scouts' wagon and stared at the armored creature waiting patiently in front of it. "What is this?"

The creature, far larger than an ox, turned a hairy and armored head to look at him with huge, sad eyes. The rest of its body was covered in an overarching piece of scaled armor that reached at least five feet in height. Its short tail, similarly armored, ended in a spiked ball. A single sweep of that thing would smash through the harness. Clanless wondered at its docility.

"It's like a giant turtle!" Sugh exclaimed, joining him. They'd finished burying the two women. Sugh had wanted to leave the Melkute scouts for scavengers, but Clanless and Nukai dug a single grave for them.

"A turtle's shell is wide," Clanless said. "This one is tall." He stepped back to study it in the dim twilight of the retreating sun. "Somewhat."

"I hope it is faster than a turtle," Sugh said. He patted the creature's side. It grunted in response.

Swift Claw came around the other side of the wagon. "The far people use these animals for many things. When they die, their armor is taken and used."

"I imagine so." Clanless rapped his knuckles on the armor. It looked remarkably thick and tough.

Kekeen climbed onto the driver's bench. "This is nicer than our cart."

Clanless frowned. He didn't like the idea of using this wagon after what had taken place within it. "Maybe we should let the creature go and burn the wagon for warmth tonight."

"I think we should take both," Sugh said. "I am tired of walking."

That was a fair point. "All right. I guess tomorrow we'll see if this thing is as fast as our ox."

"Did you just say our ox is fast?" Kekeen asked. "Have you been paying attention at all this past week?"

"You know what I mean." Clanless rubbed his temples. "What do we feed this thing?"

"We need only let it graze, like most animals," Swift Claw said. "I will unhitch it."

"You do that." Clanless closed his eyes and yawned. "I need to sleep."

"What do they call this thing?" Sugh asked.

Swift Claw cocked his head for a moment. "They say 'ghuyak,' I think."

"Ghuyak…" Sugh repeated. "A fair word." He also stretched and yawned. "Clanless has the right idea. Let us all gain some sleep. In the morning, we will see where our path leads."

((((●))))

Clanless slept longer than anyone the next morning. When Kekeen woke him, he found the others ready to depart. "Give me a minute," he grumbled. He hurried through his regular routine and joined them. To his surprise, Kekeen sat alone on the new wagon, while Sugh and Swift Claw had claimed the ox cart. They'd already hitched both animals into place.

"I thought I made it clear I didn't like this thing," he said.

"Don't be a grump, dearheart," Kekeen said. "Tuulka might take it personally."

"Tuulka?"

Kekeen pointed to the armored creature hooked up to the wagon. It turned its head to look at Clanless with the same sad eyes as the day before.

Clanless looked toward the moon. "You aren't supposed to name it!"

"Why not?"

He climbed up beside her. "It's just… ugh. Never mind." The canvas top had been removed from the wagon, leaving it much smaller. To his relief, someone had cleaned the back. Maybe it wouldn't be so bad. Even so… he picked up the reins and eyed the ghuyak dubiously.

The ox cart pulled up next to them. "We have clear space ahead of us," Sugh said. "Let us race!"

"You called it a turtle!" Clanless protested.

"But the Melkute brought it all the way here! Surely it must be faster than it looks!"

"Or they just took a long, long time to get here," Kekeen said with a grin.

"Of course." Clanless sighed. "How far is the race?"

Sugh made a show of peering ahead. "If my eyes do not deceive me, there is a creek up there. Shall we say the first animal to get its feet wet wins?"

Clanless glanced at Kekeen. "You all really want to do this?"

"We're due to have a little fun, Aldan. We can't all mope about, worrying how to save the world, you know."

He narrowed his eyes. "What do you care about saving the world?"

"I don't know. I'd hate to see all of it disappear." She made a show of looking him up and down.

"Are you ready?" Sugh called.

"We're ready!" Kekeen answered without looking at them.

"Go!" At Sugh's shout, Clanless snapped the reins. The ghuyak gave a sudden jerk and started moving at a casual pace. The ox cart outdistanced them in moments.

"Come on, Tuulka!" Kekeen shouted. "You can do it!"

"I have no idea what I'm doing," Clanless said. "I barely know how to get an ox to move. How do I make it go faster?"

The creature turned to look at the cart passing it. For some reason, that seemed to provide motivation. It picked up the pace, its hairy legs moving at a rapid clip. The ox cart continued to pull ahead.

"Alas, it appears the turtle cannot keep up!" Sugh called over his shoulder.

Clanless and Kekeen both called encouragement to the beast. "This is so stupid," Clanless muttered. To his surprise, the beast sped up again. Though several yards behind, it kept pace with the ox.

"He just needed time to get going," Kekeen said. "I'll bet he can still win."

Clanless pointed ahead. "Not likely. The creek isn't that far."

"Come on!" Kekeen cried.

"Why don't you possess it?" Clanless suggested. "Then you could control its speed yourself."

Kekeen shot him a look. "I'm not leaving this body."

He shrugged. "If you don't mind losing…"

She patted his arm. "As deception attempts go, that was not a very good one, my dear. You need to work on that." She grinned. "But if you want to cheat, you could try using your power against their ox."

"It's not bleeding. And I wouldn't do that, anyway."

"If you don't mind losing…"

He snorted and snapped the reins again. Had they gained on Sugh? Maybe a foot? Not that it mattered. The ox splashed into the shallow creek and came to an abrupt halt. Sugh and Swift Claw cheered their victory.

A few moments later, Tuulka reached the water as well. It came to an even more abrupt halt, almost throwing Clanless and Kekeen from their seats. Both creatures dropped their heads and drank.

Sugh hopped off the cart and splashed into the water himself. "Well done!" He patted the armored creature. "You moved faster than I expected!"

"Faster than it looks?" Clanless asked.

"Perhaps, perhaps. At least you will not fall far behind."

Kekeen climbed down from the wagon. "You boys need to get clean, especially after all that bloodshed yesterday. I'll go upstream a bit to do some washing myself." She smiled slyly at Clanless. "Unless you want to help me wash myself."

He took a deep breath through his nose and ignored her. "Sugh, she's right. We should clean up."

"As you say." Sugh bent, cupped water into his hands, and splashed it against his face. "Woooo! That is cold!"

"Of course it is." Kekeen pulled her bag of clothes from the back of the wagon. "It's runoff from the hills. Melted snow and ice. And High Winter has only just ended."

While Kekeen hiked up the stream, Clanless got down and joined Sugh in the water. He gasped when his feet struck the surface. Sugh had not exaggerated. Here at the edges, he waded through ankle deep frigid water, but he could see it sank to a foot or more in depth in the center. The clear water flowed fast, but not hard. He didn't think the carts would have trouble getting through, but they would need to watch the wheels closely.

Swift Claw untied the black ribbon around his beard, folded it, and set it aside with care. He removed his black skirt and tossed it beside the ribbon. He waded out into the deepest water and plunged his entire head beneath the surface. He came up sputtering, scattering water in all directions from his hair.

Clanless and Sugh joined him. After a few minutes in the water, Clanless grew accustomed to its temperature. The sun shone bright this morning with almost no wind, allowing for a pleasant experience all around. He scrubbed away the dirt, grime and blood of the previous day's battle.

"Makes you miss the baths in the arena, does it not?" Sugh asked as he waded back out of the water.

"Sure. Are you done already?"

"I have not the hair you have." Sugh grinned and set to work washing his clothes.

Clanless chuckled before dipping his own long hair into the water. It had been a while. He took his time. When he came out, he looked over his clothes. The sleeve of his tunic had been severely torn by the arrow and the subsequent treatment of the injury. He sighed, accepting that his brand would be exposed again. He glanced up to see Swift Claw tying the ribbon around his beard once more.

"Swift Claw… is there a significance to that ribbon? I don't think I've ever asked you about it."

"There is." The beastman picked up his skirt and walked to the back of the wagon.

Clanless looked at Sugh, who raised his eyebrows. Something the beastman didn't want to talk about? Curious.

He set to work cleaning his clothes. At least he had one extra pair of trousers he'd obtained while back at the clanhold. He'd just pulled them on when a scream from Kekeen jerked him around. He seized the moonblade and raced up the stream, followed closely by Sugh.

Around a bend in the stream, he found Kekeen, her hair drenched and holding her dress across the front of her body. She stood several feet from the water and stared at it. He spun to see what held her attention.

A body floated in the stream. Four arrows protruded from it.

"I was brushing my hair, and it startled me," Kekeen explained. "I didn't mean to frighten you both."

"We are not frightened," Sugh said, "except for your safety." He waded into the water and examined the body.

"Another villager?" Clanless asked.

"Yes." Sugh pulled the body out of the water on the opposite side of the creek. "He must have been running away."

"Then the village isn't far." Clanless sniffed the air, imagining he could smell the smoke and ash. "Let's finish up. We've wasted enough time."

"Should we not bury this one?" Sugh yanked one of the arrows out.

Clanless hesitated. "I suppose. But we can't bury everyone in the village."

"We will see when we get there."

They left Kekeen to finish getting dressed and returned to their own chores. The men finished as quick as they could without more discussion. The body had removed the fun from the occasion. Once they'd buried it in a shallow grave and piled a few rocks from the creek on top, they climbed back on the wagons and resumed their trip.

A few minutes later, they saw the smoke, a tall and narrow plume reaching almost straight up due to the lack of wind. As they drew closer, an ugly odor assaulted their nostrils. It smelled of old fires and burnt meat. Clanless hated it. Sugh swore by the goddess as the remains of the town came into sight.

"Why do people live out here like this?" Clanless asked. "They have no walls, no protection at all!"

"We're within the central plains of the Sar Empire," Kekeen said. "Barbarians don't come this far. These people believed they had nothing to fear."

"The cities shield them," Sugh said. "Or so they thought."

A handful of empty frames stood here and there, but most of the village had burned to the very ground. Almost nothing remained. If the road hadn't led straight through it, Clanless would have wanted to take a different route. Before long, they entered the horrors. Clanless held a cloth over his face against the smell and the persistent smoke. He caught glimpses of burnt things that could only be bodies of people. Some of them were too small.

"How far are we from Et-Baylak again?" he asked.

"Perhaps two days," Swift Claw answered again.

"These people probably traveled there to sell their goods and their crops. We might have seen some of them in the markets."

Kekeen touched his arm. "This is war, Aldan. This is what is coming to Et-Baylak itself."

A lone wolf, small and thin, darted across the road in front of Tuulka. The ghuyak snorted at it. The wolf raced off into the smoke.

"Where one wolf walks, others follow," Swift Claw said.

"More likely they've been and gone," Clanless muttered. "It's been three days, hasn't it?"

"We have to stop," Sugh said. He brought the ox cart to a halt.

"What? Why?" Clanless pulled on Tuulka's reins to keep from running into it.

"These people." Sugh gestured around him. "We cannot leave them like this."

"Sugh…"

"He is right," Nukai said. "We should not leave them for the wolves."

Clanless didn't want to be around any more bodies, but he couldn't argue with them. "Can we at least move the wagons outside the ruins?"

They hooked the wagons to a burnt tree, the only one still standing, and set to on their grim task. As they gathered bodies, Clanless wanted to weep but found he couldn't. His throat and chest were tight. Tears streamed down his face, but they came from the environment, not the emotions. It was too much.

In some ways, this was worse than the graves behind the arena. Here, he saw the bodies. Many were burned beyond recognition. Some had died from other means, and the flames hadn't found them. But scavengers had. No bodies were untouched.

Together with Sugh, he dug one enormous grave. They chose a spot within the village itself, as the heat of the fire had warmed the earth. But in doing so, they stirred up a lot of ash. Everyone wrapped damp cloths over their faces. Even so, Clanless found himself coughing often.

Swift Claw and Nukai did the bulk of finding the remains and bringing them to the site. Kekeen helped where she could. All told, they gathered around three dozen bodies.

"This is what is coming to Et-Baylak itself," Kekeen had said. Clanless wanted to vomit at the thought. His mind took this group of bodies and multiplied it by thousands. He struggled to grasp the magnitude of such a horror.

He tried to recall Nukai's words. It wasn't all up to him. But he could keep doing what he could… until hope took over. Whatever that meant.

BLACK RIBBON

Clanless patted Tuulka on the head. He'd never spent much time with any animals since he'd become a slave, aside from fighting them in the arena. In his clanhold boyhood, he'd worked with goats and oxen from time to time. His family didn't own any, but all clanhold children helped with animals owned by other families.

"You're not a goat," he said to the ghuyak. "I don't know what you want. What would make you happy?"

The beast regarded him with its sad eyes.

"Maybe it needs a challenge," Sugh suggested, stepping up beside him. "Perhaps pulling a wagon is not a task worthy of such a creature."

Clanless inhaled deeply. The cool morning air smelled clean, a significant difference from the village they'd left behind the day before. After filling the mass grave, they'd returned to the creek to clean again. From there, they'd moved on, leaving all of it behind.

On a brighter day, Clanless would have made some sort of joke in response to Sugh's "worthy" comment. But after the horrors of the village, he couldn't bring himself to express humor. He thought he'd moved on from the arena graves and even tried to get past the two murdered women. But now it all piled up into too much to accept. Lying in his bedroll the night before, he'd even been tempted to try to lock the memories away as he used to.

"We must make a decision on our course of action," Sugh said a few moments later. "Swift Claw says we are only a day's journey from Et-Baylak now."

Nukai came around from Tuulka's other side. He paused and scratched behind the ghuyak's ear. It shut its eyes and grunted in pleasure. "I am older than you all," Nukai said. "And know a little more of war than you do. If we continue on much longer, we will be discovered by Melkute scouts."

"They've already sieged the city," Clanless said. "Why would they have scouts patrolling?"

"To keep watch for other armies." Nukai regarded him with a placid look. "Not all of the Empire's soldiers are within the city walls."

"So what are we to do?" Sugh asked. "We cannot simply stop here and do nothing."

"Maybe we should send out our own scout." Clanless nodded toward Swift Claw.

"Perhaps," Nukai agreed. "But let us find a place to wait, other than a flat spot beside the road."

"You do not like our camp?" Sugh asked in mock surprise.

"I've had worse nights," the hunched man said. "But not many. This ground is rockier than usual. I think we are on the outskirts of the city's farmland, but beyond that of the village. The farmers would have relocated the rocks from their fields in this direction."

"They should have used them to build a wall," Clanless said.

"A rock wall would not have prevented the slaughter we saw." Nukai held up a hand before Clanless could protest. "I know of their importance in the clanholds. And they are helpful to discourage roving barbarians. But not against an invading army. Not unless they had many soldiers with which to man the wall."

Kekeen approached, adjusting her dress. "Have you all finished getting the wagons ready?"

"Let's move on," Clanless responded. He gave Tuulka a quick scratch behind the ear like Nukai had done, helped Kekeen climb aboard, and joined her.

About an hour later, Swift Claw pointed out a lone farmhouse off some distance to the left of the road. Upon examination, they found it furnished but clearly abandoned. The owners must have fled into the city at the approach of the enemy. Yet somehow, the Melkute army and its roving bands had not touched this single structure.

"We can stay here a bit," Clanless decided, "while Swift Claw scouts ahead."

The beastman agreed at once, gathered a few supplies, and disappeared down the road alone. Clanless watched him go. "Sometimes, I think he prefers being alone," he told Kekeen.

"We are not his people, despite your connection," she said. "I'm sure he misses his home as much as we do."

"Where is my home?" Clanless wondered.

"Well, dearheart, if I—"

"That wasn't a question for you." He turned and went to work removing Tuulka's harness. The house included a fenced-in area where some other animals had once grazed. It would do well for the ox and ghuyak.

"I told you about my home once," she whispered. "Do you remember that?"

Clanless paused. "I do, actually. You told me, and then locked that memory away, because you didn't want me to understand."

"That was a mistake."

He snorted.

She stepped closer. "Can you accept that I realize some of my mistakes and am trying to make up for them?"

"No." He stopped his work and stared unseeing at Tuulka's armor plates. "Not unless you leave that body."

He waited, but she didn't answer. When he turned to look, Kekeen had gone into the farm house. Sugh stood nearby. "It is a hard thing," he said.

"I didn't know you were there." Clanless reached for the harness again.

"You were both… focused."

"I hate myself for even speaking that way to her, because I see Kekeen when I do." He yanked the harness loose. "And I don't see any way out of it."

Sugh fumbled with the gate and swung it open. "A way will present itself. Or so we can hope."

Clanless swatted Tuulka and urged him through the gate. Sugh joined him on the other side. Once the ghuyak entered, they shut the gate and watched him wander a few feet before looking back at them.

"He has no home either," Sugh observed.

"What about you? When this is over, what will you do? I… do you have family you could return to?"

Sugh cocked his head, but kept his eyes on Tuulka. "I do not know. I have seen or heard nothing of them since I was sent to the arena." He paused. "I never knew what they thought of me, even before that. I shamed them, I suppose."

"I understand that."

"No, I do not think you do."

"What?"

Sugh looked at him. "You had a good family back there at the clan-hold. It was not a bad place."

"Sugh, I—" He stopped. Enough people knew about his uncle already.

Sugh looked back at Tuulka. "I do not have such a home. I don't think I ever did. But perhaps… when this is done, I will find a new home."

Clanless didn't know what to say, so he kept his mouth shut.

Tuulka dropped his head and took a big bite of the tall grass.

◖ ❨ ❨ ❨ ● ❩ ❩ ❩ ❩

Swift Claw's return two and a half days later brought nothing but bad news: Et-Baylak under siege, fires in the lower city, and the Melkute army's scouts roaming free across the nearby countryside. Clanless and the others listened in dismay to all he reported. When he finished, they stood in silence outside the farmhouse for a few minutes.

"What can we four do against such a thing?" Sugh asked.

"Five," Kekeen said.

"You are not on our side."

"I'm on Aldan's side."

"No one believes that," Clanless said.

"So what can we do?" Sugh repeated.

Clanless rubbed his face with both hands and pushed his hair back. "I don't know. I don't see a path forward."

"If we are patient, a path will present itself," Nukai said.

"I hate patient," Sugh muttered.

"I saw one more thing," Swift Claw said.

"I don't know if I can take more bad news." Clanless leaned against the fence.

The beastman cocked his head. "Mmh. Maybe bad. Maybe not."

"What? Tell us!" Sugh demanded.

"I saw wagons. Many. On their way to the city."

"How is that not bad? More reinforcements for the enemy!"

Swift Claw held out both hands, palms up, before returning them to his sides. "These are not of the far people." He paused. "But they come from far."

Clanless wrinkled his brow and lowered his head. "Wagons heading toward the city but not Melkute? Were they soldiers?"

"Some. Maybe. Confusing."

"I must see this for myself," Sugh declared. "I like confusion even less than patience."

"They are moving slowly," Swift Claw reported. "On the road from the Formation."

Clanless looked up. "From the north? But not Melkute? Then it must be…"

"Suirel," Kekeen said.

"Now we have something we can do!"

"A path presents itself," Nukai said quietly.

"Shall we prepare to go at once?" Sugh asked.

"How far are the wagons from the city?" Clanless asked Swift Claw.

"They are slow. Two or three days."

"Let's head out in the morning then," Clanless said. "We can intercept them before they get too close."

"What do you have in mind?" Kekeen asked.

"I don't know. But if it's Suirel, I want to know what he's doing and what's in those wagons." He glanced at Kekeen, expecting her to protest, but she said nothing.

Sugh rubbed his hands together. "At last, we can leave this place."

Clanless nodded. "Swift Claw, come with me." He led the beastman out into the field away from the others. "I have… something else to ask of you."

"Name it, Wolf Chosen. We fight as one."

"Don't agree too fast. What I have to ask is not easy." Clanless looked out toward Et-Baylak. "In fact, it's the hardest thing I've ever asked of you."

The beastman did not move. "Even so. You must ask."

"I need you to go home."

Swift Claw cocked his head. "You would send me away? Break the covenant?"

"No, no. I don't want to break anything." Clanless pointed off toward the city. "There is an army attacking my home. I need an army to fight it."

"Mmh." Swift Claw straightened up. "What you ask… is not possible."

"Not possible or not likely?"

"Not possible." He shook his head. "My people will not fight for yours."

"Maybe they will, if they know the threat."

"Wolf Chosen! Have you forgotten how we left?"

"No, I haven't." Clanless paused. "I fought Wind Tooth. You said honor was served."

"But you violated the elders' order in leaving."

"Honor is served. You said that about yourself and about Wind Tooth.

Surely that has to mean something to them."

Swift Claw squatted on his haunches and looked at the dirt. "Never. We have never fought for you."

"Then it's time to change that." Clanless knelt down to face him. "This is how our peoples can become friends. Allies. If we fight as one! Like you and I do!"

"You propose a covenant between peoples?"

"Something like that, yes."

He shook his head again. "You are not their leader. You cannot speak such a thing."

"Maybe I can't. But actions will show everyone. If the beastmen fight for Et-Baylak, my people will see who they are. They will want to be friends!"

Swift Claw kept his head down and ran his hands through his hair. "Even if it were so, I am not the speaker for this."

"There's no one better," Clanless insisted. "How many of your people have ever made a covenant with one of mine?"

Swift Claw hesitated. "None. But you are Wolf Chosen."

"Maybe I am. But I'm still just a man. And we fight as one. You are the perfect person to tell your people about this. And ask them to come help us. Tell them Wolf Chosen asks."

Swift Claw looked up. "If you ask, I will go. But they will not listen."

"We have to try."

The beastman did not speak for several moments. At last, he put his hand to his beard and touched the black ribbon there. "You asked of this. It is why they will not listen."

Clanless raised his eyebrows. "I don't understand."

Swift Claw lifted his head and looked toward the moon. "It is hard to tell."

Clanless kept his mouth shut and waited.

"You came to us in the cold times, when we live only in the Formation. When it is warmer, as now, we do not do so. We live in the Formation, but also outside. You understand?"

Clanless nodded.

"There is danger, we know. Animals. Beasts. But most dangerous is"—he looked at Clanless—"your people. We know to stay away. We teach our young. Humans. They hunt us. Kill us. Take us prisoner to fight in their cities."

Clanless winced. He knew it to be true. The disc-shaped ornament on his necklace felt heavier than usual.

"Too long ago. Eight times the winds have passed since then. Or nine." He paused. "I… am ashamed I cannot say. We were outside. The day was bright. My woman and child were with me."

The revelation came so casual and sudden, Clanless could not suppress a gasp.

"The child had only seen three passings of the wind." Swift Claw shook his head. "Too young. Too young."

A cool breeze stirred the tall grasses around them. A few yards away, the ghuyak took a large mouthful of the grass and chewed, gazing in their direction with its sad eyes.

"Tall Fang summoned me," Swift Claw went on. "He was eldest then. And I went. I believed all was safe. I was wrong."

The breeze picked up. Clanless's hair swept over his face. He pushed it back and waited for Swift Claw to continue. An ache rose in the back of his throat.

"Six of us stood in the first cave of the Formation. Tall Fang spoke of new diggings, of preparation for more young. We spoke long. The shouts came. We ran out." He paused again. "We were too late. The humans had gone."

The breeze faded, but Clanless felt colder. He rubbed his arms.

"Six were dead. Also six humans. Four were not there. Taken."

The silence lasted so long, Clanless finally prompted: "Your… family?"

"My woman lay dead. The child was gone." Before Clanless could say anything, Swift Claw pressed on: "I wear the black ribbon now for the one who died. For the one who is gone… I searched. I traveled far. I spent much time with people from far."

"The Melkute. But why would they take a child? He would be too young to fight in the arena."

"I do not know. But I searched. It is how I learned your words." Swift Claw again touched the ribbon. "I am not the only one who wears the black. Many others. This is why my people will not listen or help."

"Swift Claw, I… I'm so sorry." Clanless looked down at the dirt. "I… I can't believe you were so kind to Qara and me after that. I don't know if I would have done the same."

"Mmh. I did not want to. I wanted the elders to kill you at once." Swift Claw lowered his head. "I did not want to speak your words for them."

"Then… why?"

He raised his head. "You are Wolf Chosen. Sent by the True Wind. I could not speak against that."

Clanless tried to grasp the import. Swift Claw's belief in his god was enough to override such powerful personal feelings? Stronger than hatred and revenge? He wondered if even the Ghamba Lam had a faith that strong.

"Will you… will you search again?"

"I will. When you do not need me."

"I'm sorry I took you from that. But maybe I can help you one day. Maybe there's still hope."

Swift Claw cocked his head. "Hope? No. No hope. But I search. It is what I should do."

Eight years of searching. And yet he kept going, even without hope. Duty, perhaps? The duty of a father? Could duty and love keep one going without hope?

Swift Claw straightened up, and Clanless followed. "I will go to my people for you."

"You will?"

"This is needed, yes?"

"Yes. I… I can try to fight Suirel. I can try to rescue Kekeen." Clanless waved toward the east. "But I can't do anything against an entire army. Not without another army."

"Then I will go."

Clanless grabbed both of the beastman's shoulders. "Thank you. We will fight as one again. I know it."

Swift Claw's eyes widened, and he showed his teeth. "You have spoken it. It will be so."

"Heh. If only everything I spoke came true." Clanless embraced him. The beastman didn't quite know how to react, but he allowed it. Clanless stepped back. "We'll meet again."

Swift Claw nodded and spun. He raced away across the field, passed the grazing ghuyak, leaped over the fence, and vanished from view moments later.

Clanless took a deep breath. He doubted Swift Claw would succeed, but at least he'd be safe. If only he could send the others away too.

WAGONLOADS

Then

Sugh yanked his axe free from the body of his opponent. He reached for the Siphon on his belt but decided not to bother. He never got to spend any of his blood collection anyway. Instead, he looked up and lifted the axe to acknowledge the crowd's response to his victory.

As the roar faded, the voice of Baduhan erupted above everything else: "Sugh! Help me!"

Sugh jerked his head toward the owner's box. Some kind of scuffle took place inside. His master called; he had to obey. But how to get there in time? He took a few steps toward the exit. He would have to run through halls and stairways almost all the way around the arena to get to the owner's box by the standard route.

And then a female scream pierced the arena air. Chabi!

Sugh needed a more direct route. He raced to the side of the arena and slammed his axe into the wood. More shouts echoed from the box. The crowd reacted with their own shouts as they noticed the commotion.

Sugh hacked and chopped at the wall, ripping shattered chunks of wood out. He dropped the axe, seized a broken plank, and pulled. The solid construction of the arena wall resisted him, but his strength proved greater. The plank tore free. He grabbed the next one and pulled again. This one took longer but came loose from his brute force.

"Sugh!" Chabi's voice screamed. He grabbed up his axe and shoved his own way through the gap he'd created in the wall, in desperation ignoring the splinters that pierced his chest and back.

The stairs upward waited only a few feet away. He barreled up as fast as he could and reached the long hall behind the owner's box and other elite seats. A crowd filled the hall, either trying to find out what was going on, or trying to escape the chaos themselves.

"Out of my way!" Sugh bellowed and charged forward. Seeing the huge arena fighter coming their way with a bloody axe, the crowd scrambled to make room for him. He stormed through the hall, not caring who he trampled or shoved against the walls. He burst through the door into the owner's box.

Five or six bodies lay bleeding on the floor. Baduhan's bodyguard fell dead in front of his master, his head bashed in. Baduhan himself, on his knees, appeared unharmed, but his eyes were fixed on the other side of the box.

Two attackers remained. One stood poised to fight with a bloody mace extended. The other stood in the corner of the box, holding Chabi in front of him with a blade to her throat. A large cut on her forehead trickled blood across her face.

"Sugh!" Baduhan shouted. "Kill these men at once!"

"Ah, ah, big man," the mace-wielder warned. "Come any closer, and we'll cut her throat."

"Goddess," he whispered. "What do I do?"

"Kill them!" Baduhan commanded.

"Sir… your daughter…"

Chabi whimpered, her eyes locked on Sugh.

"Listen to me." The man with the mace kept it outstretched, his eyes darting between Sugh and Baduhan. "This horrible man is your master, slave. When I kill him, you'll be a free man."

"If that's all you want, then let the girl go!"

"Can't do that," the one holding Chabi hissed. "She's part of it too. One of the rich."

"You let her go, or I will take both of your heads." Sugh took one threatening step forward.

"Let's all wait a moment," the mace-wielder said. "W-we can work this out."

"I'll kill her, and then we both take him down," his companion said. "He's just one man."

"He's a champion!"

"Everything in the arena is for show! We can take him!"

"Enough," Baduhan said. "Kill them. Now."

"Abb?" Chabi cried.

"Sugh. You will protect me at all costs," Baduhan demanded. He fumbled at his belt and pulled out a familiar piece of metal. The bloodbond.

"You can't," the mace-wielder said, taking a step back toward his companion. "You're a slave. We'll set you free!"

Sugh didn't move at first. But the bloodbond could not be resisted. It pulled him forward against his own will.

The blade sliced Chabi's neck.

Sugh screamed in fury and charged, axe lifted.

The attacker threw Chabi's body over the railing and stepped forward to join his friend.

The mace came up like a shield.

Sugh's axe smashed through the mace and the first man's neck in one blow.

The second man stabbed at him with the blade still wet with Chabi's blood.

Sugh let the blade pierce his left hip and swung the axe back. The second man's head fell from his body.

Before it hit the floor, Sugh reached the railing and looked down. Chabi's body lay in a crumpled heap, blood spreading out to stain the sand around her. Cries of dismay and shock filled the air from people still watching from the stands.

Baduhan pulled himself to his feet. "Well, that was unpleasant. You failed to protect my daughter, but at least you did what I asked."

Sugh spun back to stare at him, wild-eyed. "I failed? You ordered me! We could have worked something out! They were talking. I could have saved her!"

Baduhan stared at him. "You are my property, and you do what I tell you. I did not tell you to talk with my attackers."

"But Chabi!" Sugh pointed.

"She was my daughter. I will grieve her in my way." The master's eyes narrowed. "But she should not have meant anything to you. Why this sudden emotional reaction?"

Sugh dropped his axe and fell to his knees beside the headless bodies. "She... I..."

"Hmp. I see." Baduhan dusted off his clothing. "Well, we are both fortunate. If I had known something was happening between the two of you, I would have arranged your death in the arena, no matter how much money you make me."

Sugh shook his head. "But… why? Who were these men?"

"What does it matter?" Baduhan looked up as several guards burst into the box, maces drawn. "Ah, it's about time. Clearly, I pay you lot too much." He started toward the door. "Clean up this mess. I'm going home."

Sugh pulled himself back to the railing and stared down at Chabi. "I'm so sorry," he whispered.

Now

Without Swift Claw, Clanless made the decision to leave the ox cart behind. But he encountered argument when he suggested they hook the ox up to the wagon and leave the ghuyak behind.

"We can't leave Tuulka!" Kekeen protested. "He would be even sadder!"

"He's an animal," Clanless said. "We leave him to do animal things."

"I don't know," Sugh said. "A big armored monster has advantages, you know. Especially if we run into more of those archers."

"Aren't we trying to avoid being noticed? An ox would be much better for that."

"Maybe. But Tuulka is our friend."

Clanless stared at him open-mouthed. "You too? We've had the ox for weeks!"

"But what is his name? Do you know?"

"No! Because we don't name our working animals!"

Kekeen shook her head. "This is a sad, sad world."

In the end, Kekeen prevailed. They left the ox in the farm's field as a present to the farmers should they return. Clanless made sure he had plenty of fodder in addition to all the space for grazing.

With Nukai and Sugh riding in the back of the wagon, they headed down the road. If they timed it right, Clanless hoped, they would meet up with Suirel's wagons on their way to Et-Baylak. After that, he didn't have much of a plan, except to discover Suirel's actions and put a stop to them.

Several hours later, they spotted the wagons. Clanless counted seven of them, though the first were far enough ahead he couldn't be sure. Most of them appeared identical. Two or three soldiers sat at the front, steering a pair of oxen. Canvas coverings concealed the wagons' contents.

"They appear to be carrying great weight," Nukai said. "The wheels sink deep in places of soft earth."

Sugh shaded his eyes. "You can tell that from here?"

"You cannot?"

Clanless toyed with the reins. "What could it be? Something heavy, but plentiful enough for so many wagons?"

"I suppose it couldn't be food for the city," Sugh said. "Or some other supplies?"

"Suirel is there," Kekeen murmured.

"You can feel him?" Clanless shot her a glance.

She didn't answer.

Clanless thought for a moment. "It's a bunch of wagons. We have a wagon too. Let's join them."

Kekeen laughed. "You don't think they'll notice?"

He shrugged. "It's worth a try."

"I like this plan!" Sugh exclaimed.

"There is one problem," Nukai said. "You are too recognizable. Both of you." He pointed at the moving wagons. "These are soldiers of the Sar Empire. They will recognize two famous members of the Dohor."

Clanless frowned. "He's right." He hated to admit it.

"But there is an easy solution." Nukai got to his feet. "I will drive the wagon. Clanless and Sugh can be here in the back and cover themselves when we get near enough to be seen. An older man and a woman will be far less threatening."

Clanless agreed and climbed into the back to make room for Nukai. "Now if only we'd kept the ox…"

Tuulka made a grumbling noise.

"All will be well," Nukai said. He climbed into position with some difficulty. "These soldiers are far more familiar with ghuyaks than you three. They may even offer to buy him."

"Twelve vials," Sugh said with a nod. "And not a drop less. V-blood, to be certain."

"Twelve? I can get two oxen for less than that!" Clanless exclaimed.

"Tuulka is worth more than two oxen."

"I don't see how." Clanless settled in as Nukai snapped the reins. "We'll be lucky to keep up with the other wagons."

Tuulka grumbled again and started forward.

Clanless sighed and watched the other wagons draw closer. Soon, maybe, they'd have a better idea of Suirel's plans. Or at the least, they'd be closer to Et-Baylak. It couldn't be far now.

$$\left(\!\left(\!\left(\!\left(\bullet\right)\right)\right)\right)$$

Suirel's arrival was not what Koland expected. In the distance, the Melkute army parted, leaving an open road leading to the city's north gate. Down the road, without any fanfare, came a series of wagons. As they drew closer, Koland could see Sar Empire soldiers on each wagon.

The cargo of the wagons quickly became a topic of much speculation among the soldiers on the city walls. Most assumed the caravan brought fresh food supplies to the besieged city. Koland shook his head. Suirel might have persuaded the enemy to let him through, but they would never have consented to a huge shipment of supplies that would only prolong the siege.

Koland headed down the stairs and worked his way through the crowds to the gate area. Curious onlookers braved the nearness to the wall to catch a glimpse of the mysterious arrivals. After the proposed champion battle, the Melkute had resumed sporadic pounding with the catapults, but it all ceased when Suirel's caravan appeared.

Nervous soldiers opened the great gates and stood ready for any betrayal. The assurances had been strongly worded, and the enemy had backed far away from the gate area, but anything could happen. A determined charge could reach the city before the gates could be closed again, if betrayal was the intent. Koland marveled that the agreement had been reached at all. But then again, Suirel and General Ghan had an understanding.

A few moments later, the first wagon came through the gates. Two soldiers sat at the front, one driving and the other scanning the crowd with wary eyes. Behind them stood a single man, mace at ready: Duurald the arena fighter. The wagon's cargo remained hidden by canvas tied down in multiple points. Some of the crowd offered cheers while others only murmured. As a whole, they weren't sure how to react. The wagon rolled on into the city.

Unlike the others, the second wagon was tall, almost like a carriage with sharp corners, but also covered tightly on the sides by canvas. A soft growl emerged from within, motivating the crowd to back up a few feet. Something lived inside it, something larger than the oxen pulling it. Koland wondered if Suirel hid within as well.

Three more wagons came through before Koland changed his mind. The fourth wagon carried a passenger in addition to the two soldiers: a cloaked and hooded figure sitting behind them. Koland couldn't make out anything about him, but a dark aura spread around the wagon. Not everyone felt it, but those who did murmured and glanced up at the moon for security. The hooded figure sat perfectly still for almost the entire time the wagon moved across Koland's vision. At the last moment, his hand stirred and lifted to point upward. One of the soldiers nodded and said something in return. The wagon kept moving.

Eight wagons in all came through the gates. The last one created a little more of a stir. Instead of a pair of oxen pulling it, a strange armored creature plodded along in front. A hunched-over man wearing a silly number of fur coverings held the reins, and a woman sat beside him. Her face turned to look back the way they'd come or into the wagon behind her. Even so, Koland knew her at once. Kekeen?

As the gate began to close behind them, a sudden motion erupted from the back of the final wagon. A man threw off some coverings and leaped to his feet. Even as the crowd surged forward at these actions, Koland knew him at once. "Clanless!"

The arena fighter snatched his moonblade from the wagon bed. He leaped forward onto the back of the armored creature and ran across it. He launched himself into the air from the beast's shoulder and landed on the back of the seventh wagon. The crowd erupted in shouts and cheers.

"Clanless!" "He'll save us!" "He's come!" "Our savior!" "Clanless!"

The two soldiers on the wagon were not so happy. The one spun around, yelling. He started to climb to his feet.

Clanless swung the moonblade down, slicing cleanly through the tight canvas covering. He grabbed one loose corner of it and yanked it aside. He stared down at the contents of the wagon, a perplexed look spreading over his face.

The crowd slammed against the wagon, shaking it. Both Clanless and the soldier wavered. Clanless pivoted and leaped back toward the armored beast. It looked like he would land on the animal's head, but at the last moment, it ducked. Clanless flailed. The moonblade ricocheted off the armored hide. Clanless smacked into it but had nowhere to stop his feet. He slid off to the street.

The seventh wagon kept moving. The soldier pulled the canvas back into place, hiding its contents once again.

Clanless found himself mobbed by the people of the lower city. He thrust the moonblade into the air, trying to avoid cutting any of them. Koland could see him saying something, but no one could hear over the shouting.

The great gates of Et-Baylak slammed shut.

A hand caught Koland's shoulder. He turned to find Captain Rakib, who leaned close to be heard. "Is that him? Clanless the arena fighter?"

"Yes! Can your men do something? The crowd is going to crush him!"

Captain Rakib turned and waved to the soldiers who'd shut the gate. As one, they pushed forward, two-handed maces held before them. The crowd, dismayed and complaining, gave back. In a few minutes, they'd cleared a space around Clanless and his wagon.

Koland and the Captain slipped between the soldiers and hurried to Clanless's side. "Are you all right?" Rakib demanded before anyone else could speak.

"I'll be fine," Clanless responded loudly to be heard over the crowd. He looked out over them. "What is going on? Why are they acting this way?"

"You've missed some significant developments," Koland said. "Let's get you somewhere safe, and I'll update you."

Clanless stared up the road after the wagons. "I need to go after Bain."

"We know where he's going," Koland said. "But for now, we need to go somewhere else." He glanced up at Kekeen, who smiled down at him. Was that truly his daughter?

"We have to keep you safe," Captain Rakib added. "You can save this whole city!"

Clanless at last looked at them. "What?"

Koland took his arm. "I'll explain. Let's go." But his own curiosity forced him to ask one question: "What did you see in the wagon?"

"Crystal." Clanless glanced up the street at the disappearing wagon. "It was full of crystal."

Part Three

ET-BAYLAK

I WILL FIGHT

It took far too long to get Clanless and Kekeen off the streets and into one of the guard stations built against the city walls. Nukai and Sugh stayed with the ghuyak and wagon. Without Clanless, the crowd grumbled and started to disperse, though quite a few remained, hoping he'd reappear.

Clanless stared out of a window on the second floor, watching the people. What beneath the moon's gaze had gotten into them? He turned to see Kekeen embracing her father and frowned. Koland didn't know about Zektel. He'd have to let him know all about that as soon as possible. But first…

"What is going on here?" he demanded, pointing out the window.

"It seems your fame has spread beyond our borders," the officer who'd come with Koland said. "The Melkute want to see you fight."

"What?"

"It's more complicated than that," Koland said. "This has something to do with Suirel."

"Bain." Clanless clenched his fist. "You said you knew where he was going."

"General Ghan has given him the arena. I assume that's where he's taking all those wagons."

"Full of crystal." Clanless looked back out the window. "What can he be up to?"

"We'll figure it out." Koland glanced at Kekeen at his side. "There are many things going on here. As soon as the other members of the council hear you've arrived, they'll want to see you at once. Captain, can your men escort us to the palace?"

"Of course," the officer answered.

Clanless could not remember a more awkward journey than the one from the guard station to the palace. Soldiers marched alongside their wagon, keeping people back. But word had spread throughout the lower city, at least. People thronged the way, calling out to him, cheering for him, begging him to save them.

"And I thought you were popular in the arena!" Sugh observed.

"This is insane!" Clanless exclaimed. A woman who clearly hadn't been eating enough held up a small child to see past the soldiers. He tried not to let his horror show in his face. "It's disgusting."

"Oh, I don't know," Kekeen said. "I think they're finally giving you what you deserve."

"I'm not their savior!"

"And yet, you hope to save them from Suirel," Nukai said quietly.

Clanless scowled at him and turned to Koland who'd joined them on the wagon. "What does this mean? Why do the Melkute want to see me fight?"

"It's a champion challenge," Koland explained. "They say if you defeat their king's champion, they'll retreat. But if he defeats you, we should surrender."

"And all these people know about this?"

"Yes…" He rubbed his beard. "That was peculiar. I'm not sure how the story spread."

"You've been performing for crowds your entire life," Kekeen said. "You know how they behave. This is no different."

"This is massively different!" Clanless protested. "Arena fights were for entertainment. This… this is real! They're cheering because they expect me to save them!"

A face in the crowd caught his attention as they kept moving. He spun, trying to keep it in sight.

"What is it?" Kekeen asked.

"I thought I saw… Salkhi."

"From Pasque House?" Sugh exclaimed.

Kekeen hugged his arm. "Forget about her. You've got me now." In a lower voice, she added, "Both of us."

"She's my friend. I want to know how she's doing." Clanless looked back at the crowd, but between the wagon's movement, the soldiers, and all the other people, he saw no more of Salkhi.

His uneasiness over the hero worship subsided when they crossed into the upper city. The crowds dwindled to curious onlookers and before long, almost completely disappeared. Their pace picked up until they arrived at the palace. Clanless looked anxiously toward the arena complex, but Koland caught his arm and guided him indoors.

"Give me a moment to send some messages to the other council members," he said. "And then we'll see what we can find out."

Nukai volunteered to make sure Tuulka found a spot in the palace stables. "Two spots, most likely," he said with a chuckle.

Sugh looked about the palace entry while they waited for Koland. "This is something, eh? The only times I've been in here was when the Hawk King wanted to talk." He gave a slight shudder. "That was never pleasant."

Kekeen sat down in a fancy chair situated against the wall. "The last time I was in here, I was running the place." She patted the arms of the chair. "I never could figure out why this chair is here. I thought maybe the Hawk King made important people wait here before seeing him, but it's nowhere near the actual throne room."

Clanless scowled at her.

Koland hurried back. "I've sent the messages. I expect the council will be here within half an hour, at the most. General Ghan will have the furthest to come, if he's at the wall."

"How is the council these days?" Kekeen asked. She stretched her arms above her head. "I do somewhat miss those arguments around the big table."

Koland stared at her a moment. "Ah. Then that question is now answered. You're not my daughter, are you?"

She cocked her head. "Why, Father. Why ever would you say that?"

"Stop it!" Clanless snapped. "We need to find out what Bain is up to. Let's go to the arena."

"I have a better idea," Koland said. "We can get a good look into the arena from the south tower windows."

"The what?"

He gestured down a hall. "This way. Up in the tower, we should have the view we need."

Clanless, Sugh, and Kekeen followed him. He led them past several turns and up a long, winding staircase. After a couple of complete circuits, they entered a barren room with windows in a circle around them. Another staircase led further up into the tower.

"No furniture here at all," Kekeen said. "I think Borde took what was here and in some other rooms and sold it in some noble gesture to feed the poor or something like that."

"Borde." Clanless looked back down the stairs. "I wonder if she's still here?"

"Forgot about her, did you?"

"I thought you wanted us to like you," Sugh said. "You've only gotten more cruel since we arrived here."

Kekeen gestured toward the windows. "I'd apologize, but it's pointless. The proximity to Suirel is affecting me."

Clanless hurried to the window and looked down. From here, they could see straight into the arena floor.

"They drove the wagons into the arena itself," Sugh said from beside him. "What an odd sight."

The sand which had seen so many fights and so much blood now held eight wagons, lined up beside each other. Workers scurried about, removing the canvas covers and exposing their contents. The sun glinted from the crystal.

"What could he possibly want with all of that?" Koland wondered. He looked at Kekeen with a fierce grimace. "What do you know about this?"

Her eyes widened. "Me? Nothing. I've been with these two."

Clanless turned toward her. "But you know how he thinks. What does he need all that crystal for?"

"I have no idea!" she insisted. "Your people use it to hold blood. Maybe he has an idea for the same thing."

"I doubt a god of chaos is interested in creating currency," Koland said. "But perhaps for storing blood for magical purposes?"

"You should ask the Ghamba Lam," Sugh suggested.

"Indeed." Koland drew in a sharp breath. "There's Suirel."

"Where?" Clanless leaned out the window to get a better view.

A hooded figure emerged from the arena doors and walked out onto the sand. From this vantage point, Clanless couldn't see his face. "Are you sure that's Bain?"

"I saw him ride in," Koland said. He glanced again at Kekeen.

Sugh peered over their shoulders. "He does not walk like a blind man."

"No." Clanless squinted, trying to make out any details. "He doesn't." Bain—if it was Bain—strode across the sand with the sure footing of someone who knew where he was going, someone who could see.

"Blood-magic cannot replace eyes. Everyone knows that."

"Assuming Suirel is all that he claims to be," Koland said, "we are dealing with a god, a creature far beyond our powers and understanding. Who is to say that he even needs physical sight?"

Clanless resisted growling in response. He'd stabbed Bain's one good eye, hoping it would cripple Suirel. But if it didn't, and Suirel ever left Bain's body, his friend would forever be blind. And it was his fault.

The hooded figure stopped in the middle of the arena. As two of the workers hurried toward him, he turned, slowly, and looked up toward the palace tower.

"Is he looking at us?" Sugh asked.

"He has no eyes," Clanless insisted.

"He doesn't need them," Kekeen said softly.

Clanless twisted to look at her. "You know his capabilities. He can see?"

"I think so." She stayed away from the window. "He can do far more than I. I'm bound to the blood. He... I don't know."

A courier appeared on the stairs. "Sirs, the council members are beginning to arrive. Your presence is requested."

"Faster than I thought," Koland said. "Well, best not to keep them waiting."

Clanless looked down at the arena one last time. The hooded figure stood still, gazing back up at him. Clanless lifted the moonblade and tapped it against the wall beside the window before he turned and descended the stairs.

ⵛ ⵛ ⵛ ⵛ ● ⵆ ⵆ ⵆ ⵆ

Clanless stood before the council and General Ghan. The General's presence came as a surprise Koland hadn't had time to explain. A few whispered words made Clanless ease off his grip on the moonblade, but he kept a narrow eye on the General throughout the conversation.

"Has the storyteller apprised you of the situation?" Ghan went straight to the point.

"He has. Do you believe the Melkute are sincere in this offer?"

"We've debated this!" Lord Ezen interrupted. "We've been over it again and again. There is only one question now: can you do it?"

"How can I answer that?" Clanless said. "I know nothing of their champion."

"I think my colleague means: will you do it?" Lord Ghayaktal said.

Clanless tried not to glare at Ghayaktal. He hadn't forgotten the man who'd abused Salkhi and broken her arm.

"How often did you know the capabilities of your opponent before you stepped into the arena?" General Ghan asked.

"Almost never," Clanless admitted.

"And did you doubt your ability to win in those cases?"

"Not usually. But I had an advantage to use in the desperate cases."

"Ah, yes. Your… ability." The General glanced at the Ghamba Lam. "Some call it an abomination, I'm told."

"Are the Melkute aware of the Taint? And how will they react if I use it?" Clanless shook his head. "Because quite honestly, without it, I'm not certain of victory." He didn't see the need to share the details of his difficulties of the past few weeks. Based on recent experiences, he doubted he would even meet the standards of one of the Dohor in his current state.

"Why not?" Lord Ulakan demanded. "You've never lost!"

"Except once," the Ghamba Lam said quietly. "Or twice."

"You're not helping," Koland whispered.

"I expect them to deny the use of blood-magic," General Ghan said. "To them, that is the abomination. But your… Taint… is not blood-magic, is it?"

"No," the Ghamba Lam said louder. "It is not."

"Even so, they might not react well," Sonkogh put in.

"Do they have no magic of their own?" Lord Ulakan asked. "I seem to remember hearing some rumors of some sort."

"Rumors!" Lord Ezen snorted. "Rumors will say anything!"

"Council!" General Ghan said sharply. "This is getting us nowhere. We must know two things: will Clanless fight for us, and should we let him do so?"

All eyes turned back to Clanless.

"I will fight, if asked to," he said with a sinking heart. "But I do not know if we can trust they will keep their word."

"Leave that to me," the General said. "I will see to the negotiations." He looked around the table. "If this is the will of this council?"

One by one, the assembled Lords and others agreed.

"Very well. I will send word to the enemy." General Ghan glanced to his side. "Since the arena is currently unavailable, I am sure sufficient lodging can be found for you and your company here within the palace. It's apparently not being used for much else. Now, if you will all excuse me, I must get on with my job." He nodded once and strode out of the room.

"If that man ever bent over, I think something would break," Sugh said in what he might have thought was a whisper.

Clanless sought for Borde within the palace but without luck. He'd almost given up when he spotted an attendant hurrying down a dimly-lit hall ahead of him. "You there!" he called. "Wait!"

The young man turned. "Clanless?"

He squinted. "Is that…?"

The attendant spread his arms. "It's Yesun! Have you forgotten me already?"

"Yesun!" Clanless sprinted forward and seized him. He lifted the young man off the ground. "How did you grow so much in a few months?"

"That's what my mother wants to know." Yesun laughed. "But what are you doing back here?"

Clanless set him down. "I'm searching for my cousin Borde. Have you seen her?"

Yesun's laugh faded. "Ah, she left." He glanced around to see if anyone else might be listening. "Fled, really. She got out of here the day after Daviland left with the priests."

"Is she still in the city?"

Yesun shrugged. "I'm sorry, Clanless. I don't know. I've rarely left the palace myself. A lot of people left after the Hawk King died, and even more left when Daviland did." He took a step, as if he needed to hurry on his way.

"I won't keep you then." Clanless waved him on. "It's good to see you, Yesun."

"And you, Clanless. I know you'll save us." He sprinted down the hall.

Clanless watched him go. He found Yesun's faith in him somewhat disturbing, but his thoughts lingered on Borde. If she'd left after Daviland, she'd wanted out. In all likelihood, she'd escaped the city as soon as High Winter faded. He might have passed her on the road somewhere. Or maybe not. Borde would seek out a different city rather than the clanhold.

He returned to find Kekeen, who showed him the room where Borde had slept. "Shall we share it?" she asked. "They're expecting us to, you know. And it's probably the nicest bedroom here. Except the Hawk King's primary suite, I suppose. Do you think we could get that one?"

"You know my answer."

She gave an exaggerated sigh and tested the bed's softness. "Well, there's an adjoining room where you can sleep. I suppose that will have to do, for now. At least you'll be close if I have to scream for help."

"Why would you need help?" Clanless gave her an incredulous look.

"You never know." She shrugged. "You have enemies within the city, you know. Striking at your dearest love would be far simpler for them than going after you."

"I'm sure if you tell them who you really are, they'll leave you alone."

"Not all of your enemies are servants of Suirel," she reminded him. "And if you fail this challenge thing, you'll have thousands of enemies."

"If I fail the challenge, I'll be dead."

"We can't allow that, now can we?" She pulled herself up onto the bed.

"Zektel, I… appreciate it, but there's nothing you can do to help this time." He opened the connecting door and looked into the other room. "This is something I will have to do alone."

"You're never alone, Aldan."

He snorted.

"I'm serious! You know Kekeen loves you, and I… I care about you too." She perched on her knees on the bed, holding on to the bedpost. "And you have such good friends on your side."

Clanless looked back at her. "None of them can enter the arena with me."

Her answer came so low, he almost didn't hear it. "I could."

He narrowed his eyes. "You would do that? I asked it before."

Kekeen looked down. "I know. I… never mind."

Clanless growled. Why even offer it if she wasn't serious? He entered the second bedroom and slammed the door behind him.

BRIEF REUNIONS

"Aldan!"

The scream jerked Clanless out of bed and across the room. He yanked the door open before the sound faded. Kekeen sat straight upright in her bed, eyes wide and staring. A single candle on the nightstand flickered light across her terrified face.

"What is it?" Clanless scanned the room for threats even as he rushed to the bedside.

"Aldan, I…" Her eyes darted around the room, still as wide as ever. "This is Borde's room. It's…"

"Yes? We talked about this. What's wrong?"

Her eyes focused on his. "Aldan. It's me."

And he understood. "Kekeen?" He put one knee on the bed. "It's you? This isn't a trick?"

Her hands shook as she reached toward him. "No, no. I don't know why or how, but I'm in control now. You have to believe me."

He scrambled onto the bed and pulled her into his arms. Clad in only a light shift, she felt like almost nothing at all, yet he held the entire world. She'd taken her hair out of its usual braid, and it fell over his arms. She held him as tight as she could, her small hands clutching at his back. "It's me. It's me," she repeated. "I love you. I love you."

"I love you," he answered, still in shock. "How, how did this happen? Where is Zektel?"

"She's still here, I think. I don't know. I don't care. Hold me."

He did. Every instinct he'd ever had about avoiding physical contact fled away in those moments. His shoulder felt damp, and he wondered about it until he realized it was Kekeen's tears. She turned her head and kissed his shoulder, kissed the salty tears away. He closed his eyes. His hands massaged her back.

She kissed the side of his neck. "We have this moment," she whispered. "I don't want to waste it."

"I don't want it to end," he said.

Her kisses moved up to his cheek. She giggled at the roughness of his scruff. "You need to shave."

"It can wait." He covered her mouth with his. They'd kissed each other before, of course, but not like this. The intensity, the passion, the need were more than he had ever experienced. When they broke free, he returned her earlier actions by kissing her cheek and down the side of her neck to her shoulder. She fell back on the pillow, pulling him down with her.

"Wait, wait, wait," she said. He stopped and lifted his head with a groan. "Aldan, if she comes back, if, if I can't stop her, I don't want—"

"No," he said swiftly. "She won't. I won't let her."

"You know you can't stop her. Listen to me. Tell Sugh. Tell him she's bound to the blood."

"What?"

"Tell him!" she insisted. "Ohhh." She arched back against him. "I think…"

"What? What is it?"

She gave a low chuckle and pulled her face up next to his cheek. "I knew I'd get you into my bed," she whispered with a warm breath against his ear.

"Zektel!" He jerked up and pushed her away.

She smiled and cocked her head. "We're here. Together. Exactly as you've always wanted." She pulled aside the blanket. "There's plenty of room for you under here."

He scrambled back off the bed, heart pounding in his ears. "What is this? What happened? Was it you all along, trying to deceive me?"

"No, dear." She sighed. "I did not have control of this body for a few minutes. I want you here with me, of course, but I won't resort to that kind of trickery. I want you in here of your own free will." She patted the bed beside her.

"Why? What happened?" Clanless kept asking questions, trying to regain control of his own thoughts, emotions, and raging heartbeat.

She straightened the blanket. "If you must know, it was Suirel. He insisted on talking with me."

"So. I can assume he knows everything you do now."

She shrugged.

"And did you learn anything from him?"

"Some. But he ordered me not to tell you." She sighed again. "You can't possibly understand, dear Aldan, how much I'm struggling here. I've served Suirel for thousands of years. I won't betray him now. But I've enjoyed our years together so much. That's why I'm here, in this body. I don't want to lose you either."

"Losing you would be the greatest moment of my life." He took deep breaths, facing away from her.

"If you lose me, you lose Kekeen," she said with a harder tone. "Don't forget that."

"How could I?" He turned back to glare at her. "For a few moments, I had what I always wanted. And you just took it away from me. Again."

She lowered her eyes and didn't answer.

Clanless spun on his heel and stalked back to the door.

"He wants you to fight the Melkute champion," Kekeen called.

He paused at the door. "Why?"

"To keep you busy," she said almost too low for him to hear. "To keep you from finding out what he's doing in the arena."

"Then that's what I'm going to do." Clanless slammed the door behind him.

((((●))))

Koland rotated the mug and watched the liquid within swirl. The honey wine had been watered down, like all drinks within the city right now. He almost thought he could see the difference. He knew he could taste it.

Sonkogh sat down across from him. "I would have thought I'd find you celebrating," he said, beckoning to a serving girl to bring him a drink as well. "Clanless has returned to fight for us. And your daughter as well!"

"My daughter is not here."

The serving girl set a mug in front of Sonkogh and poured honey wine into it. "Leave the pitcher," Koland said. The server glanced toward the eating house's proprietor, who nodded. She set the pitcher of wine on the table and left the two men.

Sonkogh took a sip and watched Koland with narrowed eyebrows. "Something is troubling you, my friend, and I don't understand. Will you let me in?"

Koland drank down his mug and refilled it with the pitcher.

"It will take some time to get drunk on this," Sonkogh pointed out, "if that is your intent."

Koland ran his hands through his hair. "Do you know I've only gotten drunk six times in my entire life? I remember each one. I try to avoid intoxication. Audiences don't find slurred stories all that amusing." He took another swallow. "But tonight may be number seven."

"Why? What has so discouraged you?"

"Six times," Koland repeated. "Three of them…" He looked up. "Shall I tell you about three of them?"

Sonkogh spread his hands. "If that will help your present state. I will listen, as I have listened to all your stories over the years."

"Have I ever told you…" Koland clenched the mug in a tight grip, staring into it once again. "Have I told you what happened to my wife?"

"She died of the sand cough, wasn't it?"

"No. She didn't. But that's the story I've told. Even Kekeen believes it. But it's not true. I've never told anyone the truth." He paused. "I think I fooled myself for a while, locking it all away."

Sonkogh took a sip of his own drink and kept silent.

"There are many ways to lose someone you love. Sometimes, you lose them while their bodies are still here." He looked up. "You've never been to Conchaga, have you?"

Sonkogh shook his head. "I've not had that pleasure."

Koland snorted. "Pleasure. My wife thought it a pleasure too, I suppose. She wanted to settle down for a while, to… raise our daughter in a single place instead of the road." He shook his head. "She loved my stories. She loved listening to me tell them. She loved telling some herself. In some ways, she told them better than I did. She loved watching the audience reactions: their laughter, their anger, their awe. She even loved the traveling we did together. But when Kekeen was born… she wanted stability. She chose Conchaga. Or rather, a smaller city not far from Conchaga. She feared the big city would lure me back into my earlier ways, I think."

Koland took a long drink. When he didn't resume the story, Sonkogh filled the silence: "Had I ever married, I doubt a wife would have taken kindly to my traveling ways either. From merchant to rebel." He shook his head. "My time here with the council has been one of the longest stays in my life. And if the Melkute have their way, it will be my final home, I suppose."

"I tried," Koland said. "I tried to be a part of the city. I joined with the elders, participated in the governance, much like we've done with the council here. My skill with words won many a day's debate." He noticed a few drops of spilled wine on the table's surface. With a finger, he traced a few random letters. "But not the one that mattered."

Sonkogh didn't speak this time.

"It was another outrage of the Hawk King's." Koland waved a hand in the air. "The details don't matter any more. He did many such things. And many people grew angry. These people, though, were foolish. Stupid. They thought they could rebel."

"Like us?"

Koland downed the rest of the mug and slammed it back on the table. "No, not like us! They had no charismatic leader, no army, nothing. But they thought they could rise up, just the same. And they wouldn't listen to me!" He poured another drink. "Or maybe I didn't try hard enough. Maybe I could have stopped them. But I didn't. And so the Hawk King's soldiers came."

"Ah."

"We were not a part of the uprising." Koland pointed at Sonkogh. "I want that clear. We did nothing wrong. My wife did nothing wrong."

Sonkogh shook his head with sad eyes. "Has that ever mattered?" he whispered.

"But my wife… her heart was too good. Too compassionate. She could not bear to see others suffer." He clenched his fist. "And so, against my advice, she ran to help someone else, someone fallen in the soldiers' attack."

"And they killed her?"

"A soldier struck her in the head. With his mace."

Sonkogh waited a few moments. Koland took another swallow of honey wine. "Then why the sand cough story?" Sonkogh asked at last. "Surely, if your wife died from a mace—"

"She didn't die!" Koland slammed the mug onto the table, sloshing more wine out. "She lived!"

Sonkogh opened his mouth but said nothing.

"It would have been better had she died in the street that day." Koland's hand shook as he shifted the mug off to the side. "But she lived. Or rather, her body lived. Her soul, her… being left it and did not return." He looked up at the rafters and let out a shuddering sigh. "I tended her. My wife. My beloved. She lay there, eyes open but unseeing. Sounds came from her mouth, but they did not form words. Her body remembered things like eating and walking, but her mind… it was not there." He turned wet eyes toward Sonkogh. "She could tell stories better than I could. I said that, didn't I? But now, she couldn't even tell me whether she was in pain. Or whether she knew who I was."

"How… how long did she live?" Sonkogh asked.

"Haven't you heard me? She wasn't alive. Not really. The priests could offer no hope of healing. Blood-magic cannot cure the mind." Koland wiped his eyes with the back of his wrist and took another swallow. "And so I watched her. I pleaded with her to recognize me. I pleaded with the goddess to bring her back. I… I did all I could. But it was no use. She wasn't there." He paused a long moment. "She wasn't there. Day by day, I watched her body, but she wasn't there. I watched and watched for weeks until even the body began to fade. Without her soul, it couldn't endure. And neither could I. It destroyed me, I tell you."

"And… Kekeen? She knew nothing of this?"

"I sent her away. She doesn't know." Koland stared into his mug again. "I almost didn't go back to her. The pain was too great. But… I did. And she has been my light, my joy, ever since."

Sonkogh put out his hand and caught Koland's before he could reach for the pitcher again. "My friend. I am so sorry for you. But I don't understand. Why tell me this now? Is something wrong with Kekeen?"

"The light is gone," Koland murmured. "Her body is there, but her being is locked away."

Sonkogh's eyes widened. "What are you saying?"

Koland stood, wavering a bit. "I will not watch again. I will not wait this time, clinging to a hope that… that will not happen."

Sonkogh pushed back his chair and got up. "I don't understand, my friend. What do you mean?"

"It is not Kekeen. It is a blood-wraith." Koland looked toward the door. "And I will not endure her presence any longer."

Clanless examined the soldiers guarding the arena side door, the one used by the Hawk King and the Dohor to go between the palace and arena. Four armed men stood in front of it, maces at ready. Suirel couldn't think such a small band could stop him. He walked closer.

"You're wasting your time!" one of the soldiers called. "The door is sealed from within."

"Then why are you here?" he asked.

"Because he commands it."

Clanless nodded. No need to ask who "he" was. He turned and exited the courtyard between the structures. The walk around to the arena's main entrance took longer than he remembered. To his relief, few people wandered the streets around the palace. Clouds obscured both moon and sun, threatening rain at some point. Chillness hung in the air.

He'd gone about halfway when hurrying footsteps came up behind him. He glanced back to see Sugh catching up.

"What do you think you're doing?" his friend asked. He held his axe in one hand and the moonblade in the other.

"Seeing if I can get in."

Sugh fell in step beside him. "Without me? Or your weapon? That is foolish."

"Suirel doesn't want me to know what he's doing in there. So I'm going to find out."

"Without me?" Sugh repeated.

Clanless laughed. "I suppose not." He waited a few more steps before adding, "Kekeen was able to speak to me for a few minutes last night."

Sugh's eyes widened. "Free of the blood-wraith?"

"Only a few minutes. But she said to tell you something."

"I am listening to your every word."

"She said to tell you that… she's bound to the blood. I think she meant Zektel." He frowned. "Didn't Zektel tell us that herself?"

"She did," Sugh confirmed. "But Kekeen wanted me to pay attention to it."

"Do you know why?"

Sugh made several clicking sounds with his tongue. "I cannot say."

Clanless took a deep breath. "Nothing is helping."

"We will find a way, my friend. Do not despair."

He didn't answer. What could he say? Nukai told him to trust to hope. Sugh always seemed optimistic. But whatever their source for their beliefs, he couldn't see it. And yet, he had to try.

A sprinkle of raindrops fell. They circled the arena until they reached the main entrance. Clanless wasn't surprised to find it shut. He pushed against one of the two massive doors without effect.

"I seem to remember these could be barred from the inside," Sugh said. He rapped against the door with his fist. "It would take a lot to knock these down. More than our weapons. More than heavy maces, even."

Clanless looked up and saw several faces staring down at him from above. Soldiers on duty watched from a perch above the gates. One waved a short bow at him. "And we'd be full of arrows before we could finish. Is there another way in?"

"Another set of doors like these." Sugh pointed down the street.

"Halfway between here and the other side of the palace."

"Probably sealed and guarded in the same way." Clanless rubbed his face. "There has to be a way."

"Clanless!" The voice echoed down the empty street. He turned, heart sinking, expecting someone looking to him as savior.

A young woman barreled into him, throwing her arms around him. Sugh recognized her before he did. "Salkhi!"

Clanless let her hug him a moment before pulling away and smiling at her. "I thought I saw you in the crowd yesterday!" He glanced up and saw three other young women standing several feet away, wide-eyed.

"I've been hoping to see you for months!" she exclaimed. "Where have you been?"

"Uh, that's a long story." He glanced at Sugh before looking her over. "You look… well."

She wagged a finger at him. "You mean you're not used to seeing me with so many clothes on. You can say what you're thinking. No secrets between us, Clanless."

"How could there be?" Sugh said.

Salkhi stuck out her tongue at him. "I haven't forgotten you either, Sugh, or your favorite scar."

"It is a wonderful scar."

Clanless shook his head. "What are you doing now, Salkhi? Are you all right?"

"All right? You set me free, Clanless! I can never thank you enough. I owe everything to you!"

She looked like she might jump on him again, so he turned to look back at the arena. "I, uh, got my freedom another way, so I needed to do something with all that extra blood…"

Salkhi slipped around and embraced him again. "You moonbent idiot. No one does something like that. Not normal people, anyway. You saved me."

Clanless swallowed. He did enjoy seeing her, but the previous night's encounter with Kekeen still filled his mind. He took both of her hands in his and gently pulled her loose.

Her face fell. "You're still… like that?" She looked down. "I saw your woman with you in the wagon. Kekeen. I'm glad you're still with her."

"I love her, Salkhi. You know that." He kept hold of her hands.

She shrugged. "A girl can hold out hope, you know."

"But you're all right. Aren't you?"

She smiled again. "Yes, Clanless. I'm all right. I had some blood of my own saved up, mostly because of you. It got me through High Winter." She laughed. "At first, I had no idea what to do. I sat around in my room in a nice inn for days. Alone. That was so strange at first. But I enjoyed it. It was the first time I'd ever been alone that long in my life."

"You had to eat, surely!" Sugh exclaimed.

"Of course I did, silly. I just had the food brought to my room. It… took me a while to start talking with other people again." She took a deep breath. "And even when I did, I felt like a fraud. Like any minute, someone would show up to drag me back to Pasque House."

"But they never did," Clanless said.

"They never did." She gave him her biggest smile again. "And now I have a job and everything. Oh! These are some friends from the job." She gestured at the other three women, who hadn't moved from their spot.

"Ladies," Sugh said with a nod. Clanless smiled at them. If anything, their eyes grew bigger. They whispered to each other but didn't come any closer.

"I was even thinking of traveling to a different city somewhere… until this army showed up," Salkhi went on. "How did you get through them, anyway?"

"Yeah… there are many things happening." Clanless looked at the arena. Could he climb the wall somewhere?

"We're trying to figure out how to get back inside the arena," Sugh said, "so we can fight the god of chaos inside."

Salkhi raised an eyebrow at him. "A god of chaos?" She glanced at the arena doors. "I suppose that's why it's shut?"

"It is," Clanless said.

"You could always try the Pasque Tunnel."

"The what?" Clanless looked back at her.

Salkhi folded her arms with a sly grin. "All these years for both of you, and you didn't know about the tunnel?"

"We never used a tunnel." Sugh scratched the top of his head. "Why would we?"

"Sometimes, the Hawk King would require the services of Pasque House but not at the House," she explained. "There's a tunnel beneath the streets, leading to two locations: the palace and the arena."

"Why the arena?" Clanless asked. "I understand why he would entertain guests in the palace, but…"

"The arena wasn't just to watch you men sweat and bleed, you know." Salkhi patted his arm. "Other things happened inside there too."

"Out in the sand?" Sugh asked.

"Ugh. No, of course not. Why would you even think that? The Hawk King has a special room for… special parties." She shrugged. "Sometimes, he liked to combine the spectacle of the arena for his guests with our kind of spectacle."

"If there's an entrance in the palace…" Clanless started to turn. "Do you know where it is?"

Salkhi shook her head. "I never saw a map of the palace or much of it at all, only the tunnel, a hallway, and a bedroom."

Clanless winced. He didn't like to think of the kind of people the Hawk King would have been entertaining and how they would have treated Salkhi and the other women.

"Then we should go to Pasque House and find that entrance!" Sugh looked ready to storm off at once.

"You… might not be welcome there," Salkhi said. "They didn't like it when Clanless freed me. And with the Hawk King dead, they haven't been getting as much business."

"We didn't kill him!" Sugh protested.

"Besides, the tunnel entrance is not at Pasque House," she went on. "The tunnel is impressive, but it's not very long. The entrance is closer than that."

"Must we drag it out of you?" Sugh asked.

Salkhi pointed down the street. "It's not far. In the basement of Lord Ghayaktal's house."

Another smattering of raindrops fell. Clanless glanced at the sky. "Would be drier in the tunnel, I suppose."

"You're going now?"

"Sugh told you. We have something to do in there."

Salkhi put her hands on her hips. "Here I thought you were going to save the city. That's what everyone believes, anyway." She glanced back at her friends.

Clanless took a step away. "I'm not going to debate my actions in the middle of the street."

"Why? Is this a more difficult place to talk than my bedroom?"

"Friends, please," Sugh interrupted. "You are both making good points. Suppose we agree to that."

Clanless threw his arms out. "What do you want from me? All of you! I'm not a savior!"

"Then why do you seek to fight Suirel?" Sugh asked.

"Suirel?" Salkhi said. "The chaos moon?"

"I'm just… I, I'm trying to do what's right!" Clanless stumbled over his words.

More sprinkles fell around them. The breeze blew dampness into their faces.

Salkhi let her arms drop. "Look, I don't know what's going on with you. At all. I know the people of this city—like my friends there—are hoping you can get rid of that army outside, but you're in here trying to get into a locked arena. Maybe that is more important. I don't know. Just… be careful. We need you, Clanless."

Clanless sighed. "The threat in there"—he pointed at the arena—"is greater than the threat outside the city."

Salkhi wiped raindrops from her face. "If that's true, it's… terrifying. I'm sorry. I only came this way hoping to see you, but this is more than I anticipated."

"And I'm, I'm so happy to see you," he answered. "I was worried about you, Salkhi. Truly."

She took several steps and embraced him again. "I told you the last time we talked that you'd made an impact in my life. And that was before you set me free. I owe everything to you, Clanless. You'll always be a part of my life." She gave him a quick kiss. "And that's still a good way to say goodbye. Or hello."

He smiled. "I've missed our talks."

"We call it 'talks' now?" Sugh inserted.

Salkhi laughed and waved at him. "You have no idea. Give me a moment." She turned and joined the other three women. They exchanged a few words and the other three dashed down the street together. Salkhi returned. "All right. Let's go."

"What do you mean?" Clanless asked.

The rain continued to sprinkle down in a slow and dreary fashion, enough to make the cool air uncomfortable.

"Do you know where Lord Ghayaktal's house is?"

"I'm sure we can find it."

"You? I'm not convinced. Follow me." She set off in the opposite direction her friends had gone. Clanless hesitated a moment, then hurried after her.

Sugh followed him. "You mean to try this tunnel now?"

"If we can get in to Bain now, before anything else happens, it's our best move. He wants me distracted by the challenge outside. That means he's worried about me stopping him now."

"Just the two of us then." He held out the moonblade.

Clanless nodded and took it. "I can't trust anyone else, Sugh. If I brought Kekeen along, she could be used against me."

"Of course. It is a shame Swift Claw will miss out on this."

"He's where he needs to be."

"Who's Swift Claw?" Salkhi asked.

"That's a long story."

The rain started to come faster. The three of them picked up their pace.

"What if this Lord does not want to let us use his tunnel?" Sugh asked.

"He will see things our way," Clanless said. "I'm absolutely certain of it."

FATHER'S DESPERATION

Sugh stared up at the dark ceiling of his chamber. Somewhere beyond it, the moon shone as it ever had.

"Did you take her from me because she held my heart?" he whispered. "Are you so jealous?"

"No." The response came almost at once.

A deep pain filled Sugh's chest, as if the tears he'd been unable to shed had filled his interior with their burning salt. It spread up into his throat and lower jaw, but he forced out the next question: "Then why?"

"The day of death comes for all. This one was a matter of sacred mystery beyond even my influence."

Sugh couldn't answer that one. When studying as a priest, he'd learned a similar theology. The goddess could kill or cause someone's death, but she did not govern over all deaths. It had always been a confusing teaching that raised more questions than it answered. And it didn't help how he felt now.

"My heart is broken," he said after a few minutes. "It beats for no one now."

And, he resolved, it never would.

Now

Koland took a deep breath and knocked on the door. Clanless had gone somewhere alone, giving him this one opportunity to make things right. His head ached from the previous night's drinking, but his thoughts could not be clearer.

"Come in," called his daughter's voice from beyond the door. The sound of his daughter's voice, he reminded himself, but not her words. It was not her. He pushed the door open and stepped into the bedroom.

"Ah, Father," Kekeen said from across the bed. She set a vase down on the desk and approached with a smile. "I wondered when we would get to talk."

"I wish to speak with my daughter."

She spread her arms. "Here I am."

"I am not a fool, Zektel." Koland turned and locked the door.

"What are you doing?" she asked, amusement in her voice.

He faced her again. "Neither of us will leave this room so long as you remain within my daughter."

She shook her head with a faint smile. "Or what? What will you do when others come? Will you keep Aldan out?"

"He'll have to break the door down."

She pointed across the room. "Or use that one. Will you barricade it as well?"

Koland seized her wrist. "I am not playing games, blood-wraith. Release my daughter."

"You have no power here, storyteller. You do not control how all this ends." She cocked her head. "In fact, you don't even control any of the major players here. You are less than nothing."

"Take me instead," he offered. "Leave her and take me. I don't control, but I influence. You could do more through me than you can through her."

"No... I don't think so. With Kekeen, I control Aldan, the most important piece in this story."

"Why? Why is he the most important? Because of the Melkute challenge? Or is he still a threat to Suirel?"

"You ask so many questions." She chuckled. "Trying to find the pieces of the story that you still lack. Frustrating, isn't it?"

Koland propelled her back several steps to the bed. He whipped out a piece of rope he'd brought along and swiftly tied her wrist to the bedpost. She watched with a bemused smile and made no protest.

"You may leave this room when you are no longer within my daughter.

I offer myself freely as your way out. I suggest you take that offer."

She tugged on the rope to test its strength. "Do you know how many times Aldan has made this same offer? If I haven't taken him up on it, why would I take you?"

"Why haven't you taken him? You spent years with him before." Koland walked to the adjoining door and examined it.

"Even if I could take him now, it's not the same. This way, I get to have a relationship with him that can lead to… more."

"You know he'll never agree to that." Koland tested the weight of the nearby desk. Its solid wood construction made it heavy enough for his purposes. "Wait." He looked back at Kekeen. "You said 'even if.' If?"

"I don't know what you mean."

He narrowed his eyes. "Yes, you do. Are you unable to enter Aldan again? Why?"

"Oh. That." She took a deep breath and let it out. "I haven't even told him that yet. Since the, uh, encounter in the cave, his blood has… changed." A distant look filled her eyes, and she stared at a corner of the ceiling. "I was going to do it, you know. Give him what he wanted."

Koland took a step closer. "You were?"

"On the road here. One night, while he was sleeping. I looked at him, and… and I wanted to make him happy. So I tried leaving this body and entering his." Her eyes refocused, and she looked down. "It didn't work."

"And it wasn't the wolf pelt?"

"No, he wasn't wearing it that night. His blood has changed. I don't know how or what it means, but I know blood." She looked up at him and smiled. "You do call us blood-wraiths, after all."

Koland considered. Perhaps this change explained Suirel's obsession with Aldan. Why would a god with untold powers worry about one simple arena fighter? "Has Aldan been able to use the Taint since then?"

"You ask the same questions Suirel does. Maybe you're smarter than you look after all." She tugged on the rope again. "Yes, he's been using the Taint. I saw him use it on some Melkute soldiers a few days ago. His eyes glowed and everything."

Koland went back to the desk and pushed it in front of the adjoining door. "I don't know what you think you're going to accomplish here," Kekeen called while he worked. "This isn't going to change my mind."

"I don't have to." Koland straightened up and wiped a few drops of sweat from his forehead. "Because you haven't figured out the most important thing yet."

"Ohhh, enlighten me, dear Father. What's the most important thing?"

"I'm not Aldan, Kekeen's lover." He walked back to face her. "I'm Koland, Kekeen's father."

She shrugged with her taunting smile. "And?"

Koland looked toward the main door. "Aldan, you see, is torn up about you. But he believes there is plenty of time to set you free, somehow. He hates it, but he thinks if he waits long enough, a new solution will present itself. In the meantime, he won't do anything to hurt you."

Her eyebrows rose. "And you would?"

"Absolutely." Koland focused his gaze straight into her eyes. "I'm not as young as Aldan. Nor am I optimistic about our survival over the next few days or weeks. And so, Zektel, you need to believe me when I tell you this." He paused, making sure he had her full attention. "I want my daughter back before I die. And if you tell me that can't happen, I would rather she died here and now than endure under your possession."

They stared at each other, neither speaking. Kekeen's smile faded.

"You're bluffing," she said at last. "You're very good at it. I suppose I should expect that from a storyteller."

"Can you take that chance?"

"Aldan is not going to be happy about you locking me in here."

In the distance, someone shouted. Three or four people ran down the hallway outside, talking as fast as they ran.

Koland drew a long knife from his belt and set it on the bed, out of Kekeen's reach. He pointed to the two doors with each of his hands. "If it appears one of these doors is about to be breached, and my daughter is not restored to me... then I no longer have a daughter. Only a deadly enemy of my people. And I will not hesitate to end her."

"You can't be serious. You wouldn't hurt Kekeen, let alone kill her."

"Is that doubt I hear in your voice, blood-wraith?"

"Humans value their children. I've learned that of your world. They—"

"You mean like Aldan's parents valued him enough to fight the priests who came to take him away?" Koland interrupted.

"They didn't. They—oh. I see what you're trying to say." She shook her head. "Different. Very different. Besides, you have only the one child. Your one, darling daughter. She means everything to you."

"As Ghouk meant everything to the Hawk King? Is that why he grew up so well?"

"Ha." She blinked in disbelief. "You can offer all the negative examples you like, but you're not like them, storyteller. I know that much. I know your relationship with Kekeen."

"Do you? Do you have access to her memories?"

She cocked her head. "Most of them. Why?"

"Then tell me, blood-wraith…" Koland clenched his fist and held it in front of his mouth, eyebrows lowered. He inhaled and tried to control the shaking which threatened to overtake his body. "Tell me what happened to her mother."

"She died when Kekeen was very young, when—" She broke off. "Kekeen isn't very clear on it. The sand cough? Is that what you call it? A type of illness here, isn't it?"

"The sand cough is what I told her when she was little. It's a common disease. People die from it. And so Kekeen accepted that story." Koland paused to let the impact sink it. "But it's only a story. It's not the truth. I've never told her the truth."

Kekeen leaned toward him, pulling on the rope. "Ohhh. You secretive man." She looked up at him with almost hunger in her eyes. "Tell me this truth. The greater the suffering, the more it interests me."

Koland clicked his teeth in disgust. "You thrive on this, don't you?"

"Tell me."

Having told Sonkogh, Koland thought repeating the story would be easier. Yet he found it harder to start. He turned away from Kekeen's eyes, reminding himself yet again it wasn't her. He swallowed and began:

"Fifteen years ago, my wife and I settled in a small city in the South, near Conchaga. She wanted to settle down for a while, to raise our… daughter in a single place, rather than the traveling of a storyteller. But the Hawk King did something and the people were outraged." He repeated the facts without elaborating. "The details don't matter any more. Hawk King did bad. People were foolish. Stupid, even."

He glanced back and saw Kekeen testing the rope again. "I know how to tie a knot. You won't pull it free."

She shrugged. "Can't help trying."

"The elders didn't listen to me back then," he went on, facing away again. "Their concerns were justified, but to rebel against the Hawk King when you're all alone? Foolish. His soldiers came to deal with it, as they always did.

"I kept us away from the fighting. But my wife…" He couldn't help glancing back at Kekeen. She looked so much like her mother. "Like the woman you've taken, her heart was too good." He clenched his fist again to control himself. "She tried to help someone. I didn't notice she'd gone until it was too late."

"Did the soldiers just storm into the city and start killing everyone?" Kekeen asked.

"The details are not important." Koland tapped his fist against his beard. "I know that's a strange thing for a storyteller to say, but it's true. None of it matters. All that matters is that my wife was struck in the head by one of the Hawk King's soldiers." He paused. "Struck by a mace."

"She died from a mace rather than an illness. I don't see—"

"No! She lived!" He paused to contain himself. "She lived. That is, her body lived. Her soul left it. She wasn't there any more."

"You realize, of course, that as you tell me this, your daughter is also hearing it for the first time?"

"I know." He turned back and let the anguish fill his eyes. "Kekeen, I am sorry for not telling you this before. But the pain was mine to bear. I sent you to stay with friends while I tended your mother. It was the darkest time of my life."

Someone shouted something nearby. He thought the voice mentioned Clanless.

"I had no hope." He stopped and took a few steps away to lean against the wall. "And I have no hope now, do I?"

Kekeen let out a long sigh. "I don't know if you're telling the truth now, or making up a story to convince me of your commitment. Are you going to tell me that you killed her? And because you could do that then, you can do it again to your daughter? Because—"

"No!" Koland spun around and glared at her. "I didn't kill her. I didn't do anything! I waited. I held on to hope, hope that was useless, worthless. It destroyed me. I will not endure that again!" He strode back to the bed and grabbed up the knife. "So when I tell you that I will kill the body you inhabit before I will let you keep it, you should believe me."

"Then do it," she whispered, staring up at him. "Kill her. You say your wife's death destroyed you? What will this do? You think you can forgive yourself? You think Clanless will forgive you? Kekeen already asked him to kill her, and he wouldn't do it. Ironic, isn't it? The arena killer values life more than either of you."

"Nnnnaarrgh!" He slammed the knife into the opposite bedpost and left it quivering. He turned away, shoulders shaking.

"To think I finally understand you." Her voice remained calm. "Ever since Aldan heard you speak in that eating house in Rochinbal, I've wondered. You weave words to entertain, to amuse, to enlighten. But you don't do it for them, do you? You speak stories to hide your own hurts. You even joined a rebellion because of it, didn't you? Because of your wife." She gave a short laugh. "You rail against Suirel for having no respect for life. Yet here you stand ready to end your own daughter's."

He didn't answer. He'd pushed himself to the limit, unsure if he could do what he said he could. Even now, he didn't know. He could turn, take the knife again, and… strike down his daughter. No. He couldn't.

"This is going to hurt, I suppose." She sounded resigned.

"No. I'm not going to—"

Kekeen screamed. Koland whirled to see her throw herself across the bed, further than she should have been able. He lunged back toward her. She snatched the knife from the bed post. Koland grabbed, but she eluded him, twisted, and plunged the blade into his chest.

She pulled it free as he staggered back. He stared at the blood gushing from the wound. It felt as though he'd been punched at first, but then the pain erupted throughout his chest. He fell to his knees and tried to stop the bleeding. His hands wouldn't stay in place. None of his limbs would obey his thoughts.

"Oooh, Aldan was not joking about this. Dislocating a shoulder is painful." Kekeen sawed the rope holding her wrist.

Koland collapsed and rolled on to his back. From the floor, he watched his daughter free herself. She gave another short cry of pain when her arm flopped to her side. Then she looked down at him. His vision darkened.

"Now what should I do?" she mused. "If I call for the priests, and they get here in time, this starts up all over again." She knelt next to him, still holding the knife. "But if you die, I need a reason. Perhaps you can help me with one more story… storyteller."

22

THE TUNNEL

Clanless glanced at Salkhi and tried not to think too hard about the last time he'd been at this house. It had been raining then too, but he'd never made it inside the house. He'd followed the Lord down the street and…

"You both must be chilled to the bone!" Lady Ghayaktal hurried into the living area and urged them toward the enormous fireplace, ignoring Salkhi completely. "Warm yourselves. It's an honor to have two of the Dohor in my home! I wish I had known you were coming. My daughter Tavuu is going to be bitterly disappointed she missed you!"

Lord Ghayaktal himself appeared in the doorway. "That's enough, dear. I suspect these men are not here for a social call."

"We need access to the tunnel below your house," Clanless said, taking a step in his direction. "We need to get into the arena."

The Lord rubbed his beard. "There is no tunnel below my house. I'm afraid you've been misinformed."

Salkhi stepped forward, rainwater dripping from her clothes. "Oh, come now. You were always there when we went through it. You came along more times than not."

He narrowed his eyes at her. "I… do not know you, young woman." He looked to the men. "Does she belong to one of you?"

"She belongs to no one," Clanless said. "You would do well to be more polite."

"I don't understand," Lady Ghayaktal said, looking from one to the other. "Husband, what—"

"The tunnel that leads to the arena," Sugh interrupted from his spot by the fire. "The one the Pasque House girls used all the time."

The Lady glared at Salkhi. "Is that who you are? One of those women? How dare you enter my house!"

"Definitely not my first time here," Salkhi said calmly.

"This is pointless." Clanless pointed at the Lord. "You will let us use the tunnel to reach the arena."

"I'm told by the General that the arena is sealed off for good reason."

"The General lies."

"That's a… bold accusation for someone who's only just returned to the city." He shook his head. "Young man, until a few months ago, you were a slave. As such, I can forgive breaches of protocol, up to a point. Regardless, you are in no position to make demands of a Lord of the city. I must respectfully ask you and your whore to leave my house."

"You will let us into the tunnel," Clanless said. "Or I will refuse the Melkute challenge."

Lady Ghayaktal gasped and put a hand over her mouth.

"That's preposterous," the Lord responded. "Why would you do such a thing?" He gestured to the side, and a boy ran up expectantly. "I will send this one to General Ghan. If he approves of your actions, then I will agree."

Clanless stepped closer and said in a much quieter voice, "You will not do that. You will not tell anyone. You will let us into the tunnel, or I will tell your wife exactly why your arm was broken a year ago."

Salkhi's sudden intake of breath filled the silence that followed. She had heard him, at least.

Lord Ghayktal froze. With a snap of his fingers, he dismissed the boy. "Very well," he said aloud. "I will allow it, but I will not be responsible for the consequences."

"What did he say?" his wife asked, hurrying across the room.

"It matters not, my love. I'll show these men the way, and then we can forget this entire incident happened."

"I'd like to forget it already," Sugh muttered. He left the fire with some reluctance.

Clanless paused for a moment. "Salkhi, I think you'd better come with us," he whispered. "I don't trust either one of them."

She shivered. "I think you're right."

Lord Ghayaktal led the way back into the rain, across the courtyard, and down a stair that led into a basement storage chamber. At the far side, barely visible in the weak light, stood a heavy wooden door with iron fittings. The Lord produced a key, unlocked the door, and pulled it open. He gestured at the dark opening. "There you go."

"We'll need a light," Sugh pointed out.

Lord Ghayaktal muttered some kind of curse involving the goddess. He stormed back up the steps. While they waited, Clanless stepped forward and peered into the tunnel. He couldn't make out much of anything.

"Do you think anyone besides Pasque House uses this?"

"I don't know," Salkhi said. "Maybe the Lord needs a shortcut now and then?"

"It's possible it hasn't been used since my fight with Daviland."

"What will we do when we reach the other end?" Sugh asked.

"Find out what Bain is up to and stop him."

"Ah. Good to know we have a plan."

"Bain?" Salkhi rubbed her arms. "He's involved in this too?"

"It's a long story."

"You keep saying that." She stepped closer to him. "And what was that about breaking his arm? Did you mean what I think you meant?"

"It was a long time ago." He gave her a weak smile. "And you know why I did it."

Lord Ghayaktal returned at last, carrying an oil lantern. He shoved it into Sugh's hands. "Be off. I want no more part of this."

"Your part is done," Clanless said. "Thank you."

The Lord pointed at him, finger shaking. "When this is all over, there will be consequences. I will not forget."

Clanless met his eyes. "I have not forgotten why your arm was broken. And I never will."

The nobleman growled and hurried back to the stairs. Sugh shook his head and stepped into the tunnel. Clanless and Salkhi followed.

The tunnel stretched ahead of them into the darkness. The walls, made of bricks, curved upward into a narrow arch. It was not quite wide enough for the two big men to walk side-by-side. "This construction style is very old," Sugh said.

"You're an architect now?"

"In my... younger days, I took an interest in construction, before I found my calling." He tapped the brick wall with his axe. "These kind of bricks have not been used in hundreds of years."

Salkhi touched one of the bricks. "I never knew that. I always assumed they'd built this for the women of Pasque House."

"Perhaps Lord Ghayaktal's ancestor built it for some other reason," Sugh said. "I wonder if the Hawk King was involved."

"It doesn't matter now," Clanless said. "Let's get moving."

They had not gone far when a creak and a resounding boom echoed behind them. All three spun around to see the door slammed shut. Lord Ghayaktal must have returned.

"No turning back now." Clanless turned back toward the darkness.

Sugh waved his axe. "We could cut it down, given enough time."

"We're leaving through the arena."

"As you say."

They walked on. Somewhere in the distance, Clanless heard water dripping. Here and there, a brick lay broken on the floor where it had fallen, shoved out by a root or the gradual movements of the earth itself. A dank, musky odor filled the air, though they saw no plant life. In fact, the only sign of life they saw were a few bugs that skittered across the floor just out of range of the light. Salkhi moved to his side and took hold of his arm. He didn't pull away.

"It seems longer than our walk down the street." The loudness of his voice surprised Clanless.

"I think we are going in a straight line," Sugh said. He turned the lantern back and forth. "It is hard to tell for sure."

"It always seems longer," Salkhi confirmed. "We're almost there."

A moment later, they came to an intersection. A large stone formed the triangular floor bordering the three directions. "The arena will be on the right, yes?" Sugh held the light in that direction.

"Yes," Salkhi said. She pointed to the left. "That one leads to the palace."

"Then we move on." Sugh plunged into the passage to the right.

They had walked about a minute longer when a dim light appeared ahead. As they drew near, they saw something sitting in the middle of the floor, blocking part of the way. The light turned out to be a metal grating in the ceiling, through which they could make out the interior of a barren room.

"A barrel?" Clanless circled the object on the floor.

"That wasn't here the last time," Salkhi said.

"It is full of…" Sugh sniffed the air. "Blood? How strange."

Clanless tried to peer up through the grating. "Who would store a barrel of blood down here? And why?"

Sugh dipped a finger into the blood and held it up to the light. "It does not appear very old. Someone put this here recently, I think."

"Then maybe Bain knows about this." Clanless gripped the moonblade with both hands. "Be on your guard."

"Always." Sugh moved past the barrel and continued on. About twenty or thirty feet later, they found another grating in the ceiling. Water dripped slowly from one corner.

"Uh-oh." Sugh lowered the lantern to examine the floor.

"What is it?"

"Sand. From the arena floor."

"Did it fall down through that grate?"

"No." Sugh pointed ahead with his axe. "There is more of it ahead."

They walked a few more feet. The sand on the floor increased, covering the entire surface of the tunnel's floor. And then the level rose until it filled the entire place, blocking their way. Someone had poured it in from the exit, however far ahead it might be.

"We cannot get through here unless we dig," Sugh said. He handed the lantern to Salkhi and tapped the back of his axe against the pile of sand.

Clanless scooped at it with his moonblade. "Maybe we should. How deep can it be?"

Salkhi frowned in the low light. "I don't think it's very far, but I'm not sure. It's been a long time."

A low chuckle came from behind them. Both men whirled, but saw no one. Salkhi lifted the lantern, eyes wide.

"My friends." An all-too-familiar voice descended from the grating they'd passed. "I'm afraid we will not be reunited through this way."

"Bain." Clanless scrambled down from the sand and glared up at the grating.

A shadowy figure stood above. "Bain is no more, Aldan. You know this. I am Suirel." He chuckled again. "Although the Melkute are now calling me Sama El. I might keep that one. It means 'blind god' in their language. Quite amusing."

"Why are you here?" Clanless demanded. "What are you trying to do?"

"Who is that with you? A girl? Why, Aldan. What would Kekeen think?"

"What's wrong with him?" Salkhi whispered. "He thinks he's the chaos moon now?"

"Not the moon. The god."

"A god? I always thought he was arrogant but... yikes."

"Ohhh, I know who you are," the figure said. "So Aldan sought out his former whore, did he? Why is that? Is one woman not enough for you?"

"Leave her out of this!" Clanless snarled. "What do you want, Suirel?"

"Sugh," the figure called instead. "You spent some time with the priests of the mines, did you not?"

"We did. They were good people. Did you kill them too?"

"I learned much from them. Fascinating. Truly fascinating their devotion to their craft."

"You want me to fight in this challenge," Clanless said. "Why? To keep me from stopping you here?"

"The priests have spent lifetimes studying your blood-magic," Suirel went on. "They've experimented with the blood of every one of your clans, exploring different combinations and uses. They've done this for generations."

"Suirel!" Clanless shouted. "Why won't you fight me directly?"

"The priests learned so many new things, some of which your priests here, even the ridiculous Ghamba Lam, have never learned."

Clanless started to shout something else, but Sugh put a hand on his shoulder. "He wants to tell us something," he said quietly.

"For example," Suirel said, "did you know that burning different types of blood can sometimes produce different types of smoke?"

"I'll burn his blood," Clanless muttered.

"The one I found most fascinating was when you mix together the blood of Clan Kurav and Clan Dendsu. Individually, their powers are healing and warmth. But when burned together…"

In the distance, something burning dropped from the ceiling. A splash followed, and then the flame grew larger. Someone had thrown fire into the barrel of blood in the tunnel.

"Together, they produce a most deadly smoke," Suirel said. "When inhaled, it leads to corruption of the lungs and then the heart. Death follows soon after."

A slab of rock fell over the grate, cutting off the light and air from above. Suirel's final words came muffled and distant: "Farewell, Clanless."

Deep, dark red smoke billowed out from the burning barrel. "Run!" Clanless sucked in a deep breath and held it. Sugh took off without waiting. Salkhi chased after him.

As they passed the barrel, Clanless paused long enough to hack a hole in its side. Blood poured out onto the tunnel floor, but the fire kept burning. Whatever they'd dropped into it wouldn't go out easy. Despite his best efforts, he inhaled a bit of the smoke through his nose. The odor of cooking meat flooded his senses. It smelled almost pleasant, making him want to take another sniff.

Sugh grabbed his arm and yanked him on. Together, they all sprinted down the tunnel until they reached the intersection. None of them could hold their breath any longer. They gasped for more air. This time, Clanless knew they'd inhaled more of the smoke. A burning spread into his chest.

Salkhi trembled and dropped the lantern. Clanless gestured for her to leave it and move on. He pushed at Sugh, and they stumbled down the tunnel to the right, leading toward the palace.

Within moments of turning the corner, they lost almost all remaining light. The tunnel seemed far longer than it should be. The darkness kept them from moving fast. Even so, Sugh tripped over some fallen bricks. Clanless struggled to help him up, conscious that either man might easily cut the other with their blades. Even if he'd been willing to part with the moonblade, he knew he might need it to get out.

At last, they reached the end of the tunnel. Salkhi searched the door with her hands. Clanless dropped the moonblade for a minute and joined her, expecting to find some kind of handle.

"The latch is gone!" Salkhi exclaimed.

"Air is… safe here?" Sugh gasped.

"For the moment. Try not to breathe much." Clanless hammered against the door with his fist. He struck wood, but he couldn't tell anything else about it. No latch, no handle, no banding. "I'll chop through it," he said, fumbling around to find the moonblade again.

Sugh's hand sought out and grabbed his shoulder. "Let me go first," he said. "I feel the poison within me, Clanless. I will chop until I can't. And then you must take over."

"All right." Clanless caught Salkhi's hand and led her back several feet. "Go!" He glanced back down the tunnel. In his imagination, he saw the dark red smoke pouring toward them.

A grunt and a heavy thunk indicated Sugh's first axe blow. Clanless watched in his mind's eye as his friend repeated the action over and over. Every blow took far too long. Salkhi whimpered. Every time Clanless was forced to take another breath, he thought he could smell the smoke again.

…Until the moment he did smell it. In that same moment, Sugh coughed and fell. Clanless ducked his head down low and took another deep breath. He set the moonblade aside, took hold of Sugh, and pulled him out of the way. Salkhi tried to help, but couldn't contribute much. Clanless felt around until he found Sugh's axe still embedded in the door. As a means to their exit, it was a better weapon than the moonblade. He took hold and yanked it out of the wood. A sliver of light burst through. Escape was in sight!

Clanless heaved and smashed the axe into the same spot. The hole widened, letting in more light… which revealed the swirling smokiness of the tunnel's air. He yanked the axe free and slammed it in again. Three more blows widened the hole, but nowhere close enough to get through. His lungs ached from holding his breath, but to inhale now would kill him faster.

He dropped to his knees and stuck his face into the hole. He caught a brief view of a palace hall, but nothing more. He sucked air into his lungs, hoping it came only from the other side. Holding it again, he got back up and resumed his axe work.

Despite his efforts, some of the poison worked within him. The burning he'd experienced earlier grew, competing with the ache from lack of air. He could feel it spreading within his chest.

One more blow broke a major piece of the door free. Clanless dropped the axe, ducked his head, and clambered through the opening. Still holding his breath, he turned around and reached back for the others. His vision swam, threatening unconsciousness. He found Salkhi first and dragged her through. Somewhere, he heard a shout.

He reached back and found Sugh's arm. He took hold of it and the shoulder and hauled the big man through the hole. Clanless turned his head away and sucked in air, trying to only take a little. But his lungs were too long denied. Air poured down his throat, not all of it clear. He coughed and fell, slipping on his own sweat. He pulled at Sugh and Salkhi, dragging them slowly down the palace hall. The red smoke drifted in behind them.

Clanless's mind reeled. The hall tilted, making it almost impossible to keep moving. The smoke appeared to move like a living thing, branching out into tentacles that reached for him and the other two from every direction.

More shouts. Pounding feet. Coughs and curses. Hands seized all three of them, pulling them away, away from the deadly smoke.

His head rolled back. His eyes focused on the sunlight from a nearby window. It grew brighter and brighter in his vision until it became… everything.

REPERCUSSIONS

The light… the light was familiar, somehow. Had he been here before? Clanless squinted to let his eyes adjust to the brightness. Was it the moon? Goddess? Was he dead?

Except the light filled with movement. His eyes couldn't quite grasp the details of motion around him. Figures moved through the brightness, some brighter than the rest of the light, while others seemed to suck the light into themselves yet never grow any brighter.

He blinked several times, and his focus improved. He saw himself lying on the ground. One of the darker figures stood above him and appeared to raise something. His mind could not grasp what he saw and redefined it into a sword, descending toward him.

One of the brighter figures intervened, colliding with the threatening figure and carrying it away. Clanless stood, trembling. All round him, he realized these figures were fighting. Light versus dark. A conflict beyond his comprehension.

As he turned in a circle, his vision expanded. Somewhere nearby, he saw a small smoke-like figure with a reddish tint. It hovered alone, isolated from the others. It felt more familiar than anything else he'd seen.

The largest figure he'd seen thus far drew his attention. This one sucked in more light than all the others, embodying darkness more than any. A crimson slash, the most color Clanless had seen, cut across the dark figure's face. It lifted hands, pointing and directing others. Both the dark figures he'd seen before and more of the reddish smoke-figures swirled around him, following his orders. It must be Suirel.

Clanless turned and saw another figure, equal to Suirel, standing outside the city, hands on his hips. He threw back his head as if laughing. Was this one of the Melkute gods?

He tried to take a step in that direction, hoping to see better. But when he did, he found himself drifting into the air. He turned in a slow circle, rising upward. He lifted his eyes and saw the moon, shining brighter than all else. It called to him. He raised a hand, reaching, reaching toward the shining orb that had dominated his upward view for his whole life.

Something caught hold of him from behind.

"Not yet, Aldan. It is not your time."

He tried to turn, caught a glimpse of golden eyes, and then…

Darkness.

"Clanless! Clanless!"

He jerked awake, gasping. For a brief moment, he thought he was in the arena with the crowd chanting his name. His vision wavered and focused on Nukai's face looking down at him.

"You're all right, Clanless." The older man patted him on the shoulder. "But I need your help, or your friend dies."

"How? What?" He struggled to pull himself up on an elbow while he looked about. How had he gotten here? A hall in the Hawk King's palace? At the far end, a trickle of red smoke puffed out of a broken door. It all rushed back on him. The tunnel, Bain, the trap, Salkhi, Sugh!

He rolled over to find Salkhi pushing herself into a seated position by the wall. She put a hand to her head, but didn't seem to be in great distress. Nukai bent over, listening to Sugh's chest. The big man lay still. "The smoke," Clanless croaked. His throat ached, but he could breathe. He coughed, adding to the pain. But at least his chest didn't burn like before.

"You didn't inhale enough of it, or else your blood is more resistant," Nukai said. He lifted his head. "Sugh here is not in good shape, though. You'll have to save him."

"How?" Clanless got up onto his knees. "What can I do? We need a priest and, and healing-blood."

Nukai grabbed his wrist. "No. We don't. It would do no good. The blood-magic heals injuries, but it can't help blood itself. Only you can."

"I don't understand."

Salkhi moaned. Clanless looked at her, but Nukai yanked him back.

"She will be fine. Focus here."

"What?"

Nukai released him and pulled out a small knife. "The poison works on blood itself. You inhale it, it goes into the lungs, and then into your bloodstream from there. That's what's happened to him. It's shutting down his heart now. He hasn't got long."

"But—"

Nukai sliced a quick cut on Sugh's forearm. Blood flowed. "The Taint. It burns, but it purifies. If you can guide it through his blood fast enough, it should burn the poison out before it can kill him."

Clanless's mouth dropped. "I, I don't know how to guide it. I just use it."

Nukai met his eyes. "Listen to me. He's dead in moments if you don't do anything. You've used your power for good before; do it again!"

Of course. The time he'd kept Qara warm and alive in the snow. He didn't remember telling Nukai about that. But he could try something similar, couldn't he? "It's going to hurt him. A lot."

"Better than dying! Hurry, Clanless!"

He closed his eyes and reached out his hand. As he'd done with Qara, he let the Taint begin with gentleness, flowing into the open wound on Sugh's arm. It pulled against him, wanting to rip through the body as he always did, but he held it back. His eyes burned behind the lids. Sugh moaned. Clanless let the Taint become a gradual flow, working up Sugh's arm and into his chest. From there, he let it go in every direction he found but focused most of it into the area of the chest where he understood the heart to be.

Other voices erupted around him, but he ignored them. He had to concentrate, focus, maintain control.

Sugh screamed in a ragged voice much unlike his own.

"Keep going," Nukai whispered.

Clanless's hand shook. A tremble ran through his own chest. It was so hard. The power still wanted to erupt, but he had to hold it and direct it. He pushed it down Sugh's other arm and his legs and then up into his head. His friend writhed on the floor, crying out. But at least he breathed! He sucked clean air into his throat over and over in between his vocalized agony.

The power of the Taint faded at last, and Clanless let the last trickle of it go. Sugh gave one last cry, jerked about, and relaxed. His breathing shook and stabilized. He lay still again, his chest rising and falling in a steady rhythm. Clanless collapsed, exhausted again, and coughed a few times. A small hand touched his shoulder. Salkhi?

"Well done, lad," Nukai said. "Well done." He sat back against the wall, looking exhausted himself. Three other palace attendants stood around them, wide-eyed and confused. "We'll be all right now," Nukai told them. "We'll be all right."

Clanless took his own deep breaths. "Salkhi. What about you?" She knelt on the floor beside him, hand still on his shoulder.

"I… I'll live."

He looked back down the hall to the broken door. He'd have to retrieve his moonblade and Sugh's axe once the smoke fully dissipated. And then what? Suirel didn't want him to know what was happening in the arena and was going to elaborate means to prevent it.

Which only made him want to find out even more.

((((●))))

"I don't understand any of this. What is happening with Bain?" Salkhi complained.

Clanless got to his feet and put out his hand. "Can you walk?"

She took his hand and rose to her feet, wavering a little. "I think so."

"If you can come with me, I'll show you."

In the time it took them to reach the tower stairs, Clanless felt the effects of the gas fading. Both he and Salkhi gained strength in their walking as they went. Even so, Salkhi hesitated before starting up the steps. Clanless wanted to ascend the stairs as fast as he could, but he moved slow for her sake. It took them only moments to reach the windows of the south tower. Clanless found the best angle and pointed to the arena.

Suirel's men were busy. Some of them tossed wooden benches from the stands down into the sand. Others dragged those benches toward the middle where they were torn apart. Still others took the parts and… they were building something.

"What are they doing?" Salkhi asked. "This doesn't help at all."

Clanless squinted, trying to figure it out. They'd built two… towers? Each stood about fifteen feet tall, but only as rough frames with platforms on which to stand. No walls or roof. In fact, it looked as if they were still going higher. A couple of long strips connected the two towers, though they served no obvious purpose.

Other workers continued to unload the crystal shards from the wagons, piling them up in multiple places, sorting them in a way he couldn't make out. None of it made any sense.

"I don't know for certain, but… it's not good," Clanless said. "Bain is possessed by Suirel, the god of chaos. He's the one who brought the Melkute army here. And now he's doing something else." He coughed.

Salkhi shivered and hugged herself. "This is all so crazy. Everything fell apart when the Hawk King died."

Clanless realized she was still wet and shaking. "I'm sorry. I shouldn't have dragged you up here. Or into any of this." He put his arms around her. She leaned into him but kept shivering.

"Maybe. I insisted on taking you to the tunnel. I thought it would be fun to tease Lord Ghayaktal. I never expected… any of this."

"Clanless?" Another voice intruded.

He turned with a scowl, but softened when he saw Yesun scramble up the stairs. "What is it?"

"Uh, uh." The young man stumbled a bit and swallowed, eyes wide at the sight of Salkhi. "There's been an, um, incident. With your, uh, woman and her father."

Clanless released Salkhi. "Yesun, this is my friend. Can you make sure she is warm and dry and, uh, anything else she needs?"

The attendant nodded.

"Go," Salkhi said. "See to Kekeen. I'll be all right."

Clanless took three steps before she called again, "Clanless!"

He turned back.

Salkhi tried to smile. "You… will save us, won't you?"

"I will do everything I can," he promised.

☾☾☾☾●☽☽☽☽

Clanless burst into the bedroom and stopped short. Koland lay on the bed, blood everywhere, with two priests bent over him. Kekeen stood off to the side, being attended to by two more priests. More blood stained the floor at the end of the bed.

"What's happened?"

"Aldan!" Kekeen cried. For the briefest of moments, she looked like herself again, as she had the night before. And then a change swept over her face. She blinked and smiled. "About time you got here."

Clanless caught one of the priests by the shoulder. "Are they all right? What happened?"

The priest scowled at him. "She is fine. A shoulder that needed fixing. The man, however…"

One of the priests by the bed straightened. "We got to him just in time," he announced. "Council member Koland will live."

"What happened?" Clanless repeated for the third time, adding vehemency to his tone.

"We were attacked," Kekeen answered. "One of Suirel's cult members, apparently. You know they were gathering down below this palace? I rescued my father from them weeks ago, with the help of your old trainer." She rubbed her wrist. "He tied me to the bed there. When Father intervened, he stabbed him." She pointed to a blood-soaked knife lying on the bed. "I screamed my head off, and he ran away."

Clanless stepped near the bed and checked on Koland. His chest rose and fell with easy breathing. Despite the blood everywhere, he appeared all right. "Thank you, priests. I cannot possibly repay you for saving them."

The priest by the bed bowed. "We but do the will of the goddess. Moon's stability to you, clanless one."

He nodded in return, taken aback. No priest had ever treated him so polite. The scowl on the other one's face was much more normal. Either the Ghamba Lam had told them to be nicer, or… like everyone else, they were hoping he would save the city.

The priests gathered their things and left, promising to send servants to clean the room and replaced the ruined bedclothes. Clanless waited until he shut the door before turning on Kekeen. "What really happened?"

She put a hand to her chest. "I just told you!"

"Why would a cultist come after you? You're on their side!"

"And how would they know that? He wouldn't believe me, anyway." She pulled up the nearby chair and sat down. "Forgive me. The priests fixed my shoulder, but magic won't solve the exhaustion that comes from such an experience."

"You could have left Kekeen and possessed the cultist," Clanless grumbled. "That would have solved everything."

"It's not that easy, you know." Her eyes darted to Koland. "Switching to another body and then back is quite a strain."

"If there really was a cultist." Clanless folded his arms. "I'll get the truth from Koland when he wakes up."

She shrugged and winced. "You're welcome to. He won't contradict me."

"We'll see." He leaned against the wall, ready to wait as long as it took. "Your story makes no sense."

"Neither do half the things that have happened to you in your life."

He couldn't argue with that.

"Where have you been, anyway?" she asked. "If you'd been close, this wouldn't have happened."

Clanless shifted and glanced at the door. "I tried getting into the arena. Bain was ready for us."

"Us? Where's Sugh?"

"He'll be all right." He looked at the bed. "Like your father."

Strange that two of the only men he trusted had both nearly died in the past hour, and in completely unrelated ways. Or was it? Maybe Suirel sent the cultist to attack Koland as another distraction for him, and the timing didn't quite work—if there had been a cultist, which he still doubted. If one had been here, why stab Koland and leave Kekeen alone? What purpose could it serve?

He turned away and coughed hard. This one had been building for a while.

"That doesn't sound right," Kekeen said. "Are you well?"

"I breathed some poison. It's going away."

"Sounds like a… story." Koland's soft voice came from the bed.

Kekeen stood. She and Clanless moved next to the bed from opposite sides.

"Koland. What happened here?"

The storyteller blinked a few times. He felt for his chest and found the remains of his shirt torn and bloody. His eyes darted around as his brows knitted. "I don't…"

"We were attacked," Kekeen said. "Remember?"

"No. I…" He closed his eyes. "I was coming here, to this room. That's the last thing I remember."

"You were stabbed, man!" Clanless exclaimed. "You don't remember that?"

Again, Koland's hand felt for his own chest. "No. I… don't remember anything. I should get up." He started to move.

"You rest a bit." Kekeen put her own hand on his. "Whether you remember it or not, you almost died. Give yourself time to recover."

"She's right," Clanless said. "Rest. We'll talk more later. I'm… thankful you lived." He nodded to Kekeen and left the room.

Out in the hall, he stopped and leaned against the wall. The morning's exertions had taken a toll. After only a moment, he bent over and put his hands on his knees to hold himself up. He coughed again. If this kept up, he'd become like Hagh.

Hagh. He hadn't thought of him in a long time. Zektel had killed him when she'd been possessing Daviland. He couldn't forget that. Yet if she hadn't hesitated to kill Hagh, why hadn't she killed Koland? Even if her story about the cultist were true, she could have delayed things long enough for Koland to die. She'd let him live. Why? Did Kekeen exert some control somehow? He hoped that was the case.

He needed help with this. Spiritual help. And that meant talking with the man who'd destroyed his whole life at the very beginning.

A SPIRITUAL PROBLEM

"This is your room." The guide, a young woman scarcely old enough to have such a job, turned in a circle. "Does it meet with your approval?"

Sugh looked around, mouth agape. The room was three times the size of his chamber at Baduhan's arena. "It is too much," he managed to say. The bed was larger than any he'd ever slept on. He also had his own table and chairs; even his favorite axe leaned against the wall. They trusted him with it in here?

The guide smiled and tossed back her long, sable hair. "I am Qara of clan Dalbai. The Hawk King takes care of his own. You'll see. There are many other… perquisites of serving the Hawk King this close."

"I can only imagine." Sugh shook his head, marveling at the circumstances that had brought him here.

After Chabi's death, Baduhan had given him harder and harder battles every week. He'd acted as though he didn't care about his daughter's death, but his actions made it clear he wanted Sugh dead as well. But Sugh defied the odds, triumphing over each challenge. Six weeks later, the Hawk King himself arrived, witnessed Sugh's epic battle against eight opponents, and bought his bloodbond on the spot.

"Ah, I am Sugh of clan Ghamkiin," he said, suddenly feeling embarrassed.

"Yes, I know." Her smile grew. "It is my honor to serve the Hawk King by attending to the needs of the Dohor. Every one of their needs, whatever they may be."

"Every... need?"

"Every one."

Sugh looked away, trying not to think of the obvious implications. He'd continued to enjoy the female visits to his chamber, but he could never form a relationship with them. But if this girl lived here... No. He couldn't do it. Not again.

"Shall I give you a tour of the rest of the facility?" Qara asked.

"I am... tired from my journey," he said. "Perhaps tomorrow."

"Of course." Her smile faded. "Shall I have some dinner sent to your room then? I assume you haven't had time to eat yet."

"Uh, that would be amazing. Thank you."

"The Dohor generally eat in the dining hall. I'm usually there myself, in case they need anything." Qara headed for the door. "Should you need more, you can send an attendant to find me. Or...." She paused and glanced back. "My room is the last door to the right, near the exit. You're welcome to come find me there... at any time."

"Thank you," he said again. When she had gone, Sugh fell onto the bed and groaned.

"Goddess, this is a wonderful place. Thank you."

She did not answer, but he didn't expect one.

"Perhaps I will continue to live a bit longer." He looked toward the door where Qara had left. "Perhaps..."

Now

Koland massaged his forehead with his thumbs. "This may be the most frustrating thing I've ever experienced."

Sonkogh poured a mug of zokin and passed it across the table. "I'm afraid I don't understand." He glanced around the eating-house. Only two other customers sat at a table on the far side of the room. "You can speak freely here. No one will hear."

"I was going to Kekeen's room. I was going to confront the blood-wraith and demand it leave her." Koland ignored the drink and held out his hands to stare at them. "And then I don't remember anything until I woke up."

"Memory loss after trauma is not unheard of," Sonkogh pointed out.

"Trauma." Koland put a hand on his chest. "They said I was stabbed. By a knife that I brought with me. Something is not right about the whole thing."

"It wouldn't be the first time someone was injured by their own weapon. Whatever would possess you to carry a dishonorable weapon like that, anyway?"

Koland chuckled and took a sip of the zokin. "I think we're far beyond questions of honor any more, old friend, at least as it relates to blood. Many of the old ways will be falling away from us." He looked in the direction of the city walls. "Assuming the Sar Empire survives this present crisis, of course."

Sonkogh looked down and swirled the liquid around in his cup. "Have you ever thought maybe the Empire doesn't deserve to survive? That perhaps we've brought all this on ourselves?"

"It's certainly possible, but unless the goddess herself tells me otherwise, I will continue to fight for our people. I will not see this city fall if I can prevent it in any way."

"When you speak like that, I can almost believe it myself." Sonkogh sighed. "If only Daviland were here. The old Daviland, I mean. He would have this entire city fired up and ready to resist the Melkute to a man."

"I fear he is lost to us for good. But in his absence, we must do our part." Koland pushed the mug to the side and leaned closer. "For now, the assault on the city has paused. General Ghan negotiates with them over this champion fight. Now, should Clanless fight and win this battle, perhaps the Melkute will leave us be. Or perhaps not. I cannot say. Should he fight and lose… we have no other strategy upon which to fall. The assault on the city walls will begin in earnest, I fear."

"I've been quietly moving as many people into the upper city as I can," Sonkogh said. "And reminding everyone else that they should be ready to flee that way themselves if the time comes."

Koland nodded. "If the outer walls are breached, the upper city will be our last defense. Those walls are just as thick, if not thicker. And it will take a good deal of time for them to be able to assault it."

"What good does that do us? We have no hope of help from other quarters."

"I don't know. But I will fight for our lives to the very end. And as long as we live, there is still hope."

Sonkogh snorted. "Look, here you are speaking of hope after all you told me yesterday. You amaze me, my friend."

Koland paused. "I… did, didn't I? Curious how it comes and goes."

Sonkogh drained his cup and poured some more. The two friends sat in silence for several minutes.

The door opened, and a young man entered. He glanced around the room, then came straight toward their table.

"Ah, let me guess," Sonkogh said. "We are summoned to the council."

The messenger bowed. "My lords. The council is gathering. Your presence is urgently requested."

Koland took a deep breath. "Let's see if anything new has come from the General's negotiations." He grabbed the mug and took a quick drink. "At the very least, we've gained time." He grinned at Sonkogh. "And time is hope."

((((●))))

Getting in to see the Ghamba Lam proved more complicated than he'd anticipated. The priests within the palace claimed no knowledge of his whereabouts. Clanless went next to the nearest and largest temple. Several more priests rebuffed him, either claiming ignorance or outright refusing to speak with the "abomination."

After raising more of a commotion, Clanless finally drew the attention he wanted. Visitors to the temple recognized him and gathered around. Many people had come to the temple seeking aid from the goddess for the city. Seeing Clanless there convinced some their prayers had been answered. The crowd grew larger and louder. He stood unmoved in the midst of it, waiting.

A Daghilch appeared and pulled him aside. "The Ghamba Lam is unavailable," he explained. "He is in the middle of a spiritual retreat, entreating the goddess for us all."

"Either I get an audience with him," Clanless said slowly, "or perhaps I will be 'unavailable' when I am asked to fight for this city. Maybe I need a spiritual retreat too."

The Daghilch sputtered. "You would threaten the safety of everyone over this?"

"If I am to fight for all the city, shouldn't I first have the blessing of the spiritual leader of the city? How am I to fight against the Melkute and their god without the aid of our goddess? Why would you deny me this?"

The Daghilch looked around at the crowd and let out an exasperated groan. "Very well. Come with me."

He led Clanless behind the main court of the temple, down some stairs and to a side door. He opened it and gestured. "You will find the Ghamba

Lam out here."

Clanless stepped out onto a stone path in the midst of a side garden. He smiled, remembering the last time he'd been here. He followed the path through the lush array of trees and flowering plants until he reached the statue of the goddess perched on the moon. The Ghamba Lam sat on a stone bench beside it, gazing up at the flame burning within the moon. At Clanless's approach, he stood and adjusted his robes. He turned, and his eyes widened.

"You are not who I expected to see today," the priest observed. "The goddess is ever full of surprises."

"Who were you expecting?" Clanless asked. "Suirel, perhaps?"

"Not him but one of his agents, come to end my interference in his plans." He turned away from Clanless and looked back up at the statue.

"What good would it do them to kill you? You would be replaced by another, wouldn't you? And then he would cause just as much trouble."

"Would he?" The Ghamba Lam reached a hand toward the moon, feeling the warmth of the fire within. "I would like to believe that. But between the cult's infiltration of the priesthood and the intransigence of the Council of Daghilches, I am less inclined to think so."

Clanless didn't answer. He couldn't say he understood any of the priest's words, other than the reference to Suirel's cult.

The Ghamba Lam sighed. "I'm sorry. Obviously, you came here for a different reason than to hear my whining. What can I do for you… Aldan?"

He reacted with a step back. "Why do you call me that? You took that name from me."

"One of many errors throughout my career. Were I given enough time, perhaps I could correct some of them. As it is…" He looked back at Clanless and lifted his hands.

For a moment, Clanless wanted to demand those corrections. He wanted to understand why he'd suffered so much as a child. This man had taken his future and put him in the arena. But he held back. No matter what the Ghamba Lam said, it would never change anything. The past happened. It was time to move on.

"I came to ask for your help. My beloved is held by a blood-wraith. How can I free her?"

The Ghamba Lam's eyebrows rose. "Why do you think I can help with this?"

"You're the spiritual leader of the Empire, aren't you? This is a spiritual problem!"

"Ah." He shook his head. "Would that I could do such a thing. But the only person I've seen cast out a blood-wraith is you."

"That won't work on her."

"Then I have nothing to offer."

Clanless pointed at the statue. "You are supposed to be the one man closest to the goddess! Are you saying you have no influence with her? Or that she has no power over the blood-wraiths?"

"Careful, Clanless." The Ghamba Lam's eyes narrowed. "If you resort to blasphemy, I cannot help or support you in any way."

"It seems you cannot do so anyway."

"I am but a man, despite my position. I spend many hours a week in earnest prayer to the goddess." He turned back to the statue. "That does not mean she answers me." In a lower voice, he added, "I would give anything to change that."

Clanless stared at him. "Do you mean to say she speaks more to me than she does to you?"

The Ghamba Lam's head jerked back toward him. "What do you mean? We both know the voice you heard as a child was not the goddess!"

"No, that was Zektel. The blood-wraith. But I have heard her speak. Twice now, at least."

"Tell me. When did this happen?" The priest took a step toward him.

"The, uh, first time was when I lost the fight to Daviland. I lay dying, and she came to me."

"What did she say?" The Ghamba Lam's voice was eager and hungry.

"She said she chose me, gave me the Taint. And she said something about a war in the heavens. It involved Suirel."

"You were… unconscious when this happened?"

"Yes."

The Ghamba Lam lowered his eyes. "A dream then. It is said she speaks in dreams sometimes, but dreams contain many things. Most often, they are only… dreams."

"It wasn't a dream the second time. I wasn't asleep."

"Where was this?"

"In the Throat, when I fought Bain. She said she couldn't intervene, but those above her could. That's when my blood dripped into the rest and gave me all the powers."

The Ghamba Lam held up a hand. "You speak blasphemies. There are no others above the goddess."

"And yet she said she was assigned to our people."

"This is pagan teaching. Not ours. You must not repeat it."

"She—"

"I will not hear it!"

Clanless shut his mouth. He would never understand the ways of priests. He would have thought the Ghamba Lam would be thrilled to hear the words of the goddess.

The Ghamba Lam sighed. "I know the difficulty you face. I have been doing a lot of reading in our archives on this very subject."

"What have you learned?"

The priest returned to the bench and seated himself again. "In the early days of the Empire, we became aware of blood-wraiths. For many years, they were considered fables, folktales to frighten the ignorant. Or perhaps a way to explain when someone's mind was damaged." He tapped his forehead. "When at last we took them seriously, we tried many ways to deal with them."

"Such as?"

"It was the early days, you must remember. A much more… violent time. The early priests tried various cures that today we would regard as… horrifying. And none of them worked." He paused and glanced up at the statue. "They are not called 'blood-wraiths' for naught, you know. If they were some form of spirit alone, perhaps we could cast them out by calling on the goddess. Or if they possessed one part of the body, perhaps it would be worth it to sacrifice that part." He held up his hand and wiggled his fingers.

"But they're in the blood," Clanless said.

The Ghamba Lam nodded. "In perhaps the most horrific experiment in those ancient days, the priests took a man possessed by a blood-wraith and tried to drain the creature out of him."

"They drained his blood?"

"Yes. I suppose they thought the creature would be drained out with it soon enough, or that he would be able to replace the blood as fast as it drained." He rolled his eyes. "The knowledge of the human body was not so well known, either."

"So they bled him to death."

"Yes, but… the last part of the story was interesting. It seems that just before the man died, he looked up and his eyes were clear. His last words were, 'I'm free! Free!' Thus, it appears that draining the blood did work to rid him of the wraith. Unfortunately, it also killed him." He shrugged. "Their methods were horrendous, of course. But that is how we know for sure that the wraiths exist within the blood itself."

"Kekeen said the same thing, that Zektel was bound to the blood. But

I can't remove her blood without killing her, just like I can't use the Taint without killing her."

"Have you tried offering it something else it wants?"

"Blood-wraiths want a body to control." Clanless looked up at the moon. The sun's retreat was well underway. Evening approached. "They lost their own. But I've tried offering her a different body, my own."

"You can't do that! We need you!"

"She won't take me, anyway. She… wants a relationship with me."

The Ghamba Lam did not answer at first. "Do you mean to tell me that a blood-wraith has possessed your girlfriend out of a desire to… copulate with you?"

"Something like that."

The Ghamba Lam chuckled, then laughed a bit harder. "Thank you, Clanless. I thought I'd seen and heard all of the absolute nonsense this world has to offer. And then you come to me with this." He laughed again. "The world is a bizarre place. I needed something to laugh about."

"You're no help at all." Clanless stalked down the stone path back toward the temple.

"But you are!" the Ghamba Lam called after him.

TERMS

Hagh demanded Sugh's attention the day after his arrival at Et-Baylak. At first, Sugh thought his fellow member of the Dohor was like Raki, the older fighter who'd dispensed wisdom at the last arena. But he soon learned different.

"One of Baduhan's, eh?" Hagh asked upon meeting him. "I've not heard good things about him."

"He was…" Sugh gestured at the dining hall. "It was nothing like this."

"Yah." Hagh set his plate on the nearest table. "Join me?"

"I… would like to eat in my room."

Hagh shrugged. "Suit yourself."

Sugh turned to go and met another fighter entering the dining hall. The new man smiled broadly without showing his teeth. "Uh, hello," Sugh said, but the other did not respond.

"That's Silence," Hagh said behind him. "Lost his tongue in a fight. But he hasn't lost anything since."

Over the next few weeks, Sugh learned much more about his fellow Dohor. Hagh proved especially unique. Faithfully religious yet wantonly indulgent in the pleasures afforded to their status. He coughed like a horribly sick woman but could fight better than anyone Sugh had encountered for the past three years in the arenas. He also liked to talk and pry information out of others. Sugh resisted as much as he could.

Silence, of course, said nothing. But he smiled and acted friendly most of the time.

In fact, both of them did their best to include Sugh in everything they did, inviting him to join them when they went out into town. Sugh went along but resisted their attempts—especially Hagh's—at closer friendship. An arena fighter's life was fleeting. The deaths of two other members of the Dohor in a single week emphasized this truth. Making friends with other fighters was asking to be hurt. Better to keep his heart closed.

He kept this attitude for three months. And then the most ridiculous thing changed his mind.

Now

Clanless entered the throne room alone but found the council table already full. Apparently, they'd gathered together before summoning him. After receiving the summons, he'd found Yesun to ask about Salkhi. Satisfied that she'd been treated well, he took his time getting to the throne room. With any luck, he'd missed out on the boring parts.

He gave a short glance to Lord Ghayaktal. The Lord didn't act surprised to see him, but his face narrowed, and he clenched one of his fists resting on the table. Clanless got the impression that if he wasn't needed for this champion fight, Ghayaktal would be calling for his head.

General Ghan stood apart from the table, hands behind his back, as seemed his usual position. He waited until Clanless came to a stop a few feet away before speaking: "Clanless. We have asked you to fight for this city, and you agreed. I ask you now to repeat that agreement. Will you fight for us?"

"I have said that I will, if asked. Here I am."

The General nodded and turned to those at the table. "As this council requested, I spent yesterday in negotiations with the Melkute over this champion battle. We each made proposals that the other rejected, and we each made proposals that the other accepted. After many hours, I think we have a compromise that will work… somewhat."

"What does that mean?" the Ghamba Lam asked.

"It means that I was negotiating from a position of weakness. They have us surrounded. If we refuse all their terms, they shrug their shoulders and resume the attack. They lose nothing. Their king may be disappointed that he doesn't get to see the champions fight, but I'm sure he'd get over it as his troops plunder our city."

"So we are doing everything on their terms?"

"Not everything. I was able to obtain some minor concessions. They were most concerned about the use of blood-magic. They will insist on searching you and anyone accompanying you to be sure you are not bringing blood vials with you."

"And the Taint?" Clanless asked.

The General half-smiled. "I made sure to define blood-magic as explicitly as possible. Your ability does not fall under that definition."

"What of the use of magic by their champion?" Lord Ulakan demanded.

"They have no magic!" Lord Ezen said.

"Since I did not wish to give away Clanless's Taint, I could only accept the ban on blood-magic," General Ghan said. "If indeed they possess some other form of magic that does not involve blood, I suppose it is possible they may use it."

Ulakan and the Ghamba Lam expressed concern over this development while Ezen continued to argue it was pointless. Clanless stood silent. He'd fought foreigners in the arena. Only one, a sorcerer from some island, had possessed a bizarre kind of magic that appeared to involve blood as well. Now that he thought back to the fight, he realized the magic was similar to the blood-magic of Clan Ghamkiin, but elevated in some way. Curious. Did that mean the island peoples came from Clan Ghamkiin, or were related in some way? In addition, Koland once told a story where the Melkute people and those of the Sar Empire had come from the same place. Why wouldn't they have blood-magic as well?

He was so lost in these thoughts that he missed General Ghan's next statement. "I'm sorry. What was that?"

"I said: the battle will be fought in a space they are building not far from the north gates."

"I have to go out there to them?"

"We cannot invite their king and his entire retinue inside our city. They would never agree to such a thing. Besides, our arena has been… co-opted for another use."

"Yes, what use is that, exactly?" Koland asked.

"There is a special project ongoing. I am told it is vital to the safety of this city."

Clanless snorted.

"Regardless," the General went on, "when the time comes for the fight, two days from now, Clanless will exit the city through the north gate. He will be allowed to take two others to serve as his assistants and witnesses. I have been given the strongest possible vows a Melkute can make that all three will face no danger, save Clanless from their champion, and that they will be allowed to return to the city unharmed, regardless of the battle outcome."

"Sugh will be one of the two," Clanless said at once.

"I can be the other," Koland offered.

"No," General Ghan said. "I mean no disrespect, storyteller, but I want someone from the military there, to make observations and report back. I would go myself, but…" He gave a very slight inclination of his head. "To give the Melkute the person in charge of the city's defenses would be too much of a temptation for them, I fear. Captain Rakib shall represent me."

"Very well, We march out into the middle of their army, just the three of us." Clanless shifted his stance. He didn't know how the General could stand so still all this time. "They'll want to search us for blood. And… then what? I fight this champion of theirs?"

"That is the plan. No doubt they will present you before their king. He may ask you questions. I need not tell you that anything you say may impact the safety of this city's inhabitants."

"I won't reveal any of your military secrets. I don't even know any."

"Nevertheless, you may say more than you realize. I caution you to say as little as possible about anything within these walls."

"Of course."

"And then the battle will take place." General Ghan inhaled deeply and let it out. "They were most insistent that it begin during the 'red hours.'"

"When the moon is red?" Koland clarified.

"Indeed. Clanless, you should be ready in the morning when the sun's pursuit begins. They call it the red hours. Apparently, it is a time of religious significance for them. I gave them this, as I could see no harm in it."

The Ghamba Lam muttered something to himself.

"By agreement from both sides," the General went on, "there will be no interference in the fight from anyone on either side. No one will enter the designated 'arena' area save the two of you, until the fight is ended by the death of one of the combatants."

"And then?"

"It depends on who wins, of course. If their champion wins, the two escorts will be allowed to return to the city, and they will demand our surrender."

Lord Ghayaktal leaned forward. "And do you intend to surrender in that scenario, General?"

General Ghan waited a moment before responding: "That decision will be up to this council."

"And if I win?" Clanless asked.

"The original offer said they would withdraw in that case," Lord Ezen said.

"That is what they claim," the General agreed. "We can only wait and see. And be prepared for any eventuality." He paused and looked around the table. "Any other questions?"

"I have one," Clanless said. "I need to prepare for this fight. Since our arena is being occupied, I need a place, large enough to exercise and move about. Can you suggest anything?"

General Ghan frowned deeper. "We have such a space at the barracks, but it is currently filled with additional tents for my soldiers."

"Ah, I can help, perhaps," Lord Ezen said, lifting a hand. "I will instruct my servants to clear out the courtyard. It should suffice."

"Ezen!" Lord Ulakan exclaimed. "You have the finest courtyard in the city. It would be a shame to ruin it."

"What good is the finest courtyard in the city if the city is destroyed?" Koland asked with a straight face.

Lord Ezen gestured to the throne room about them. "It is a bit larger than this space. Will that be enough?"

Clanless glanced around and nodded. "Certainly. Thank you, Lord Ezen. Sugh and I will come tomorrow morning. We will probably train most of the day." He would need it. He'd fought so little in the past weeks. Months, really.

General Ghan again asked for further questions. When none came, he dismissed the council and left. The others followed more slowly, talking amongst themselves.

Clanless stepped near Koland and whispered, "I thought of something about the Melkute I'd like to ask you and the Ghamba Lam about."

"I'll ask him to stay behind."

The three Lords and Sonkogh made their farewells and departed. The remaining two men looked to Clanless.

"I'm not sure about any of this," Clanless began, "but Bain—Suirel—told me he'd sent a prophet to the Melkute, which is why they're here in the first place."

"Yes, you told us," Koland said.

"I've been thinking. If he sent this prophet, isn't it likely that it's someone controlled by a blood-wraith?"

"Probably," the Ghamba Lam answered. "But does it matter?"

"What if I were able to expose this prophet in front of their king?" Clanless asked. "What if I used the Taint to pull the wraith out of him?"

Koland frowned. "I see some problems. First, how will you know the right man?"

Clanless held out both hands. "I could just ask."

"Second, if I understand correctly, he would have to be bleeding for the Taint to work on him. How do you expect the king to allow that?"

"Not to mention their aversion to blood-magic," the Ghamba Lam put in. "The king might accuse you of using it and call the entire fight off."

"Not if I do it after the fight," Clanless argued.

"You would have to win first. And if you do, they're either going to keep their word and leave, or… break it and probably start by killing you."

Koland nodded. "He's right, Aldan. It was a good thought, but I don't see it helping."

Clanless sighed. "You're probably right. I'm still trying to think of a way to keep this from being necessary. Suirel wants me to fight, for some reason. It can't be a good thing."

"Maybe he's trying to keep you busy, like Kekeen said. Whatever he's doing in the arena, he wants to keep you away from it."

"Maybe." Clanless looked in the direction of the arena. "Or maybe there's something else going on with this fight, and we just haven't figured it out yet."

((((●))))

Lord Ezen's massive home was not far from the palace but further than Lord Ghayaktal's. Clanless and Sugh arrived early the next morning where a serving girl admitted them through the front gates.

Inside the walls, they stopped to stare at the remains of what must have been an impressive courtyard. Marble pillars, statues, and numerous plants in huge pots had all been shoved to the sides. Four men spread and raked sand across the surface.

"It's… big enough," Sugh observed.

Lord Ezen appeared from a side door and hurried over to meet them. "I apologize, gentlemen, that the work is not quite finished." He gestured toward the working men. "We had to remove the central tree, which left a big hole, as you can imagine."

"You didn't have to pull up a tree," Clanless said. "We could have practiced around it."

Ezen waved a hand. "I'd rather you do your work here than have those Melkute barbarians tear it apart."

"Lord Ezen, I…" Clanless hesitated. "I owe you a debt of gratitude."

"For this? It is nothing, I say."

"No, not this." Clanless looked down for a moment, took a deep breath, and looked back at the Lord. "I am told that you saved my beloved, Kekeen, from the Hawk King's wrath on the day he died."

"The singer? Ah." He snapped his fingers. "That was the storyteller's daughter? Of course. Sorry. I am just making all these connections." He chuckled and shook his head. "It was through no heroism on my part, I assure you. With all that was happening, I simply could not stand still and let him slaughter an innocent girl in front of everyone. He nearly took my own head off for it. Fortunately for me, Daviland attacked him." He shrugged. "The rest is now history."

"It is heroic to me," Clanless said.

"And me," Sugh added. "Most men in this city will not stand up for a woman, or so it seems to me."

"Yes, well." Lord Ezen shifted his feet. "They're almost done here. If you have need of anything at all, please let one of the servants know. I'll make sure someone is near at all times." He laughed. "Though I strongly suspect many of them will want to watch the two of you. If you'll excuse me, I still have business to conduct… even within a city under siege." He nodded to them both and hastened away.

"What a peculiar man," Sugh said.

"He sounded almost embarrassed that we praised him for being a hero." Clanless scratched his chin. "I don't understand."

Sugh leaned his axe against the wall and stretched his arms over his head. "Humility is not a common trait among the rich. That's why he's peculiar."

The servants finished their work and hurried off to the sides, leaving the former courtyard open and empty. Clanless and Sugh wasted no time in getting to their own work. They started with light exercises before moving on to detailed practice maneuvers. High Spring was still young, giving them a cool morning in which to work. Even so, sweat soon appeared and poured from their bodies from the exertion.

After two hours of this, they stopped to rest, setting their weapons aside. Sugh gestured to one of the servants who'd been watching wide-eyed. "Some water for our throats and towels for our sweat, if you please."

Clanless crouched and then sat on the dirt. "I am not keeping up with you like I should."

Sugh waved a hand without looking at him. "Nonsense. You were the greatest of all of us. You are just out of practice."

"But I don't have time to get in practice." Clanless slammed his fist against the ground. "The fight is tomorrow, Sugh!"

Two servants hurried across to them, carrying water and towels. Sugh thanked them, giving assurances that he and Clanless could drink on their own and wipe their own sweat without assistance. The servants backed off but waited until the fighters were done with the towels. They took the damp cloths back as if they were treasures and hurried away, giving Sugh much amusement.

"Clanless, my friend," Sugh said, this time looking down at him. "Even out of practice, you are better than almost anyone. Stop this doubt."

"Not since the mines." He didn't get up. "It should be you, Sugh. You have a better chance at this than I do."

Sugh threw back his head and laughed. "What nonsense is this? You are the mighty Clanless! It is true: I could probably defeat any champion these foreigners could throw at us. But you are better! So much better. For one thing, I do not possess this power you have over your enemies' blood. It makes you invincible!"

Clanless pushed himself up. "If I'm forced to use that, it may ruin everything. We don't know how the Melkute will react."

"Their king has heard tales of the great Clanless, yes? Surely, he has heard of your strange power in those tales. He will be expecting it!"

Clanless dusted himself off. "I hadn't considered that." He frowned. "That makes it even more suspicious. If he expects me to use the Taint, then either he has no intention of honoring his word when I win with it, or…"

"Or what?" Sugh took up the practice weapons they'd brought along: two short staves of polished wood. He handed one to Clanless.

"Or he believes his champion can win even if I do use it."

Sugh put a hand to his forehead. "You are finding the worst possibility in everything lately," he complained. "It makes it hard to be happy around you."

Clanless smiled. "And yet you do it, anyway. I'm lucky you're around, Sugh."

"Indeed you are. Without me, you would sit around feeling sorry for yourself instead of doing something about it. It is foolishness. Come!" He gestured toward himself. "Let's see if you can beat me with nothing but a stick. Whoever loses must feed Tuulka tonight!"

"You've been keeping track of that beast?"

"Nukai takes good care of him." Sugh chuckled and waved his staff. "But I've checked on him a couple of times."

"I do not understand your obsession with that animal. All of you!" Clanless took a defensive stance.

"It is good that you will be feeding him tonight then." Sugh stabbed at him and danced back to avoid a counterattack. "Then you can get to know him better!"

"We'll see about that!"

FEEDING TUULKA

Silence's chain whipped around the ankles of the barbarian and yanked him off his feet. As he dragged the opponent across the sand, Sugh leaped forward and slammed his axe into the man's chest. The crowd roared its approval.

The remaining seven barbarians charged with cries of rage. Silence and Sugh stood back-to-back and fought, dispatching the enemies one by one. In short order, they stood alone and victorious.

"Sugh and Silence, citizens! Triumphant yet again!"

Sugh couldn't help but notice that the presenter listed his name first. He'd become a bigger star than Hagh or Silence in only three months.

A few moments later, they jogged back inside where Qara and a priest met them. The fighters handed their Siphons to the priest for the tithe and accepted towels to wipe their sweat. Hagh nodded to them both and headed out for his own fight.

"No injuries needing healing?" Qara asked, trying not to look too closely. Sugh thought it odd she disliked the sight of injuries so much while working in an arena.

"Nothing but a scratch or two," he bragged. "We were unstoppable out there!" He grinned at Silence.

The other fighter smiled back and licked his lips.

Sugh wiped blood from his axe before it registered. His head jerked back up. "You do have a tongue!"

"Shhh!" Qara warned. She glanced to the priest, who didn't act as though he'd heard. He finished with the Siphons, returned them, and left.

"Hagh said he lost his tongue!" Sugh stared at Silence, who continued to grin.

"It's the story he's asked us to tell," Qara said. "When he trusts someone enough, he reveals the truth." She chuckled. "If they don't notice, he finds another way."

Sugh kept staring. "Can… can you talk then?"

"No." Qara slipped over next to Silence and touched a scar on his neck. "Something in here was severed and didn't heal right. But he thought the tongue story was more fun." Silence put his arm around her shoulders and squeezed.

Sugh chuckled and shook his head. "So I am trusted, it seems."

"Yes, and you should be honored." Qara slipped out of Silence's embrace and stepped over to Sugh. "Aside from myself, the only other people who know are Hagh and a couple of the girls at Pasque House."

"High company."

Qara frowned. "I'm serious, Sugh."

An enormous roar from the crowd interrupted them. Hagh must have done something spectacular.

"Silence is basically telling you he wants to be your friend. That he trusts you with the truth." Qara motioned from Sugh to Silence.

"Oh. Ah, thank you, Silence. I…" Sugh hesitated. "I haven't had friends since I entered the arena. It's—"

Before he could finish, Silence lunged forward and embraced him. Sugh gasped, and the smaller man released him. He punched Sugh's shoulder and walked away.

"That was… unusual." Sugh watched the other man saunter off toward the baths.

"Let your friends in," Qara said, picking up the discarded towels. "Our lives are short and miserable enough in this world, Sugh. Don't spend it alone."

Her words occupied his mind for the next few days. He could think of little else.

Now

"I won that bout!" Sugh proclaimed as they left Lord Ezen's property. "You must feed Tuulka."

"But I won the next three," Clanless answered.

"We did not agree on who won the most but on who won the first one!"

"I didn't agree to anything." They started walking back toward the palace.

"Now, now." Sugh shook a finger at him. "I laid out the terms, and you started the fight. That is agreement."

"I don't even know where the stables are."

"That is easily remedied. I shall show you."

They continued their banter, but Clanless noticed a small group of people watching them from the other side of the street. None of them looked as though they lived in this rich area of town.

"That's him!" someone said.

"Sugh, watch it," Clanless warned.

The group rushed across to them with cries of "Clanless! Clanless!" Both men backed up against the nearest wall and held up their hands, keeping their weapons out of reach.

"Hear, hear, hear!" Sugh shouted. "What is all this? What do you want?"

"Save us, Clanless!" The speaker was an older man dressed in ragged clothes and leaning on a crutch.

"I'm doing what I can," he answered. "The fight is tomorrow. Please, let us go on, and you go back to your homes."

"Are you staying at the Hawk King's palace?" someone demanded.

"At the moment, yes."

A woman pushed to the front of the group, dragging a small girl who couldn't have been more than five years old. She thrust the child toward Clanless. "Please! Take my daughter with you!"

"What? No. Why would I do that?"

The woman fell on her knees. "Please! We have no more food or blood to buy any. My daughter will starve. If you take her into the palace, she will have food. She can work for it. She's strong for her age!"

Clanless stared, mouth agape, at the teary-eyed woman and her child. The girl looked back and forth between her mother and Clanless, as if she wasn't sure what was happening. He looked to Sugh, who appeared equally stunned. "What do we do?" he whispered.

Sugh knelt to face the woman. "Your child should not be separated from you, madam. Come with us, and we will have some food brought out for you to take home."

"And how long will that last? She needs more than food for today alone! Please! Take her!"

The girl put her thumb in her mouth, eyes wide. She whimpered. The rest of the group watched, silent now, to see how this played out.

Clanless put on his most disarming smile. He patted the girl on the head and reached a hand out to the mother. "I had no idea food supplies were running so low," he said.

"Maybe not for people living up here," someone muttered.

"As Sugh said, come with us to the palace. We'll get food for both of you, enough to last several days. Tomorrow, I fight the Melkute champion. If I win, and they keep their word, the siege will be over and, and there will be food for all again."

She took his hand hesitantly and let him pull her back to her feet. She gathered her daughter close.

"And what if you lose?" the first older man asked.

Sugh stood up. "He will not lose! This is Clanless! Have you seen him lose?"

"I heard he lost to Daviland."

"Because he wanted to!" Sugh shook his axe in the air. "This man, I tell you, does not lose!"

Clanless took a deep breath. He wanted to argue with Sugh and tell him not to work up these people's hopes. But what did it matter? If he won, their hopes were justified. And if he lost… well, he wouldn't be around to see their disappointment.

Or their deaths.

Sugh put a hand on his shoulder and gestured at the people with his axe. "This is what you are fighting for tomorrow," he said in a quiet voice near Clanless's ear.

"Follow us," Clanless told them. He started forward, hoping they wouldn't block his way. To his relief, the people stood aside and let him lead. Sugh walked beside him, and the entire group trailed along behind. The promise of food was enough of a lure for all.

Upon reaching the palace, Sugh waited outside with the people while Clanless went to make good on his promise. With the help of Yesun, he found the palace kitchens. It took some persuading, but he convinced them to send a load of food, both freshly cooked and some to store, to the group outside.

"The cooks say you've started something that could be a problem," Yesun said as they walked back.

"What's that?"

He gestured toward the doors. "These people will go home and tell their friends what you did. Tomorrow, there will be a bigger crowd."

"Then we'll feed them too." Clanless stopped and waited near the doors for Sugh to return.

"Then what about the next day?" Yesun asked. "And the next? The palace has a good store of food, but not enough to feed everyone. If we could, we'd have already done that. The Hawk King's not here to stop us, after all."

Clanless leaned against the wall, feeling the exhaustion from the day's workout setting in. "I hear you. But with luck, this will all be over tomorrow."

"Goddess willing." Yesun nodded to the servers coming from the kitchen and hurried off to help with other chores.

((((●))))

The stables were on the opposite side of the palace, not far on a normal day, but after this day's exertion, Clanless didn't enjoy the walk. Nukai met them at the entrance. "I've been wondering when you would come," he said to Clanless.

"Nukai!" Sugh exclaimed. "Clanless has agreed to feed Tuulka tonight. I leave him in your capable hands. I'm heading to the baths myself."

Clanless groaned. "I need a bath."

"Then finish your duties here." Sugh slapped him on the back with a big grin, nodded to Nukai, and headed back into the palace.

"This way." Nukai led Clanless inside. They walked through an entire room of stalls. Horses peered out as they passed. "We had to keep Tuulka as far from them as possible," Nukai explained. "He makes the horses nervous."

They passed through a short hall and entered another identical room of stalls. All of the stalls on the right were empty while the ones on the left had been converted into one large stall in which the armored ghuyak waited alone. At their approach, he lifted his head and regarded them with his enormous eyes.

"We have people starving outside, and we're feeding this thing," Clanless said.

Nukai pointed to the empty stalls on the other side. "Fortunately, Tuulka is quite happy to eat hay. I don't think sharing it with the poorer populace would help their situation."

Clanless opened one of the stalls and found bales of hay piled high.

He lifted one, carried it across and tossed it into the beast's stall. Tuulka meandered over to the fallen bale and started to munch.

"How many?" Clanless asked.

"Five bales should be sufficient for now." Nukai slipped inside the stall and patted Tuulka on the head. The beast grunted and kept chewing. Clanless went back and forth, delivering the fodder.

"Tuulka is quite fortunate here," Nukai said. "There is enough hay to last for many days."

"I don't quite know why we're keeping him," Clanless said.

"What would you do with him? Set him free inside the city?" Nukai chuckled. "That would create a stir. Someone might get hurt." He pointed to the back of the stall. "When I first put him in here, Tuulka got agitated. His tail smashed through the wall there. We repaired it, but he could easily knock it back down if he wanted to."

Clanless paused and looked. "His tail is something like a giant mace. I suppose the Melkute find that useful sometimes."

"What of you, Clanless? Are you prepared for tomorrow?"

"As much as I can be, I guess. Sugh and I spent all day practicing. You know what that's like."

Nukai found a spot where he could reach under Tuulka's armor plate and scratch. The ghuyak twisted its neck and closed its eyes in response. "You know this fight is a distraction from the true battle, don't you?"

"Yes." Clanless threw the fifth bale of hay into the stall. "Suirel probably staged the whole thing, telling the Melkute King about me. It's to keep me busy while he does whatever he's doing in the arena."

"Do not forget what we discussed before."

Clanless brushed hay from his clothes. "I'm sorry. Which discussion?"

"Hope."

"Oh." Clanless put both arms over the stable door and leaned against it. "To be honest, I still don't see much hope. It feels like I'm fighting and running as hard as I can just to keep up with everything that's going wrong. Between Bain and Kekeen and the city itself… I don't see a way out. It's getting darker by the day."

"And?"

"I know, I know. It doesn't all depend on me. You said do the next thing I could and keep going until…"

"Until hope takes over." Nukai gave Tuulka another scratch under his armor.

"I hope it's soon." Clanless laughed.

"Why do you laugh?"

"Because I basically said I hope in hope."

"Is that so strange? Many have done the same."

Clanless pulled a splinter from the stable door. "Swift Claw says he has no hope left, but he keeps searching for his lost child. I guess it's a matter of duty for him. He keeps going because he thinks it's the right thing to do."

"Is that so different?"

"It's not really hope, is it?"

"He does the next thing he can and then the next…"

"Until hope takes over. I get it." He sighed. "I hope that happens for him. But it's more likely we'll all die here, I suppose."

Nukai looked up at him. "When the time comes, Clanless, I must go with you."

"To the fight? I'm limited to only two companions, and—"

"No. When you enter the arena."

"Nukai… I don't even know if I can get into the arena. He's thwarted my attempts already."

The hunched man sighed. "Open your eyes, Aldan. Sometimes, you simply cannot see what is right in front of you."

Clanless frowned. "What do you mean, old man? There's nothing in front of me but you and this creature."

Nukai rolled his eyes. "Must I explain everything?" he asked, addressing the ceiling. "Why is he so blind?" He looked back at Clanless. "You said it yourself a moment ago."

"What?"

Nukai pointed at Tuulka, then at the stable's back wall.

Clanless slid behind the stall door and groaned. "You're right. I'm a blind idiot." He opened the door and stepped into the stall. "Why wait? Let's do it now."

"No, no. The people are counting on you."

"You said do the next thing. This is the next thing."

Nukai stood. "The champion battle awaits you tomorrow. You have trained and prepared for it. It is getting late, and you are tired. You cannot go against Suirel in this condition."

Clanless pulled at his hair. "Ugh. I know. I just…"

"One fight at a time, Clanless. Deal with the Melkute champion. Suirel will still be there afterward. He will not complete his work so soon."

"Do you know what his work is? What is he doing in there?"

"I… can guess. But I can only guess. Let's move on with what we know. Do the next thing."

"Fine. What's my next thing?" Clanless growled.

"You said it when you came in." Nukai moved past him out of the stall. "You need a bath."

☾☾☾☾●☽☽☽☽

Clanless set the moonblade on the nightstand and stretched. The workout and the bath had both helped. He almost felt like his old self on the eve of Arena Night.

"Aldan?"

He sighed and turned to see Kekeen standing in the doorway. For a moment, she looked so small and fragile, her form framed by the light streaming from her room, he almost went to her. Instead, he closed his eyes. "What do you want?"

"That's the problem, isn't it?" He heard her take a short step into his room. "I've always thought I knew what I wanted, but… you changed everything."

He didn't want to deal with this. "Zektel, I'm very tired, and I have the biggest fight of my life tomorrow morning. Please… just let me rest."

"I can't. Not without telling you how I feel."

He opened his eyes and looked at her without saying anything.

"For… longer than you can imagine, all I wanted was power. And a body of my own again. Suirel wasn't even a factor; we never thought he'd make it here. All of us—the blood-wraiths, I mean—we were doing our own thing." She put her hands together in front of her and bowed her head. "And then I met you."

Clanless didn't move. He wouldn't fall for any of her tricks, not tonight.

"I, I grew to love you, Aldan. We spent years together."

"But you left me as soon as you had a chance at greater power. Don't try to rewrite the past. I can remember it all now."

She looked up with wide eyes. "Yes, I left you. And regretted it immediately. But… everything came together so perfectly, and you wouldn't do what I wanted, and, and I could feel Suirel's influence growing as the moon appeared, and—"

"Stop." He shook his head. "The excuses don't matter. None of this matters."

"You have to understand me!" She took three steps closer and dropped her hands to her sides. "Please, Aldan!"

"Leave me alone."

"Yes, I did everything Suirel wanted!" She waved to the side. "While I controlled Daviland, I did everything necessary to bring about his coming. I delighted in behaving like I used to, for a while. I even killed Hagh."

Clanless stiffened.

"And I know, I know that means you hate me even more. So when I had a new opportunity, to maybe fix things, I took it." She gestured at Kekeen's body. "I'm here because of you, Aldan. Because I have to be near you, no matter what Suirel wants."

"Do you mean that?"

"Yes!"

He stepped toward her and stared into her eyes. "Then leave Kekeen. Now. You want me not to hate you? That's the only way. Because as long as you are within her, you are my greatest enemy, Zektel. Not the Melkute champion. Not Suirel. You. I hate you and will keep hating you, unless you leave her."

She wrapped her arms around her. "But… if I leave her, you'll be with her. You won't want me around. I'll lose you forever."

He opened his mouth to deny it, but… he couldn't. He wanted her gone not just from Kekeen but from his life.

She sighed and stepped back. "I wanted to tell you all this before the fight. So you know. I don't want you to die."

With that, she turned and hurried back into her bedroom, leaving the door open. Clanless stood still until the light in the doorway went out. He sighed and crawled into bed himself. He stared up at the ceiling, wrestling with the words of Nukai and Zektel. He could come to only one conclusion, born either of hope or stubbornness: "I don't want to die either."

Part Four

ARENA

CHAMPION DUEL

"A new fighter will be joining you tomorrow."

Sugh looked up from his plate at the voice. He'd continued to eat in his room for almost every meal. Sometimes, Hagh could persuade him to eat together, but he tried to avoid it… because of Qara. Everywhere he went within the arena, he saw her. She would always smile and engage him in conversation. Though she'd told him to let friends in, he did his best to keep it casual, and nothing more. He wanted more. Oh, how he wanted it. From the moment, she'd showed him his new room, he'd wanted her. But the memory of Chabi forced him to keep his distance. His heart had broken and not healed yet. Better to keep the girls at a distance, like the ones at Pasque House. No emotional connection.

On the other hand, he'd opened up with Hagh and Silence. For the first time in years, he had friends, true friends. And it felt… good.

"Goddess? You haven't spoken to me since I came here," he said toward the ceiling.

"He will need friends, Sugh. I have chosen him for a purpose. He will be good for you."

Sugh raised his eyebrows. "Do you speak to him as you do to me?"

"No. Only you."

"Oh." He paused. "If you do it for my heart… it may be yours again someday. But not yet."

"I know. I am not asking yet. Let it beat for others, Sugh. Until I need it."

"I don't know if I can do that."

"Guard your heart, but do not enclose it in a cage. You have friends here. Enjoy them. And make a new one. The new fighter will need you."

He looked back down at his plate. "I will try."

"That is all I ask… for now."

Now

Koland claimed his spot on the city wall next to the north gate. Once he'd learned of the champion fight location, he'd arranged with the soldiers for this spot to be reserved. Kekeen, Qara, and Sonkogh joined him.

"Oh," Qara said. "It's right there. This is almost like having prime seats at the arena."

"It's further away than the arena floor," Kekeen said, "but this is as good as it's going to get without going out there."

"I wasn't trying to be that specific." Qara rolled her eyes.

Kekeen put her hands on the parapet. "A few thousand of their army has assembled to watch, but I suppose the others are still spread around the rest of the city."

"How can you be so calm?" Qara demanded. "It's your beloved going out there! Aren't you worried?"

Kekeen looked at her with widened eyes. "Aldan is the greatest arena fighter in history. Do you doubt him?"

Qara made a disgusted noise and turned away.

Koland made a mental note to let her know about Zektel, if they made it through this day. He leaned in close to Kekeen and whispered, "Are you able to discern anything out there in the, uh, spiritual realm?"

"What do you mean?"

"Can you see others of your kind? Gods or wraiths?"

She chuckled. "I see only what this body can see."

"So you have no other supernatural senses, then?"

"I suppose." She shrugged. "I mean, when someone is up close, I can usually tell if they're possessed by a blood-wraith. But certainly not from this distance."

Koland accepted that and looked back toward the city. "He should be coming soon."

((((●))))

Clanless and Sugh rose before the sun. Once they prepared themselves, three squads of soldiers escorted them to the north gate of the city. Crowds lined the streets even at this hour, cheering for Clanless as he passed.

"If you put all these people together, it would be a larger crowd than any arena," Sugh pointed out. He turned his head and gave a small cough.

"That's not very helpful," Clanless said.

"Why not?" Sugh flexed his muscles and grinned. "I always did my best with an enthusiastic crowd."

"This crowd isn't here to see me entertain them. They're expecting me to save their lives!"

"They expect it because you will. They have faith in you."

"I don't have faith in me."

Sugh lost his smile. "Then you will lose. As will we all. You need not have faith in yourself. But have faith in your training, in your experience, in your past record. All of it adds up to a powerful and impressive arena fighter, perhaps the greatest that has ever lived."

Clanless ran a hand back through his hair but didn't answer.

"You must do your best," Sugh said. "That will be enough."

"If I can talk to the Melkute King, maybe the whole thing can be resolved."

"I would not count on it." He coughed again, harder this time. "Your pardon. I appear to be taking Hagh's place."

"It's the poison you inhaled. It'll clear up." At least Clanless hoped it would. Even blood-magic could not heal internal damage if it couldn't get to it.

They reached the gate and waited. Clanless looked up at the moon. The sun rose in the distance, beginning its daily pursuit. A red hue colored the moon, as often happened during the early days of High Spring. It would dissipate as the sun's pursuit grew nearer, then reappear briefly in the late evening when the sun retreated. Clanless had never thought much of the redness; it was such a simple part of the changing seasons. Now, it appeared ominous, as though blood overshadowed the goddess.

Captain Rakib pushed past their escort and joined them. He nodded to the two Dohor and wiped sweat from his brow.

With a roll of drums and a giant creaking, the massive gate of Et-Baylak opened. Dozens of soldiers surged forward, spears at the ready, while archers above drew their bows, all prepared in case the Melkute charged at this moment. When no such attack came, an officer signaled for them to make their move.

The crowd behind roared their encouragement as the three men walked past the soldier and through the gate. Once they passed through, the gate swung closed again as fast as the soldiers could move it.

Clanless looked out at the mighty Melkute army. When they'd come through on the wagon, he'd been hiding and unable to observe much. Now he stared at the dramatic change that had taken place here outside the city.

A wide empty space stretched in front of them, a deference to the opening of the gate. But beyond it, thousands of enemy soldiers stood rank upon rank, watching the three men walk forward. Massive siege weapons were stationed at equal distances from each other in a ring that stretched off as far as he could see in either direction. They sat silent and still now but ready to resume their assault at a command from the King. As he, Sugh, and Rakib began their descent from the gate, he could see scores of tents and wagons beyond the army, a veritable city in itself.

Cheers came from behind. Clanless took a quick glance back and saw watchers lining the top of the gate and the walls on either side. He couldn't make out faces from this point, but he knew Kekeen and the others would be there, along with the council and anyone else who could squeeze in or persuade the soldiers to allow their presence.

Turning back, he saw the Melkute army split apart and march in either direction, opening a large area before him. To his left, an open area had been marked off by a short wall of stone. It looked about the size of an arena floor. From this angle, it also looked red, for some reason. To his right, a huge pavilion had been erected. Above it flew a red flag decorated with a stylistic saber.

Four men broke away from the crowd and hurried to meet them. When they drew close, all bowed and came to a stop. One stepped forward, a younger man with a short beard. All of them looked and dressed similar to the scouts Clanless and Sugh had fought.

"We are honored by your presence," the young man said, focusing on Clanless. "I am Ghenbish. I will be your mouth and your ears for this morning's events. I have no doubt that I am addressing the famous Clanless, warrior of the arena. May I know the names of your companions?"

"This is Sugh and Rakib," Clanless answered, gesturing to each. "Before the fight, may I have the honor of speaking to your king?"

"The mighty King Kataat Ghun is most eager to see your prowess in battle," Ghenbish said. "Should you prevail in the fight, he will welcome you to his presence and listen to your words. But for now, he wishes the fight to begin while the red hours are still upon us." He gestured toward the makeshift arena.

"Very well. Lead on." Clanless hid his disappointment, but Sugh had been right. The King did not want to talk. At least, not yet.

"I apologize, but under the terms of our agreement, all three of you must be searched for blood."

"You're welcome to do so, but the only blood we bring with us is what flows within our veins."

"Nevertheless." Ghenbish gestured and the three other Melkute men stepped forward. They searched Clanless, Sugh, and Rakib in moments. Finding nothing, they stepped back.

"One last question," Ghenbish said. "You mentioned your own blood. How can we know you will not shed some yourself and use its magic?"

"It doesn't work that way," Captain Rakib said. "Only the priests can use the blood-magic."

Clanless didn't see the need to bring up his own blood's catalyst properties.

"Very well. I suppose we must trust you in this." Ghenbish snapped his fingers and the other three shifted behind Clanless and his companions. Sugh chuckled, and Clanless smiled. Were they genuinely trying to prevent a retreat? Where would they retreat to? Ghenbish motioned for them to follow and walked toward the short stone wall.

Clanless picked up his pace and walked beside the translator. "Tell me," he said, "has your king brought spiritual advisors with him? Are there prophets in his, uh, presence?"

"The mighty King Kataat Ghun always seeks the wisdom of his prophets, both those of Taichi Denkri and those of Sama El," Ghenbish answered. "He understands that true wisdom can be found in an abundance of counsel."

How would he know which prophet Suirel had sent? It would make sense to be one of those claiming to serve Sama El, the latest name he'd claimed, but it could also be one of the others. Koland was right: finding the right prophet might be impossible.

They reached the arena "wall," made of stacked stones about three feet in height. It wouldn't stand up to any kind of serious impact but was impressive, nonetheless, for being so hastily constructed. Now Clanless could see the arena surface. The Melkute had brought sand from somewhere and spread it across the dirt. Unlike the sand he'd fought on for years, this sand had a reddish hue to it. "Your companions may wait and watch from this side," Ghenbish said, indicating the southern wall of the arena, nearest to the city. "I will remain here should further translation be needed. Our people will watch from the two sides, while the King and his retinue will be opposite here."

"Moon's stability to you, Clanless," Captain Rakib offered.

"And to you two." He glanced at Ghenbish, then lowered his voice. "If I lose this, or if something happens to me after the fight, I want the two of you to run for the city as fast as you can."

"We will not abandon you," Sugh said with a cough.

"It's not about abandonment. You can't abandon a dead man."

"He's right and wrong," the Captain said. "If he dies, our lives aren't worth an ounce of blood to these people. But running for the city probably won't help us. The archers will cut us down long before we get there."

"Do what you have to." Clanless turned and vaulted over the stones. Puffs of red sand erupted where his feet landed. It felt softer than normal sand, as well. He turned his attention to the far side where an imposing man stood alone. "Is that—?"

"Ular awaits the start of the battle," the translator said. "Once the ritual is completed, the King will signal the start of the fight."

"What ritual?"

Ghenbish pointed to the other side with his palm. Clanless squinted, trying to get a better look at Ular. The champion stood head and shoulders taller than any of the other men near him. He wore a spiked helmet that appeared to have been made from the tail tip of a ghuyak like Tuulka. His chest also looked to be covered by armor from a similar creature. Crimson paint—or maybe tattoos—decorated his arms and legs. He held an enormous saber in his right hand, and a spear protruded from the ground beside him.

Two Melkute soldiers climbed over the wall to join the champion. Another man, struggling against his captors, was handed over to them. From this distance, it looked like the struggling man wore a Sar Empire uniform. The crowd of Melkute soldiers murmured, creating a discordant cacophony.

"What is this?" Captain Rakib demanded.

The prisoner was thrown to the ground in front of Ular. Clanless took a step forward, but before he could do more, the champion brought down his huge saber. The prisoner's head rolled clear from his body. The crowd fell completely silent.

"This is outrageous!" Rakib exclaimed. He started to climb over the wall, but Sugh stopped him. "Do not throw your life away as well," he warned.

One of the Melkute soldiers knelt beside the fallen body for a few moments. He stood and handed Ular a bowl. The Champion lifted it in the air. "For Taichi Denkri!" he cried, his voice booming across the open arena. He brought the bowl to his lips and drank.

The crowd of soldiers responded with a chant of, "Taichi Denkri. Taichi Denkri." They repeated the god's name over and over.

Clanless turned on the translator. "What was that for? Is this how you treat all your prisoners?"

Ghenbish cocked his head. "The red god of war demands sacrifice. Every obligation met. Does not your goddess demand blood sacrifices as well?"

"Not like this!" Clanless pointed the moonblade toward Ular. "The sacrifices for the goddess are freely given, not taken by execution!"

"I am confused," Ghenbish said. "I was told that the blood of those fallen in the arena fights was given to your goddess as well."

"Those are men who choose to fight! Prisoners seeking freedom, or those trying to win glory or blood," Sugh broke in. "Not helpless prisoners being murdered!"

"You"—the translator gestured at Clanless and Sugh—"chose to fight? Are you not slaves?"

"Taichi Denkri!" Ular screamed above the sound of the chant. At his cry, the rest of the soldiers fell silent again.

"The fight begins," Ghenbish said, stepping back.

"What?" Clanless spun around to see Ular yank his spear out of the ground and charge across the arena. "Sands!" Clanless snarled the curse and hurried to meet him. The crowd erupted in raucous cheers.

As the Melkute champion drew closer, Clanless wondered if he'd underestimated the man's height. He might be seven feet tall! The height plus a spear and huge sword gave him an enormous reach advantage.

Blood still trickled from Ular's mouth and ran down his chin. In anger, Clanless activated the Taint. His eyes burned. Ular jerked his head. He must have experienced a bit of a shock on his tongue, if nothing else. He shouted something in his language and came to a halt a dozen yards from Clanless.

Clanless shifted to his right. Ular did the same. Clanless smiled and continued, creating a slow circling of the opponents. He much preferred this start to a fight, rather than a headlong charge. Now, he could evaluate his opponent and decide on the best opening maneuver.

Ular began to speak. At first, Clanless took it for some kind of antagonistic aggravation. But as it went on, he realized the Melkute champion was slowly chanting the same lines over and over. He caught the name "Taichi Denkri" in the middle of it. Another religious ritual, then?

A breeze swept across the arena from the north. Ular smiled, revealing not four canine teeth, but eight. Or, more likely, he'd sharpened four of his other teeth to match. Clanless had fought someone who'd done something similar in the Et-Baylak arena. He could see no point to it.

The breeze grew into a significant wind. The Melkute army continued to shout cheers and encouragement toward their champion. From time to time, Clanless also heard shouts coming from the city walls: his own people cheering for him.

Ular grew tired of pacing first. He lunged forward a few steps and thrust his spear forward. Clanless sidestepped it easily. He swung a quick parry, hoping to damage the spear, but Ular pulled it away too fast.

The wind increased its strength. Clanless narrowed his eyes to protect them from the red dust being picked up and thrown into his face. With a start, he realized Ular was not doing the same. His eyes remained wide open above his sharpened smile while he kept chanting. Were his eyes immune to dirt, or...? The wind. It wasn't natural. This was the Melkute magic! A wind that affected only one man, even when the two of them moved about? Definitely magic.

And if he could use magic, then there could be no objection to the use of the Taint. Clanless's confidence rose with the knowledge. He took a step toward Ular. The wind grew stronger, as if trying to force him back. This could be a problem. At this strength, the wind could limit not only his footwork but also the movement of the moonblade. He took a step back instead. The wind subsided. Interesting. The intent of the magic was clear: controlling his movements while giving freedom to Ular's.

ᴄ ᴄ ᴀ ᴄ ● ᴅ ᴅ ᴅ ᴅ

"Something is wrong," Kekeen and Qara said almost simultaneously.

"What do you mean?" Koland asked.

"He's not fighting like he usually does," Qara answered at the same time Kekeen said, "Aldan's moves are too slow." They glared at each other.

Koland squinted, trying to get a better focus on the two battling figures in the sand below. The taller one, the Melkute champion, did appear to be moving faster than Clanless. "What do you think is the problem?"

Qara didn't answer. After a moment, Kekeen said softly, "It's Melkute magic."

"How can you tell?" Koland didn't take his eyes off the fight.

"I can't. But I can't imagine anything else that would do this to him. He fought normal a few days ago."

Koland ground his teeth. The Melkute had rigged the fight from the very beginning, forbidding blood-magic but not their own, whatever it was. If Clanless could use the Taint, he still had a chance. But to do that, he had to make his opponent bleed...

"This is what Suirel wanted," Kekeen whispered. "He orchestrated all of this."

☾ ☾ ☾ ☾ ● ☽ ☽ ☽ ☽

The champion kept chanting. Was his magic dependent on it? If Clanless could disrupt the voice, would it disrupt the magic? One of Zaluu's throwing knives would come in handy right now... if he could get it through the wind barrier.

Ular stepped several steps toward him and swung his saber. Clanless tried to bring the moonblade up to strike back, but he couldn't move it fast enough. Instead, he was forced to parry the blow. The impact of the two weapons colliding made him stumble onto one knee. With his other hand, Ular stabbed with his spear beneath the other two blades. Clanless gasped as the edge of the spearpoint sliced across his left side. It wasn't deep, but it was first blood. The crowd's cheers increased in volume.

Clanless rolled back and onto his feet, creating a wider gap between them. Ular resumed his chanting, and the wind against Clanless picked up again. Unless he could find a way to counter it, he couldn't do much.

"Goddess," he muttered, "or whoever else is listening, I could use some help here."

At that, something changed. He couldn't be sure what, but he experienced a change within his chest, a rhythm coinciding with his heart beat. It hadn't been there before. It almost felt...

The spear came at him again. This time, he moved faster and smacked it aside with the moonblade. "Haaaaa!" Ular's annoyed cry came out like a hiss, interrupting his chanting. Clanless took full advantage of it to leap forward and launch his own attack. The moonblade slipped past Ular's attempted parry. It would have struck home if it hadn't been for the armored breastplate. Sparks flew from the scraping impact.

Ular dropped the spear and caught Clanless's right arm with his hand. Clanless released the moonblade to his left hand and swung a quick uppercut to prevent Ular from bringing the saber back too soon. He tried to twist free, but Ular's grip proved stronger than he'd anticipated.

"I will drink your blood for Taichi Denkri!" Ular snarled down at him. "And then we will flood this land with the blood of this city!"

Clanless ignored the words, though he was surprised the champion could speak his language. He pretended to focus everything on twisting free of the grip again. Instead, he shifted back and aimed a kick at Ular's left knee. He didn't create enough of an impact to do damage, but Ular let out a grunt of pain, and his grip weakened. Clanless broke free, ducked under a wild swing of the saber, and spun around to deliver a two-handed blow. The moonblade struck the side of Ular's armored breastplate. It penetrated deep but not deep enough to hit flesh. Clanless had to twist and yank hard to get it free in time to avoid a more precise saber strike.

He backpedaled and achieved some separation again. He returned to a circular pacing, regaining his own breath. He'd fought opponents taller than himself before, but not this tall. His eyes could not keep track of his enemy's entire body at once. If he focused on Ular's eyes or his hips, he could easily miss movement elsewhere.

Ular chanted again. Clanless saw the dust swirling from the magic wind, but he felt no more than a breeze now. Whatever was helping him now, supernatural or not, it made a significant difference.

Advice from those he'd trained and fought with over the years swirled through his mind. "When your opponent is larger than you, stick to the basics. Wait for him to make a mistake!" Kan warned. "Narrow your focus. Where is his weakest point?" Badaar asked. "Your words are weapons too. When will you learn that?" Bain taunted. "Fight as one!" Swift Claw insisted.

Only Badaar's advice sounded relevant right now. Ular's potential weakest points were his legs. He wore plates of hard leather on the front of the legs, but they didn't reach all the way around. A hit to the side or back of the leg could draw blood. That's all he needed to do.

But he needed room. He tried to widen the circle of his pacing, but Ular caught on right away. "Coward! Why you try to run?"

"If I run, it will be right at you," Clanless answered calmly. Why had he entered this fight with such trepidation? It was an arena fight like any other. He'd fought hundreds like this and never worried. The only difference was that he had no obligation to entertain any of the watchers. He could end this as soon as possible. That didn't mean Ular wasn't a challenge. If this man had fought in the Sar Empire's arenas, he would have risen to the very top.

The blood trickling down his hip reminded Clanless of one other important difference. Should he suffer a serious injury, he couldn't be healed right away. They would have to get him back to the city. He put that aside. He'd been hurt before; he could deal with it.

Ular paused next to the fallen spear. He shifted his weight as if he were going to reach down for it. Clanless charged. An almost overwhelming urge came over him to leap into the air and bring the moonblade down at Ular's face. Instead, he stayed low and delivered a flurry of quick strikes at multiple angles, designed to keep his opponent on the defensive. Ular parried a couple and dodged the rest, moving surprisingly fast for someone so big and armored.

When the champion shifted from defense to attacking back, Clanless broke free again. He'd learned what he needed from the engagement. After catching his breath, he could finish this.

The crowd noise washed over him, competing with the bloodrush pounding in his ears. In some ways, he had to admit he'd missed this. Even when he'd fought in Ulken, he'd been teamed with Swift Claw. He hadn't faced an opponent in an arena setting like this since Daviland. He pushed back against the threatening excitement. This wasn't a game. Thousands of lives might be at stake.

This time, he let Ular make the move. By now, the Melkute champion had grown frustrated and wanted to end the fight fast. He swiped his saber in an arc toward the ground in front of him while shouting something in his language. Red dust erupted upward, concealing his movements… but it also concealed Clanless. Undoubtedly, Ular would be rushing forward and swinging his blade at where he believed Clanless to be.

Instead, Clanless also charged forward a couple of steps before dropping flat and sliding through the dust. He felt, rather than saw, Ular's legs passing by him. On the ground, he twisted and swung the moonblade. He smelled the blood from the moment he sliced the champion's ankle, even before Ular roared in anger.

But before Clanless could roll free, the saber came back down at him. A burning pain erupted on the right side of his head. He scrambled to his feet and staggered away. Blood poured down over his ear and into his right eye. Agony clouded his vision even more than the dust. The crowd erupted, though they probably couldn't quite tell what had happened.

The dust settled, exposing the situation for all to see. Clanless, barely on his feet, struggled to stay conscious and aware. Ular bled from his left ankle, limping toward him, mouth open with inarticulate rage. He lifted the saber with both hands.

Right before he could bring it down again, Clanless used the Taint. His eyes burned, surprising him with clear vision for a moment. Ular screamed and stumbled. Clanless brought the moonblade up to meet him, but it barely connected. Ular fell, writhing. The saber tumbled from his hands. The helmet rolled away from his head.

With his own head pounding, Clanless fought for focus. He screamed himself, lifted the moonblade, and brought it down on Ular's head. With the same motion, he fell forward over his defeated opponent.

OBLIGATION

"He did it! He won!" Qara screamed.

Koland closed his eyes and let out a deep breath while a tumultuous celebration broke out all over the city wall. In moments, the news spread to the crowd gathered in the street below. Their voices added to the cacophony. Koland opened his eyes and saw his hands gripping the stone of the parapet. He released it and turned to look at the others.

Kekeen, despite her earlier confidence, appeared the most relieved of all of them. She sank down behind the parapet, resting her forehead against it. Qara would have danced if there had been more room. As it was, the soldiers around her were delighted with her antics, especially when she hugged two of them.

"Now the real question," Sonkogh said for all of them. "Will they honor their word?"

Clanless heard pounding feet coming his way, but he didn't move. A moment later, hands grabbed his shoulder. "On your feet," Sugh said. "A victor should not bow."

"I won?" He spat on the ground, not sure if the red came from the sand or from his own blood, which continued to run down his face. Howls of outrage filled the air, but distant cheers came from the city.

Captain Rakib caught up to them. "I've never understood why you don't wear armor of your own," he muttered. He joined Sugh in lifting Clanless to his feet.

"Not used to it." Waves of pain washed over his head. "How bad?" he gasped.

Sugh leaned close to get a better look. "It is a severe cut, but I do not think it got through your thick skull." He made a clicking sound with his tongue. "The head always bleeds so much."

Rakib tore his own shirt off. "Here. We'd better bandage that as well as we can. It will take some time to get to a healer."

Sugh yanked the moonblade free from Ular's body and held it up for Clanless. "They're coming this way," he warned.

"I told you two to run," Clanless mumbled.

"That was if you lost," Sugh said. "Hold still."

Ghenbish the translator and a dozen soldiers surrounded them while Captain Rakib bound up Clanless's head. The makeshift bandaging covered his right eye.

"You have triumphed," Ghenbish said. "The mighty King Kataat Ghun will speak to you now."

"Will he keep his word?" Clanless demanded.

"He will speak to you now," the translator repeated. He stood to one side and gestured toward the other end of the arena.

Clanless took a step forward and almost fell. "Lean on me," Sugh said, gripping his shoulder. Side-by-side, they made their way across the wide space. Clanless hated to show weakness before the monarch, but he had no choice. His legs did not want to support him alone. The sounds of the Melkute crowd grew uglier the further they traveled.

A massive open-walled tent stood beyond the arena. Sugh and Rakib helped Clanless over the stone wall and into the tent. Shielded from the morning sun, the air beneath provided a welcome coolness. The red sand from the arena also covered the floor within. The King, easily identified, sat alone atop a huge throne in the middle of the tent. Clanless couldn't help wondering about how it had been transported all this way.

The King himself stared at Clanless with cold eyes beneath a high, unadorned forehead. He wore a multilayered outfit consisting primarily of various shades of red. Silver trim around his neck formed a high ridge and also decorated his shoulders, wrists, and a wide band down the center of his chest. The silver bands contained intricate engravings Clanless couldn't make out in the shadowed tent. He wore heavy boots of dark leather decorated with what looked like scales from a ghuyak.

In fact, as he glanced around the tent, he saw the ghuyak scales in various patterns on a number of the others present. Advisors, presumably. Maybe military leaders and other high-ranking officials. Two pairs of women, all with veiled faces, stood to either side and behind the throne. Wives or concubines?

Four robed men to the right drew his attention. Their attire resembled that of the Ghamba Lam and his Daghilches, though there were subtle differences in the shades of red. While the servants of the goddess wore red to symbolize blood, Clanless suspected these wore it to match the strange sand. Then again, the champion had drunk blood. Maybe there was more of a connection between the cultures than he'd at first assumed.

Ghenbish took a position at the foot of the king's throne and faced Clanless. The King spoke and Ghenbish translated: "You have defeated Ular, and yet I am not impressed."

"He fought well," Clanless answered. "Will you keep your promise?"

Sugh coughed.

"You were warned against the use of your heathen blood-magic, yet you did so anyway," the King accused.

"Not so," Clanless said. "I used no blood-magic. Your men can attest they found no blood vials on us."

"Regardless. Your own blood can provide the power. What did you use? Which of the magics did you employ?"

"I have no blood-magic!" Clanless insisted. "I am clanless. My blood does not possess any power that could affect the battle. Your champion used magic against me!"

"It was not blood-magic."

"Neither are my skills. It was a fair fight. Will you withdraw your army now?"

One of the robed men on the right rattled off a long diatribe of some kind.

"Is this the prophet of Sama El?" Clanless asked. "If so, he deceives you, mighty King! He lies to provoke you!"

"How would you know this? Are you a servant of Sama El also?"

"No. But I spoke with him. He told me about sending a prophet to convince you to invade." Clanless slipped and almost fell again. Sugh shifted his grip to stabilize him. "He is the god of chaos. He wanted a war for his own ends!"

The robed man again spoke rapidly. The King laughed and answered.

"The blind god always works to his own ends," Ghenbish translated. "This does not change our reasons for coming here. Your Empire oppresses the slave and the poor. We are here to punish them for this. For many years, the great King Kataat Ghun has listened to the stories of your people. He has heard of children taken from their families and forced to fight and die in arenas. Of others who are slaves because their parents made poor decisions. The King said to himself, 'are we not all children of the red god? Do I not have an obligation to these, my brothers and sisters in the South?' So we have come to meet this obligation."

"We overthrew the Hawk King ourselves! We're working to get rid of slavery and change things!"

"Do you deny the stories? Is it not as I have said?"

"No, I don't deny them! But they don't tell everything. We're changing it."

The Melkute King leaned forward. "Then surrender your city to us now. We will kill only the leaders and oppressors. We will set the rest free."

Clanless tried to point back at the arena, but his hand shook. "I won the fight. The agreement was that you would withdraw."

King Kataat Ghun waved his hand dismissively. "You used the magic. The fight is not valid."

Captain Rakib stepped forward. "How many do you call oppressors?" he asked.

"What are you doing?" Clanless pulled himself straighter with Sugh's help.

Rakib glanced back at them. "If they only want the council and the military leaders, maybe it's a price worth paying."

After a consultation with the King, Ghenbish spoke again. "The city has two circles, yes?" He motioned with a finger to illustrate. "Those in the upper circle: they are the oppressors. We will deliver the oppressed, the ones in the lower circle."

Captain Rakib's face paled. "That's almost half the city's population!"

"Once this city is freed, we will leave. We will move on to the next city. And the next. Until all of the Sar Empire is free of this oppression. And then we will let those who are free join with the mighty Melkute Kingdom."

Clanless looked around at the other officials in the tent. "You have your own rich," he pointed out. "What's the difference?"

"If you will not surrender the city, then we will take it by force. We will then be unable to determine who is an oppressor and who is not. They will all be treated alike."

"Meaning you'll kill everyone. How is that deliverance?" Rakib said. "Even if we wanted to, we don't have the authority to surrender the city to you."

"And you made an agreement!" Clanless cried. "You gave your word. I won the fight! Is that not an, an obligation?"

"It is not. You violated the rules with your use of the blood-magic. Every obligation met. The contest is invalid."

The Melkute King stood and made a proclamation. Soldiers swept in and surrounded the three men.

"You will be kept safe with our other prisoners while we deal with the city," Ghenbish said. "We will bring deliverance." He gave a short bow. "Every obligation met."

((((●))))

The tension among the watchers on the city wall grew with each passing moment after Clanless and the others disappeared inside the king's tent. Confused murmurings swept through the crowds. Those in the street shouted questions to which those on the wall had no answers. Koland paced behind the others, struggling with his own thoughts. For some reason, the incident with Kekeen in the palace kept circulating through his mind. The missing part of the story ate at him. He knew what he'd gone to do, but something else had happened. Why? And why couldn't he remember.

"Something is happening," Kekeen said.

Koland turned to see.

"The soldiers are on the move." Sonkogh pointed at the activity.

"They don't look like they're leaving," Qara said.

"They're not." Koland stepped up to the parapet. "They're preparing for a new attack."

"They're readying the catapults!" a soldier yelled.

"Clanless failed," Sonkogh said. "Or they broke the agreement."

An officer pushed his way through the other soldiers on the wall. "Clear the way! Clear the way!" he shouted. "If you're not ready to fight, you need to leave. Now!"

Koland stood aside and let the others go ahead. Before following them down the stairs, he took one last look outside the city. A sudden wind struck him, knocking him off-balance momentarily. A distant motion caught his eye. A huge rock flew through the air, launched by a Melkute catapult. Before Koland could turn and run, it struck the north gates. The crowds below screamed and panicked at the impact. The wind increased.

Koland grabbed the officer's arm. "How long can the gates hold out if they focus on them like that?"

"I don't know." He shook loose from Koland's grip. "It's never been tried."

After one last look confirming his thoughts, Koland scrambled down the stairs. At the bottom, he caught Qara and Sonkogh. "Spread the word. It's time."

"Time?" Kekeen asked behind him.

Koland ignored her. "Get the people moving. We don't know how much time we have." He glanced back at the sound of another impact against the gates. "If I'm right, the Melkute wind-magic is propelling those stones harder than ever. It's time to abandon the lower city."

The others stared at him in shock.

"Wind-magic?" Qara repeated.

"Go!" Koland ordered. "Tell everyone to hurry!"

Kekeen seized his arm. "What are you saying? What happened to Aldan?"

He looked down at her, wishing she truly was his daughter. "Our only hope now is that the inner walls will be harder to breach."

"But what about Aldan?"

"I don't see how we will ever see him again. Let's move!"

PANIC

"Hagh was the best friend a man could ask for."

"Can you… tell me about him?"

"I will." Sugh got to his feet. He did not know Kekeen very well, save that Clanless loved her. He sat with her at a table and described his friendship with Hagh.

This day, this woman had suffered as well. She'd seen a man she respected, now possessed by an evil entity, murder another man in front of her. And that entity had made disturbing insinuations about Clanless, the man she loved. Sugh could see the evidence of her own tears. She had suffered this day. And yet… she'd sought Sugh out to attempt comfort. She cared about others.

His mind went over all this while they talked. This woman impressed him more than any he'd known, even his beloved Chabi. She possessed a heart for others and a fire to resist evil, truly a powerful combination.

Which is why Sugh slid off his chair and knelt on the floor before her. Maybe his friendship with Hagh had softened his heart enough to want more. "Noble lady of song," he declared, "I will serve you until we find Clanless, or you have no need of me."

Kekeen's mouth fell open. "You're not a slave any more! I'm not your master!"

His eyes twinkled. "I am not asking to be a slave. I am a free man. And

I can choose my path. I choose this."

"This is a good idea," the goddess whispered in his mind while Kekeen looked around the room. "But be careful of your feelings toward her."

Fascinating. She'd never spoken to him when others were around. This must be a very good idea.

"Clanless is my friend," Sugh said, "perhaps the only one I have left. Since we cannot go find him now, I can help him by serving you." He shrugged. "Besides, she said it would be a good idea."

"Thank you, I guess?" Kekeen blinked. "Who is 'she'?"

"The goddess." Sugh grinned and got to his feet. Before Kekeen could ask anything else, he picked up his axe and left the room.

Until they found Clanless, he would stay by Kekeen's side unless she sent him away. And while he would never wish for Clanless to die, if the worst happened, he could envision himself staying by Kekeen's side forever. Or maybe Qara would come back.

"Be careful..." the voice whispered again.

Now

With desperation adding to his strength, Koland pushed through the crowd. He held tight to Kekeen's hand, pulling her along with him. The throng moving up the street toward the upper city had become a dense pack of humanity. People shouted at each other. Soldiers along the road shouted at everyone. And behind them came the roar of magic wind propelling stone against the north gate.

"This is insane!" Kekeen cried. "Tell the soldiers you're a member of the council. They can get us through!"

"My life is no more important than anyone here," he answered. Someone stepped on his foot, and he almost stumbled.

"What about the life of your daughter?"

Koland gave her a narrow-eyed glance. Kekeen would never have said something like that, but the blood-wraith within her cared little for anyone else. "We're moving," he said, more to himself than her. "We'll make it."

Ahead, he could see the gates into the upper city. Only about a hundred yards remained now, but the space grew tighter and tighter with the masses. Their forward progress slowed almost to a complete stop. Too many frantic people tried to cram through one narrow space. Koland pulled Kekeen closer to himself so they could stay together.

The crashes behind escalated in frequency. Only fifty yards remained now. They could make it. They would make it. They still had time.

And then one final, tremendous crash echoed across the city, followed by a gust of wind sweeping over their heads.

"They're through the main gate!" someone cried. Screams filled the street, and the crowd surged forward in a panic. Koland saw a couple of people go down in the massed throng, trampled underfoot by their desperate neighbors.

Thirty yards. Twenty. How long would the soldiers keep the gates open? How long would it take the Melkute army to reach them? He certainly wouldn't be able to tell by the sound: between screams, shouts, and everything in between, he wouldn't know if Melkute soldiers had arrived unless he saw them.

Ten yards. Kekeen stumbled and started to fall. He grabbed her with both hands and pulled her back to her feet. Others pushed past him in that brief moment, leaving him further from the gate. The soldiers on top of it screamed something, trying to be heard above the crowd.

Five yards. To his horror, Koland saw the enormous gates starting to close, pushing inward onto the masses of humanity. The gap between them became smaller. The desperation of the crowd erupted even higher. People were pushing so hard, Koland almost felt like he could ride their pushing all the way. But it was a deceptive thought: if he lifted both feet from the ground, even for a moment, he would fall and never get back up.

They plunged through the final few feet and made it past the slowly-closing gates. Almost in unison, everyone around Koland let out a gasp of relief. The pressure of the crowd subsided as people spread out. Most had no idea where to go, but they hastened to get as far from the walls as possible. Many would probably end up near the palace and arena. The streets would be full of displaced people everywhere, assuming the upper city's gates could hold for long.

Koland pulled Kekeen off to the side near the entrance to a massive estate. Five servants stood near the entrance, armed with maces, keeping out any of the "rabble" attempting to enter their master's property. Koland almost laughed. If the crowd decided, as a whole, to enter the estate, these five wouldn't be able to stop anything.

"Get back to the palace," he told Kekeen. "I need to get up on the wall and see what's happening."

"But what about Aldan?"

Koland glared at her. "If Aldan is still alive, he's a prisoner. And even if he escapes, he can't possibly get through to us. Waiting at the palace is the best and safest option." He narrowed his eyes further. "Unless you're ready to leave my daughter now."

For a moment, she hesitated and a tiny thrill of hope stabbed through Koland. Zektel had entered Kekeen to be close to Aldan, or so she claimed. If he was truly gone, why stay? Why even remain in a city about to be overrun?

"Suirel doesn't believe he's dead," she said. "His great project is almost complete, and he's counting on Aldan to show up before the end."

"What project is that?"

She didn't answer.

Koland gave her a gentle shove. "Get to the palace. I'll come when I can."

Without a glance back, she hurried away. Koland took a deep breath and watched the way they'd come. Even as he did, the gate slammed shut with a thunderous boom. He winced at the cries of anguish from the other side. People of his city had been left behind to die. The Melkute would not spare them. He could only hope everyone he knew had made it inside.

Koland turned and working his way through the milling crowd. He identified himself to a guard and climbed the stairs to the inner wall of the upper city. It wasn't much different from the outer city wall, though a bit smaller. It had never been intended to hold off an enemy indefinitely, only as a last resort while awaiting a rescuing army. Or, Koland considered, the Hawk King had it built to hold off a rebellion of the lower classes.

Near the gates, he found General Ghan. Spatters of blood and dirt decorated his usual spotless and immaculate uniform, along with multiple tears and holes. He'd been involved in some fighting Koland knew nothing about.

"Storyteller," he said. "Come to see the city's final downfall?"

"You've given up then?"

Ghan snorted. "Never. Not so long as a single one of my soldiers draws breath." He looked back into the lower city. "But it does not seem likely we will long survive this. With the north gate breached, the Melkute will open the others from within. Their forces will pour in from all sides."

"What of your god? Do you still trust Suirel's plans?"

The General did not answer. He turned to one of his officers and issued orders to be carried around the upper city.

Koland stepped to the parapet and looked down, afraid of what he would see. The enemy army had not reached this wall yet, of course. But he could see fires erupting all over the parts of the lower city nearest the outer gates. And the sounds… he wished he couldn't hear the sounds. Below him, people pounded on the gates, pleading to be allowed entrance. Others gave themselves up to their fate and sat in the street, weeping or staring off into the distance. Beyond, he heard sounds of destruction, doors and windows being smashed, fires igniting, and endless feet pounding down the streets. Above it all, he heard screams: screams of the dying and abused, screams of victory and debauchery from the enemy, screams of despair and screams of exultation.

In all his life, Koland had never felt such an overwhelming sense of dread and despair. Hope had truly vanished forever. Nothing could save Et-Baylak now. He stared out over the very end of the Sar Empire.

He lifted his eyes to look beyond the city. He could see the last few hundreds of Melkute soldiers pushing toward the fallen gate, waiting their turn to enter the city. Such a contrast with the crowd Koland had just escaped: a crowd desperate to enter and save their lives. This crowd pushed forward, desperate to enter and end lives. Beyond them, the camp lay empty, the siege engines abandoned and quiet.

"Seen enough?" General Ghan asked from behind him.

Koland blinked and turned around. He'd lost track of himself and his position in the last few minutes. He had no idea how long he'd stood there.

The General stepped up beside him and looked down as well, putting his hands behind his back. "I had hoped and believed we would receive some relief," he murmured. "A small force from Ulken, perhaps, or even Conchaga. Or the port cities. They might not have accomplished much, but…" He trailed off.

"But it would have been something," Koland said.

"It would have been something."

Neither spoke for a while. The screams below grew louder.

"Is there nothing we can do for the people below?" Koland gestured to the ones locked outside.

"It will be a little while before the enemy's soldiers arrive here," General Ghan answered. "They will be preoccupied with what they can find below. Our archers will be ready to make them pay for coming too close, but in the end, there will be nothing we can do."

Koland forced himself to look again at the trapped people. His eyes locked with someone else's, and he felt his knees go weak. Two of the figures outside the gate stared up directly at him, their faces lined with despair.

Sonkogh and Qara.

ALSO WOLF CHOSEN

"At least they let us keep our weapons," Sugh said. He shook his axe at the guards outside their cage. "Don't come too close! My axe is thirsty!"

Clanless would have laughed if he had the strength. His head pounded with pain. He set the moonblade aside and stretched out on the dirt. His one uncovered eye stared up at the moon. It shone bright and free of the morning's red tint, not that it seemed to matter to the Melkute. They were attacking the city again. He'd failed.

They'd been escorted to the back of the enemy camp, the farthest section from the city itself. Soldiers forced them to enter a massive wooden cage the size of a small house. Eight other disheveled prisoners watched them enter but made no moves. Captain Rakib crossed the space to speak with them.

"We could break out of here very easily," Sugh continued. "My axe could do it in a few good swings." He coughed.

"Too many… soldiers," Clanless said.

"Not for the three of us. We could—" Sugh turned around and slapped his head. "Ah, fool that I am! I forgot. Captain Rakib! I am in need of your assistance!"

Out of the corner of his vision, Clanless saw Sugh kneel beside him. Captain Rakib's footsteps came from the other direction. "I spoke with the other prisoners," he said. "Most of them have been here since before the siege began."

"We can speak more of them later. For now," Sugh said, "I need some of your blood."

"My blood?"

"You are clan Kurav, are you not? My friend here needs healing."

"Yes, but… we don't have a priest. The blood-magic doesn't work that way."

"In most cases, you would be right." Sugh gently took hold of the blood-soaked bandaging. "But this is Clanless. His blood combined with yours will be enough. Qara told me everything I need to know."

"Who is Qara?"

Sugh looked up at him. "Someone who is very knowledgeable about these things. Now. I need some blood. A good amount, if you please."

"Ahhh!" Clanless couldn't help the cry of pain when Sugh started to remove the bandage.

"Sorry, my friend. I'm afraid this is going to hurt a lot more before it gets better."

"Do it," he gasped.

Sugh continued to work with the bandage. He turned Clanless's head to the side to expose the wound.

"How do I give you any blood?" Rakib asked. "I don't have any vials on me or anything."

"Once I have the wound showing," Sugh said, "cut yourself and let it pour."

"Pour? I can't cut myself that deep!"

"A few drops won't be enough. Give me what you can." Sugh pointed at Clanless. "We need him. Unless you wish to give up right now. Maybe they will cut your head off and drink your blood too, eh?"

Rakib made grumbling noises. "Give me your axe."

"It's over there." Sugh pulled the last of the bandage away to another pained cry from Clanless. "Oh."

"What is it?" Clanless asked.

"A large piece of your scalp has torn free. I, uh…" Sugh touched something, and Clanless screamed. "Oh, goddess. Please help my friend here." He lowered his face to look into Clanless's eyes. "The magic should still heal you, but I am no expert. You may have a scar. Or a bald spot. Even so, I'm afraid we cannot wait."

"Whatever… it takes."

"Very well. Captain Rakib, if you please." Sugh straightened up and climbed on top of Clanless. "I will hold him down. Please dispense the blood." He put both hands on Clanless's shoulders. "Take courage, my friend. This is like any Arena Night. A few moments of pain, and all will be normal again."

Clanless couldn't see what was happening, but he heard Rakib wince as he cut himself.

"Let it gather in your hand if you can," Sugh said.

"It's already dripping."

A moment later, the pain on the side of his head erupted anew, worse than ever. Clanless screamed. His muscles tensed, but Sugh's weight held him down and kept him from thrashing. "Keep going!" Sugh shouted. Voices of the guards shouted from outside their cage, demanding answers.

"How much?" Rakib gasped.

"More!" Sugh ordered. "It's working!"

In every other case, the healing blood-magic had been as painful as the original injury. This time, because of the slower application, the pain dragged on far longer. Ular's saber strike had been a moment's intense agony. This was far worse. Clanless jerked his head about. Blood dribbled over his face.

"Hey! Can't you hold his head?"

"I am too busy holding his body!"

"Enough!" Clanless shouted. "It's enough!"

Captain Rakib backed away, muttering something.

"Are you sure?" Sugh asked. "I cannot tell if—"

"It's enough! Let me up!"

Sugh climbed to his feet and stepped out of the way. Clanless sat up and took deep breaths. Sugh knelt beside him and tried to look at the side of his head. "I do not think it is fully healed."

"I'm all right," Clanless insisted. "It's enough."

A guard poked a spear into the cage, yelling something. "It is none of your business!" Sugh shouted back. He picked up the moonblade and waved it at him. The guard backed away and exchanged words with two others.

"If this keeps up, I will run out of clothes to bind wounds," Rakib said. Clanless looked up and almost laughed. The Captain had torn a strip from his trousers and used it to bandage his own arm. Combined with the loss of his shirt, the soldier looked very much out of uniform.

"Thank you," Clanless told him. His head ached with a throbbing fierceness, but he could endure it now. The worst was over. He put out his hand. Sugh took it and pulled him to his feet. He wavered for a moment as his vision blurred, but the sensation passed.

Sugh helped brush dirt from his clothes. "No red sand in here," he noted.

"Maybe it has something to do with their god," Rakib suggested. "They talk about 'red' a lot. It's the only word of their language I can understand."

In the distance, Clanless could now hear a lot more shouting and an occasional boom. "They're attacking the city, aren't they?"

"They are," Sugh confirmed. He handed the moonblade to Clanless. "What should we do?"

"What can we do? I fought to save the city, and it didn't matter."

"We are, in effect, powerless," Captain Rakib said, joining them. He returned Sugh's axe. "We are but three. We could break out and attack them from behind, but…" He shrugged.

"Even such mighty warriors as we would be overwhelmed in time." Sugh let out a big sigh, followed by a cough. "There must be something we can do to help, even so."

"I don't see what." Clanless watched the guards. Others had joined them, bringing the number to well over a dozen. "If only…" He felt a twinge in his chest. Had he felt that before? A few minutes earlier? Maybe even during the fight.

"If only what?" Rakib asked.

"If only we weren't alone." He was sure now. A smile spread over his face.

"What are you saying?" Sugh asked.

"Be ready." Clanless positioned himself next to the cage wall, holding the moonblade in preparation. Sugh joined him, axe also at the ready. In response, several guards aimed their spears at the duo, preparing to throw if they made any further moves.

A scream of horror seized everyone's attention. Both guards and prisoners spun to see… nothing. Two of the guards stood apart from the others, looking around as if confused. One of the others shouted something to them. One turned and held out his arms in a shrug.

And a beastman landed on his back, taking him to the ground while driving a sword through his neck. Beside him, another beastman killed the second guard.

The others spun their weapons away from the prisoners and toward this new threat. But before they could do anything, six more beastmen erupted from concealment behind them.

Clanless and Sugh attacked the cage walls and cut through it in moments. By the time they stepped out, the fight was over. All of the Melkute soldiers lay dead. Eight beastmen stood triumphant. One of them bounded forward and stopped in front of Clanless. "Wolf Chosen," he declared. "I have returned."

Clanless grabbed Swift Claw by the shoulder. "I knew you would." He looked to the other beastmen. "Did you bring more than this, or…?"

The beastman motioned for them to follow. "Come. There is much to see."

"Wait, wait, wait." Clanless held on to him. "Swift Claw, the city is about to fall. We must do something. They have their own magic. They—"

"They twist the winds," Swift Claw interrupted. "We know. It is why you must come. There is much to see. And do."

Captain Rakib came up behind the two fighters. "What is this?" he whispered. "You control the beastmen?"

"Control? No," Sugh answered. "But this one is our friend, Swift Claw. I think we should do as he says."

Clanless turned and looked back at the other prisoners. "You are all welcome to come with us," he called. "It will be frightening, but you will be safe. Or you can make your own way of escape. Or stay here, I suppose."

The prisoners talked amongst themselves, then hurried out, one or two at a time, and ran off in different directions.

"I suppose I'll come with you," Rakib said. He eyed the beastmen uncertainly.

Swift Claw and the others led the way behind the cage and over the nearest hill. Despite the haste the beastmen encouraged, the journey seemed to take far too long. As they walked, Clanless and the others couldn't help looking back at the battle.

One of those times, Captain Rakib stopped. "I think the gate has fallen."

Sugh shaded his eyes to look. "Are you certain? I cannot tell."

With lowered shoulders, Rakib shook his head. "They are moving forward. Either the gate has fallen, or… or nothing. There is no other reason."

"Then we're too late," Clanless said.

"They will fall back into the upper city," Rakib said. "The walls there will still hold… at least until they can get their siege weapons and that accursed magic into position."

Clanless patted Rakib on the back, knowing it was a weak gesture. He stared down at the city. Kekeen, Qara, Salkhi, Koland… and so many thousands of others. They might be dying even now. A hollow pit formed in his stomach. All that they'd done, all that he'd tried to accomplish… it had been useless. Suirel triumphed.

"We must hurry!" Swift Claw urged.

With a last look at the surging army pouring toward the city, Clanless turned away.

◖◖◖◖●◗◗◗◗

The beastmen crowded in close as they came over the hill. Staring down at his feet, Clanless didn't notice much of anything until Sugh murmured, "Goddess!"

He looked up and gasped. Hundreds of beastmen stood assembled below, all of them armed and ready to fight. At the sight of the humans, several of them let out howls of celebration.

"Swift Claw! You convinced the entire… the entire army?"

The beastman shook his head. "Not I, Wolf Chosen. When I found them, they were ready." He pointed. "Because of him."

A lone man limped toward them, leaning on a crutch. Clanless's mouth fell open. "Daviland?"

The rebel leader grinned. Behind him, the leaders of the beastmen followed. Clanless recognized Wind Tooth at their head.

"Greetings, Clanless," Daviland called. "It seems you and I share more than either of us thought!"

"He also," Swift Claw explained, "is Wolf Chosen."

They came together and grasped hands. "I never thought to see you alive again," Clanless said.

"I thought I was dead too. But then that wolf—"

"It appeared to you too?"

"It saved my life. And then—" He swept an arm back.

"They found you?"

"Yes. And now we can save Et-Baylak."

"But, but how?" Clanless stared out over the assembled beastmen. "They wouldn't listen to me!"

Daviland shrugged. "I'm told I have a way with words."

"We must hurry," Captain Rakib broke in. "They have breached the front gates."

"Ah, Captain." Daviland smiled at him. "Rackhim, is it?"

"Rakib."

"Yes, Rakib." He chuckled. "I almost had it. I am grateful you are here. We need these two fine warriors, of course"—he gestured at Clanless and Sugh—"but I need you."

"Me?" Now Rakib's mouth fell open. "Why me?"

Daviland shifted on his crutch and put a hand on the captain's shoulder.

"These beastmen are amazing fighters. And for some reason known only the goddess, they're willing to follow me. But I am no military strategist."

"I, I'm not either. I'm just a captain."

"Nonsense. As I recall, you must have been in charge of the defense of the city. If not for you, it would not have been prepared for this attack at all."

"But General Ghan—"

"Pfft. He built on what you had already done. Come!" Daviland pulled him closer. "Help us. Direct this fearsome army in the right way. Let us save this city."

Clanless's mind had been racing since he'd seen the army. Hope filled him, a strange feeling after so long. But something else weighed on him. "Daviland... I need to get inside the city. Suirel is there, in the arena. We don't know what he's doing."

Daviland nodded. "I wondered where he went."

"I will tell you, Aldan."

Clanless turned in surprise, because the voice was Sugh's. "You've never called me that."

Sugh let out a long sigh. "I didn't want to say anything for so long. I hid for so long. But... you need to know."

"What do you mean? You haven't been hiding," Rakib said.

Swift Claw let out a hiss. "His wind is not his own."

"What?" Clanless lifted the moonblade.

"Wait, wait, wait." Sugh held up a hand and lowered his own weapon to the ground. "You know me, Aldan. It's, it's Yul."

"Yul? Have you been inside Sugh this whole time?"

"After Suirel threw me out of you, I had to find another body. I just wanted somewhere to hide, you know. I haven't controlled him until just now."

"Wolf Chosen!" Swift Claw drew near with his claws lifted. "Should I make him bleed?"

"No, not yet. Thank you, Swift Claw." Clanless glanced around. "Tell your people we'll be with them in just a moment."

"What does this mean?" Captain Rakib asked. "What is happening?"

"We're talking to a blood-wraith named Yul," Clanless said, lowering the moonblade. "He was inside me for a long time. He... doesn't want to serve Suirel."

Sugh nodded and lowered his head. "And... I'll leave this one if you want me to."

Clanless winced. "Yes. I don't think you should stay inside my friend.

In fact, you shouldn't stay inside anyone who doesn't want you there."

"I'm so tired," he mumbled. "I just want it all to be over."

Clanless set down the moonblade and removed the wolf pelt from his shoulder. "Maybe you should come back into me, Yul."

Sugh looked up. "I would like that, Aldan. But you've changed since… the crystal cave. No one can enter you now."

"This is fascinating," Daviland said, stepping near them. "But you said you could tell us what Suirel is doing?"

"He's building a new portal to our… home," the blood-wraith said through Sugh. "That's why he took all the crystal. You destroyed the old one with your battle against him. But if he gets it built out here, in the open, your people can't shut it down like they did before."

"How is that?" Daviland asked.

"They flooded it with our blood," Clanless said. "It's why the priests have taken blood sacrifices all these years. They used it to control the portal and keep the blood-wraiths from coming to our world."

"He's almost done building it now," Yul said. "I don't know what he has to do to activate it, but once he does, the rest of my people will come."

"How many are there?" Daviland wanted to know.

Sugh turned and looked him in the eyes. "Millions."

For a moment, no one said anything.

"I don't understand," Captain Rakib said. "Someone wants to release millions of blood-wraiths?"

"In the arena," Clanless told him. "That's what's happening in there. Where General Ghan hasn't let us interfere."

"All the more reason to save the city now," Daviland declared. "Come, Captain. Let's give our army here their orders." He pointed at Clanless and Sugh. "And there is a special job for you two. Swift Claw will explain."

"Haven't you been listening?" Clanless exclaimed. "We have to get inside and stop Suirel!"

"Exactly. And the only way for you to do that is to get this army out of the way. Work with me, Clanless. We're on the same side now." Daviland smiled. "It's good, isn't it? For us to fight together for once?" He shifted his crutch and leaned closer. "The wolf said I could be one of those who would save this land. I'm pretty sure you're included in that."

"What is happening? Did I miss something?" Sugh said. "How did I drop my axe?" He bent to pick it up.

Clanless rolled his eyes and looked back at his friend. "Yul! You need to come out of him now."

Sugh's face shifted ever so slightly. "Aldan… let me stay just until you defeat Suirel. After that, it won't matter."

"You'll have to talk to Sugh about that. It's his body." He paused. "On second thought, no. No. I can't have you taking control of him at a crucial moment, like you tried to do to me. Suirel can still order you."

"The answer to that is in your hands," Yul said. "And it will protect him from others of my kind."

Clanless looked down at the wolf pelt. If what Yul said was true, he didn't need it himself any more. He held it out. "Prove you still want to help. Put it on yourself."

Sugh took the wolf pelt and draped it over his own shoulders. "What am I doing? This is…" He paused, listening now to a voice no one else couldn't hear. "A Siphon? Yes. Why do you ask?"

While the internal dialogue continued, Clanless turned back to Swift Claw. "All right. What does Daviland want us to do?"

Swift Claw pointed in the direction of the Melkute army. "Those who twist the winds. We must stop them. They helped break your city's gate. Now they try to break the next one."

"The priests or prophets or whatever they are? All right. We take them down and head into the city ourselves. As soon as Sugh is done talking, we can go."

"I do not understand," Swift Claw said. "He has another wind, but you do not cast it out?"

"It's complicated," Clanless answered. "I think they can work together. For now. Where do we find these priests?."

Swift Claw again pointed back the way they had come. "Beyond where we found you, there is a… cloth enclosure?"

"A tent?"

"That is the word, yes. The ones who twist the wind are there. We must end their work."

"We will. Sugh, are you ready?"

The big man adjusted the wolf pelt on his shoulder. "I am ready. This looks better on me than it did on you, anyway."

"I will want it back when this is over," Clanless warned.

"We'll see."

AT THE GATES

"That's a member of the council down there!" Koland insisted to General Ghan. "There must be something we can do!"

"We can't open the gates again. It's far too dangerous."

"You just said we had some time! That the enemy is preoccupied with pillaging."

The General shook his head. "We cannot risk it. There are too many people. They would all try to get inside, and the enemy would arrive to find our gates open. The slaughter would then begin for all of us."

Koland looked back down. Sonkogh and Qara had broken free of the rest of the crowd and moved along the wall below him.

"A rope!" he exclaimed. "Do you have a rope?"

General Ghan hesitated. "We can try," he conceded. "But if people swarm our attempt, or enemy soldiers show up, we drop it."

"It's worth a try, at least!" He turned and waved at the two below, directing them further along the wall. To his chagrin, a handful of others saw the motion and started to follow them.

The General dispatched a soldier to find a rope. Koland continued to move along the wall, guiding Sonkogh and Qara further away from the gates. Others followed out of curiosity and desperate hope.

The soldier returned a few minutes later, carrying a thick rope wrapped around his own body. He started toward the parapet, but the General stopped him. "Don't let anyone see the rope until you're ready to throw the whole thing at once," he warned. The soldier nodded and unwrapped it.

Koland gestured for Sonkogh to wait.

An archer a few feet away called out to the General: "Sir! The enemy is approaching!" He pointed before putting an arrow to the string.

"Stand ready," General Ghan ordered. He turned to the soldier with the rope. "It's now or never."

The soldier stepped to the edge, looked down, and heaved most of the rope over the parapet. Sonkogh and Qara caught it. The others rushed toward them, shouting.

"I was afraid of this," the General muttered.

"Hurry!" Koland shouted.

Sonkogh shoved the rope into Qara's arms and turned to confront the others. He held out his arms to stop them.

"Pull!" Ghan commanded.

Three soldiers caught hold of the rope and started to pull it back. Qara wrapped it around herself and held on as tight as she could. Her feet left the ground. Sonkogh argued with another man, trying to hold him back. The other man punched him. Another younger man darted past both of them and grabbed at Qara's legs. She screamed.

"Sir?" the archer asked, aiming down.

"We don't release arrows on our own," General Ghan said.

"Qara!" Koland looked around for something—anything—to throw.

She shrieked again as the young man pulled her back toward the ground. Her hands slid along the rope.

Sonkogh pushed the other man aside and dove at her attacker. He managed one quick punch to the younger man's side before he was grabbed from behind again.

An arrow pinged off the wall near Qara. Koland looked up and saw Melkute soldiers running forward while two of their archers pulled arrows back to launch. More shouts and screams.

"Release!" Ghan shouted. His own archers let loose a flurry of arrows at the oncoming foes. Three of them went down.

The young man below tried to lunge past Qara to grab the rope himself. She took advantage of the moment to kick at him. He broke free, and the soldiers yanked Qara up several feet.

Sonkogh struggled to his feet. He shoved the young man aside again as he tried to leap for Qara. An arrow struck him in the back.

"Sonkogh!" Koland cried. His friend looked straight up at him and smiled. Then he turned to protect Qara one last time from two men who rushed forward.

Arrows whined from both sides. A second one struck Sonkogh. The impact jerked him around, and he fell to his knees. Koland could only watch as his friend toppled over face-down into the dirt.

A moment later, the soldiers pulled Qara over the top. Her hands were torn and bleeding, her clothes ripped and filthy. Freed, she rushed into Koland's arms, crying. "Thank you, thank you," she whispered.

Koland looked past her to General Ghan and nodded his appreciation.

"We, we tried to get everyone," Qara said into his shoulder. "Sonkogh wouldn't stop until we'd swept through almost the entire lower city."

"You both saved hundreds," Koland said. He pulled her free of his embrace. "Let's get your hands taken care of."

He started to turn away when a new sound echoed across the screams and chaos. For reasons he didn't understand, a chill ran up his back. The hair on his arms stood on end. He paused and looked out past the city. "What was that?"

"It couldn't be." Heedless of enemy arrows, General Ghan leaned across the parapet, staring.

The sound came again. This time, Koland recognized it. A horn of some kind, blowing in the far distance. "The Melkute do not use horns... do they?"

General Ghan's arm shot out as he pointed to the north. "Storyteller! Should you survive, you will have a great tale to tell of this day!"

"What is it? Some of our soldiers from another city?" Koland squinted. He could see a crowd of figures coming over a hill in the distance, but he couldn't make them out.

"Goddess above," the General breathed. "If I weren't seeing it with my own eyes, I would never believe it."

"Who is it?" Qara asked.

"Beastmen! They're attacking the Melkute from behind!"

Koland and Qara's eyes met. "Clanless must have done it," she gasped. "He went back and convinced the beastmen to join us!"

Koland wrinkled his brow. "When would he—?"

General Ghan ran down the wall. "Assemble a force!" he shouted. "We must launch a counterattack immediately!"

"Are we... are we saved?" Qara asked, her voice shaking.

"I don't know." Koland looked back. The horde of beastmen charging forward looked awfully small compared to the vast Melkute army. But maybe, just maybe...

Led by Swift Claw, Clanless and Sugh hurried back over the hill and into the fringes of the Melkute camp. They scurried in between several smaller tents. At first Clanless wondered about their purpose, but then he saw a scantily-clad woman peaking out from one of them. She had deep-set sad eyes that reminded him of Tuulka. A bruise darkened her cheek. Anger filled Clanless's chest. The Melkute King claimed to care about the oppressed, and this was how they treated women?

They passed by larger tents, those used by the soldiers. These were empty, of course, a reminder to hurry. The occupants were all shoving their way into Et-Baylak.

Everywhere they went, red sand sprinkled the ground. It didn't cover everything like within the king's tent or the arena, but they'd made an effort to spread at least a little throughout the camp except in the prisoners' cage.

Once they reached the end of the soldier's tents, he spotted the arena where he'd fought. It stood empty now, as did the tent where the King and his entourage had been. No doubt they had moved nearer the city to watch its fall.

A snort erupted to the right. Clanless whirled, moonblade at ready. He relaxed upon seeing several large creatures penned up at this end of the tents. They were as large as Tuulka, but without the ghuyak's armor. Instead, they stood tall on long legs with tight muscles, two large horns curving up from their heads, and thick fur covering their entire bodies.

Sugh leaned in and spoke quietly: "Maybe we release those things and let them cause problems?"

It sounded fun, but… "No." Clanless turned away. "Chaos is what Suirel wants. Let's stick to what we know to do."

Another large tent stood near the king's. Six guards stood outside, but their attention focused on the city, no doubt wishing they could be a part of the pillaging. Swift Claw pointed at the tent and waved his hand back and forth. Clanless took a closer look. The tent's entire surface undulated as if moved by unseen winds from every direction. A low chanting came from within.

The three of them crouched together to consider their strategy. Clanless had been concerned about detection, but aside from the guards, who would raise an alarm? And who would come in response? The camp was largely deserted. "Let's do it fast," he told the others. "The longer we let them do their work, the greater the danger to the city."

"We don't know how many are within," Sugh pointed out.

"We'll take the guards down first," Clanless said. "Then you and I will make a big entrance, while Swift Claw goes around the back, just in case they can stop us with this wind magic."

"I will cut a new door," the beastman said.

"Yes, and then cut as many of them inside as you can. I'll do the rest with the Taint."

"It does simplify things: this Taint of yours," Sugh said.

Clanless didn't answer. Swift Claw slipped off in the opposite direction while he and Sugh made their way as close to the large tent as they could. With the guards focused on the city, they were able to get almost within striking distance before one turned and noticed them. He let out one quick shout before Sugh's axe silenced him. Clanless took down a second before the other four could join the fight.

Both Clanless and Sugh had fought multiple opponents many times in the arena. Four against two was not even a challenge for them. With blood dripping from their weapons, they threw open the tent's door.

Clanless caught a brief glimpse of around a dozen men and women, most wearing the robes he'd seen in the king's entourage. The one nearest to them threw up his hands as if warding them away.

And the next instant, a wind hit Clanless and Sugh with such force, it threw them into the air. For a brief moment, Clanless remembered Suirel using a similar power to lift him off his feet in the cavern. Both of them smashed into one of the soldier tents. It collapsed beneath them, and they rolled clear. Sugh groaned and pushed himself up. "Where is my axe?"

"It's here somewhere." Clanless found his own moonblade and looked back to the big tent. A commotion came from inside. Swift Claw!

Clanless scrambled to his feet and almost fell right back down. Pain erupted in his gut. The impact of hitting the ground had aggravated his old injury within, whatever it was. He gritted his teeth and staggered back. Snarls from Swift Claw and shouts from the wind users drew him on. As soon as he got close enough to the tent again, he activated the Taint.

Cries of pain answered his action, followed by silence. Clanless pushed the tent door open again and stared.

Every one of the Melkute magic users lay on the ground. Most didn't move, but two or three twitched and groaned. Swift Claw stood on the right, panting, his sword and claws red. "Well done, Wolf Chosen."

"Well done yourself." Clanless squinted in the low light provided by a handful of lamps scattered around the rim of the tent. The magic users had been standing in a wide circle. Strange markings decorated the ground, which was covered with more of the red sand. Each of them had apparently stood in a kind of circle with lines stretching out to the other circles and toward the center of the tent. Two bodies lay on a large, flat rock in the center, their throats cut. Blood pooled beneath the bodies and dripped over the sides of the rock.

"Those two were dead," Swift Claw said, gesturing at the bodies as he joined Clanless at the entrance.

"Sacrifices for their dark arts," Clanless guessed. The Melkute condemned the blood-magic of the Sar Empire, but their magic seemed to require blood as well. Clanless couldn't understand it.

"Is it done?" Sugh came up behind them. "Did I miss it?"

"It's done." Clanless turned and stepped away from the tent. Part of him wanted to walk through the tent and kill all of them. It might even be the best course of action in the long term. But they'd disrupted the magic, and that's what mattered right now. "Let's get to the city."

Sugh looked toward Et-Baylak. "Ah. That will be an adventure."

Clanless paused at the sound of horns. "What is that?"

"It is the horn of the wild ones," Swift Claw said. "Your people call them rams, I believe."

"I know what horns are," Clanless muttered.

"The beastmen attack!" Sugh pointed to the left.

The three of them moved out past the last of the tents and watched a large portion of the beastmen army rushing toward the city gates. In the distance, Clanless spotted a smaller band circling toward the west: Captain Rakib's strategy in action, no doubt.

"They look… smaller than I'd thought," he said out loud.

"We are powerful fighters," Swift Claw replied. "And your people will fight too, yes?"

"If there are any left." Clanless took a deep breath. He well knew the ferocity and skill of the beastmen warriors, but the Melkute army was so large… He shook his head. "None of this matters if we can't get to Suirel and stop him."

"Then let us follow our bestial comrades into the fray," Sugh said. He pointed his axe toward the city. "Shall we?"

Together, the three of them jogged toward the city. They moved at an angle to the beastmen attack, which would reach the broken gates long before they did. The charge had not gone unnoticed, either. Already, large numbers of Melkute troops turned from their attack against the city and formed lines to defend against the beastmen. Clanless wanted to run as hard as he could to join the fight, but arriving exhausted would be worse than arriving late.

Somehow, the trip from the Melkute camp to the city felt longer than when they'd come out early this morning. Clanless had no sense of how much time had passed. He glanced at the sun's position. It had pursued the moon and given up already, now in full retreat. How had so many hours passed?

Ahead of them, the beastmen met the Melkute. The enemy's leaders wisely put spearmen in the front ranks, but they'd underestimated how far the beastmen could leap. While a few were caught and impaled, most launched themselves over the line of spears into the crowded mass of soldiers beyond. Howls and shouts filled the air.

"We fight our way to the upper city," Clanless said. "No matter what, we have to get to the arena."

"Fight as one," Swift Claw answered.

As they charged into the fray, Clanless experienced the bloodrush and the connection with Swift Claw all at once. In moments, he found himself leaping and slashing side-by-side with the beastman. Together, they cut a swathe through the enemy soldiers. Sugh followed closely, making sure no one found room to attack them from behind. Clanless used the Taint again and again, his eyes blazing. The Melkute soldiers, who'd shown admirable courage in facing the beastmen attack, fell back from this strange onslaught.

Other horns sounded from within the city. More fighting must be happening within. "To the gates!" Clanless shouted. Between all of the magic at work in and around him, he felt energized like he hadn't felt since the cavern of blood. This fighting was far different than the arena or even fighting the soldiers during their journey. If anything, it resembled the day he'd fought the barbarians in Ghoyor. But on that day, he didn't have Swift Claw.

At one point, he caught himself trying to claw at an enemy soldier with his fingernails. He laughed at himself, swung the moonblade, and used the Taint. The soldier fell, and he moved on.

But even the ferocity of the beastmen had its limits. The sheer size of the Melkute army slowed their assault bit by bit, until they came to an almost complete halt. Clanless wanted to push on to the gate, but too many soldiers stood in their way.

All at once, he heard an odd whistle in the air above. A huge rock sailed over his head and crashed into the assembled soldiers near the gate. Sugh let out a whoop. "Captain Rakib! He uses their own weapons against them!"

Of course. With the enemy camp mostly deserted, Rakib and Daviland would have been able to take command of one of the siege weapons.

A small squad of beastmen would be all they needed to load and use the device.

A few minutes later, a second boulder flew overhead. This one went further, passing through the broken gate itself and into the crowd of soldiers inside. Clanless couldn't even guess how many went down.

At another time, he might have experienced compassion for the enemy soldiers. He wasn't killing many himself, but he knew they were dying in great numbers. But after his arena battle, interview with the Melkute King, and Suirel's words, he felt nothing over these people. He wondered briefly where the King and his followers had gone within all of this chaos. Had they entered the city already? Or had they circled around in one of the other directions, perhaps?

When fighting multiple opponents in the arena, he'd learned to isolate and separate them. That wasn't possible in this kind of fight. Nor could he rest between opponents. No one stopped to pace around each other, evaluate an opponent, or show off for the watching audience. Here, he fought one man after another after another. No breaks, no rest. Find a way to cut, then use the Taint. Move on.

Without a shield or armor of his own, Clanless couldn't stop all the thrusting spears. He soon bled from a dozen different wounds, none of them serious alone. But if this kept up, the blood loss would slow him down and eventually kill him. He needed a break, time to wrap up the worst ones to stop the bleeding. But no such break came his way.

They'd moved closer to the gate, but everyone crowded in against each other. Captain Rakib couldn't risk using the catapult again without hitting some of the beastmen.

The fading sunlight mixed with a growing red tint. At first, Clanless thought it came from all the blood. He wiped at his face, hoping to get the redness out of his eyes. But it persisted. In the briefest of moments between one opponent and the next, he realized the red came from within the city. It wasn't the same as the glow of a fire, but something else. It could only be magic. And if so, then Suirel's plan within the arena might be coming to an end.

With that thought, he lunged forward side-by-side with Swift Claw. "Don't stop!" he shouted. They hacked and pushed forward, hacked and pushed forward.

And suddenly, they stumbled past the enemy and stood inside the gates of Et-Baylak.

THE LOWER CITY

Far sooner than Koland would have expected it, the gates of the upper city opened again. He and Qara had chosen to remain on the wall for now, anxious to see the course of the battle.

Dozens of archers on the wall cleared the way as General Ghan led his counterattack. A thousand men joined him in charging back into the lower city—a thousand trained Sar Empire elite soldiers. Every one of them would be using blood-magic even now, probably a mixture of Berge and Dalbai at least. With that kind of power, they would be worth over twice their number. It took only moments for them to clear out the Melkute soldiers who had ventured as far as the upper city walls. They hurried down the streets toward the north gate, hoping to join the massive fight the beastmen had begun.

The gate swung closed once more, reminding everyone that nothing was guaranteed yet. The counterattack might prove completely futile. The beastmen might not stand firm in their first war with men. Anything could still happen.

As if to illustrate that truth, Qara gasped. "What's happening in the arena?"

Koland spun around. A reddish glow rose from within the king's arena beside the palace. The sight of it sent a chill down Koland's spine.

"Suirel."

The lower city of Et-Baylak burned. Clanless paused and stared at the remains of the city he'd called home for over two years. Fires blazed in every direction as far as he could see. Heat blasted his face. The aroma of burning wood mixed with blood filled his nostrils. Debris and bodies inundated the streets—far too many bodies. He couldn't help but think of the small town they'd discovered, but on a much larger scale. Only a few men had destroyed the town. Hundreds—maybe thousands—had poured through these streets, killing, ransacking, devastating everything in their path.

And they hadn't stuck to one path. They'd fanned out in all directions, down all the side streets and alleys, searching out whatever they could find to destroy, rape, or kill. Even if the Sar Empire and the beastmen were victorious today, it would take months or years for the city to recover from this.

"Keep moving!" Sugh said behind him with a short cough.

Clanless tore his eyes away from the devastation and took note of the Melkute soldiers converging on their position. He sprinted down a side street, followed by the others. At the next intersection, he paused and glanced back. "Sugh! You've lived here longer than I have. Which way do we go?"

Sugh shook his head and leaned on his axe. "Up. That's all that matters. Keep circling and moving up."

One of the great horned creatures with three Melkute riding galloped past the intersection, but didn't turn toward them. Clanless thanked the goddess for that much.

He sucked in a breath and started running again. He turned to the left, the direction that appeared to lead toward the upper city, and found himself in a poorer region where he knew he'd never been. The destruction here was far more complete. The homes, made of lesser materials, burned easily. A few, by their appearance, had fallen prey to the earlier catapult bombardments. Very little remained save smoke and ash.

A small band of Melkute soldiers came around another bend just ahead of them. Swift Claw barreled into them at once, hacking and slashing. Another use of the Taint and they went down.

"Very handy again," Sugh said. "Is there no limit to how much you can use this power?"

"I don't know," Clanless said. "I've never reached one." In the fight with the barbarians, he'd used it until he could no longer remain conscious, but it hadn't stopped working. He'd struggled with it at times, feeling like it wasn't working as well, but there seemed no trouble with it today.

He took a moment to catch his breath and looked at his companions.

Like him, Swift Claw was covered in cuts and scratches, though none of them looked serious. Sugh had made it through the battle at the gates with fewer overall injuries, but one wound near his left hip appeared worse than the others.

"Are you all right? That one doesn't look good." Clanless pointed at the injury.

"Ah, a spear from a dying man," Sugh said. "I will be fine." He coughed and spat. "But if you happen to find a priest with healing blood, I would not object."

"Bandages," Clanless said. "We need to stop the bleeding. For both of us."

Together, they tore up what left of Sugh's shirt. Clanless insisted on binding Sugh's hip injury first. After that, they took turns bandaging several more wounds. Clanless took deep breaths. At least now, his body would not keep losing blood. He could keep going.

They set out again but no longer ran. They made good progress, moving up and up. Every so often, Clanless thought he caught a glimpse of the inner city walls and the red glow beyond, but a bend in the road or a new plume of smoke always took the view away. He grew impatient, pushing the other two to walk faster. They were all exhausted by now and could not maintain the pace for long.

At last, Sugh came to a stop and leaned against a wall. "You go on," he gasped. "I will wait here."

Clanless took a couple of steps before stopping and groaning. He turned back. "No, no. We can't leave you alone. Too many enemies are still around."

Sugh waved with the back of his hand. "You must stop Suirel. What is one life to that?"

Swift Claw crouched between them and looked to Clanless for his answer.

"One life—" Clanless began.

A scream erupted from across the street. Without a thought, Clanless tore across the road and burst into a small house. The front room, a living space, had been torn apart, but he saw no one. "No, no, no!" A woman's voice cried from behind a curtain leading to the next room. Clanless ripped it aside. Behind him, Swift Claw bounded into the house.

A Melkute soldier held a woman by her arms while a second stood in front of her. She bled from a gash on her forehead. Half her clothes had been torn off, and the soldier was in the process of removing his own. He spun around at Clanless's entrance.

"Release her," Clanless growled.

"Clanless!" the woman screamed, recognizing him. "Help me!"

The soldier holding the woman said something to the other in his language, but Clanless heard his name mixed in. The first soldier laughed and picked up his spear. The other tossed the woman to the side and drew a sword.

Clanless's eyes narrowed. "There will be no Taint for you," he said, not caring if they understood. In response, both of them charged him.

Despite his fatigue, Clanless ended the fight in moments. Two soldiers trapped in a room with him: they never had a chance. By the time Swift Claw forced his way into the room behind him, they were dead.

Clanless motioned the beastman to leave and turned to follow him. "Get dressed," he called back to the woman. "We'll wait for you outside."

A few moments later, she staggered out into the street to join them. She stared around at the devastation. "I… has the city fallen?"

"Not yet. And help has arrived," Clanless said. "We'll get you to the upper city. You'll be safe there."

"Thank you." She hugged a coat around herself, despite the heat. "I, I tried to hide, but they found me. I didn't know what to do. And, and…"

"It's all right. What's your name?"

"Amitral. I… friends call me Ami."

Clanless tried to smile. "All right, Ami. Come on. We need to move before more soldiers find us."

Sugh, who'd been sitting on the ground throughout the entire thing, got to his feet with a groan. "One life, eh?"

"One life is worth it," Clanless answered.

Sugh nodded. "Let's go."

When they arrived at the inner city wall, Clanless stared up at it and paced nervously. The smoke obscured the afternoon sun, but the red glow from within had grown brighter, casting an eerie red-tinged darkness over everything. "How do we get inside?"

Sugh looked from side to side. "I think the gate is that way." He pointed to the left. "Perhaps they will let us in?"

"They closed the gates," Ami said. "That's why I ran back home and hid." She glanced back down the street and took a step closer to Clanless.

Swift Claw pointed up. "Someone watches us."

Clanless could barely make out a silhouette against the red background. "Hello there! Is there a way inside?"

"Who is that?" the guard answered.

Clanless held up the moonblade. "It is Clanless! I have friends here who need to get to safety."

The guard leaned over to peer down at them. "Clanless? We thought you dead in the Melkute camp. How are you here?"

"Is there a way inside?" he repeated.

"The gate is closed. General Ghan has joined the battle. We cannot open it again without his presence."

"We waste time," Swift Claw said. He leaped up onto the wall and scrambled upward. The others watched, open-mouthed, as he moved up the stone surface as if it were a gentle incline. His claws somehow found places to grip that no human fingers or toes could ever grasp. In a few moments, he vaulted over the parapet.

The guard backed away, mace at ready. "Stay back!" he warned. "I-I'll call for help!"

"Swift Claw will not harm you!" Clanless called. "He is a friend."

The guard looked back and forth between them and finally lowered his mace.

Swift Claw leaned over the parapet. "Wolf Chosen. If you cannot climb, how will we bring you up?"

"We helped someone up with a rope earlier," the guard suggested.

"Why did you not mention that first?" Sugh shouted. "Fetch the rope, boy! We have places to be."

"Why is it red in there?" Ami asked.

"We don't know," Sugh said. "But we will find out."

She shrank back. "Maybe it's safer out here. If we all stay together somewhere, we can wait for it to be over…"

"We are going over," Clanless said. "I must get inside. If you want to be safe, you need to come with us."

Ami whimpered and looked up and down the wall. Sugh stepped over to her and placed a hand on her shoulder. "Fear not, little one. You are with the mightiest warriors in the Empire. We will protect you. Come, I will help you up the wall."

She looked up into his eyes and nodded. A moment later, the rope fell down to them.

"You first," Clanless offered.

NO CERTAINTY

Koland and Qara worked through the crowd outside the palace doors. The guards recognized Koland and let them through.

"Did my daughter arrive?" he asked as soon as the door shut behind them.

"Yes, sir, but then she left again," the guard reported. "We've been anticipating your arrival, sir. You're wanted in the throne room."

"What?"

"The council is in session. They are hoping you will be able to join them."

Qara shivered, despite the warmth of the interior. "The council is meeting? Now? Whatever for?"

"I'm sure I don't know." Koland set off through the hall.

"Uh, what should I do?" Qara asked.

He motioned her to follow. "You can wait inside. They haven't minded when Kekeen sat in."

"I'm not your daughter," she muttered but followed anyway.

Upon entering the throne room, Koland strode toward the council table while Qara stayed near the door. The three Lords waited for him, but the Ghamba Lam sat apart from the table, head down. In his place stood two Daghilches in red robes.

"Ah, Koland," Lord Ezen said. "I'm glad you turned up. What of Sonkogh?"

"I just witnessed his death." Koland stopped at the table and stared at the Daghilches. "What is going on here?"

"The Ghamba Lam is facing removal from his post," one of them said. "We are here to represent the priesthood in this crucial moment."

"Now? You're choosing now to do this?" Koland demanded. "This is despicable."

"Here now," Lord Ulakan said, "it is not our place to interfere in religious matters."

"Ironic for a cultist to say that."

Ulakan bristled but did not respond.

Koland pointed outside. "We're in the middle of a battle for our very existence! Is now really the time for leadership changes? Or even a council meeting, for that matter?"

"Your pardon," one of the Daghilches said. "You accuse Lord Ulakan of being a cultist. Exactly what cult would that be?"

"You know as well as I do. The cult of Suirel."

"Ah, I see. The superstition about a so-called chaos god. Surely an… educated man such as yourself knows what manner of nonsense this is."

Koland stared at him. "Am I to believe you not only do not accept Suirel's existence, but that his cult doesn't even exist?"

The Daghlich folded his arms in the most smug manner possible. "It is patently ridiculous."

Koland looked around at the rest of the table. "What else is going on here, then? Is this meeting for nothing more than listening to these red-robed buffoons?"

"Storyteller!" Lord Ghayaktal exclaimed. "Regardless of opinions about cults and such, they are still priests of the goddess and should be respected as such!"

"The council is not listening to us," the Daghilch said. "We are here to listen to them. And you. We are seeking final evidence in order to complete the trial of the Ghamba Lam."

"So he has not been removed yet?"

"It is all but certain."

"Tell us," said the second Daghilch, "have you anything to add to our investigation?"

"This is preposterous." Koland took a few steps away. "The fate of our city could fall either way in the next few minutes, depending on the actions of the beastmen, of all people. I need to find my daughter. And right now, in the arena—" He broke off.

"Haven't they seen the red glow?" Qara asked from the corner, just loud enough to be heard.

"What about the arena?" Lord Ezen asked.

"If your lordships will permit me…" Koland came back. "And you Daghilches, as well. I have one final request as a member of this council. I wish to move our meeting to another location."

"What's wrong with this one?" Lord Ulakan asked.

"Humor me in this," Koland said. "If after moving our location and hearing what I have to say at this new spot, you find me as ridiculous as these two do"—he waved at the Daghilches—"then I will resign from this council and leave you all to do as you please."

The other men all looked at each other, some clearly perplexed. Koland noted a more pointed look traded between one Daghilch and Lord Ulakan.

"I, uh, see no objection to this," Lord Ezen said, standing to his feet.

"Nor I," said Lord Ghayaktal.

"I do object to this pointless posturing," Lord Ulakan countered. "And with the support of the Daghilches here, you are overruled."

"They have no vote in this council," Koland pointed out.

"But I do." The Ghamba Lam stood up. "Until I am officially removed, both from council and my position as leader of the priesthood, I can make my own decisions. I wish to hear what the storyteller has to say."

"Four to one, my friend," Lord Ezen said to Ulakan. "Even if we gave the other two a voice for this, you'd be outvoted."

Lord Ulakan rolled his eyes. "Fine. Let this be his last act." He shoved his chair back and got to his feet.

Koland nodded and gestured toward the door. "We will reconvene in the south tower."

"The south tower? If I'd known you meant that far away…" Lord Ghayaktal trailed off on a harsh look from Ezen.

Koland led the strange assembly through the halls and up the winding stairs. Qara followed at a slight distance. After two complete circuits of the stairs, Koland brought them to the barren room with the windows. The red glow suffused the entire space.

"There aren't even any chairs in here," Lord Ulakan complained. "What are we doing?"

"Your lordships," Koland said, stepping near the window. "Noble priests. I would like to draw your attention down there." He pointed to the arena. "For if Suirel does not exist, and his cult is a myth, perhaps you can explain what is taking place in our arena."

Everyone except Lord Ulakan crowded near the windows to stare down at the source of the glow. Koland stared himself, taken aback. He'd expected something strange but… not this.

The wooden frame had been torn back down, its pieces scattered across the sand floor. In its place stood the crystal construction Suirel and his workers had been building. It appeared to be a huge, vertical circle. Crystal shards pointed off in every direction from its shape, giving it a spiky appearance. The red glow came from within the circle itself. Though the angle was difficult to observe, the interior of the circle looked like glistening red liquid, not quite water but not quite blood either.

Movement caught Koland's eye. Unlike the last time, he didn't see any humans working in the arena. Instead, a large creature of some kind prowled around the crystal structure, never staying in one place for very long. Koland had no doubt it was the thing he'd heard inside the covered carriage.

"What… what is this?" Lord Ezen asked.

"Several of us know exactly what it is," the Ghamba Lam declared, arms folded. "Wouldn't you agree, my colleagues?"

One Daghilch turned to face him, horrified. "Are you saying they brought the crystal from the mines and rebuilt the portal here?"

"Ridiculous!" the other snapped.

"Then what is that?" Koland asked him.

The Daghilch opened his mouth, paused, and snapped it shut with a glare.

"The rest of us are ignorant here," Lord Ghayaktal said. "Would one of you please enlighten us?"

"For generations, we have taken vast quantities of blood north to the almaz mines," the Ghamba Lam began.

"Stop!" the angry Daghilch interrupted. "You are not authorized to reveal these things!"

"I am the leader of the priesthood," he responded. "I am the only one who is authorized."

"The time for secrets is past," Koland said.

"Within the mines, there was a crystal cave where a… portal existed." The Ghamba Lam pointed toward the arena. "By flooding it with the blood of our people, we prevented its usage. For the most part."

"Usage? What is this usage?" Lord Ezen demanded.

"The blood-wraiths. It's where they come from."

Everyone turned to look again. "And there is no blood that can stop it," the other Daghilch murmured. "What will happen now?"

"The sureness—the certainty—of the blood is what protected us all these years." The Ghamba Lam shook his head. "Now it is gone."

"We must stop this!" The reasonable Daghilch moved toward the stairs. "We will storm the arena and destroy this thing!"

"And how will you do that?" Lord Ulakan turned with a grim smile. "Our soldiers are all engaged in the battle or defending the walls. My lord holds the arena with troops of his own, as well as the beast you see below. And in the unlikely event you make it inside, what will save you from the blood-wraiths themselves?"

"Ulakan!" Lord Ghayaktal gasped.

"The truth comes out," Koland whispered.

"Are you saying the portal is already active?" the Daghilch asked.

"If it's not already, it will be very soon." Lord Ulakan gestured to the windows. "You see the evidence all around us. It is the dawning of a new age. The weak and useless goddess of old is being swept away. Suirel, Lord of Chaos, is our god now."

"It won't even be us any more," the Ghamba Lam said. "The blood-wraiths will take over and do as they like with our bodies. No one is safe from them."

Koland frowned. He'd heard something about that... something he couldn't quite remember. Something about someone being immune... A strange feeling swept over him. He took a step back from everyone as the other two Lords shouted at the gloating Ulakan.

Kekeen. She'd said... but not her. Zektel. The blood-wraith. She'd been unable to enter Aldan. She'd told him that when... when... images rushed into his head. Tying Kekeen. Threatening her. Telling her about her mother. The blood-wraith refusing to leave. And then... she stabbed him. She'd used his own daughter to stab him. All of the memories came cascading back into his head. He staggered and leaned against the staircase.

"Zektel," he murmured. "She left Kekeen and entered me. Long enough to hide my memories before going back."

"What was that?" the Ghamba Lam asked.

"It... doesn't matter right now. Except I know who can stop Suirel. If he's still alive."

The Ghamba Lam raised his eyebrows. "I'm assuming you mean our mutual friend. You think he survived the Melkute camp?"

"If anyone could, he did." Koland pushed himself back toward the other arguing men. "This is getting us nowhere."

"You're right. Allow me." The Ghamba Lam stepped past him and lifted both arms. "Quiet, all of you!" he bellowed. To Koland's surprise, the Lords and Daghilches obeyed.

"Lord Ulakan, by your own admission, you are a heretic and a cultist!" The Ghamba Lam turned both his upright hands in circles, tracing the moon above. "As the Ghamba Lam of the Sar Empire, I hereby cast you out."

"You think I care—"

"Be silent! I am the supreme spiritual authority of the Empire. My word is law in this regard." He pointed to the angry Daghilch. "As for you, we have no confession yet. But your actions today have indicated your true loyalties." He looked to the second Daghilch. "Am I right?"

"You are, your holiness." He nodded with a grim look. "I will see to this one."

The Ghamba Lam turned back and fixed his gaze on Lord Ulakan. "As I said, I have spiritual authority. But beyond that, I am a member of this council, the ruling council of Et-Baylak. And I charge you with treason against this city. You have conspired against our people, hoping to turn them over to a conqueror even worse than the Melkute Kingdom. Do any of the other council members agree?"

"I do," Koland said. Lord Ezen immediately added his agreement. After a moment's hesitation, Lord Ghayaktal murmured, "Yes."

"Then by a decree of the council of Et-Baylak, you are to be tried on this charge! Guards!"

Before any guards could answer the call, if any were even in earshot, Lord Ulakan bolted toward the stairs. Standing beside it, Qara stepped back out of his way but put out her foot. Ulakan tripped right as he reached the stairs. He gave a short cry before tumbling down, down, down. He made no sounds after that.

Koland raised his eyebrows at Qara. She shrugged. "I've heard enough stories of how he's treated women. That was for them."

Lord Ezen sighed and headed toward the stairs himself. "I'll make sure he's healed and kept secure."

Koland glanced around at those left. The Ghamba Lam had things under control now. Lord Ghayaktal wouldn't be any trouble by himself. And with these memories restored, Koland couldn't help feeling more anxious about finding Kekeen. Where would she have gone? He suspected he'd find the answer, one way or another, at the arena.

"Gentlemen, now that we've settled things for the moment, I'm going to see what I can discover myself."

"Are you going down there?" the Ghamba Lam gestured toward the arena.

Koland nodded.

"Wait." The Ghamba Lam pulled a pouch from within his sleeve and fumbled to open it. "You may need help. This isn't much, but…" He pulled out a vial of blood and examined it with a chuckle. "On the other hand, this is probably the most appropriate for you, storyteller."

Koland accepted the vial, a taller and thinner version of the usual blood currency. "What do I do with this?"

"The magic is already activated, but it won't last long. If you use it, do so within the next hour or so."

Koland nodded, took a closer look at the vial's label, and tucked it away.

"Go with the goddess." The Ghamba Lam bowed his head.

Koland hesitated, but for once, he had nothing to say. He headed down the stairs with Qara following.

(((((●)))))

Clanless pushed open the stable door and hurried inside, followed by Sugh and Swift Claw. "Nukai? Nukai, where are you?"

They passed through the first set of stalls. Several of the horses reacted with snorts and other nervous noises at Swift Claw's presence. After the short hall, they entered the second set. Clanless stopped, surprised to see large outer doors open beyond the area where the ghuyak had been housed.

"Out here, Clanless," Nukai's voice called.

Outside, Tuulka stood still, chewing a huge wad of hay. As Clanless drew near, the beast turned his head and looked over the three of them. His eyes still looked as though they drooped in abject sadness. Nukai sat on top of the ghuyak. He waved at them.

Clanless stared up at the hunched man. As usual, he wore several fur pelts piled on top of his back. But he sat on top of a leather seat of some kind with room for another rider in front of him. "You built a saddle for that thing?"

"Please, Clanless. Stop calling him a 'thing.' You do want him to help you, yes?" Nukai gestured to the spot in front of him.

"Um, all right. Sorry." Clanless patted Tuulka on the head. "I'm not sure why we need to ride…"

"How else are we to get him to the arena gates? Pull him there?"

Sugh laughed. "If you aren't climbing up there, Clanless, I will!"

"Fine. Hold this." Clanless shoved the moonblade into Sugh's hands. He caught hold of the leather strap and pulled himself up. He swung into place on the saddle. Nukai handed him the reins, and Sugh handed up the moonblade.

Still unsure about the entire thing, Clanless flicked the reins. "Let's go,

Tuulka." The beast snorted and started forward.

"You will need to turn right at the intersection," Nukai said.

"I know," Clanless growled. "I lived in this city for over two years."

Sugh and Swift Claw had no trouble keeping up with the plodding pace of the ghuyak, but Clanless ground his teeth at the lack of speed. Even so, he admitted the ride did him some good. He'd gotten up early to meet the Melkute champion in battle. After the consequences of that fight, he'd fought at the gates to the city for what had to have been hours. He glanced at the sky and saw the sun nearing the end of its retreat. If not for the red glow radiating from the arena, twilight would be upon them soon. Riding now gave him a few brief minutes of rest before what was sure to be another fight.

"Have you found any hope?" Nukai asked behind him.

"I… don't know." Clanless waved the moonblade at the sky. "This doesn't look very hopeful."

"And yet the siege has been broken. Help unforeseen arrived. Is not hope working even now?"

"Maybe so," he conceded. "But—"

"One thing at a time, Clanless. One thing at a time."

"Nukai…" He hesitated. "This will be dangerous. Even when we arrive, there are archers. They will try to stop us."

"This is the moment. I must be here. It is the reason I came with you."

Clanless shrugged. "Very well."

Though the streets remained crowded with the lower city's refugees, Tuulka had no trouble getting through. No one wanted to stand in the way of the armored ghuyak, a creature most—if not all—had never seen. Many, however, did recognize Clanless atop it. Cries of both gratitude and condemnation filled the air. At first, it confused him.

"Some believe you failed this morning, leading to the attack," Nukai said. "Others know the truth."

"I should be used to people yelling at me."

"And yet?"

He didn't answer.

At last, they reached the arena doors. Clanless turned to slide off, but Nukai stopped him. "I see no archers."

Clanless looked up above the gates and around. Nukai was right. He didn't see any soldiers at all. What did it mean?

"Swift Claw," he called. "You can climb into this place, can't you?"

"Of course, Wolf Chosen. Should I enter ahead of you?" The beastman reached for the arena wall.

"No. I want you to go all the way around and climb in from the other side. We may need any surprises we can against Suirel."

Without another word, Swift Claw ran down the street to the left. The refugees made a wide path for him.

"Stay back, good people. Stay back!" Sugh shouted, waving at the onlookers. "Give us room."

Clanless turned Tuulka until his back faced the doors. "How do I make him swing his tail?" he asked over his shoulder.

"Ask him to," Nukai suggested.

"Uhh…. Tuulka. Will you swing your tail for me?"

Nothing happened.

"Did I ask wrong?"

Nukai laughed, a dry and wheezing noise. "I'm joking, Clanless. I just wanted to hear you try it." Before Clanless could say anything else, the other man slid off the ghuyak.

"What are you doing?" Clanless tried to turn to see.

"Patience." Nukai did something near Tuulka's back hip. A moment later, the ghuyak grunted. His tail whipped through the air and slammed into the arena doors. Wood splintered, but didn't break. The onlookers exclaimed.

"Again, Tuulka, if you please," Nukai said. The tail swung again. This time, it smashed through the doors and even yanked some of the pieces back with it.

Sugh rushed forward to push the remaining bits of the doors open. Clanless pulled hard on the reins. With a loud snarl, Tuulka turned around. Nukai scrambled to get out of the way, calling, "Clanless! Watch yourself!"

"It's time to end this," Clanless growled. He urged the ghuyak on, pushing him to a more rapid pace into the arena tunnel. Sugh was yelling something to the onlookers, warning them, he supposed, but Clanless didn't listen. The tunnel here had been used to bring larger things into the arena on special occasions, but it had another set of doors into the arena floor itself. Or at least it used to. Those doors no longer blocked his way. Instead, an increasing red light filled the tunnel ahead of him.

And then one silhouette of a dark figure moved into view. "Suirel!" Clanless shouted.

"No," came the answer. "I would think you could recognize me by now, Clanless, you stupid taichin."

Duurald?

SUIREL'S GUARD

Sugh caught up to Tuulka in time to see Duurald step into view. He glanced up at Clanless and considered. Suirel mattered, not this one. But Clanless had a personal connection with this man.

"Duurald?" Clanless leaned forward in Tuulka's saddle. "Is it you or a blood-wraith?"

"Suirel set me free from the wraith," the arena fighter answered. "I'm my own self again."

"He's the one who put the wraith inside you!" Sugh exclaimed. "And me! If not for Clanless, I would still be held by that thing!" In fact, if not for the fur pelt on Sugh's shoulder now, he suspected he would already be possessed again. Though he couldn't see them, he knew blood-wraiths would be lurking nearby.

"It was a temporary thing," Duurald said, with a brief glance at Sugh. "Suirel set me free and enlightened me. I serve him now. Truly, Clanless, you should join us. We—"

"Prove it!" Clanless challenged. "Cut yourself and let me use the Taint on you. We'll see if you're really free of blood-wraiths."

Duurald laughed. "Expose myself to your taichin power? I don't think so. Your blood, however… Suirel wants your blood. That's why I'm here."

"You think you can beat me?"

"I don't have to beat you. I just need some of your blood, that's all. Give it to me here, and"—he glanced over his shoulder at the red arena—"you won't have to face what's in there. Trust me, Clanless. It's for the best."

Clanless hesitated. Sugh knew he wouldn't surrender his blood, but he must be thinking about whether he could still persuade Duurald to his side, or find some way to save him, like he wanted to save Bain. That was Clanless's weakness: he thought he could save everyone.

Sugh stepped forward. "Let me deal with this one, Clanless. You go on."

Duurald laughed again and pointed his mace. "Don't be ridiculous."

"Sugh… he's one of us. An arena fighter," Clanless said. "We should be on the same side."

"But we're not," Sugh said. "He's either still possessed, or he's joined Suirel. He will not change again."

"At least this one understands." Duurald took a step toward Sugh. "Stop wasting our time, Clanless. Don't you know people are dying outside? With Suirel's help, we can stop it. We can save the Sar Empire! Sands, we can rule the Sar Empire!"

"The city is already being saved now, no thanks to Suirel. The beastmen have come."

"What nonsense is this?" Duurald laughed even louder. "I know you've spent time with a storyteller, Clanless, but that doesn't mean you can do it. Beastmen? Really?"

"It's true," Sugh said. He swung his axe in a lazy circle and moved toward Duurald. This was taking too long. He needed to take action and let Clanless get to the real threat. "Come, Duurald. You were champion of Ulken's arena, no? Show me how you fare against one of the Dohor!"

"I was far better than you pampered Dohor!" Duurald growled.

"Show me!" Sugh waved back at Tuulka. "Move on, Clanless. I will deal with him."

"He's right, Aldan," Nukai's voice came from further back. "Suirel waits for us."

Sugh half-expected Clanless to argue more. He was a stubborn one. Instead, Tuulka started moving again.

"Fine. I'll deal with you first." Duurald charged at Sugh. He swung his mace at the last moment, bringing it in an arc from below. Sugh dodged, but Tuulka's tail swung past at that moment. Both men threw themselves to the ground to avoid it. Sugh hit a little harder than he meant to and scraped both knees on the rough floor.

He rolled away to give himself room to recover his footing. Duurald had the same idea. They came to their feet facing one another ten feet apart. From his peripheral vision, Sugh noticed curious onlookers crowding in at the broken doors.

"We have an audience!" Duurald proclaimed.

"He's lying, you know," said a voice within Sugh's chest.

"Yul? You can speak to me again?"

"When you're bleeding. It's… difficult, but possible."

Sugh paced to his right, circling Duurald, who did the same. Both fell into standard arena tactics and stances.

"Duurald hates blood-wraiths with a passion, more than any of you," Yul went on. "He is not free."

"You mean he has a blood-wraith controlling him after all?"

"Either he is under its control, or it is there all the same, threatening him."

Sugh grunted in response. He envied Clanless riding off on the ghuyak. It had been a long day. After all the earlier fighting, he wasn't sure he could deal with Duurald. He certainly couldn't be sure about taking him down without killing him. Clanless would be sorrowful about that. But it couldn't be helped now.

"Why do you wear Clanless's fur now?" Duurald called. "What was it the beastman called him? Are you the 'wolf chosen' now?"

"I won it from him in a bet," Sugh answered. "We were bored and played a game. He lost."

"He has the Siphon," Yul whispered.

Sugh's eyes darted to Duurald's belt. Sure enough, one of the standard arena Siphons hung there. Exactly what he needed. New motivation surged through him. With a whisper to the goddess, he lunged forward.

Duurald met his attack with his own moves. He was fresh and rested. Sugh was tired and bloodied. If Hagh had been here, Sugh would have made a bet against himself on this one. Except… he had a reason to fight. Duurald fought only to serve Suirel, to serve chaos and evil. Sugh fought to save those he cared about.

Duurald's mace slammed into the sand next to his foot. Sugh's axe clipped the other man's left shoulder as he dodged. If he had the power of the Taint like Clanless, he could end this now. But no. He'd won every arena fight by his own strength and skill. This would be no different.

They circled each other again. What a strange arena. Dark walls on two sides and a dark roof above. From one twilit side, a crowd watched, mostly silent. From the other, a crimson glow threw an eerie light on the combatants, casting elongated shadows across the ground.

Every arena fight for Sugh until now had been about one thing: survival. Live to fight another day. Live to enjoy what pleasures he could find between fights. Except the one time… he'd fought to save Chabi. And he'd failed.

He would not fail today. No matter the cost.

"My father complains about how much healing you require," Chabi had told him.

"What does it matter if I win?" he'd answered. He'd become famous for accepting huge injuries in order to get close enough for a killing blow. As he grew in prowess, Sugh hadn't needed to use that tactic, except in desperate situations, such as when the Hawk King was displeased.

The cost would be high indeed today. There were no healers here.

"We're both survivors," Duurald growled. "It doesn't have to be this way."

"Then step aside," Sugh said. "Let us stop Suirel."

A hideous roar echoed from the arena inside. Sugh cast a quick glance toward it. In that moment, Duurald leaped forward. Sugh let him come, prepared for this moment. He feinted upward to the left with his axe, as if to block the incoming attack.

Duurald's mace swept down, striking Sugh's left thigh. The bone inside shattered from the impact.

Sugh's axe arced around in a twist, striking under Duurald's left arm. The blade cut deep into his chest.

Duurald staggered back. He dropped the mace.

Sugh fell, the pain overwhelming. His axe remained in his opponent's chest.

Duurald's mouth opened and shut several times. "It wasn't…" he said at last. He fell to his knees. "I didn't want this. I only wanted…" He collapsed forward, his face into the sand. The impact knocked the axe loose. Blood poured from his side. He didn't move again.

((((●))))

Koland slowed his pace outside the palace. The crowd in the streets, made up of refugees from the lower city as well as those curious about events in the arena, had become almost a solid block of humanity in his way. Without other options, he started pushing his way through.

"Excuse me. Excuse me. My daughter. I need to get to my daughter!"

Qara stayed right behind him, following his footsteps and being even more antagonistic in her demands. "Get out of the way! Didn't you hear him? It's his daughter in there!"

A handful of people in the crowd recognized him and helped push him along, making paths. In the moments where he got through several feet, he left Qara behind. When he realized they'd been separated, he stopped and looked back.

"Keep going!" she called. "I'll catch up!"

At last, he made it to the arena doors. Pushing his way through the final members of the crowd, he burst into the passageway in time to see Sugh and Duurald both fall.

❰ ❰ ❰ ❰ ● ❱ ❱ ❱ ❱

For a few moments, Sugh thought he would never move again. He closed his eyes and felt the cool sand against his cheek. So tired. Such a long day it had been.

"Get the Siphon," Yul whispered.

He inhaled sharply through his nose. His job wasn't done yet. He lifted his head and tried to pull himself toward Duurald's body. His mangled leg dragged in the sand. Pieces of bone poked through his skin, spilling his own blood. He almost passed out from the agony.

"Sugh!" A hand grasped his shoulder. "Don't move. That looks horrible."

He tried to turn his head. "Koland? What?"

The storyteller wasn't looking at him but toward the arena. "Clanless is in there?"

"Yes. Help me. I need that—" He tried to point to the Siphon on Duurald's belt.

"You need healing, but we don't have any right now." Koland stood up. "Rest now. I'll be back, if I can."

"Where are you going?"

Koland drew a dagger and started toward the arena. "I'm going to kill my daughter."

❰ ❰ ❰ ❰ ● ❱ ❱ ❱ ❱

Clanless stared at the transformation of the arena. The portal loomed large in the center of the sands, a crystalline structure far greater than he'd anticipated. He guessed it to be at least thirty feet tall. A red liquid, thinner-appearing than blood, formed a kind of vertical watery surface within the crystal circle. From it came the red glow, reminding Clanless of the cave beneath the Throat of the Goddess. The wooden frame that had encased it during construction had been torn down. Fragments of it lay strewn across the sand.

"Maybe we should go back and help Sugh," he murmured.

"Be wary, Clanless," Nukai said from the ground to his right. "Suirel is not alone."

A roar echoed across the arena to illustrate his words. Clanless and Tuulka turned their heads at the same time to see a huge creature approaching them from beyond the portal. To Clanless, it looked like a much larger version of the lizard creatures he'd fought before, both in this arena and in the snow near the mines. He'd lost a toe to the one in the arena; this one looked like it could bite off his entire leg. As it gained speed in its charge, it spread its powerful forearms out as if to embrace. But each forearm ended in enormous claws, especially the first one on each hand, curving out like giant scythes.

Tuulka answered the beast's roar with a high-pitched "Rannhh!" of his own. The ghuyak lumbered toward the monster before turning its side to face the oncoming assault. Clanless realized his position in the saddle put him level with the beast's teeth-filled mouth. Before it reached them, he slid off the opposite side and rolled free from Tuulka.

The ghuyak swung his tail, but the monster leaped high. It crashed into Tuulka's armored side and back. The massive fore claws scrabbled against the armor, trying to cut and grip. The largest claws gouged slight furrows in the plates as it slid back down. Tuulka screamed a response, whipping his tail back and forth.

Wary of the tail, the creature backed away a few steps. It kept its head low, watching Tuulka's movements with an intense glare. Then it caught sight of Clanless on the other side. It spun and ran around the front of Tuulka, moving faster than the ghuyak could turn to follow.

Clanless readied himself, unsure how he could even fight against a creature this size. He waved the moonblade in front of him, trying to appear larger and more dangerous. The beast paused only a few feet away and lifted its head, surveying this smaller prey with a big claw.

Unimpressed, the beast lunged forward, its jaws open. Clanless waited until the last second, swung the moonblade once, and dove to the side with the momentum. The moonblade cut a short gash on the tip of the beast's lower jaw. Blood spurted as it jerked back.

Clanless activated the Taint as the creature stepped back. It displayed no signs of being affected. He'd expected as much but still had to try.

With another high-pitched roar, Tuulka barreled into the beast, knocking it off its feet. It fell with its head only inches away from Clanless. He rolled away, narrowly avoiding another snap of the jaws.

Tuulka spun around. His tail bounced off the other beast's hip, eliciting a yelp of pain. The creature sprang onto all fours and lunged at Clanless again, right as he got to his feet.

A chunk of wood bounced off the beast's snout, distracting it in time for Clanless to dodge out of the way. It snarled and turned in the direction the wood had come from. Clanless looked as well and saw Nukai struggling to pick up another discarded shard of wood.

"Nukai! Look out!" Clanless broke into a run as the beast lifted itself up to charge the other man. It limped from the blow Tuulka had given it but would reach Nukai in seconds.

"Clanless, use the Taint!" Nukai shouted, lifting a large plank. "Focus it, like you did with Sugh!"

The creature's head shot toward Nukai. He broke the plank over its nose before it knocked him aside.

Clanless activated the Taint and tried to focus as he'd done before. He kept it from racing through the creature and instead moved it slowly and deliberately up through the lower jaw.

Too slow. The beast snapped down at Nukai. The jaws closed on the pile of furs on his back and lifted him into the air.

Tuulka squealed and rumbled toward them.

Clanless gritted his teeth from the exertion of maintaining control. His eyes burned hotter than ever. He pushed the Taint up inside the beast's head, focusing it harder and harder into that one area, that one spot, where its brain must be.

The creature shook Nukai like a rag doll, frustrated at the mass of fur.

Clanless screamed, pushing the Taint again and again into the same spot, building it stronger and stronger.

Tearing the pelts apart, the creature jerked its head one more time. Nukai flew loose from its jaws and landed hard in the sand.

Tuulka ran full-force into the creature's injured hip. It went down again, screeching. Tuulka tried to turn, but the beast clamped its jaws on the ghuyak's back left leg. Tuulka shrieked.

Clanless released the Taint and fell to his knees. The beast released Tuulka and jerked its head upright. It trembled. Strange noises came from its throat. Clanless looked up and pushed the Taint one last time.

Something exploded in the creature's head. Blood spurted from its right eye. The jaws clamped closed. The enormous head slammed into the sand. The rest of its body twitched and fell still. Tuulka nudged it with his nose and snorted.

Clanless pushed himself back to his feet, breathing hard. He wasn't sure what he had done with the Taint, but it had taken a lot out of him. He turned and jogged as best as he could over to Nukai's fallen form. The hunched man lay still at first, but as Clanless bent over him, his body lifted in a deep breath.

Some of the creature's teeth had made it through all the furs and cut long gashes across Nukai's back. His right arm twisted at a bad angle. There was no telling how much more damage he had taken. Clanless hesitated, not sure what he could do to help.

"It's… all right, Clanless," Nukai wheezed. He turned his head to the side and coughed. Sand and blood flew from his mouth. "It's all… the way… it should be."

"What are you talking about?" Clanless caught Nukai's left arm as he twisted and lifted himself. Together, they managed to get him into a sitting position.

"I'll wait here," Nukai said, pulling his arm loose from Clanless's grip. He pointed past him. "While you deal with him."

Slow claps came from behind. Clanless stood and turned. A single figure stood in front of the red portal.

Bain. Suirel.

BLOOD OF THE TAINT

"Well done!" Suirel called across the arena, clapping again. He wore leather armor across his body, much like Bain had worn in the duel years ago. But he wore no helmet, exposing his scarred face and empty eye sockets. "I wondered if you would have a chance against my pet. I'm very impressed. Do you know how much work it took to capture that thing and bring it here?"

Clanless tightened his grip on the moonblade and started walking toward the portal. Exhaustion pulled at his limbs, but he had no choice. This was why he'd come. He had to stop the Lord of Chaos here and now.

"So many close calls," Suirel went on. "The gas in the tunnel. The fight with the champion. And now this. I needed your blood, and I could have obtained it then if you'd failed. But you… you outperformed even my expectations. I say again: well done!"

Clanless stopped. "My blood?" But hadn't Suirel been trying to keep him away?

"It's the final ingredient, you see." Suirel gestured at the portal behind him. "It's open now, and my children are beginning to slip through again. But to truly activate it, to open it wider than it has ever been… I need the blood of the Taint." He spread his arms wide. "And here you are."

"You mean… your plan depended on me getting here and giving you my blood?"

Suirel laughed. "Of course not." He dropped a small bag into the sand. It landed with a familiar clink of crystal. "Zektel already brought me your blood. But it's so much more satisfying to have you here for this. And I prefer to get it fresh."

"There's nothing special about my blood." Clanless stepped to one side. Bain's head turned to follow. The empty sockets where his eyes had been didn't seem to matter.

"Oh, we both know better than that." Suirel chuckled. "After what happened in the crystal cave… well… You know that without all that blood-magic, you have no chance against me now."

"I'm not alone this time."

Bain's head turned back and forth as if looking. "You're not? Sugh is occupied. The storyteller might show up at some point, but he's useless. That leaves… who? The old man crawling in the sand over there? I can't fathom why you brought him along. Some bizarre attempt at nostalgia? Bain barely remembered him."

Clanless took a quick glance back at Nukai. He had crawled a few feet from where he'd been but appeared motionless now. Suirel was wrong, of course. Clanless had one other ally working his way closer, if he could keep the enemy distracted a little longer.

"Bain?" Clanless called, taking a step closer. "Are you still in there? Can you hear me?"

"You know the answer to that. Bain can't respond to you any more than Kekeen could." Suirel snapped his fingers. "And speaking of your beloved…"

Kekeen appeared from behind the portal, escorted by a soldier. Her hands were tied in front of her for some reason.

"Here she is," Suirel said. "And thus, I await your surrender, Aldan. If not, she dies, of course."

"If you kill her," Clanless said slowly, "you remove everything that holds me back. If she dies, I will tear you apart."

"If this body still had eyes, they would be rolling." Suirel shook his head. "Your threats mean nothing. If she were not a part of this, you would try to kill me. And fail. But you would try. Telling me what you'll do if she dies does nothing. So if threatening her doesn't affect you, then I suppose she should die and get it over with. Zektel, would you—"

"Wait!" Clanless held up a hand.

"Ah, so it does matter. Good."

"Zektel," Clanless called. "Would you really kill her, knowing what she means to me?"

Kekeen hesitated. "I don't want to kill her, Aldan. But if you won't do as he says, I'll have no choice."

"You always have a choice."

She lowered her head. "No. I don't. Surrender, Aldan. Or I'll stop her heart."

Clanless didn't move. He only needed a few more seconds.

"We're waiting," Suirel said. "But I won't wait long. Put down the moonblade, if you please."

Clanless let out a sigh, not an exaggeration considering his exhaustion. He lifted the moonblade high in the air, keeping Suirel's attention focused on him.

Swift Claw leaped from behind the portal, his own blade high. His feet struck Suirel in the back and drove him down into the sand. Kekeen broke free of the soldier and ran toward the arena wall. Clanless leaped forward. The soldier swung around to help Suirel. Swift Claw brought the sword down at Suirel's head.

And froze, the blade barely an inch from contact. An unseen force seized him and lifted him off the ground. Clanless ran. Suirel stood and gestured. Swift Claw flew through the air and smacked into the unfortunate soldier. The soldier went down, but Swift Claw kept moving across the arena, past Kekeen, where he slammed into the wall. He fell to the ground and didn't move.

Clanless raised the moonblade to strike, but Suirel put out a hand. A strong wind struck Clanless and pushed him back. He strained against it.

Suirel wiped sand from the front of his clothes. "Nothing has changed here, Aldan. Surrender, or she dies." His eyeless head looked toward the arena wall and Swift Claw's body. "Ah, those beastmen. I will admit I was surprised you brought an entire army of them. However did you manage that?"

Clanless didn't answer, pushing against the wind.

"Oh, that's right." Suirel gestured, and the wind stopped. Clanless stumbled a few steps forward. "Now you can answer me."

Clanless glared at him. "I didn't bring the army." He switched to a small smile when he realized he knew something Suirel didn't. "Daviland brought them."

"Really?" Suirel stood silent for a moment. "How in the moon's name did he manage to survive?"

Clanless took a step.

"That's far enough. Drop the moonblade. Now. Or she dies."

Kekeen screamed.

Clanless looked back at her. She trembled, standing near the arena wall, then sank to her knees. She held out her tied hands toward him in petition.

He closed his eyes. How much of it was Kekeen, and how much was Zektel? He had no way of knowing. But he knew the threat was genuine. He opened his eyes and looked down at the moonblade. He took a deep breath and lowered it down toward the sand.

"Very good." Suirel tossed an empty bowl into the sand beside the moonblade. "Now fill this with your blood."

That wouldn't be difficult. Clanless looked at his left arm. One of the cuts he'd received in the battle before the gates had started to scab over. He picked at it to start the bleeding again, then held it over the bowl. Blood dribbled down his fingers and dripped off the tips. He could have accelerated the process but saw no reason to do so.

"Don't do it, Aldan!"

He turned in surprise; the voice was Koland's.

The storyteller stood beside Kekeen with a dagger to her neck.

"Suirel, now I have a proposition for you. Free my daughter. Now. Or I will kill her and remove your leverage over Clanless."

Clanless stopped breathing, his mouth frozen as he stared at his beloved and her father.

Suirel folded his arms over his chest. "You are bluffing, storyteller. You would not do this."

Clanless worked his jaw and managed to whisper, "No! You can't!" He wanted to scream. This could not be happening.

Koland nudged Kekeen. "Tell him."

"He's not bluffing!" she cried. "He almost did it before, but I made him forget it."

"Hm. Well, it makes no difference. Do what you will."

"No!" Clanless snatched up the moonblade and lunged at Suirel.

Suirel dodged his swing and snatched up Swift Claw's scimitar where it had fallen. "It was always going to end this way, anyway." He dashed a few paces away before turning back to face Clanless. "Come, my friend and enemy. Let us end it here in the arena sands. Can you think of a more appropriate place?"

"No. I can't."

The two combatants paced around each other, feinting, dodging, attacking. For unending minutes, they fought without a word, demonstrating why both of them were true champions of the arena. Though the stands were empty, the arena had never witnessed a more balanced struggle. For every move Clanless made, Suirel countered. For every attack Suirel made, Clanless eluded. Twice the moonblade snagged Suirel's armor without drawing blood. Twice Suirel's scimitar scratched Clanless's bare skin, adding to the dozen or more wounds on his body.

Clanless resisted the urge to go for Suirel's head. He'd left it unprotected as a taunt, daring Clanless to try it. A simple cut to the face would give him the opportunity to use the Taint. Anything harder, though, would risk killing Bain. Or would it? Suirel moved and fought as if he possessed perfect vision, though both eyes were gone. Would damaging Bain's body in any other way even impede him? Could he keep a body alive indefinitely? Clanless still held a tiny spark of hope that he could somehow free Bain from the chaos lord's influence. The Taint drove blood-wraiths out. He hoped it could do the same against Suirel. But if so, he couldn't damage the body too much.

All these thoughts whirled through his head but did nothing to affect his actual fighting. He couldn't afford to try any risky tactics. Bain had always been good, almost the equal of Clanless. And he hadn't been fighting all day. The scales were balanced.

He saw nothing but his opponent and sand particles, kicked up by their shifting feet and suspended in the air, illuminated by the white light of the moon above and the red light of the shimmering portal. He felt nothing but the sand below, the moonblade's handle, and the bloodrush within. He smelled and tasted nothing but sweat and blood.

Ultimately, the loss of blood proved his undoing. Too many injuries. Too much bleeding. Though he had the will and desire to fight forever, his body simply could not keep going. He faltered at a key moment, and Suirel seized it. With a twist and a half-spin, Suirel whirled around and drove the tip of the scimitar into Clanless's right side, halfway between his shoulder and hip.

His vision went black for a moment, and the moonblade slipped from his hands. When his eyes cleared, Suirel held the moonblade. Clanless fell to his hands and knees in the sand.

Suirel shook his head. "A shame, really, that such a battle would go unnoticed." He made a show of looking around and snorted. "The storyteller. Our sole witness. Unless you count the crawler over there."

Crawler? Nukai still moved? At least he lived. But if Koland watched, what had happened to Kekeen?

Suirel tossed Swift Claw's scimitar away. He found the discarded bowl and returned to Clanless. "You're bleeding much faster this time. This shouldn't take long."

Clanless struggled to breathe. He wanted to resist, to at least say something defiant, even if he couldn't fight. But his strength was gone. His arms held him up, but they quivered from the effort.

Suirel held up the bowl and laughed. "Blood of the Taint! The final piece to my victory."

"Wait!" Koland called.

Suirel strode toward the portal. "You used your only gambit, storyteller. I don't have time for you any more."

He slung the blood across the surface of the shimmering portal.

SACRIFICE

Then

Sugh took the wolf pelt and draped it over his own shoulders. "What am I doing? This is…"

"Hello, Sugh. My name is Yul. You have one of the arena Siphons, don't you?"

Sugh paused. The voice came from… within him. "A Siphon? Yes. Why do you ask?"

"You want to help Kekeen, Aldan's beloved. I can tell you how. But it won't be easy."

"I don't understand. Who are you?" He glanced around at Clanless talking with Daviland and the beastmen. "And what is going on here?"

"We don't have time for the full story. I am a blood-wraith. I was inside Clanless for years, and I entered you when you were camped outside the mines. I've been hiding, not influencing you in any way." He hesitated. "Well, except for that one time."

"What?"

"I saved your life in a fight. But never mind. I promised Clanless I would leave you when Suirel is defeated. He's the best one to do that, but he can't. Not if he's too worried about the girl."

Sugh nodded. "This I have seen."

"You have a Siphon. You know why and how they work better than anyone. And you're Clan Ghamkiin. All of these things together mean we can help her."

"How?"

"I'll explain as we go. But if you can find another Siphon, it will be better."

Sugh looked at the others. "Clanless no longer carries one. I am not sure if we can find another."

"Maybe we can do it with just one."

"This is a very strange feeling: talking to someone inside me. You do not sound like the goddess at all."

"No, we are not the same." Yul seemed to sigh. "She is far above me, like Suirel."

"I am beginning to understand Clanless better. Or at least how he used to be." Sugh touched the wolf pelt. "And why am I wearing this?"

"To prevent Suirel from exerting control over you through me. And to keep out any other blood-wraiths. Even now, it is affecting me. I won't be able to speak much longer. Will you let me help you, Sugh? Or do you want me to leave now?"

He hesitated. "You really think we can save Kekeen?"

"I do."

Clanless called, "Sugh, are you ready?"

Sugh adjusted the wolf pelt on his shoulder. This was a very strange circumstance, but everything had been strange since the Hawk King died. What would happen next? "I am ready. This looks better on me than it did on you, anyway."

Now

Sugh groaned and dragged himself to Duurald's body. He almost screamed every time his leg touched anything. "Goddess, please," he whispered.

Instead of the goddess, Yul answered: "I, I can't help you, Sugh. I don't even know if this will work any more."

"It has to," Sugh grunted. He yanked the Siphon from Duurald's belt and hooked it on his own beside the other one. Rolling over, he pointed himself toward the arena.

Sugh had endured pain many times. Early in his arena career, Baduhan had left him to suffer from wounds for a few days in order to create scars.

Everyone knew arena fighters used healing blood-magic after their fights, but scars added to their appearance and mystique.

Even so, none of those injuries had been like this. Every inch he crawled caused almost enough pain to knock him out. If he stayed still, he could bear it. He could rest. But if he stayed still, Kekeen would die.

"Sugh? Oh goddess! Sugh!" A rush of steps and skirts came near him. He knew the voice. Qara.

"What are you doing? Stop! I, I'll find some healing blood. Wait here."

"No." He reached out to pull himself forward again.

She fell to her knees in front of him. "You're killing yourself! Stop!"

"I can't. I… have to stop Koland."

Qara glanced over her shoulder to the arena. "I'll go stop him."

"He won't listen to you. I can save her."

"I'm not letting you drag yourself any further." She grabbed hold of his outstretched hand.

"Then help me up." He pulled at her hands.

She looked at his leg. "You can't put any weight at all on that. And I can't carry you. Maybe I can help, but you would have to hop on your good leg."

"Hopping is better than dragging."

"Maybe." She didn't look convinced. Sugh pulled at her hands again. "All right, all right. We'll try it. Unless…" She looked back toward the street. "Can one of you men help me? Anyone?"

Another roar echoed down the hall, coming from the arena. The crowd at the doors murmured and moved back.

Qara groaned. "No one wants to go near the terrifying sounds and end-of-the-world lighting. Guess it's up to me."

She crouched on his right side and helped him get his arm over her shoulders. Getting up on his right knee almost took them both down. From there, transitioning to standing took far too long for his liking. He tried to balance on the one leg. When he let the other dangle, the weight of it stretched his broken bones further apart, creating another intense bout of pain.

"Move," he gasped. They had to do this before he lost the ability to stay conscious, or before it was too late.

Qara took a hesitant step forward. Sugh hopped once. The dangling leg shook with the motion. By now, he knew it would be excruciating, no matter what they did. He hopped again before the pain could overwhelm him.

"You're so heavy," Qara complained.

Somehow, they kept moving. Step by hop by step by hop. Every movement an agony. Every moment a struggle to keep the darkness away and stay awake.

At last, they reached the corner. Qara let Sugh lean against the edge while they both looked out into the arena. Sugh took in the fallen beast, Tuulka, the portal, Clanless, and Bain. And only a few yards away stood Koland, holding the knife to Kekeen's throat. Before Sugh could say anything, Clanless launched an attack on Bain.

"Koland!" Sugh shouted. He followed it with coughs that bent him in half.

Koland turned to see them. "This is the only way, Sugh. I won't allow it any longer."

"You can't." Qara stepped toward Koland, holding out her hand. "Koland, this is not like you. The man I know would never do something like this."

"I want my daughter back." Koland's eyes darted from Suirel to her. "And if she can't come back, then I don't want this thing parading around in her body."

"So you'll kill her?" Qara walked closer. "Come on, Koland. Go help Clanless. You're the only one left who can."

Koland glanced toward the fight. "I failed once already. I shouldn't—"

"I can save her!" Sugh called.

Koland's head jerked his way.

"I know it," Sugh said. "Just let me try."

Koland took the knife from Kekeen's neck. "Ah," she gasped. "You almost convinced me that time, Father dear."

Qara grabbed the rope dangling from Kekeen's tied hands. "Over here, you."

"I need the dagger," Sugh added.

Koland tossed it in the sand near Sugh then turned toward Clanless.

Sugh collapsed to the ground. Qara gasped at his fall. Blackness embraced him, but only for a moment.

Kekeen snorted. "It doesn't look like he'll be doing much of anything."

"That's… where you're wrong." Sugh lifted his head. "Bring her here, Qara."

Qara yanked Kekeen next to Sugh and made her kneel beside him. Sugh took one of the Siphons from his belt.

"The largest blood vessel in the thigh," Yul said. "It's a direct line to the heart."

With the dagger, Sugh first cut a slit inside the Siphon's bladder and then stabbed into Kekeen's thigh. She barely had time to exclaim in pain before he jammed the Siphon's punch tube into the cut.

"What are you doing?" She tried to pull away, but Qara held her down. "You're taking my blood?"

Sugh lifted his head and looked into her eyes. "Zektel. I know you're bound to the blood. I'm removing you from her forever." He coughed again, spitting out some of his own blood.

Kekeen's face twisted in confusion. "You would have to drain too much of her blood. She'll die. And, and if she doesn't, I can go right back in."

"You'll… do nothing. Ever again." He looked up at Qara. "The fur."

Qara understood, though her eyes were wide. She lifted the pelt from Sugh's shoulders and placed it on Kekeen. "Will this work, Sugh?"

"It has to." He fumbled for the second Siphon.

Kekeen gasped and shook her head. "Oh, she's angry. So angry. But she can't do anything right now. You're pulling her out!"

Blood filled the Siphon's bladder and spilled out onto the sand.

Qara knelt beside both of them. "It… it's so much blood. Sugh, will she survive?"

Sugh yanked the punch tube free of the second Siphon. "Give me… your arm, Kekeen."

Shaking, she extended it toward him. He inserted the punch tube into her vein, then brought the other end to the largest open wound on his arm. "Qara, help her lie down."

Qara took Kekeen's shoulders and guided her down onto the sand. Both women stared at Sugh with wrinkled brows and open mouths.

"Sugh, you've lost too much blood already," Qara said. "You can't—"

"Quiet! I need… to concentrate." But concentrating hurt even more. His mind wanted to give up, to go to sleep and never wake again.

"Qara has to do this," Yul whispered. "If your blood isn't activated, it won't flow to her."

Kekeen's face grew pale. She rested her head on the sand and mouthed, "Sugh… don't…"

"Qara," Sugh said, stumbling over each word. His mouth felt thick and clumsy. "I need… catalyst."

"What?" Qara shook her head. "No! You can't ask me to do that!"

"Now!" he begged. "Or she dies!"

"I, I don't have any of Aldan's blood with me."

Kekeen lifted a hand and pointed out into the arena. "There," she whispered. "The bag."

((((●))))

Qara looked into Sugh's eyes. If she didn't do this for him, both he and Kekeen would die. But if she did…

With a curse, she scrambled to her feet and ran out into the arena. Bain—Suirel—bent over Clanless near the portal. For a moment, a wild thought entered her head of charging to his rescue. But Sugh and Kekeen needed her, and Koland was heading that direction anyway. She hurried toward the fallen bag of blood vials.

Winds whipped past her from the portal, catching her skirts and dragging at her steps. She stumbled and reached for the bag.

At the same moment, a hand seized her left arm. "What are you doing out here, girl?"

Qara fell to her knees and looked up to see Suirel's soldier. The beastman's claws had scraped across his forehead, sending blood trickling down his face. He wiped at it with his other sleeve while he glared down at her.

"Let me go! My friend's life depends on it!"

"I don't think so. Not until Lord Suirel—" He broke off, staring at the portal.

"Idiot." Qara drew her dagger from its hidden sheath in her skirt. "I stabbed a beastman. You're nothing." The soldier twisted at her movement. Instead of stabbing him in the chest as she intended, she buried the dagger into his thigh. He yelled and released her arm.

Qara grabbed the bag of vials.

"No, you don't!" The soldier yanked the dagger from his thigh and reached for her again.

Qara swung the bag of vials and smacked him in the head. The bag burst open, scattering crystals full of blood across the sand. The soldier fell with a last moan.

The wind grew stronger. Qara fell to the sand and grabbed one of the blood vials before the shifting sand could bury it. She pulled herself to her feet and staggered back to Sugh and Kekeen.

Both of them looked almost dead.

((((●))))

Sugh watched Qara fall to her knees beside him, holding a small blood vial. Aldan's blood. "You'll die!" she whimpered. "There has to be another way!"

Across the sand, someone shouted.

Kekeen's eyes closed.

Sugh sought out Qara's face. Grains of sand filled her hair, disheveled by the wind. Flecks of blood covered her skin from the encounter with the soldier. Had she ever looked so beautiful and alive? His own eyes were rimmed with red and darkness. "Qara. You… must."

She turned the vial and let a single drop of the Clanless blood fall into Sugh's wound. A warm rush spread throughout his entire body. Immediately, he could sense all of his own blood as well as Kekeen's as it spilled out. The power of Clan Ghamkiin: controlling the blood itself. He focused and sent his own blood through the tube and into Kekeen's veins.

"It's working!" Yul cried.

The growing stain of blood in the sand swirled, almost forming a face. "Stop this!" Zektel hissed.

Sugh ignored her and kept his focus. Enough of Kekeen's blood had to leave to fully remove Zektel. And enough of his own blood had to enter her veins to keep her alive. His chest grew tight and resisted his breathing. His heart kept beating, but it slowed. He only had to hold on a little longer…

"Sugh…" Qara's skirts rustled as she moved beside him. She lifted his head onto her lap. "You… you…" She sniffed and caressed his head.

"I cared… for you too," he said.

"I know." She bent and kissed his cheek.

"Tell me… when it's… done," Sugh whispered to Yul.

"Almost…"

The darkness blended with the redness and took away his vision. At least the pain was fading. And he felt cold, the coldest he'd ever felt on these hot sands.

"No, no," Qara murmured. A warm drop struck Sugh's face. She wept for him. Had anyone ever wept for him before? He blinked, trying to see her, but the darkness grew colder.

"My… heart…" he managed to whisper.

"It worked! She's gone!" Yul shouted.

Sugh did not answer. He could no longer focus on moving the blood. And his heart. He'd never known it to beat so slow. It… oh.

It stopped.

Koland stumbled back. Winds rushed outward from the portal, but none of them touched him. The watery and now bloody surface undulated,

as though someone had tossed a pebble in a puddle. Suirel's laughter filled the air.

"They come!" he shouted. "My triumph is complete! Across the endless void, they come!" He pointed past the steadfast moon toward the faint image of the chaos moon beyond, so faint Koland almost couldn't make it out. "From the prison of the gods, the abyssal rock, our dwelling for millennia, they come!"

Koland looked around. Qara had returned to Sugh and Kekeen. Whether Sugh could truly help his daughter now didn't matter in the face of this calamity. Nukai, bleeding himself, appeared to be trying to crawl toward the portal, but he would not reach it for a very long time, if ever. Tuulka the ghuyak whimpered to himself near the arena wall.

Only Clanless remained. Beaten, wounded, bleeding, and barely conscious. He watched Suirel and the portal from his hands and knees.

"Suirel!" Koland called against the wind. "I have one last story to tell!"

"You are nothing, Koland." Suirel turned his head, a rictus of pleasure on his eyeless face. "But I will grant you this last wish before one of my children takes you forever. What story is this?"

Koland fumbled with his hands in front of him as he walked forward. The vial from the Ghamba Lam came open, spilling its contents onto his hands.

"It's the story of your triumph, the true reason for it all. But it is for your ears only."

"Who is there to hear?" Suirel spread his arms.

"Your ears only," Koland repeated. He stopped, bowed his head, put a bloody hand to his neck, and tapped his beard.

Suirel stalked to him. He seized Koland's neck with his right hand and lifted him off the sand. He waved the moonblade at him. "Or maybe I'll cut off your head with the blade of Clanless, this blade that represents a failed goddess. An adversary who couldn't muster a single ally against me. None of any consequence, at any rate."

Koland's mouth moved without sound.

"What's that? What is your final story, storyteller? Tell me." Suirel brought Koland up near his head.

Koland smiled. With Clan Torov's blood-magic enhancing his voice, he opened his mouth, and said:

"THIS IS NOT YOUR WORLD."

Bain's ear drum exploded. Blood burst from within.

And Clanless activated the Taint.

37

PRISON OF THE GODS

Suirel screamed and threw Koland away, his wind-magic tossing the storyteller across the arena.

Clanless's eyes burned as always. He focused the power like never before. The Taint roared through Bain's body. He screamed and staggered like a drunken man. The moonblade fell to the sand.

More blood called to him. Clanless turned his head and used the Taint again, this time against his own blood, the blood glistening on the surface of the portal. It hissed, sending red-tinted steam drifting outward. For a moment, he felt pulled toward even more blood; Nukai wasn't far. Swift Claw… others…

Clanless took a deep breath and pushed the Taint back at Suirel instead. The god of chaos screamed again. He fell to his own hands and knees only a few feet away. Clanless let the Taint rush through his enemy's body one last time before letting it go. He lowered his head, eyes still burning.

"Clan… less…"

He lifted his head. Bain lay on the sand. "I can't see, Clanless. I'm… blind."

"Bain? Is that you?"

Bain's head turned in the direction of his voice. "It's… me. For the moment. You hurt him. But he'll be back. Soon."

"I'll do it again, then. I'll drive him out completely, Bain." Clanless pushed against the sand and sat up. More blood gushed from his side. He put one hand against the wound and groaned.

"No. I told you before. It's too late for me. It's all I can do to keep my one last secret from him." Bain put his hands into the sand and pushed himself up as well. "He knows almost everything I know, but I've kept one or two things to myself. And somehow, this one might actually matter." He winced. "He-he's angry now. Raging. He'll take me back very soon."

"No, no. Fight him, Bain. I'll drive him out for good. I'll destroy the portal. I'll—"

"You can't destroy it, Aldan." Bain chuckled and spit sand out of his mouth. "Even now, you're blind. Like me. Sort of."

"What are you talking about?" Clanless walked on his knees to get closer. The pain in his side grew dull. Was that good or bad?

"He-he's coming back." Bain reached out a hand, flailing. Clanless caught it and held it. Bain smiled. "We were almost friends, weren't we?"

Clanless nodded before realizing Bain wouldn't see it. "Yes. Yes, we were."

Bain's breathing grew labored, as though he struggled to do something. "Do you… do you want to know a secret, Aldan? I haven't known it for long… only since you came into the arena."

"What are you talking about?"

Bain pulled at his hand, drawing him close. Clanless leaned in near Bain's head to hear the faintest of whispers. "That… is not… Nukai."

Bain's body spasmed. He released Clanless's hand and fell back to the sand.

"Bain, I…"

Bain's body jerked and tensed. He opened his mouth and hissed, "Remember!" And then he collapsed and lay still.

Clanless stood confused and alone, still holding the wound in his side. Remember what? He turned to see Nukai, not far away. The hunched man had crawled almost all the way to them, leaving a trail of blood behind him. He lifted his head and looked at Clanless.

And a memory rushed back.

Then

Clanless snuck down the hall, leaving the other boys sleeping. As he so often did, he wanted to speak with Zektel. Only a few days remained until graduation. His own anxiety was reflected by all the other boys.

Despite boasts to the contrary, none of them were ready to kill or die.

"No, no, no!"

Clanless stopped. Another boy was awake. The voice came from around the corner at the end of the hall. He'd never gone that way before at night. It led to Nukai's quarters. He took a few steps closer.

"I won't let you! You can't!"

He knew the voice now. Bain. Who was he yelling at? Clanless crept to the corner.

Bain burst around the corner and almost ran into him. He shoved Clanless aside and raced down the hall. Clanless pulled himself back up and stared. Bain had been… crying? Bain?

"Clanless. Why are you out of bed?"

He turned to see Nukai watching him. "I'm sorry. I'll go back."

"Wait." Nukai held out a hand. "Don't speak with Shool Baina about this. He is… proud. He will not admit anything."

"Is… is he all right?" Clanless glanced nervously back down the hall.

"He is fine. I had to tell him a truth he did not want to hear."

"I don't understand."

Nukai sighed. "Bain is my nephew. He was hoping I would leave here with him after graduation."

"He never told us." Clanless rubbed his face. "Why… why don't you go with him? Do you like it here?"

"Sometimes, it doesn't matter what we like. Can you keep his secret, Clanless?"

Clanless wrinkled his brow. "Yes. I still don't understand, though."

Nukai patted him on the shoulder. "I'm dying, Clanless. Kan is leaving after you graduate, but I'll stay… for one more class, though I may not see them graduate. Bain… did not want to accept this."

Clanless didn't want to accept it either. "This place is horrible, but you… you've been almost kind to me. Can't you get healing? From the blood-magic?"

"The magic cannot heal what is wrong with me. Go to bed, Clanless. Say nothing of this to your friend."

Clanless nodded and hurried back toward the bunk room.

"In fact, try to forget it!" Nukai called after him. "Forget the whole thing!"

Now

He had forgotten. Had Zektel done it for him, or had he buried that memory himself?

Bain screamed behind him. "Enough! This world will burn!" Suirel was back in control. Clanless knew he'd lost far too much blood by now. He'd be unconscious soon. And it would all be over. But no one else remained to stop the god of chaos.

"Now, Clanless," Nukai said. "This is the moment. Let it take over."

Let it take over? Let what take over? Hope? He couldn't be serious. Who was this man, anyway? Clanless looked down at Nukai. Their eyes met.

And Nukai's brown eyes shifted to gold. "This is the moment," he repeated. "Get me to the portal."

Something changed. Clanless didn't understand, but he stepped forward. He released the wound on his side and helped Nukai to his feet. Together they moved, step by bleeding step, toward the glowing red surface of the crystal portal.

Suirel clambered to his feet. "What are you doing?" he snarled. He stepped toward them, and then staggered back two steps, as if his own body fought him. "Agh. Give it up, you fool."

"Fight him," Clanless whispered. If Bain could give them a moment longer...

"He took the blood of the Taint to activate this, just as he did ages ago," Nukai said. "It took the blood of your people for generations to keep it closed. Now, the blood of a god will seal it."

They stopped at the base of the portal. The crystals here had been embedded into the ground. The glowing surface started at the height of their knees and rose far above their heads. "Who are you?" Clanless asked.

"You have nothing to fear from me, as I told you the first time we met." The voice came not from Nukai's mouth, but within Clanless's head.

The golden eyes. The Wolf. And... something else. Another memory tried to resurface. Shining. Glowing beings. Thrones. The Goddess. And the golden eyes.

Suirel rushed at them, wielding the moonblade. Clanless had time only to try to push Nukai away. But the Wolf seized his arm and pulled himself back, right as Suirel brought the sword up.

The moonblade lodged into Nukai's chest. He smiled, the largest smile Clanless had ever seen. His blood gushed from the wound. And he fell back into the portal.

The moonblade clanged off the crystal and fell. Clanless didn't see where it landed.

Where Nukai had fallen, a splotch of his blood, richer in color, remained on the surface of the portal. As Clanless stared, it grew, doubling in size in seconds. Darker and thicker than the watery portal surface, the blood spread faster and faster. In moments, it would cover the entire thing.

"No, no, no." Suirel grabbed at the blood, trying to stop it. His hands came back dripping. "How could he have been here? How?"

The portal trembled. The red glow faded. The light of the moon filled the arena, shining brighter than any evening Clanless could remember. For the first time since entering the arena, he heard the distant sounds of battle. Soldiers and beastmen still fought over the fate of the city.

With a rush that whipped through Clanless's hair, the portal, now covered in the Wolf's blood, shifted. Instead of a flat surface, it pulled inward, and the wind pushed into it. The blood swirled, turning like a giant whirlpool on its side.

Suirel staggered, as if the wind hit him hardest. He threw out his hands, attempting to counter it with his own power. The wind did not change. He spun to face Clanless, a look of rage twisting his features.

And then he laughed. "This… this will not stop me. Regardless of who wins the battle outside, I have supporters everywhere. We'll rebuild the portal, and—"

Another burst of wind struck him, knocking him off balance. He wavered but recovered.

"The wind is not yours any more," Clanless said. The beastmen would be pleased about that.

Clanless caught hold of one of the crystals around the edge to stabilize himself as the power of the wind increased. But it seemed to be pushing Suirel with more force, driving him toward the portal. His eyeless face turned back toward Clanless. "If I am to leave… you will come with me!" He lunged with the wind and seized Clanless, one hand grabbing his arm and the other wrapping around his torso.

In that instant, the full force of the wind struck, pushing them both into the portal. Clanless gasped, and the air was torn from his lungs. He held on to the crystal with his left hand and struggled against Suirel with his right.

"Come. With. Me!" Suirel pulled with the wind. Clanless wanted to fight harder, but his injuries and general exhaustion threatened his ability.

"Where?" He searched the reaches of his vision for any of the others. Sugh, Swift Claw, Koland, Kekeen… he knew nothing of any of them. The wind and brightness all around made it impossible to see beyond a few feet.

"I told you! The prison of the gods! You see it every thirty years." Suirel pushed his eyeless face close. Clanless tried not to stare at the empty sockets and jagged scars. "But we see it forever." He pulled harder. Clanless's foot slipped to the very edge of the crystal. "You and Bain. You'll be the only humans there. But you'll have plenty of company. Come with me! Escape this life forever."

The horror of the thought overwhelmed him for a moment. Life in a barren place, tormented by millions of blood-wraiths until he couldn't take it any more. As horrible as his life had been for so many years, it couldn't be as bad as what awaited on the chaos moon.

The wind's power grew even stronger. Suirel tightened his grip… or tried to. Blood flowed from Clanless's side wound again, making his torso slick. Suirel's hand slipped free. He flipped over the edge of the crystal and spun in a circle. In an instant, his lower body disappeared into the blood-covered portal. Only his grip on Clanless's arm kept him from disappearing. In spite of his fear, Clanless gripped him back. His hair flowed around his head and pulled toward the portal.

"Let Bain stay! Leave him! You don't need him on the other side!" Clanless had to shout to be heard over the rushing wind and a growing roar from the swirling portal itself. He braced himself, wrapping his left arm as far around the crystal as he could. His knees pressed against the crystal frame on the bottom.

"Don't be ridiculous. Bain chose me. I would never leave him behind!" Suirel's grip slipped down to Clanless's wrist. He tried to bring his other hand up, but the portal pulled it back.

As Clanless stared, a red mist gathered around Suirel's face. In moments, it formed another face overlaying Bain's scarred visage. It opened its mouth and laughed again. "This isn't the end, Clanless. Join me on the other side. And when the time comes around again, we'll return here. It will be glorious!"

Clanless didn't answer. The strain of holding on to the crystal and resisting the wind and suction was becoming too much. Darkness clouded the edges of his vision. He almost didn't notice the red mist-face starting to dissolve around the edges.

"Not… over…" Suirel's words almost didn't reach his ears.

Clanless blinked, and his vision cleared for the moment. The red mist separated and swept into the portal's vortex.

"Aldan. It's all right."

"Bain?"

"It's me. He-he's gone."

"Hold on, Bain. Don't let go."

"No." The roar from the portal intensified. "It's all right, Aldan. Let me go."

"No! Hold on. Someone will come." Clanless tilted his head to yell over his shoulder: "Help us!"

"It's too late, Aldan. It was too late long ago." Bain turned his blind head, trying to aim it toward Clanless. "This is it for me."

"I won't!"

Bain's face stopped moving, and he smiled at last. "And I won't take you with me."

Clanless clenched his teeth and strained.

Bain chuckled, an odd sound against the roar of the portal, yet one that somehow reached his ears. And then he let go.

"No!" Clanless held on to Bain's wrist with the grip he'd used on the moonblade thousands of times. "Don't go!"

"Aldan."

He looked into Bain's empty, scarred eye sockets. His body trembled with the strain. Blood and sweat rolled down his arm.

"Trust me."

Clanless caught his breath. He'd never— His grip slipped. Bain's fingers slid through his.

And he was gone.

The portal's surface undulated for a moment but returned to its swirling vortex at once. Clanless would have wept if he'd had any strength. Something struck his shoulder before flipping into the portal. The impact knocked him off balance. He lost his footing and fell over the edge.

In a second, his legs disappeared through the portal's surface. A horrible cold crept up from his feet, colder than he'd experienced even lost in the snow. He wrapped both arms around the crystal he'd been holding.

The wind swept around him, now carrying voices, voices calling, pleading, begging, mocking.

"Come with us, Clanless."

"No! I don't want to go back!"

"Save us!"

"All your fault."

"We want you, Clanless."

"We can be together, forever."

"Allldannnn! Pleeease!" Zektel?

"Suirel is waiting for you on the other side."

"Darkness. Death. Fire. So cold."

"Not again."

"Come with us."

"Come with us."

"Come with us."

He closed his eyes. His hands were slipping. It wouldn't be long now. Over the roar of the portal, he heard a new sound: the crystals cracking. The portal was starting to come apart. Even if he held on, he would be swept in eventually. But Bain was there. Maybe they could fight together one last time in this dark and frigid place beyond. Maybe it would be their last duel. Forever.

"Aldan!"

It wasn't a wraith's voice. He opened his eyes. It took a few moments to blink away the darkness, the blood, and the tears.

Another pair of hands grabbed on to his arm. His vision cleared at last, and he saw a tear-streaked face staring at him framed by wolf fur and her own pale brown hair streaming toward him and the portal.

Kekeen.

"It's me, Aldan. Don't leave me. Please."

A moment later, Koland appeared beside her, looking dazed and shaken. He seized Aldan's other arm.

And then Swift Claw was there too, extending his clawed hands.

Aldan released the crystal, let them grasp him… and grasped back.

They pulled him out, bit by bit. His knee smacked against one of the crystals. And then he fell forward, his face striking the sand, the same sand he'd fought and bled upon for so long. But never again.

His eyes closed, and he drifted away.

A GLEAM OF MOONLIGHT

Soft light and warmth enveloped Aldan. He relaxed, recognizing the setting this time.

"Goddess?"

"I am here, Aldan." A brighter light drew near, almost in the shape of a person.

Aldan shook his head. The warmth felt so good, especially on his legs after the portal's icy grip. "Why do these meetings only seem to happen when I'm asleep and badly hurt?"

"You have shed your blood for the sake of others." The goddess paused. "And that is why he is here too."

What? Aldan turned and saw another human figure who appeared to step out of the light into view. "Sugh!"

"Clanless!" The two men embraced as if they hadn't seen each other in years. "You have triumphed then," Sugh said. "Suirel is defeated?"

"I… think so." He turned back toward the goddess. "Suirel is gone, isn't he? What happened to him?"

"He has been returned to the place from which he came. Your people call it the chaos moon."

"Can he ever return?"

There was a long pause. "The portal is closed. His access to your world is cut off."

"But can he come back some other way?"

"If he does, it will not be for a very long time. Beyond that, I cannot say."

"Then—"

"Even the gods do not know all the answers, Aldan." She paused. "At least most of the gods."

"Goddess!" Sugh exclaimed. "I have come to you now?"

"For now, my faithful one."

"What of…" Aldan stumbled over his words. "What of the Wolf? Is he dead? Who was he?"

"He gave his all. Do you remember the last time you were here?"

Aldan glanced at Sugh. "I, I remember pieces. The light. You were there. And he was. The gold eyes. And there were others."

"Yes. That is enough for now."

"You're not answering any questions. Not really."

"She does that," Sugh said.

Several moments went by without words. Aldan wanted to ask more, but everything felt so calm, so pleasant.

"I have loved the both of you for so long," the goddess said at last. "I have watched you both, attempted to guide you in my own way. And now… everything changes."

"I don't understand," Aldan said.

"You don't have to. Not yet."

"Then why did you bring me—us—here?"

"I brought you here to say goodbye."

"Oh. Well… goodbye, I suppose. I won't see you again?"

Aldan couldn't explain it, but something like a wave of sadness washed over him, as if it came from the goddess herself.

"No. Not to say goodbye to me."

"Then…"

"She means me." Sugh coughed a little.

Aldan turned slowly. "No."

"It is not for us to decide, Clanless." Sugh smiled and looked down. "Although I suppose I did choose this."

"What do you mean?"

Sugh lifted his head and looked toward the goddess. "I will not see him again, will I?"

"No. But others are waiting to see you."

"Hagh?"

"I can barely keep him back."

Despite the environment, Aldan felt a deep ache settle into his chest.

He longed to see Hagh again. And maybe others too. Badaar. Nukai—the real one. Zaluu. And Tunt. And he didn't want Sugh to leave. Not without him.

"It is not your time, dear Aldan." She knew his thoughts. Of course she did.

"Why not? Haven't I bled enough?"

"You have others who wait for you on your own side. And time enough left to enjoy them. To enjoy her."

Kekeen.

"And you owe that to Sugh."

"What?"

Sugh shuffled his feet. "It was Yul mostly. He told me what to do, how to free her from the blood-wraith. What about him? What happened to Yul?"

"I do not know his fate. But I know that he also told you what it would cost," the goddess said. "And you still did it."

"Yes, well. It seemed like the right thing to do."

"It was."

Aldan looked back and forth between them. "I don't understand."

Sugh shrugged. "I don't either."

"If you saved Kekeen, then… I owe my future to you. Everything."

"You don't owe me, Clanless." Sugh looked him in the eyes. "We are brothers. We do what we must for each other."

"The essence of love," the goddess whispered.

Sugh shrugged again. "I think my life proves I don't know much about love."

"You know more than enough. There is none greater than this."

Aldan felt a shimmer, as if his entire body shifted ever so slightly, along with a twinge in his side. He suspected his time in this place would soon be ending.

"What happens next?" he asked.

"You will return. And you will live," she answered.

"Then I won't have to fight any more?"

"Not now. And perhaps not ever again. I do not know all things." She paused. "Come, Sugh. It is time."

"Wait." Aldan grabbed Sugh and pulled him into another hug. "I don't… I can't…"

"Farewell, brother. Live."

Aldan choked back a sob. He had no more words. At last, he released Sugh and stepped back. Sugh smiled at him and turned toward the goddess.

He put a hand to his chest. "My heart—" He stopped. "Do I still have a heart?"

"My child, you have one of the strongest—no, one of the greatest—hearts I've found among your people," she answered. "Come." She gestured, and Sugh stepped toward her.

Aldan caught a brief glimpse of something opening up beyond them. He saw it for only a moment, but he knew he would never forget it. A landscape with no sand. A wide river of flowing, clear water. Trees. So many trees. Green and blue everywhere. And in the furthest distance, a gleam of moonlight reflected from a city whose beauty took his breath away.

"Home!" Sugh cried.

The light faded.

Aldan bowed his head. Grief and joy warred within him.

"Aldan."

He looked back up to see the shining form of the goddess still present. She held out her hands, displaying something. Aldan took a step forward and squinted against the light. Only then did he recognize the moonblade.

"It would have been swept to the chaos moon with Suirel and his followers had I not stepped in," she said. "But even so, it is no longer a part of your world. I can return it, but… it may be some time."

"I… I don't need it." He swallowed against another lump in his throat. "I mean, I don't want to need it."

He felt a distinct impression of pride radiating toward him. "I will keep it for you then, unless a day arrives that you do need it. Since your sword is of the moon, to the moon it shall return."

Aldan's view shifted, and he saw the moon once more. It looked just as it had the first time he'd met the goddess. He saw details he'd never glimpsed from the ground: mountains and valleys, riverbeds and vast plains. His view rotated and drew closer to a mountain range.

"From the Sar Empire, these mountains can be seen as a dark patch on the northernmost portion of the moon," the goddess said. "Here, on its highest peak, I will keep your sword. It shall be preserved without harm."

Aldan saw a pinnacle of a high and steep mountain. His moonblade stood at the very tip, embedded into the rock. He spun and turned around it, seeing it from all sides, though he had no sense of actual movement. The vision and the light itself began to fade.

"Farewell, Aldan. I do not think we will speak again like this."

Aldan tried to hold on to the light, but it vanished into the darkness. He returned to sleep, a deep rest without pain.

Aldan wanted to wake up. He wanted to see Kekeen. Nothing remained to keep them apart now. And despite the assurances from the goddess, he worried they might have to flee the city right away. But though his brain cycled through these thoughts over and over, he couldn't seem to find his way back to full consciousness.

And then he heard her.

"...surrendered,
I found my love in shadows long.
Though the winter winds were blowing,
We knew our love would make us strong."

Kekeen was singing. He hadn't heard her sing since... since the night before Ghouk forced him and the others out of the city. How long had it been? Five months? Six? Was it still High Spring, even? In some ways, nothing communicated how horrible things had been than the simple fact that Kekeen hadn't been singing.

He tried to open his eyes, tried to speak... and succeeded at neither.

"On the day the sun surrendered,
My love and I walked in the light..."

Aldan managed something between a grunt and a moan.

Kekeen broke off. "Aldan?"

"I... I'm..." As he struggled to open his eyes, new sensations swept over Aldan. Pain erupted from all over his body. Deep agony radiated from his side, but it competed with intense burning on every inch of skin across both legs. He let out a short exclamation of pain.

"Aldan!" Cool, soft hands touched his face. It created such a contrast with the pain, he wanted to turn off everything else and just enjoy the feeling.

"Isn't there anything we can do for him yet?" Kekeen asked.

"Not yet." It was Koland's voice. "Every person in Clan Kurav that can be found is donating blood. But we have so many on the brink of death, I don't know when any will get here."

"Hold on, Aldan," Kekeen pleaded. "Help is coming."

"F-fin-finish..." he managed to whisper.

"Finish?"

"The song," Koland said. "Finish the song."

Kekeen hesitated a moment. Then, after humming a bit, she sang the last two lines:

"With pain and trials now overcome,
We have no fear to mar the night."
Aldan smiled and let himself drift off.

(((●)))

When Aldan woke again, he heard only silence. The pain in his side remained but nowhere near as intense. His legs still burned, but even as he thought about it, he felt some kind of lotion being spread on his left calf. Cooling spread with it. "Ohhh," he murmured.

"Aldan?" Kekeen's voice again. The hands stopped spreading the lotion.

"Don't stop," he croaked.

"It's not Kurav blood," she said in a hurry as she resumed, "but Qara says it's helpful with burns."

"It feels… nice."

"No one really knows what happened to your legs," Kekeen said. "They look like someone who sat in the sun of High Spring for hours and hours. But worse, somehow. There's lots of bruising, or something like bruising. I'm not sure. It's, uh, very ugly."

Aldan took a few deep breaths and opened his eyes. The canopy above told him they must be in the Hawk King's palace. It looked like the room where Kekeen—Zektel—had been sleeping before the battle.

"Just give me a minute to finish up with this, and I'll get you some water," Kekeen went on. "Things are still crazy around here. We got a few drops of healing blood yesterday. I hope your side feels better. And, and maybe there will be more by the end of the day. Or first thing tomorrow. That's what they told me, anyway."

When she brought the water, Aldan almost didn't drink it. He stared up at Kekeen's face until she blushed and looked away. "Drink the water, idiot."

"It's really you, isn't it?" he asked a few minutes and a lot of water later. "She hasn't come back."

"It's me," she whispered. "I think Zektel is gone for good now. Thanks to Sugh."

Remembering the moments with the goddess, he couldn't think of the right words. Sugh was gone. The enormity of his friend's sacrifice overwhelmed Aldan.

"What… what happened with the battle?"

"Oh! We won! I mean… I don't know much about the details. I know a lot of people are dead. But the Melkute are gone, at least."

"Their entire nation is crippled," announced a voice from the direction of Aldan's feet. He turned his head enough to see Daviland drawing near the bed. He still moved with a crutch. "It's good to see you awake, Aldan."

Aldan nodded. The arrival of Daviland and the beastmen made so much sense now, since he understood a little more about the Wolf. Thinking about them made him realize he could sense Swift Claw. The beastman couldn't be far away.

Daviland stopped next to Kekeen. "Of course, our nation is crippled, as well. Neither of us possess an army large enough to threaten the other, perhaps for a very long time. I'll be sending an ambassador north in a day or two to see what we can salvage from all this." He paused. "But that may be more information than you were wanting."

Aldan tried to shrug, but it hurt his side.

"I'll let you rest," Daviland said. "I just wanted to check in on you. We'll have healing blood soon, I'm told. Most of the life-or-death injuries have now been handled, and they'll be moving on to the ones that are less critical." He shook his head. "The priests are doing an amazing job, working with all the injured, classifying the needs and rushing here and there to take care of everyone. The Ghamba Lam is directing it all. It's very impressive.

"Even so…" He paused. "There are limits. I'm afraid many of us will bear scars for the rest of our lives, at the least. And we've lost far too many."

He moved away. "I may not see you again for some time, Aldan. So much to do. But you're in my thoughts. Without you, we wouldn't even have what we do."

"Not me."

"No modesty from you now. I know what you did. Thank you. I mean that. Truly." He stopped and lowered his head. "We… haven't had the best of relationships since we met, I know." He glanced at Kekeen. "And then the arena. And Zektel. I did horrible things while under her control. I know. And yet, in a way, I've found redemption. Someday, I'll tell you the whole thing. The divine move in strange ways."

Aldan didn't answer, not trusting himself with words again. Daviland nodded and left.

Kekeen moved closer and offered water again. "And now you need to rest," she told him. "I've been told not to upset you or give you any stress. So… go back to sleep, my love." She leaned over and kissed his forehead. "We'll talk more when you're better."

He wanted to argue, but sleep stole over him again. He couldn't resist its pull.

RESOLUTIONS

Aldan felt much better the next time he woke up. The pain in his side had vanished, and even his legs didn't hurt quite as much. A dozen other smaller injuries still ached, but he could handle that kind of pain.

Kekeen helped him drink and eat a little bit. She apologized for the simple food, especially the lack of bread. Apparently, there was a shortage throughout the city. And with the fields destroyed by the Melkute army, Et-Baylak would be short of many things for some time to come. Another crisis that Daviland and the other leaders would have to resolve.

"Your father?" Aldan asked. "I remember hearing his voice. He's all right? And Qara?"

"They're fine," she said. "Father got banged up pretty bad but nothing that required any healing magic. He's sore, but he's already out helping others. So is Qara. Daviland has asked her to be his assistant, but she comes by to check on you—us—every day."

"Every day? How long have I been asleep?"

"Three days? No, four. The battle was four days ago, and it's almost the middle of the night right now." She smiled. "Your waking times aren't exactly on schedule yet."

"Middle of the night? And you're still here?" He lifted a hand to rub his face, surprising himself that he could move it so easily. He'd been healed with blood-magic thousands of times, but his body always expected to hurt more afterward than it did.

"I want to be here."

He pulled himself up onto his elbow to look at her. "I want you to be here too. Always."

Kekeen looked down and wrung her hands together. "I want to be here, because… because I don't want to miss anything else myself. She stole so much from me, Aldan."

"I know."

She looked up, tears forming. "No, you don't. Not fully. I know you carried her around for years, but she didn't control your body like she did mine."

"She stole memories from me." He paused. "But I guess she thought she was helping me with some of those."

"She stole real memories from me! She experienced things that I never will, not the same. I won't get to meet your family for the first time, because they think they've already met me. I won't… won't…"

"I'm so sorry," Aldan said. "I tried everything I could think of."

Kekeen shook her head. "I don't blame you."

"You should. Everything she did, she did because of me."

"Maybe." Kekeen paced to the other side of the bed. "I could experience some of her feelings at times. She hated you. And she loved you. It was so complicated! At times, I couldn't tell where her feelings ended and mine began. Sometimes, I think I hated you."

"Kekeen…"

"No, don't talk. Let me get this all out."

Aldan closed his mouth.

Kekeen paced back the other way. "I love you, Aldan. I do. When you woke up while I was singing… that was the perfect moment. It would be the ending in one of my father's stories, and everyone would applaud and be happy. But real life is more complicated. Or at least our life is." She collapsed into the chair. "My own father tried to kill me to save me. And then Sugh…" She choked up for a moment. "Sugh died for me. I mean, I know he did it because of how much he loved you, but it's the same thing. How… how do I go on after that?"

"He cared about you too. He died for both of us," Aldan said. "So we could be together."

Kekeen wrinkled her brow and looked up with a fierce gleam in her eyes. "I watched him die! I saw the life leave him! And Qara… Qara cried and cried. And then I left them. I left them to run to you."

"You saved me. You and your father and Swift Claw. I was almost gone too."

"I know! I know…" She buried her face in her hands. "It's just all too much. I don't know what to think any more."

"I… I don't either." A deep ache settled into Aldan's gut. The moments with Sugh and the goddess had made him think everything would be all right now. But…

"You're both forgetting some things." Aldan turned to see him Koland standing by the door, arms crossed and leaning against the frame.

"Have you been listening to us?" Kekeen demanded.

"Long enough to understand," Koland answered. He uncrossed his arms and walked across the room. "Daughter, why do I tell stories?"

"To make money."

Koland chuckled. "Yes, there's that. But I could just play music and let you sing. That would be enough. But I tell stories, especially if there are younger people present. Why?"

"To teach," Aldan said.

Koland nodded. "I can teach all kinds of lessons through stories. Anyone can. But almost every story I tell has a similar purpose. A similar lesson. Do you know what it is?"

Kekeen sniffed. "You tell stories with monsters and, and enemies to fight, and heroes."

"Is it courage?" Aldan asked. He shifted on the bed and winced as the bedclothes rubbed against the ravaged skin on his legs.

"Maybe. Look at it this way: everyone knows evil exists." He held out his palm and gestured outside. "We live in a dangerous world. Barbarians. Beastmen. Monsters. Evil Kings. And more. Everyone knows this." He caught hold of a bedpost and swung around to point at Aldan. "But they need to be reminded of the other side. They need to be told about brave heroes who stand against the evil. From this, they draw courage. And maybe…" He smiled. "Maybe they become the brave heroes the rest of us need."

Aldan considered the words for a few moments. "My first trainer, Kan… he said everyone, deep down, wants to be the villain. It's why they cheered for us in the arena."

Koland answered with slow words. "There is no question that evil is alluring. It is why so many fall to it. People like Duurald, Lord Ulakan, or… Bain." He paused. "But does everyone want it? I don't believe that. Did you want to be the villain?"

"At times, yes," Aldan said.

"You wanted to turn on your friends? Betray them? Join Suirel in his chaos?"

"No, not like that. But… I wanted to give up. Turn away from, from fighting so hard."

"Despair is not the same thing as evil, Aldan." Koland waited a few moments before adding, "And it can be countered by the other thing I usually try to include in stories."

"Hope," Kekeen whispered.

He nodded. "You suggested courage a moment ago, Aldan, but courage only comes from hope: the belief, however small, that evil will be overcome. That's what all heroes share in common. Hope. And I will admit I lost it myself. I should have listened to my own wisdom."

"Hope," Aldan repeated. He took a deep breath. "Someone told me, not long ago… that we were never without hope. That not everything depends on me." He looked at Kekeen. "On us. Because there are other powers at work."

"Very wise," Koland agreed. He examined both of them. "Well. I've talked enough. I will leave you two alone again."

"Wolf Chosen is never alone," came Swift Claw's voice from the door.

Koland laughed. "Of course. Not when he has such a faithful guardian outside." He winked at Aldan. "Now there's a source of stories I need to explore further." He laughed again and left the room.

Aldan and Kekeen sat in silence for a few minutes. At last, she reached out and took his hand. "Maybe… maybe we don't need to know everything or solve everything yet. I mean, if it doesn't all depend on us."

He smiled, though it took an effort now. Exhaustion crept up on him again. "We can leave some of it to hope?"

Kekeen squeezed his hand. "Hope. I lost it while Zektel controlled me. Most of the time. But sometimes… sometimes, it would come back."

"When?"

She released his hand and reached up to touch his cheek. "When I would see your face and see your determination. I knew, then, that you would keep fighting to save me. No matter what it took. And it would help… for a while."

"Nukai—the Wolf—reminded me at one point that even though Zektel was in control, you were still watching me. I tried to remember that. Every time I said something rude to her, I felt guilty, because I was saying it to you too."

"It's all right. I understood."

He put his hand over hers. "The first story I heard your father tell—"

"You remember that?"

Aldan smiled. "I remember everything about that evening. It was the first time I saw you. Zektel couldn't take that memory away, even though she never liked you."

She leaned in closer and ran her other hand through his hair. "I got that impression over the past couple of months."

"The story he told… I don't remember all of it, because I got distracted by you. But I do remember the ending." Aldan swallowed. Kekeen's nearness was a distraction now too. "The, uh, hero in the story returned to his true love and learned she wasn't just a prize, but a companion."

Kekeen nodded but didn't say anything.

"That's what I want. A companion. For the rest of my life."

"Are you asking me to marry you?"

"I think I am. That is, if you think we could. I mean, that it would work, after all we've been through." Why couldn't he get his words out?

"Hmm." Kekeen pulled back. "We jumped from not being sure about anything to marriage pretty quick."

"I'm sorry. It doesn't have to be right away. We can… we can spend more time together. Get to know each other better. I don't know." Aldan knew he was babbling, but he couldn't stop.

Kekeen grinned. "Then let's get to know each other." She took his hand and pretended to bow. "I'm Kekeen."

"Uh, I'm Cl—Aldan."

"Clawdan?" She giggled.

"A fine name," came Swift Claw's voice from the door.

Kekeen rolled her eyes. "Swift Claw! If you're going to listen to everything, you may as well come inside!"

"I will not," he responded. "Wolf Chosen may still have enemies within this city. I will guard this room."

Aldan smiled. "I wonder if he'll come along if we get married."

Kekeen's eyes widened. "He won't be listening to us for the rest of our lives, will he?"

"Sands, I hope not." He pulled on her hand, and she sat on the bed beside him. They laughed together. And kissed. And laughed some more.

In a quieter voice, Aldan told her Swift Claw's story and how he'd promised to help search. "I don't know how long that will take," he said. "But I have to try."

She agreed. "You owe him that much. But maybe I can come with you too."

Their conversation drifted through more pleasant topics, though Aldan could still see occasional flashes of worry in Kekeen's face. He didn't want their time to end, but exhaustion eventually won over. Kekeen admitted to being tired herself. She leaned against the pillow, as if she would sleep beside him.

"If you do that, I'll never fall asleep," he said.

"I probably wouldn't, either," she admitted. "I'm just afraid to leave you."

"I'll be fine." He waved toward the door. "Swift Claw. Remember?"

Kekeen gave him another kiss before sliding off the bed. "I'll be next door if you need me."

He caught her hand again. "For now. But someday soon… I want… I don't want us to be apart."

"We'll talk more about it tomorrow," she promised. She kissed his hand and pulled free.

Aldan let his head slip back on the pillow and closed his eyes.

（（（●）））

When Aldan woke again, Kekeen still slept. He had Swift Claw check on her to be sure. A few minutes later, Koland arrived, bringing food and more conversation.

From him, Aldan gained more information about events outside the room. Yes, the Melkute had been defeated by the combined forces of Daviland's beastmen and General Ghan's troops. Only a few thousand of their troops—and presumably their king, though no one had seen him—had escaped the battle and fled north toward their own country.

The cost had been high. Much of the lower city of Et-Baylak lay in ruins, burned or broken. No one could even begin to count the number of dead.

Once the fight ended, the beastmen appeared ready to pursue the fleeing Melkute soldiers. But Daviland convinced them to remain and help protect the city in its broken state. Should any barbarians or other enemies seek to take advantage of the city's weakness, they would be quite surprised by its defenders.

"Most of our citizens are still trying to understand how the beastmen could come to help instead of attack," Koland said. "It will take some time for them to learn to trust… on both sides." He brightened. "Still, Daviland's arrival to rescue the city with such an army has catapulted him back into favor. The remaining Lords don't dare speak against his leadership now."

"What of the General?" Aldan asked. "He served Suirel. And his cult is still around."

Koland nodded. "General Ghan led the counterattack on the Melkute. He fought at the head of our soldiers until the enemy was completely routed.

He is almost as much a hero as Daviland or yourself now. Fortunately, he rejects any claim to leadership other than what he possesses now. In the presence of the council, he swore a new oath of loyalty to the Sar Empire. He seems genuinely repentant for his part in Suirel's actions."

Aldan grunted.

"We'll keep an eye on him, anyway. As for the cult... with the loss of Lord Ulakan, they've disappeared into the shadows." Koland paused. "Huh. Their leader, Demujin, did not return from the mines with Suirel. I don't know what happened to him."

Suirel's portal in the arena had shattered moments after they'd pulled Aldan out of it. Nothing remained save crystal shards scattered in the sand. "We would all probably have been torn apart by broken crystal if not for your animal," Koland explained.

"My animal?" Aldan wrinkled his brow.

"The big one, with the armor."

"Tuulka?"

Koland shrugged. "Whatever you call it. In spite of a hurt leg, it managed to get close enough to shield us from the explosion."

"Is he all right?" Aldan hesitated. "Uh, Kekeen is quite fond of him."

"Uh-huh. He's fine, except for that leg, of course." Koland shook his head. "Remarkable. You and Kekeen can go see him when you're able."

"I would like that."

A knock at the door heralded the arrival of a red-robed priest who bowed upon entering. He displayed a large crystal full of blood. "I am here to provide healing."

"Ah." Koland jumped up. "They finally procured enough Kurav blood then."

Aldan raised his eyebrows at the priest. "You are... willing... to heal me?"

The priest blinked, appearing shocked. "You are Clanless, aren't you?"

"Yes..."

He nodded. "Then it will be my honor to heal the one who saved our city."

Aldan didn't know what to say.

The priest gestured, and Yesun joined him, carrying a pile of towels. "We will do our best to protect the bed from the blood," the priest explained. Aldan almost laughed. That had never been a consideration in the arena.

The priest approached the bed and pulled aside the bedclothes. For the first time, Aldan got a good look at his legs. Kekeen had called it bruising, but that put it lightly. Purple and yellow splotches covered his skin in wide patterns, swollen in ugly bulges. Where the surface wasn't bruised, it burned a bright red. Looking at it caused bile to rise in Aldan's throat.

The priest had a similar reaction. "Oh. I, uh, I've never seen, um, anything like this before." He took a step back.

"Does that matter?" Koland asked.

"I don't know. I don't know whether the blood-magic will work here."

"I don't expect my lost toe to grow back, if that helps," Aldan said.

The priest frowned and stepped back beside the bed. With the help of Yesun, they positioned towels beneath Aldan's legs and side. The attendant stepped back against the wall but kept watching. The priest murmured a prayer and unstoppered the blood. "Prepare yourself. This will undoubtedly hurt."

"I know how it works." Aldan took hold of the nearest bedpost to brace himself.

"Of course you do," the priest muttered. "You're Clanless. You've probably been through this a thousand times over."

With that, he began.

At Aldan's first cry of pain, Kekeen rushed in from the adjoining bedroom. Koland caught her and held her while they watched. Swift Claw peeked around the door as well. Even Yesun, who'd seen the process before, stared wide-eyed.

The full healing of Aldan's side proceeded like every other healing he'd experienced: the pain of the healing matched the pain of the injury. But the pain was momentary. Once completed, it faded away.

"What about his head?" Kekeen asked.

"Hm?" The priest took a look. "Ah, I see. An injury was healed, but the scalp was not reattached properly. If the scar is a problem, the only alternative I can offer is to tear it open again and re-heal it."

"I can live with another scar." Aldan looked to Kekeen. "If it's all right with you?"

"Of course it is, silly. I love you no matter what you look like."

When the priest worked on Aldan's legs, things did not work the same. He felt the cold again, cold beyond snow and ice and wind. More, he felt something happening to the blood within his legs. It was like the Taint, but worse, as if the blood were boiling. He cried out much louder than he intended.

Kekeen broke loose from her father and dashed to his side. She wrapped her arms around his as he held the bedpost.

"Blood is life. Blood is precious. Blood is power," the priest repeated as he worked, but sweat broke out on his face. He wiped it off with his forearm and pushed his hood back.

"Is there a problem?" Koland asked.

"I'm… not sure." The priest stepped back. He took the last towel from the wide-eyed servant and wiped the blood from his hands. "I think it worked, but…"

Aldan released the bedpost and let himself relax. The pain subsided, but not as quickly as he would have liked. Kekeen held his hand with both of hers.

Together, the priest and Yesun cleaned the Clan Kurav blood away and removed the stained towels. Aldan examined his legs. The burned skin appeared new and whole. The swelling and bruising had diminished. But tiny dark lines remained in the skin, tracing his veins.

"How do they feel?" Kekeen asked.

"Achy and tingly." Aldan wiggled his toes, all nine of them.

"Can you stand?" the priest asked. "The Ghamba Lam will want a full report from me."

"Let's find out." Aldan sat up and swung his legs over the side of the bed. As he did, the smell of the blood and his own body struck him. He coughed. Had it been this bad since he came here? No wonder Swift Claw stayed outside the room. How did Kekeen stand it? "I need a bath."

"If you can walk, I'll take you there," Yesun offered.

Aldan placed his feet on the floor and leaned forward, letting them take some of his weight. He gasped as a Taint-like burning ran through his calves. It wasn't severe enough to impede him, but it wasn't pleasant.

"Are you all right?" Kekeen shifted one of her hands to his elbow.

"I'm not sure." Aldan gritted his teeth and stood up. The burning shot through his calves again but immediately subsided. He took a step. The pain repeated itself but only in the leg he'd moved. A few more steps gave the same result. He tried to describe what he felt to the others.

"It sounds as though something has been damaged within your blood system," the priest mused. "Ordinarily, the blood-magic should have healed it. We can heal almost anything other than completely lost body parts."

Koland tapped his beard. "If that gateway truly led to the chaos moon, then Aldan's legs were exposed to something beyond our world. Either the air of the moon or something else in-between."

"That is beyond our understanding." The priest nodded.

Aldan took a few more steps, Kekeen at his side. "I can bear it," he said.

"Aldan, are you sure?" Kekeen looked to the priest. "Maybe you should try again."

The priest inclined his head. "I am sorry, dear lady. I have used all the blood that I had. Perhaps when our stock is restored…"

"There are others who need it more, I'm sure. I can live with a little pain. Thank you, priest." Aldan took another step. "And thank the Ghamba Lam for me."

The priest bowed. "I will be sure to do so. Thank you for your service, Clanless."

Aldan waited until the priest and servant left, then turned to Koland. "That… was strange. A priest has never thanked me before."

Koland chuckled. "Consider what you did from their point of view. You drove back a false god. What greater service is there to them?"

"You're everyone's hero," Kekeen put in.

"That's… uncomfortable. Yesun, let's go get that bath."

((((●))))

Koland hesitated at Aldan's door. He didn't want to do this, but it needed to happen. He peeked in. As expected, Aldan had fallen asleep again. Kekeen sat by the bed, trying to read a book by lamplight. Koland tapped the door, and she looked up. He gestured for her to join him.

They left Swift Claw by the door. The beastman showed no interest in their movements. They chatted for a while about Aldan's recovery, concern over his legs, and the state of the city. All the while, Koland guided them through the palace and up several stairs until they found a door which led out onto the roof.

"I've never been up here before!" Kekeen exclaimed. She turned in a circle. Aside from the towers, they were higher than anything else in the city. "You can see so far in every direction!"

"I wanted somewhere as private as possible," Koland said. He glanced up at the moon. Only an hour past sunset, its brightness filled the sky, seeming especially large tonight.

"Oh." Kekeen folded her arms and looked at him. "I was wondering when we'd have this conversation."

Koland looked down toward the lower city. Fires burned in all directions, but not the blazing buildings from a few days ago. Now people burned debris, both to get rid of it and to provide heat and light for the cold nights. "I suppose you want an explanation for my actions."

"You mean when you tried to kill me? Twice?"

He looked back at her. "I didn't harm you either time. I don't know if Zektel allowed you to remember all the details…"

"I'm pretty sure I remember everything. I never learned to hide things from myself like you and Aldan."

Koland winced. That made sense. "I am here to apologize, though maybe not as you might expect. I apologize, daughter, for losing hope. I despaired, believing I would never get you back."

Kekeen shivered in the cool air and looked down. "I suppose… I suppose you had reason, after what happened to Mother."

"As soon as I knew you'd been taken, it was all I could think about." He shook his head. "Those were the most horrible days of my life."

"I wish you'd told me."

"You were a child. I couldn't do that."

"Maybe not right then. But you could have told me when I was old enough."

Koland looked back up at the moon. "By then, I'd repeated the lie so often, I almost believed it myself. And the longer you tell a lie, the harder it is to tell the truth."

Kekeen didn't answer.

"I am sorry," Koland said. "I was wrong."

Kekeen shivered again. "I forgive you. Can we go back inside? It's getting cold out here."

He stepped toward her and held out his arms. "Come here."

She didn't hesitate. Koland wrapped her up in the best father hug he could. "I've tried to keep you warm and safe all your life," he said. "But it looks like that won't be my job for much longer."

"Will you be all right with that?"

He chuckled. "I don't think I have much choice. But it's hard to surrender a job I've loved for so many years."

"Are you talking about me or storytelling now?" Kekeen tapped his beard for him.

"Maybe both. Daviland has asked me to help with the new government. Again."

"At least this time, it's actually him." She paused. "But will you be all right if I leave with Aldan? I don't think he wants to stay here."

Koland took a deep breath. "I lost you for a few months. And now I've had you back for only a couple of days. Am I ready to lose you again? No. Definitely not."

"It's not the same thing."

"I know. I know. And I know you and Aldan belong together. I… let me deal with it in my own way. I'll be all right. Eventually."

"If you say so." She didn't sound convinced.

"Just… don't leave too soon. Give me a few days, at least."

She turned within his arms and looked out over the city. "At least."

"And I do have a suggestion about all this…"

"Am I going to like it?"

Koland smiled. "I think you'll love it."

UNDER THE MOON'S GAZE

For the next two days, Aldan learned to walk again. Or more accurately, he learned how to endure walking. The burning pain in his calves bothered him with every step. After the first day, he downplayed the pain when Kekeen or others asked. When he considered Sugh and the Wolf's sacrifices, he decided the pain was a small price for him to pay.

Even so, he tried to avoid long walks if he could. But the day came when he couldn't avoid a significant one.

"Why is it so far out there?" he grumbled.

Kekeen straightened the wolf pelt on his shoulder. When she'd returned it to him, he'd considered putting it in a chest and never wearing it again. But he remembered Nukai's words the first time: "Honor me, Aldan." Wearing the fur would honor Nukai, the Wolf, and Sugh. He might never go without it after all.

Despite finding him finer clothing than he'd ever worn, Kekeen insisted he keep the brand open as he used to. She cut off the sleeve on his shirt herself. Though he didn't quite understand, he didn't mind… except the shoes. It felt wrong to wear them into the arena.

As for Kekeen, she wore an outer robe of maroon and blue, with a simple inner dress of maroon. Both were trimmed in gold. She'd braided her hair and woven in a handful of blue beads. She'd never looked lovelier in Aldan's eyes. He wanted to take her and escape this event right now. Satisfied with the positioning of the pelt, she stepped back and said, "You walked and ran out there hundreds of times."

He looked past her into the arena. "That doesn't mean I want to do it again."

"I'll be with you every step of the way." She took his hand. "Ready?"

He returned his gaze to her outfit. "You wore something very much like this when—"

"When we had our first kiss," she finished. "It wasn't easy to find this, either. But Gogeku came through."

"Oh, you've seen him? How is he?"

She patted his shoulder. "Moaning about the loss of business from the war. Now stop stalling. Shall we go?"

"No. I don't want to do this."

"Too bad."

With a gentle push, she encouraged him to step out into the open. As soon as he did, the crowd erupted in cheers. He'd heard the same sounds in this same place so many, many times, yet today it sounded different. These cheers weren't for the entertainment he could provide but for what he'd done for these people. Or at least what they believed he'd done. The truth seemed far more complicated.

He tried to smile as he and Kekeen walked slowly across the sand toward the low platform erected in the center of the arena. Here and there, Aldan spotted chunks of half-buried crystal the priests had not yet retrieved. But did they need the crystal any more? Without the need to fill the cavern, what would happen to the entire blood sacrifice system? It would already be crippled by the ending of the arena system. So many changes were coming to the Sar Empire. He wondered what it would look like once everything settled down.

Daviland stood waiting for them on the platform. Beside him on one side stood Lords Ezen and Ghayaktal, the Ghamba Lam, two Daghilches, General Ghan, Koland, and Qara. On the other side stood four beast-men. Aldan recognized Swift Claw and Wind Tooth but not the other two.

"This is all so unnecessary," he muttered.

"After everything the city has been through, the people need reasons to celebrate," Kekeen said. She waved at someone in the stands. "This is not just about you. Now stop being so grumpy."

Aldan lifted his face and scanned the crowd. The numbers rivaled anything he'd seen in the days of the Hawk King, but the makeup of this crowd was different. There had been no charge for this event, so far more of the audience came from the lower city.

"Here he is, everyone!" Daviland's voice, enhanced by blood-magic, resonated across the arena. "The one you've known as Clanless! The greatest arena warrior in history!"

Aldan had to give Daviland credit: he could have mentioned how he'd won the fight here last time.

"But we are not here to honor him for that, but for what he did for our city in its time of need."

Aldan and Kekeen reached the platform. It was only two steps up, but pain shot through his calves on each one. Aldan made a mental note to avoid all stairs from now on.

"When the Melkute foe demanded a singular battle, Clanless accepted the challenge," Daviland went on. "He fought for us all, without knowing what he was getting into or whether he would survive. And he triumphed!"

The crowd cheered, though Aldan was sure some of them wondered about that particular story. Only a few could have seen from the walls during his fight with the Melkute champion.

"But our enemy betrayed us and attacked the city anyway. And yet…" Daviland turned in a circle to include all of the crowd. "This man has done far, far more than that. The stories of what he did over the past few weeks will one day be told in every eating house and inn across the Empire and beyond!"

Aldan glanced at Koland, who winked. At least one storyteller would know all of it. He didn't much care for that idea.

Daviland pointed at Aldan. "This man befriended the beastmen months ago. Without his influence among them, I would never have been able to secure our new alliance and bring them to the aid of Et-Baylak!"

Aldan wasn't sure that part was true. The Wolf had more to do with it than he did.

"Once the battle began, Clanless was one of only a few who knew about the greater threat happening here within this arena," Daviland explained. "He fought his way back into the city through the Melkute forces. He made his way here and won the greatest victory ever achieved. For in this arena, he defeated Suirel, the chaos god himself!"

The crowd murmured. Some had heard rumors and whispers, but few knew any of the details. Blood-wraiths had swept through the city, possessing dozens. But then most had been freed soon after. The chaos of those minutes were only a part of the greater battle.

"It was Sugh and Nukai," Aldan said. "They should—"

"They will be honored later," Daviland said in a non-enhanced voice. "This moment is for you."

"I don't need to be honored."

"Nevertheless, it is our desire to do so," the Ghamba Lam put in. "All of us. Would you deny us?"

Aldan closed his mouth.

Resuming the enhanced voice, Daviland declared, "Everyone here wishes to honor Clanless in their own way. First, we turn to our new allies. Wind Tooth?"

The beastman leader stepped forward to face Aldan. "Wolf Chosen," he said, then continued in his own language. Swift Claw stood beside him and translated. Daviland then repeated his words for the crowd to hear.

"You have shown honor to our people. You hold the honor of Swift Claw. You have covenanted with blood. You have served the True Wind well. Because of this, you are welcome in the Formation at any time."

"We can visit their city?" Kekeen asked.

"That is what he is saying," Swift Claw said.

But then, Wind Tooth removed his belt with the sword and scabbard and held them out. He spoke again. "You have lost your weapon. Please take this one in its place."

Aldan's mouth dropped open. "You can't mean it. Your… your weapons are for life!"

Swift Claw dipped his head. "This is the greatest honor he can offer you, Wolf Chosen. Please accept it."

"I can't! It's… too precious!"

"You must. To refuse it now would be the greatest dishonor you could pay him."

Aldan swallowed. He took the proffered weapon and bowed to Wind Tooth. He drew the scimitar and held it up to a new chorus of cheers from the crowd. Like all of the beastmen weapons, the sword was an absolute work of art, unique from all others. He looked forward to examining it more closely. After letting the crowd cheer, he sheathed it and bowed to Wind Tooth again. Satisfied, the beastman retreated. Swift Claw stayed long enough to be sure Aldan strapped the belt on to himself and then stepped back.

Lord Ghayaktal was next. "I have consulted with the other leaders of Clan Kurav. Should you wish travel anywhere within the Sar Empire, you have only to ask." He pointed to Aldan's shoulder. "Your brand is the key to transportation and lodging anywhere our influence extends."

"And within Et-Baylak as well," Lord Ezen added. "You are welcome to stay or eat anywhere within this city at no charge for the rest of your life. Your brand is the only identification you need."

"Let's hope others don't get the idea to start branding themselves," Kekeen murmured.

"The brand is one-of-a-kind," one of the Daghilches spoke up. "No one else living possesses one now."

"And no one else will," General Ghan said, taking his place beside Daviland. "From this day forward, by the authority of the new ruling council of the Sar Empire, I proclaim the branding of slaves, especially the brand of no clan, to be outlawed."

"Why not outlaw slavery itself?" Aldan asked. He looked at Daviland. "Isn't that what you said you'd do?"

"Arena slavery is now outlawed as well, throughout the Empire," Daviland said. He switched to a quiet voice to add, "Step by step, Clanless. I don't have the power to shut it all down just yet." He glanced back at the Lords. "But give me a couple of months, and we'll get it done."

"I think it's my turn now," Koland said, springing up beside them. He grinned and looked at Kekeen.

Aldan glanced at her. She brightened and held his arm a little tighter.

"Clanless, it is my turn to honor you." Koland paused and took a deep breath. "And I can bestow no greater honor than to accept you as a son. I consent to your request for the hand of my daughter."

"You didn't actually ask," Kekeen whispered in his ear as the crowd roared, "but he knew you would, when you thought of it."

"This is a joyous occasion indeed!" Daviland thundered to the crowd's delight. "In the sight of all of you, these two will now be joined by the highest official in the service of the goddess, the Ghamba Lam!"

Aldan almost fell to his knees as the Ghamba Lam stepped in front of him and Kekeen. This was happening so fast, but it was exactly what he wanted.

The priest lifted his hands until the crowd grew quiet. "I am here to join these two as one," he proclaimed, his voice also enhanced by blood-magic. "But though we have many witnesses, each must also be accompanied by a companion witness. Kekeen, daughter of Koland, do you have such a companion?"

"She does," Qara said. She slid past the others and stood at Kekeen's side. "I bear witness under the moon's gaze."

"And does the husband-to-be have such a companion?"

Aldan looked to Koland. "I…"

"Of course you do," Koland said. "You have a friend closer than a brother to you." He smiled and moved behind the couple. "But I am the father who bears witness. My place is not at your side."

Aldan wrinkled his brow, until another voice said, "It is mine."

To his surprise and absolute delight, Swift Claw stepped out from the other beastmen. He came to Aldan's side and faced the Ghamba Lam. "I bear witness for Wolf Chosen."

"Thank you," Aldan whispered. "And I promise you: we will find your child someday."

"You cannot make such a promise."

Aldan clapped him on the shoulder. "Then you hold my honor until we do."

Swift Claw did not visibly react, but his shoulder trembled beneath Aldan's hand.

The Ghamba Lam made an expansive gesture. One Daghilch took position beside Qara and the other, somewhat more hesitantly, beside Swift Claw. "And we have the required representatives of the goddess." The Ghamba Lam paused. "But there is a problem."

"What?" Aldan almost started forward.

"Kekeen, daughter of Koland, your proposed spouse has been banished from his clan, and his name has been stripped away. He is forbidden from marriage or the fathering of children. This was to be known throughout the Empire and under the moon's gaze."

Aldan tensed. At the moment of his heart's desire, this priest would steal it? He reached for the new scimitar's hilt, but Koland caught his arm. "Wait."

The crowd reacted in anger, raining down their displeasure.

"There is but one solution to this problem!" the Ghamba Lam shouted as he turned to look at the audience. He looked back at Aldan and smiled. "The bloodline must be restored and the name returned."

Aldan gasped. "You can do that?"

"I am the servant of the goddess, and she has decreed this must be done!" He leaned in closer and whispered without magic, "She told me so herself." He winked. "In a dream, no less."

Kekeen squeezed his arm and bounced a little in excitement. She and Koland had clearly known this would happen.

"In the holy and hidden name of the goddess of the moon," the Ghamba Lam cried, "I restore you… not to clan Tokuur… but to all clans of the Sar Empire. You, who have bathed in the blood of all, shall belong to all bloodlines, and all shall call you their brother. Let it be known throughout the Empire and under the moon's gaze!"

The Ghamba Lam put his hand against Aldan's branded shoulder. To his own surprise, he did not flinch. "And I restore to you the name that was taken from you—" In the quieter voice, he added, "that I took from you." He looked up at the crowd and shouted, "Aldan!"

Aldan trembled at the crowd's reaction. He'd heard cheers within the arenas for over eight years. He'd won unbelievable victories and received the accolades that were his due. But now… their thunderous cheers resounded louder than he'd ever heard. His eyes rose to the sky. The moon itself appeared to tremble at the sound. Maybe it did.

Tears formed in his eyes and broke free as the crowd's tumult turned into a chant, a chant so similar to ones he'd heard a thousand times… but so much more. Because this time, they chanted, not "Clanless," but:

"Aldan! Aldan! Aldan!"

The End

For more information on Clanless & his world,
upcoming books and more,
visit timfrankovich.com

(Sign up for the newsletter and
you'll get access to free short stories)

If you enjoyed this book, please post a review on Amazon,
Goodreads, B&N, or wherever you find books!
There's no better way to spread the word.

On the Day the Sun Surrendered

Lyrics & theme by Tim Frankovich. Musical notation by Bradford Eide.

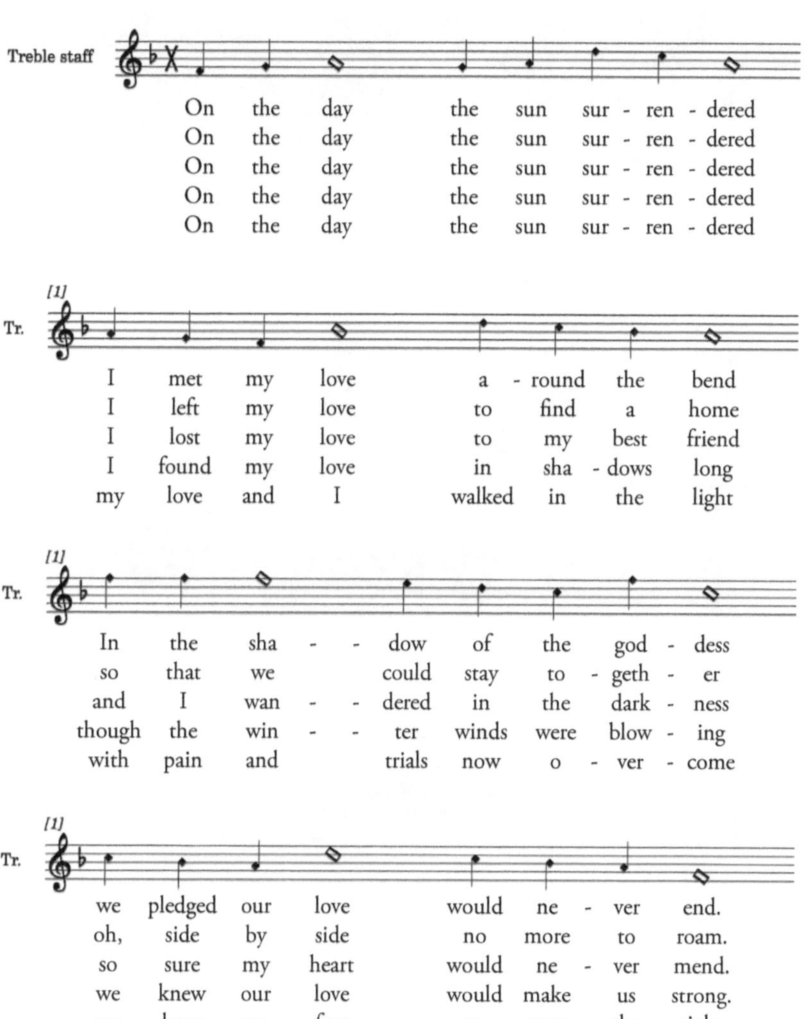

Clans of the Sar Empire
(This includes spoilers for the end of *Wolf Chosen*.)

The Sar Empire consists of twelve clans of various levels of power and influence.

Clan Shukan - One of the four most powerful clans, vying for power within the capital. The Hawk King comes from this clan, which gives them the greatest prestige. They also have a great deal of influence over the priesthood. Owns a large portion of the city.
Blood-magic: Life extension

Clan Ghutalta - Second of the most powerful clans. Controls most of the banking system within the capital, and has significant influence over the priesthood.
Blood-magic: Duplicates other blood-magics

Clan Kurav - Third of the most powerful clans. Has arrangements with many smaller clans to bring in their goods, thus controls much of the market within the capital.
Blood-magic: Healing

Clan Torov - Fourth of the most powerful clans. Owns the largest portion of the city, and has bits of control throughout everything. Diversifies their influence, but is always scheming to increase it.
Blood-magic: Voice

Clan Zavi - Their richest family owns a mansion in the capital, but their primary influence is over the harbor city and the shipping industry.
Blood-magic: Speed

Clan Shasin - While they only have small influence over the priesthood in the capital, this clan virtually controls religion in most of the other cities and quite a few clanholds.
Blood-magic: Accelerates thought

Clan Dendsu - Richest members own a couple of large homes in the capital and another city. But they control the largest amount of farmland in the country, via several clanholds.
Blood-magic: Heat (and light)

Clan Dalbai - Operates the arenas in all of the cities. (Shares capital city arena management with Clan Torov.) Has some influence within the priesthood to help them find new gladiators.
Blood-magic: Endurance

Clan Berge - Military-focused. Highest officers are all from this clan. Also maintains a very large blacksmith guild throughout the land.
Blood-magic: Strength

Clan Tokuur - The low clans, agricultural, mostly live in clanholds.
Blood-magic: Drains strength, but revitalizes blood

Clan Dariachin - The low clans, agricultural, mostly live in clanholds.
Blood-magic: Enhances hearing and vision

Clan Ghamkiin - The low clans, agricultural, mostly live in clanholds.
Blood-magic: Controls the movement of blood

Acknowledgements

This is it. I think I've agonized over this book more than any other. I knew how I wanted the story to end, but I hadn't worked out a lot of the details. It took many hours of plotting, re-plotting, and so on until I was happy with the results. Even then, I think the first draft of this book was the roughest first draft I've had since the very beginning of this writing journey.

More than any previous book, my beta readers (Allen Perkins, Stephen Tallman, and Ben Stringer) were absolutely invaluable this time. All three offered suggestions that made this story so much stronger than before, from small details to entire character arcs. I can't thank them enough. And here, three books later, I was still pulling in new details from the notes I took at that one lunch with Dr. Sonny White, whose understanding of a world with a geostationary moon was off-the-charts brilliant. (But I will beat you at the next Twilight Imperium game!)

Continued thanks to all those I listed over the past two books, including Tys Grenz, John Hart, Scott Foster, Bradford Eide, & Chris Vaughn. And I'm sure I've forgotten someone else along the way. When people ask how I can keep so many stories in my head, I always answer that it's because I can't remember people's names.

Is this the end? Let us say it is the end of this story. There are more to tell, and I hope to tell them at some point. Do Aldan and Swift Claw find the lost child? What happens when the chaos moon completes another 30-year cycle and comes within view again? These are obvious hooks that are ready to be explored. I have other books to write first, but I do believe I will return to this world. And it may be soon.

Let it be known throughout the empire and under the moon's gaze.

About the Author

Tim Frankovich has been exploring fantastic worlds since third grade, when he cut up a grocery sack and drew a Godzilla-meets-superheroes story. Since then, he's gotten a little bit better at the writing part (not so much with the drawing).

His goal as a writer is to transport readers to another world, make them care deeply about characters in dire situations, and guide them deeply into life itself.

At the moment, he is suitably conscious somewhere in Texas with his beloved wife, awesome kids, and a fool of a pup named Pippin.